She had no intention
of removing his briefs

There was no reason to. But like a fig leaf on a statue, they drew Rachel's attention inexorably to the area they covered. The first time she and Sandor had been together in this room, he'd been furious and she'd been terrified. Tonight, he was battered, and she was full of conflicting emotions wavering from anxious concern to unruly desire.

Third time's the charm? her inner voice queried.

Maybe so, she admitted to herself with surprise. Unfortunately, tonight—their second time in her bedroom—was not the night. What Sandor Pulneshti needed right now was a friend, not a bedmate.

But I want you in my bed, she thought, gazing down at him. *I want you in my life. I just don't have any idea whether that's going to be possible....*

ABOUT THE AUTHOR

Julie Meyers, a 1987 Golden Heart award winner, makes her Superromance debut with *In the Cards*. Julie has published previously with Harlequin Temptation and already has two more books in the works. Not bad—especially since she was moving into a new house, caring for her infant daughter and beginning research on the new projects while working on *In the Cards*. Julie, her husband John and their daughter Jessica make their home in California.

In the Cards

JULIE MEYERS

Harlequin Books

TORONTO • NEW YORK • LONDON
AMSTERDAM • PARIS • SYDNEY • HAMBURG
STOCKHOLM • ATHENS • TOKYO • MILAN

Published March 1990

First printing January 1990

ISBN 0-373-70396-1

Printed in U.S.A.

To the Sacramento Chapter of RWA,
with thanks for their generous friendship
and encouragement.
And to Dorothy, Doris, and John,
whose loving help
gave me forty-eight-hour days
just when I needed them most.

CHAPTER ONE

IT WASN'T RIGHT. Midnight, and it still wasn't right.

Sandor Pulneshti lifted the fragile sheet of yellow tracing paper from his drawing board and crumpled it into a small, tight ball. He'd been designing houses for years, and had helped to construct dozens of them with his own hands. In all that time, no project had fought and tantalized him so mercilessly. Never before had he cared so deeply.

Too bad caring wasn't enough.

Sandor looked down at the detailed drawing in front of him, but his eyes, stinging with sweat and weariness, refused to focus properly. Thwarted, he rubbed his aching temples with fingertips made rough by long weeks of physical labor at the building site.

The rented room that served as both his office and his living quarters was hot and muggy. There were no motels with handy ice machines and air conditioners to be found in the little farming community of Dalewood, Ohio. Strangers looking for a place to stay were directed to the town church, where a list was kept of private homes with rooms to rent.

Sandor supposed he should have minded all the attendant inconveniences, but except for the heat, life at the boardinghouse was a welcome change from staying in a motel with paper-thin walls and eating all his meals at a diner. His landlady was a sweetheart, friendly without being intrusive, and the streets around her home featured a cross section of architectural styles diverse enough to delight his builder's eye. An air of genteel neglect infested many of the town's homes, but that neglect had not yet deepened into true decay. The beautiful old buildings could still be salvaged; he intended to see to it.

In fact, he intended to see to more than that. Out beyond the edge of town there rose a wooded hill. The first time he'd chanced upon that rise, while out walking, he'd found himself picturing the home that deserved to stand there, half-hidden among ancient oaks, as proud and tall as the surrounding trees. In his vision, there had been a deeply satisfying integrity to it, a singular unity that satisfied the eye and nourished the spirit.

Right now, however, that unity was just an image in his mind. In order for it to come to life, he had to finish translating it into drawings his crew could work from. The current plans were nearly complete, but while he was satisfied with the layout of the place, there was something jarring, something inappropriate, about the design of the actual facade. He could do better. He knew he could.

Unfortunately even if he failed to capture his vision accurately on paper, construction would go on. The house would take shape as a well-constructed, competently designed structure, despite the flawed "face" it presented to the world. Everyone would pronounce it a success. Everyone would be satisfied.

Everyone but Sandor.

"Bed," he told himself, and shut off the light over his drafting table. But he couldn't shut off his mind as easily. In less than six hours, the eastern sky would brighten, heralding another workday. Beams would be cut, hammers would strike, carpenters would progress in their work on the new building. It was no fault of theirs if the plans they worked from were wrong, if the result took dozens of man-hours to correct, assuming it could be corrected at all—

"Go to bed," Sandor repeated harshly to short-circuit the pointless cycle of worry. And yet he knew that the failed elevation he had spent so many hours drafting and redrafting would haunt him as he sought sleep, would project itself maddeningly on his closed eyelids.

He felt a strong urge to escape from his room and slip out into the hot, still night, where he could walk the streets of Dalewood until his sense of frustration eased. But it was after midnight, and there were other people sleeping in the rooms around him. It wasn't fair to risk disturbing them just because he was a *vadni ratsa* who breathed easier under the open sky. He'd left the wandering life of the "wild goose" behind years ago, and it had been a wise choice, the right choice for him, even if it had sometimes proven a difficult choice to live by.

Sandor pulled his T-shirt off over his head and stripped out of his jeans and undershorts, enjoying the brief feeling of coolness caused by the night air touching his sweat-damp skin. *You can rest even if you can't sleep,* he told himself, turning back the chenille bedspread and lavender-scented top sheet provided by his landlady. *Take it easy, Pulneshti.*

Stretching out, he closed his eyes and took a deep breath, consciously unclenching his muscles. The night was silent, except for the distant barking of a dog. He counted his heartbeats, willing them to slow.

Maybe if the entryway windows were more symmetrical—

"No!" he said aloud, and the tension of the past few hours flooded back into his thoughts.

Exasperated, he reached out and flicked on the bedside lamp. For a moment more he hesitated. Then he sat up, slid open the drawer of the night table and reached inside.

His fingers closed around the soft chamois pouch, and with a resigned smile, Sandor opened the drawstring and carefully removed the contents, setting the bag aside.

What he held in his hands was his heritage, the single legacy left to him by the family he could scarcely remember. Resting on his broad palm, it looked like a simple pack of playing cards, slightly dog-eared and somewhat larger than a conventional deck. It was only when he turned the cards over and began manipulating them that the jewel tones of their glowing faces were revealed, still vibrant despite their obvious antiquity, embodying the complex mysteries of the Tarot.

Shuffling the deck, Sandor closed his eyes, taking pleasure in the smooth coolness of the cards. Their touch evoked memories of his earliest years, when his grandmother had spent hours displaying her knowledge of the Tarot to the child he had been.

"One card for the days gone by, one for the present hour, and two to light the path into tomorrow."

Sandor's voice was a quiet rumble in the late-night stillness; his tongue caressed the angular syllables of the Romany words. At the age of four, he had been convinced that his grandmother saw the fate of the world in their measured spread. His use of them was less ambitious: they acted as a distraction from the worries of the day and were a means of honoring his ancestry and his memories of a wise and loving old woman.

Cutting the oversize Tarot deck with his left hand, as she had taught him, he drew the first card from it.

One card for the days gone by...

The Five of Pentacles.

The card depicted a glowing stained-glass window, with drifting snow on its bottom ledge. Below it, an impoverished couple trudged along, shut out from whatever lit the window so gaily. According to his grandmother, the Five of Pentacles represented isolation and poverty, a need for refuge long denied.

Startled by the aptness of the image, Sandor put it aside. Yes, his childhood had been a hard one, but there was nothing to be gained by dwelling on it. His hopes and ambitions involved today—today and all the bright tomorrows.

Warily he revealed the face of the second card.

One for the present hour...

The Two of Pentacles.

He smiled grudgingly at the card's cheerful juggler. Lately he had indeed been balancing two ways of life. It wasn't always easy, but it had its rewards. Again the symbol was disconcertingly appropriate.

And two to light the path into tomorrow.

Traditionally the third card represented positive forces influencing the future. Half-reluctant, he turned the card faceup... and whistled in surprise at what he saw there.

The High Priestess. She smiled at him enigmatically, a symbol of the unrevealed future, representing the perfect woman of a man's dreams.

What the hell was a card like that doing in a reading of his? The High Priestess was meant to foretell the appearance of the one woman in all the world best suited to complete his happiness. His match. His mate for life, if he had the wisdom to recognize her value and win her to his side....

Sandor shook his head in reluctant dismissal. He wanted to believe such a woman existed; a part of him hungered desperately for her presence. It was hard going through life so alone...but, for him, the true tragedy would be to find such a woman now, at a time in his life when he couldn't do a thing about it.

Depression settled over him as oppressively as the heat. If finding his "true love" was the good news, he wasn't sure he was ready for the bad. Reluctantly he turned the fourth card, the card designated to speak of the obstacles and negative forces looming ahead.

The Tower, reversed.

Sandor looked down at it, jolted. The Tower, reversed, foretold troubled times ahead and warned him of false accusations, perhaps even false imprisonment. More disturbingly yet, it cautioned him against a lack of insight that might make him too stubborn to avoid the trouble that stalked him.

But I'm not that obstinate, he reasoned uneasily. *Decisive, sure, but not inflexible....*

The jagged lines and brooding colors of The Tower remained unchanged, threatening. Where, in all those dark warnings, was his perfect lady? Was he meant to find her and protect her from harm, or was she the one, somehow, who would bring the danger into his life?

Slowly, troubled, Sandor gathered the cards and slid them back into their protective pouch.

As a diversion, the self-administered "reading" had been a rousing success. As a way to lull himself to sleep, however, it left a lot to be desired. He wanted to laugh the warnings off... and yet, to his consternation, he couldn't. The cards had awakened old hopes and memories, raised issues in his mind that weren't easily dismissed.

Feeling drained, he placed the pouch on his bedside table and switched off the light, ordering himself to fall asleep. But as he began to drift, he found himself wondering what she might be like, this woman of his dreams....

COMPULSIVELY Rachel Locke unfolded the innocent-looking sheet of beige stationery and read the typed words again.

My dear Miss Locke:

You should be warned that your aunt has taken up with a group of people who can only be described as "undesirables." It cannot be wise or safe for her to consort with juvenile delinquents and vagrants. These people are set on taking advantage of a gentle-hearted woman, and it must not be allowed.

Knowing of her many kindnesses to you over the years, I must assume that your continued absence is due to ignorance of your aunt's situation, not indifference. Although I respect her right to privacy and self-determination, my conscience would never let me rest if she came to harm because I had failed to write to you.

The letter had arrived in a plain envelope with no return address, and was signed, simply, "A Friend."

Sighing, Rachel slipped the anonymous letter into her purse and leaned back against the shabby upholstery of the bus seat. She ought to have learned, in the frantic hours since she'd first opened the envelope, that rereading the incredible words wouldn't change them. Aunt Carrie was in some kind of trouble—again—and this time it sounded serious.

"What's your sign, dear?"

Rachel jumped at the unexpected question. "I beg your pardon?"

The elderly woman sitting beside her leaned closer. "What's your sign?" she persisted in a conspiratorial tone.

"Excuse me," Rachel said, trying to sound firm, "but I don't—"

"When's your birthday?"

Something in the woman's childish air of enthusiasm made it hard for Rachel to snub her. Besides, it would take nearly an hour for the bus to reach Dalewood, and there was no polite way to climb over the woman and find another seat. She might as well be pleasant.

"July."

"Early or late?"

"The fourth," Rachel admitted.

"Independence Day. How wonderful! Let's see now, July... July...." The older woman ran her finger down a column of the newspaper she held. "Here we are. Oh, my!" She looked up, her eyes alight. "'*A tall, dark stranger is about to enter your life,*'" she intoned. "'*Prepare for romance.*' Isn't that exciting?"

Rachel swallowed a caustic reply. Horoscopes were nothing but superstitious nonsense. If people wanted a better life, it was up to them to *make* it better, not to wait for stars and planets to magically align. And considering the embarrassment she'd suffered in the past semester at the hands of a visiting professor of performing arts at Giblin University, where she worked as a librarian, the only place she wanted to find "romance" was in the dictionary.

Her seatmate patted her arm. "That's twice I've heard you sigh as though your heart was about to break. I hope that letter of yours wasn't bad news. What was it? A note from your boyfriend?"

"No," Rachel said brusquely, abandoning her attempt at good manners. Being pleasant to a stranger was one thing; submitting passively to the third degree was quite another.

For a moment, silence reigned. Then a bony finger poked at her arm. "That boyfriend of yours isn't married, is he?" the woman asked. "Nothing but heartache can come from dallying with another woman's man, you know. Why, I once knew a girl who—"

"I don't *have* a boyfriend," Rachel interrupted her, then wished she hadn't when she saw the woman's expression melt from prurient interest to pity.

"Well, then, no wonder you look so sad. But don't you worry, sweetheart. A pretty girl like you is bound to find a husband. And remember, Madame Zora says you're going to meet somebody soon, and her horoscopes are almost never wrong. So what was it, then?"

"What was *what*?" Rachel asked, disconcerted by the scattershot conversation.

"Your letter. The one that had you so upset. If it wasn't a man, then it must be family troubles."

Rachel bit back a groan. Didn't she have enough problems without having to deal with an aspiring Sherlock Holmes?

"Not a death, I hope," the woman rattled on. "Nothing's more upsetting than a death in the family, especially if it's unexpected. Why, I remember when my Uncle William—" She broke off abruptly, shaking her head. "No, never mind me and my stories. It's you who's got a problem that needs fixing. Tell me all about it and we'll figure something out, I promise. Two heads are better than one, y'know. My friend Myrtle McCreedy claims I should be writing one of those newspaper advice columns, seeing as I can always find a way out of other people's problems for them. Myrtle's known me nearly forty years, so you can probably imagine—"

"Thank you," Rachel broke in, forcing a smile, "but it really isn't necessary. I'm just on my way to spend my day off with my aunt."

The older woman beamed at her. "Your aunt? Well, isn't that nice. I wish my nieces would come and visit *me* sometime. I bet your aunt will be tickled to see you."

Rachel hoped so. Arriving home from her work at the university library that evening, she'd unlocked the door to her apartment and opened the day's mail, reading for the first time, with disbelief, the now familiar words: *My dear Miss Locke, You should be warned...*

Before she'd even reached the closing lines, she'd been dialing her aunt's number in Dalewood, listening as the phone rang and rang until, just as she was about to hang up, a gruff male voice answered, saying, "Locke residence."

"I'd like to speak with Caroline Locke," Rachel said as soon as she recovered from her initial surprise.

"She isn't here."

Then why are you there? she wanted to shout. Instead, trying to control her uneasiness, she asked, "When do you expect her?"

"I don't know exactly. Late."

"It's late now," Rachel pointed out anxiously. "Where is she?"

"I'm not sure. Did you want to leave a message?"

"Who *is* this?" she demanded, exasperated.

"Who is *this*?" he asked. When she didn't answer immediately, he said, "Look, I'm in the middle of something important here. I don't have time for phone games. Is there a message or isn't there?''

By that time, the message she wanted to leave was unprintable. Thoroughly disconcerted, she hung up. Then, hastily packing an overnight bag, she had grabbed her purse and hurried to the bus station, just in time to catch the last Greyhound of the night. Wisely or not, she would be arriving on her aunt's doorstep unannounced, unsure what she would find waiting for her there.

Rachel gritted her teeth, willing the bus to go faster. A year after moving to Cleveland, she had sold her ancient Volkswagen, thinking it a clever economy since she lived at the edge of the university campus, with the shopping district within easy walking distance of her condominium. But now, with the anonymous letter burning a figurative hole in her purse, it no longer seemed so clever.

"Do you have much farther to go?" her seatmate inquired. "Where does your aunt live?"

"In Dalewood."

"Dalewood? Why, that's where *I* live! What a small world. What a small, small world, I do declare. What's your name, child?"

"Rachel."

Twisting in her seat, she grasped Rachel's hand and shook it. "Pleased to meet you, Rachel. I'm Agnes Denihee. Mrs. Walter Denihee. Walter and I moved there last April, and we've already become *very* involved in the community. What's your aunt's name, dear? Maybe I've made her acquaintance."

In a town the size of Dalewood, it was almost inevitable. Although Rachel knew that volunteering her aunt's name was bound to add fuel to a conversational bonfire she would have loved to extinguish, she couldn't think of a way to refuse without exciting Agnes Denihee's curiosity even further. Grateful, at least, that she hadn't told the woman anything about the anonymous letter, Rachel said, "My aunt is Caroline Locke. She lives on Spruce Street. Do you know her?''

For the first time in ten minutes, the woman beside her seemed at a loss for words. Rachel watched in surprise as Mrs. Denihee's cheeks grew red, then pale. "Why, yes," she quavered at last, smoothing her dress over her narrow lap as she avoided Rachel's gaze. "Yes, I...I do believe I've heard the name."

"What's the matter, Mrs. Denihee?"

"Nothing," the old woman replied, much too quickly. "Nothing at all."

"Then why—"

"Now, dearie, it really isn't any of my business."

"*What* isn't any of your business?"

"Any of it," Agnes Denihee said firmly, and glanced pointedly down at her watch. "My heavens, look how late it's gotten. But I do believe I still have time for a little cat-nap before we get to Dalewood. Be sure to wake me when we get there, won't you, dear?" And with that she folded her hands and closed her eyes, pursing her lips together as if to prevent any further words from leaking out.

THERE WAS NO BUS STATION in Dalewood, just a curbside bench at the north end of Main Street, in front of the town's one gas station. It came as no surprise to Rachel that she and Agnes Denihee were the only passengers to climb down from the bus when it stopped.

"Well, there's Walter," Mrs. Denihee said, nodding across the street to where a car was idling, its headlights illuminating twin swarms of moths and mayflies. She took a step, then looked back over her shoulder at Rachel and said, "I'd offer you a lift, dear, but we have to hurry home. Walter gets so cranky when he's out past his bedtime!"

As excuses went, it was one of the lamest ones Rachel had ever heard. Riding the last miles beside her obstinately silent seatmate, Rachel's anxiety over Aunt Carrie's safety had built to a point where she *had* decided to ask the woman for a ride to her aunt's house. But Agnes Denihee's silly outburst made it clear how eager she was to see the last of Rachel. *It's only a few blocks,* Rachel reasoned. *Not worth causing a scene. Just start walking.* "I understand perfectly," she said, and saw by the woman's uneasy expression that she sensed the truth in Rachel's words. "Good night."

"Lovely meeting you," Mrs. Denihee gushed nervously, and scuttled across the street to where her husband waited.

Rachel waved goodbye as the Denihees' car pulled away, then rotated her stiff shoulders. It was late, well past midnight, and there wasn't another soul in sight. Under other circumstances, she might have been nervous about walking the deserted streets alone, but somehow the urban caution she had acquired in the past four years seemed pointlessly paranoid in the quiet country night.

Turning right at the corner, she started briskly down Maple, leaving behind Main Street's single block of stores. Despite the late hour, it was still hot and humid, with only the slightest breeze. Overhead, a three-quarter moon shone silver in the cloudless sky.

It could be worse, Rachel told herself as she walked. *At least you aren't lugging a full-size suitcase.* Although she'd been living in Cleveland for four years, returning to Dalewood only for occasional visits, Rachel knew she would find her room just as she'd left it, down to the clothes in her closet. Aunt Carrie would probably even have fresh sheets on the bed, although Rachel was arriving unannounced and hadn't been home since Christmas.

Her conscience writhed. Six months without a visit was shameful. But the university's latest round of budget cuts and layoffs had pared the library staff to the bone, requiring longer hours from everyone. Unable to get away, Rachel had tried to fill the gap with letters and telephone calls to her aunt.

She knew, though, that calls and letters were no substitute for being together, face-to-face. Somehow she should have *made* the time to come to see her aunt...and she probably would have, at least once, if she hadn't been so caught up in her attraction to Douglas Chadwick. If something terrible had happened to Aunt Carrie as a result of her neglect—

Rachel realized that her pace had quickened almost to a run. Her blouse was clinging clammily to her spine. *Slow down and catch your breath,* she counseled herself sternly, *or you'll scare Aunt Carrie to death when you do get there.*

With luck, she was getting all worked up over nothing. In the past, her aunt's ''adventures'' had been harmless enough, the result of a deep zest for life and an overly generous nature. For almost as long as she could remember, Rachel had been the cautious, reasonable member of the household, the practical tail on Aunt Carrie's sometimes erratic kite. It had fallen to Rachel to amend the Girl Scout cookie purchase from fifty boxes down to five, to arrange neutering and vaccinations for the endless parade of stray kittens and puppies, and most recently, to cancel the order given to ''that nice young man'' for a thousand-dollar set of unwanted encyclopedias. Still, none of Aunt Carrie's impulsive acts of charity over the years had had truly serious consequences.

But none had ever elicited an anonymous letter, either.

At the corner of Maple and Sycamore, Rachel turned left. By the light of the street lamp, she saw that the weather-beaten For Sale sign was finally gone from the front lawn of the old Gilcrest house. Someone had even begun repairing the damage brought on by three years of the house standing vacant.

Good. It was a crime for such a beautiful old place to be allowed to fall into disrepair. Besides, it was the first indication she'd seen that Dalewood might be shaking off the doldrums into which it had fallen over the past ten years. It seemed to her that the town, like so many small farming communities, had become solely a place people came from, not one to which newcomers were apt to move. If that was beginning to change, then perhaps a buyer could be found for Aunt Carrie's house, too.

A buyer for Aunt Carrie's house. It was a dream Rachel had not yet confided to anyone. The anonymous letter had been right in that respect: it wasn't right for Aunt Carrie to be living alone. Big houses required constant upkeep, especially older ones. It was too much work and too much expense for her aunt to shoulder indefinitely. If she sold the family home, she could use the money to buy a place in Cleveland—a condominium, perhaps, where the upkeep of the grounds and the building's exterior would be taken care of by others.

And, totally aside from the house and all of the work it entailed, there was the question of companionship, of family. If Aunt Carrie moved to Cleveland, she and Rachel could spend time with each other again. It wouldn't be the same as when Rachel was growing up, of course, but they could be close and caring, all the same—together, as the last two members of the Locke family should be.

There hadn't seemed to be any point in tackling the subject as long as real estate sales were at a total standstill in Dalewood. But if a run-down structure like the Gilcrest house could sell, Rachel mused, then certainly there ought to be a market for her aunt's spacious old Victorian, with its high ceilings and gleaming hardwood floors.

She nodded decisively. She'd start pricing condominiums as soon as she got back to Cleveland.

Rounding the corner of Sycamore and Spruce, Rachel looked ahead to her aunt's house, the third from the corner. Its windows were all dark, as were those of its neighbors, but the glow from the streetlight was enough to show her the outline of the house where she had grown up. It stood tall, as if priding itself on its posture, and Rachel could see that some helpful neighbor had rescued the porch swing from winter storage and rehung it, now that summer had returned.

Stepping carefully along sidewalks that had buckled under the slow, steady pressure of tree roots, Rachel wondered how many hundreds of hours she had spent in that swing while she was growing up. How many library books had she devoured there, absently swatting at the flies and mosquitos while she read? How many evenings had she sat, sipping lemonade while she listened to her aunt spin stories about Rachel's parents and grandparents and great-grandparents? The summer she turned fifteen, Tommy Gaines had bestowed her first real kiss on her while they sat side by side on that swing, and it was there, four years ago, that she had broken the news to her aunt, as gently as possible, of her impending move to Cleveland to work at the university.

Rachel shook her head sharply. Memories; they were the blessing and the curse of each homecoming. Every street, every house, every person she encountered in Dalewood carried an association. Some were pleasurable, others decidedly were not. In Cleveland, each day was a new beginning. But here, the past was an ever-present part of life.

And is that such a terrible thing?

She mounted the porch steps with that unanswered question echoing in her mind.

She was exasperated to discover the front door was unlocked. How many times had she cautioned her aunt on the dangers of leaving the house unsecured at night? Yes, this was Dalewood, but it was no longer the Dalewood of her aunt's childhood. The present world was a chancy, violent place, even for the strong. Like it or not, a woman needed to be watchful and prudent if she wanted to keep herself safe.

Then why didn't you put your pride aside and ask Mr. and Mrs. Denihee for a ride instead of walking here alone in the middle of the night?

"Oh, shut up," she muttered in exasperation as she eased the big door open and slipped inside.

Admit it. There's something special about Dalewood. You feel safe here. You always have.

In answer, Rachel took elaborate care in locking the door behind herself. As she did, the familiar scent of the house filled her nostrils, a comforting blend of lemon oil and lavender that relaxed her against her will. In the darkness, she put out her hand and reached into the little cut-glass bowl of wintergreen candies that Aunt Carrie always kept on the entryway table. Then, with the clean taste of the lozenge melting on her tongue, Rachel took off her shoes and started up the stairs.

Out of habit, she avoided the fifth step with its resident squeak. Now that everything seemed peaceful, she would simply peek into her aunt's room and make sure she was all right. There was no need to startle her awake in the middle of the night. Tomorrow morning would be soon enough to tell her about the anonymous letter and find out the identity of the man who had answered her phone.

The upstairs hallway was hot and still. Rachel reached out in the darkness and bumped her hand against her aunt's bedroom door, which, uncharacteristically, was closed. Turning the knob slowly, she let herself inside.

Tucked beneath the sheet on her big bed, Aunt Carrie was sound asleep. A pool of moonlight illuminated her plump face and created an illusion of youth. Her hair, loose on the pillow, curled in the same soft nimbus that Rachel's did, although its deep chestnut color was now streaked with gray. Her lips quirked upward in a smile, even in sleep. Rachel smiled back as she listened to the steady rhythm of her aunt's breathing, then grinned as she saw that Gertrude, the elaborate "French lady" doll her aunt had had since child-hood, lay beside her on the pillow.

"One o'clock and all's well," she murmured as the grandfather clock downstairs chimed the hour.

Relieved, Rachel tiptoed out into the hallway. Now that she had made certain that her aunt was safe, she could afford to come down from the adrenaline high that had gnawed at her since her hurried departure from Cleveland nearly three hours earlier. At the far end of the hall, there was a firm mattress and a soft pillow waiting for her.

And in the morning she could put on denim shorts and a halter top and let her hair flow free. Nobody in Dalewood cared whether she looked knowledgeable and professional. To most of the town's inhabitants, she would forever be "Caroline's little niece," and to the rest she was "that Locke girl, graduated first in her class but then what do you expect from somebody with her nose in a book all the time?" Few of them knew or cared what she did for a living. Once she'd moved away from Dalewood, she had largely ceased to exist for them.

Just like most of them ceased to exist for you as soon as you hit the Cleveland city limits.

Irritably Rachel shrugged the thought away. Sleep was her first priority. Everything would look better in the morning.

The door to her room was closed, as well. Rachel sighed. Her room faced south and west. If the door had been shut all day, it would be like an oven inside. She'd just have to open the windows wide and hope that the fledgling breeze could force its way through the branches of the big catalpa tree.

And if it can't?

Rachel grinned. As a girl, she had sometimes removed the window screen and climbed out to sleep on the roof of the porch, under the stars. Somehow, she'd never worried about rolling off; it had felt as safe to her as her own bed.

But she knew she wouldn't be doing that tonight, no matter how hot the room was. Her childhood was past—not as far past as Aunt Carrie's, but past, all the same—and she no longer gave in to indulgent or dangerous impulses. One stuffy night wouldn't be the death of her.

Rachel opened the door to her room . . . and heard the unexpected rustle of catalpa leaves. The windows were open after all, and the breeze seemed to be on the rise, leaving the room warm but not unbearable.

The tree outside her windows blocked out the moon, making the room almost totally dark, but this was familiar territory. Rachel had no need of light here. Bending down, she set her shoes on the floor beside the bed, followed by her purse and overnight case. Then, unbuttoning her sweat-damp blouse, she let it slip from her shoulders and reached for the button at the waistband of her skirt.

If she'd been thinking more clearly when she left her apartment, she would have taken the time to change out of her work clothes into something cooler . . . but then she would probably have missed the bus. All things considered, it was better to be here, hot but reassured, than still to be in Cleveland, physically comfortable but unsure whether Aunt Carrie was all right.

Of course, neither extreme would have been necessary if Aunt Carrie had just been home to answer Rachel's anxious telephone call herself. Where had she been at nearly ten o'clock at night? In Rachel's experience, the sidewalks of Dalewood rolled up shortly after sunset. Choir practice wasn't until Thursday night, and ten o'clock was far too late to have been out visiting. And yet, wherever Aunt Carrie had been, she was all right now, sleeping soundly in her own bed, unaware that her earlier absence had caused Rachel to spend a long bus ride working herself into a froth over nothing.

No, not quite nothing. There was still the anonymous letter to consider. There had to be a way to track down its author. If she could just think of it . . .

Lost in speculation, Rachel stepped toward the closet to hang up her skirt and blouse.

Crash! Without warning, she found herself painfully entangled with an unexpected, sharp-edged obstacle that tumbled to the floor with her, making a clattering sound loud enough to wake the dead.

"Damn!" Rachel scrambled gingerly to her feet again, then froze as she heard a rustle of movement in the darkness behind her.

A cat, she told herself to combat the fear squeezing her heart. *One of Aunt Carrie's strays.* But it hadn't sounded like a cat. It had sounded . . . bigger. Much bigger.

Instinct told her to run, but how could she leave Aunt Carrie behind, asleep and defenseless? Dry mouthed, Rachel turned to face the intruder, wincing as a floorboard creaked beneath her feet. *Don't panic. Maybe it's nothing. Fear can play funny tricks on—*

Before she could finish the thought, however, an unseen hand came out of the darkness, its fingers closing around her wrist in a bruising, viselike grip.

CHAPTER TWO

TRYING TO PULL AWAY, Rachel opened her mouth to scream but all that came out was a hoarse cry.

"Hold still," a rumbling voice warned. "Don't make me hurt you."

Hold still? Rachel thought wildly. *Like hell!* If something horrible was about to happen, she didn't intend to be a passive victim.

Wishing she still had shoes on, she kicked her attacker and threw herself to one side, trying to knock him off balance. Undeterred, he began to drag her toward the bed; in answer, she dropped to her knees and sank her teeth into his arm.

His only response was to curse her in some language she didn't recognize as he continued to pull her forward.

Rachel fought him, inch by inch, but his strength made a mockery of her efforts. Desperate, she tried to bite him again. He stopped her by hauling her roughly to her feet and crushing her against him in a sudden bear hug that forced the air from her lungs.

Then, inexplicably, he released her.

She tumbled unceremoniously to the floor. Gasping for breath, she crawled away, groping in the darkness for something she could use as a weapon, but all she found was a bundle of cloth. Rachel pulled it to her, with a half-formed notion of trying to strangle him with it, or at least of throwing it in his face when he launched his next assault.

Instead the light came on, half-blinding her. Blinking painfully, she squinted up at her adversary.

Silhouetted against the glow from the bedside lamp, he was a towering, shadowy form, something from her worst nightmares, faceless and formidable. He stood motionless, watching her, and fear gathered like a fist in Rachel's stomach. *This can't be happening. Not to me. Not here, in my own house, in my own room.*

It made it worse, somehow, that he had turned on the light. He didn't seem to care whether she saw him well enough to identify him. Why? Because he had already decided that she'd never have the chance?

He took a step toward her.

I love you, Aunt Carrie. The words ran through Rachel's mind like a prayer. *I love you. I'm sorry I stayed away so long, sorry I couldn't keep you safe, sorry this is happening....*

"I thought cat burglars wore black," the deep voice said, cutting across her desperate thoughts. "But pink is nice. Very nice."

Rachel glanced down at her peach silk teddy, feeling sick. Depressed over Douglas Chadwick, she'd worn the frothy piece of lingerie to bolster her battered feminine pride, never dreaming that her impulsive self-indulgence might later raise the stakes in a perilous game of wits and nerve. Trying not to betray her fear, she said, "Who are you? What do you want?"

He shook his head. "You're the one with questions to answer," he said sternly, and came a step closer.

With a sick feeling of foreboding, Rachel realized that he was clothed only in the massive muscles that had allowed him to overpower her so easily. So then, he *was* a psychopath, a man whose twisted, troubled mind prompted him to break into people's houses, naked, in the middle of the night. That made him dangerous and unpredictable... but it might also mean that he could be frightened away.

"You don't belong here," she said forcefully. "If you leave right now, you can be gone before my husband gets home. If he finds you here, he'll call the police."

He shook his head, rejecting her words. "Lady, you're as crazy as a loon—and you bite like a pit bull. Believe me, if it's police you want, it's police you'll get. But first, I want my pants back."

Looking down, Rachel realized that the bundle of cloth she was clutching so tightly to her chest was a faded pair of denim jeans. Her own skirt and blouse were crumpled on the floor a few feet away.

Two minutes earlier, convinced that she was in danger of losing her life, her sole concern had been survival, not modesty. But she was beginning to suspect, with relief and consternation, that she was safe, just entangled in a misunderstanding of cosmic proportions. If that was the case, she was nearly as embarrassed by her own lace-trimmed teddy and panty hose as she was by her tormentor's nudity.

It was an insane situation, one for which she could imagine no likely explanation. If she hadn't seen Aunt Carrie sleeping so peacefully, Rachel might almost have been able to convince herself that she had somehow blundered into the wrong house. But she hadn't. This was her home. Her room. For that matter, the antique four-poster bed was hers as well, although its rumpled sheets seemed to indicate that her assailant had been sleeping in it. "Who *are* you?" she demanded again, averting her eyes from the provocative sight of his naked body.

"Ladies first," he insisted grimly, making no attempt to cover himself. "Who the hell are *you*?"

Before Rachel could reply, the sound of a tentative knock on the bedroom door made her nerves jump. Then Aunt Carrie's familiar voice called softly, "Mr. Pulneshti?"

"My pants!" the big man demanded of Rachel in a stage whisper, holding out his hand in implacable demand.

"Mr. Pulneshti? Are you all right?"

"Just a minute, Miss Caroline," he said firmly, and snatched his jeans out of Rachel's benumbed grasp. Sitting down on the edge of the bed, he stepped into them hurriedly.

Finally free to remedy her own state of dishabille, Rachel untangled her clothes from the tumbled wreckage of the spindly-legged table on the floor and began to dress, her mind racing.

Mr. Pulneshti, Aunt Carrie had said. So the monster had a name. Moreover, it seemed that Aunt Carrie had expected to find him in Rachel's bedroom in the middle of the night. *Curiouser and curiouser,* she thought gloomily. How many other surprises would she have to face before the long day was finally over?

Shimmying to coax her narrow skirt over her hips, Rachel felt a sudden prickle of awareness and looked up to find the man watching her. "Need a hand?" he asked softly, a glint of amusement brightening his dark eyes.

"No." Cheeks burning, she turned her back on him, trying to ignore the shaking of her fingers as she tugged the zipper of her skirt closed and worked her way down the long line of blouse buttons.

"Ready?" he asked rhetorically, and opened the room door a discreet few inches, his broad back blocking Rachel's view of the hallway. "Hello, Miss Caroline," she heard him say as she tucked her blouse into her waistband. "Sorry if I disturbed everyone's sleep. The rest of you may as well go back to bed now. The excitement's over."

"But what on earth was it, Mr. Pulneshti? What happened?"

"Come on in, Miss Caroline, and I'll explain."

He opened the door farther and Aunt Carrie stepped hesitantly into the room. The sight of her, swaddled in her old blue bathrobe, brought unexpected tears to Rachel's eyes. Fighting to control an upsurge of affection and relief, she hurried forward, eager to wrap both arms around her aunt's plump form.

"Dear heaven," Aunt Carrie exclaimed, the initial look of surprise on her wrinkled face giving way to an expression of incandescent joy. "Rachel! Where—"

And then there were no words, just the sweet security of Aunt Carrie's welcoming embrace and the feathery tickle of her graying curls beneath Rachel's cheek as they held each other close.

"What on earth are you doing here?" her aunt asked at last. "I didn't know you were coming home."

"No, I can see that," Rachel said. Stepping back, she met the eyes of the man at the door. He'd closed it again and stood with one bare shoulder braced against it, watching them, his expression unreadable.

"Oh, dear," the older woman said, following Rachel's gaze, "you're upset. It must have been a terrible shock for you. For both of you. I'm so sorry if—"

Rachel shook her head. "I don't need apologies, Aunt Carrie. I just need an explanation. Who *is* this man?"

"That's Mr. Pulneshti, dear. Sandor Pulneshti. Mr. Pulneshti, I'd like you to meet my niece, Rachel Locke."

He straightened from his lounging stance and inclined his head toward Rachel in a mocking little bow. "Pleased to make your acquaintance," he said, and Rachel saw that he was having a hard time keeping his face straight. "Life is full of surprises. I never would have taken you for a research librarian, Miss Locke, considering—"

She glared at him as dauntingly as she could, forbidding him to even think about mentioning her underwear.

"—how young you are," he concluded blandly.

Rachel dismissed him with a glance, turning her attention back to her aunt. "That answers *who* he is, but why is he here? And why did you put him in my bedroom instead of one of the guest rooms?"

"Well, you see, dear, the other rooms were all…taken."

"Taken?" she echoed, and her memory suddenly retrieved Sandor Pulneshti's earlier words: *The rest of you may as well go back to bed now. The excitement's over.* Rachel's heart sank. From the sound of things, the "excitement" was just beginning.

Aunt Carrie patted her hand. "You don't mind sharing my room for the rest of the night, do you, Rachel? If only you'd called to let me know you were coming…."

"But I did," Rachel protested earnestly. "I called at ten, as soon as I got home from work, but some stranger answered."

"That was me," Sandor Pulneshti said.

Rachel turned to him in surprise. "You?"

"But, Mr. Pulneshti," Aunt Carrie said reproachfully, "you didn't tell me that Rachel called."

He shrugged. "How could I? She wouldn't leave her name."

"Because you wouldn't give me yours!" Rachel flared, and said to her aunt, "He wouldn't tell me where you were or who he was. I was afraid something had happened to you. I had to come to make sure you were all right."

"You've had a hectic night," Aunt Carrie said sympathetically. "But as you can see, I'm fine. There was really no need for you to take the bus here in the middle of the night. Even considering the phone call, don't you think you may have overreacted just a little?"

Under normal circumstances, Rachel might have agreed, but an anonymous letter didn't qualify as "normal circumstances." Still, the letter wasn't something she wanted to discuss with her aunt until they were alone. "Where were you?" Rachel asked instead, hoping to be convinced that she had embarked on a wild-goose chase.

Aunt Carrie avoided her eyes. "As it happens, Max and I didn't get back from Milford until a little after eleven."

Rachel stared. "You were in Milford? But why? You hate to drive at night! And who on earth is—? No, wait," she said, and looked pointedly at Sandor Pulneshti, who looked right back, apparently unabashed. "Aunt Carrie, can't we talk about this in private?"

"Of course," her aunt said cooperatively, then ruined it by adding, "It's time we left so that Mr. Pulneshti can get back to sleep."

"In my bed," Rachel couldn't resist adding.

Aunt Carrie ignored her. "Will we see you at breakfast, Mr. Pulneshti?"

"I wouldn't miss it," he assured her, opening the door for them.

Aunt Carrie smiled on him with gentle approval. "I do hope you and Rachel will have a chance to get acquainted while she's here."

"Oh, I'm sure we'll be seeing a lot of each other," he said as Aunt Carrie passed by him and started down the hallway, then added quietly, for Rachel's sole benefit, "Of course, our first meeting may be a tough act to follow."

"Very funny," Rachel said, trying to edge past him.

"Don't look so glum. You drew first blood."

Glancing down, she saw that he spoke the literal truth: tiny dots of blood were beading along several of the scratch marks she had inflicted, and imprints of her teeth were still clearly visible on his tanned flesh.

"Lucky for you I've had my shots," she said, rubbing her aching forearm. She was damned if she'd apologize for what she'd done. At the time, she'd believed she was fighting for her life. And he had left his fair share of marks on her, as well—bruises rather than bites, but by morning she was sure his handiwork would be as clearly visible as her own. "My aunt is waiting. Good night, Mr. Pulneshti."

"Pleasant dreams, Miss Locke. Try a hot bath."

"What?"

He gestured toward her arm. "If you're stiff in the morning, try a hot bath. It can work wonders."

The words might have been meant as friendly advice or as a further jibe; his neutral tone made it impossible for Rachel to tell.

She looked up at him assessingly. His expression was impassive, his ebony eyes unreadable in the dim light. His curly hair was as dark as his eyes, and his swarthy skin completed the picture, making him look like a denizen of the night, the sort of creature who could move with ease through a midnight world, gliding unseen from shadow to shadow. He looked like a powerful man. Perhaps even a dangerous one. Not someone who belonged in Dalewood. And definitely not someone she cared to have sleeping under her aunt's roof, regardless of whose bed he was using.

Until she could talk to Aunt Carrie and learn the full story behind his presence, however, there was little she could do about it. Certainly a staring match wasn't going to help. "Good night," she repeated, trying to match his noncommittal tone, and turned away.

But she was uncomfortably aware that he was watching her every step of the way as she walked the length of the hallway to Aunt Carrie's door.

MISS CAROLINE'S NIECE, Sandor observed, looked as though she'd just swallowed a mouthful of thumbtacks, but even in defeat she carried herself proudly as she retreated down the hallway.

He admired that. Truth to tell, he admired a great many things about Rachel Locke, ranging from her bravery in battle to her taste in lingerie. Despite the late hour and his landlady's good wishes, he doubted whether he would find it easy to fall asleep again. After all, it wasn't every night that a man woke from a sound sleep to grapple with an intruder who turned out to be . . .

" . . . the woman of his dreams?" Sandor mused, and began, slowly, reluctantly, to laugh. If that sharp-toothed, tart-tongued spitfire was the woman the Tarot cards had foreseen in his future, it was going to be a long, hot summer.

CHAPTER THREE

"ALL RIGHT, Aunt Carrie," Rachel said as she stepped into her aunt's room and shut the door securely behind herself. "Why is Conan the Barbarian staying in my room?"

Her aunt looked up from straightening the bed. "Conan . . . ? Oh, you mean Mr. Pulneshti! You shouldn't call him that, dear. He's really very nice. The two of you just got off on the wrong foot. Entirely my fault. I imagine you must have been startled to find him there."

"Startled?" Rachel dropped onto the edge of the bed. "Aunt Carrie, I was terrified. I thought he was some crazed burglar who was going to kill me and then come down the hall and kill *you*. When he grabbed my arm, I thought my number was up."

"He grabbed your arm? Why did he do that?" Aunt Carrie asked, sounding more surprised than alarmed.

Honesty compelled Rachel to give the devil his due. "I guess he thought *I* was a burglar. He didn't say, and I didn't ask. There wasn't any time for words. He just came at me, out of the darkness, before I even knew he was there, and . . ." She gestured helplessly, powerless to translate the raw fear of those minutes into words, but a reflection of it must have shown on her face, because her aunt dropped the pillow she'd been fluffing and made her way around the bed to embrace her.

"I didn't realize," Aunt Carrie said faintly. "Oh, my. I should have known something like this might happen eventually, but I was afraid you'd fuss at me if I told you about

Mr. Pulneshti and the others, so I kept finding reasons not to mention them. I am sorry, dear. Forgive me?''

"You know I do," Rachel insisted staunchly. "Don't look so stricken. I'm fine...or I will be, once I've calmed down." She managed a wry smile. "With luck, my heart rate may even drop back to normal in a month or two. But if you want to make me feel better in the meantime, you can sit yourself down right here," she said, patting the bed, "and tell me what it is that you've been so busy not mentioning to me. I'll try not to 'fuss' at you, but I do think I've earned the right to hear the truth, don't you?''

"Yes, of course...but wouldn't you rather wait until morning?''

"Do you honestly think I'll be able to sleep a wink until you've told me? Besides, what could be more appropriate than a bedtime story? Lord knows, I've already played the part of Baby Bear tonight, asking 'Who's been sleeping in my bed?' "

Aunt Carrie folded her hands. "I'm not sure where to start."

"That's easy—begin at the beginning."

The indulgent smile she knew so well deepened the lines around her aunt's mouth. "All right, Rachel. But I think you should get ready for bed first. That way, it won't matter if you nod off while I'm talking."

Rachel had no intention of so much as closing her eyes until she'd gotten to the bottom of her aunt's latest escapade, but there was little point in arguing. "I'll need to borrow a nightgown," she said. "I don't intend to knock on the Barbarian's door and ask him for my overnight bag. Is my toothbrush still in the bathroom?''

"Of course, dear. For that matter, some of your old clothes are here in my bureau. I believe I put your nightgowns and underwear in the third drawer."

"You moved all of my clothes into your room?" A renewed rush of indignation heated Rachel's blood. "How long is this guy planning to stay, anyway? For that matter, how long has he *been* here?"

"That's all part of the story," her aunt replied. "Get settled for the night, and then I'll tell you about it."

Rachel did as she was told, looking over her shoulder more than once as she padded barefoot down the darkened hallway to the bathroom. The silence of the house was misleading. Strangers were sleeping behind those closed doors, and their presence in Aunt Carrie's house left her deeply uneasy.

Once she was safely barricaded inside the bathroom, she saw that her toothbrush was in the rack beside Aunt Carrie's, where it had always hung...but there were four unfamiliar ones hanging by it, as well.

She soon found other evidence that she and Aunt Carrie weren't alone. A long auburn hair clung to the bowl of the sink, and the bottom shelf of the medicine cabinet held a battered tube of denture adhesive and three brands of toothpaste. Whoever the invaders were, they seemed to have settled in for the duration.

Rachel pondered that as she brushed her teeth and scrubbed her face. If they were overnight guests, she would see shaving kits or makeup cases on the counter beside the sink, not individual items stored away on shelves. Rinsing the offending strand of auburn hair down the drain, she tried to reconcile herself to the growing realization that Aunt Carrie was committed to some ongoing arrangement that involved strangers sleeping in her house.

Boarders, Rachel thought unhappily, drawing the pins out of her hair. *Aunt Carrie has taken in boarders.*

When her hair was free of restraints, tumbling in curly disorder down her back, Rachel reached for her brush, remembering too late that it was in her purse, and that her purse, too, was still down at the end of the hall, in her—correction, in Sandor Pulneshti's—room. *Wonderful,* she fumed. *The perfect ending to a perfect day.*

With her foul mood renewed, she walked back along the hallway, wondering sourly which rooms held Redhead and Toothless. She knew all too well where Conan was spending the night. He was probably asleep by now, his long, muscled body relaxing on the mattress that had been hers for so many years, his raven head cradled by her down-filled pillow, his bare skin warm between the soft laundered cotton of her sheets....

That's no way to ease your blood pressure, she warned herself impatiently, and slipped back into her aunt's room.

Aunt Carrie, already tucked into bed, offered a drowsy smile of welcome. "I'll only be a minute," Rachel assured her, and searched hastily through the third drawer of the bureau until she found a summer nightgown. After undressing, she pulled it over her head and hung her skirt and blouse in the crowded closet with the other outfits that had been transferred there. "Mind if I borrow your brush?"

"Of course not, dear."

Rachel lifted the silver-back brush from its place on top of the bureau and tugged its firm bristles quickly through her hair, working out the tangles. When she was done, she turned off the light and slid into bed beside her aunt. "Well, I'm all ears. 'Once upon a time...'" she prompted, settling back against her pillow.

"Now, Rachel, there's really no huge, outrageous secret to tell, so don't be disappointed," her aunt cautioned her. "I've just rented rooms to a few people, that's all."

"I knew it! Oh, Aunt Carrie, how *could* you?"

"Hush, dear. You'll wake the others. And remember, you promised not to fuss at me."

Rachel took a deep breath, counted slowly to ten, and exhaled. "All right," she said, lowering her voice to a tense murmur. "No fussing. Just a few basic questions—like *why?*"

"Well, for a lot of different reasons."

"Pick one."

"In part, for the extra income."

It wasn't an answer Rachel had expected. "But you have the check from your annuity every month, and the money I send home. Isn't it enough? I can send more if—"

"Certainly not," Aunt Carrie said with surprising firmness. "That's your money, and you have your own future to consider. Now that you know about my boarders, I won't need to take anything from you at all. If you're making more than you need to live on, you should be saving up for when you get married and start a family."

"Believe me, that isn't going to happen any time soon."

"Can you be so sure?" Aunt Carrie asked, her tone light and teasing. "What about that professor who called you when you were home for Thanksgiving? Donald . . . or was it David? Oh, you know who I mean."

"Yes, I know who you mean," Rachel acknowledged heavily. "Douglas Chadwick. Don't worry about remembering his name—you won't need to. Now that the school year is over, he's gone back home to Colorado."

"Oh," her aunt said, sounding abashed. "I'm sorry, dear. But I wouldn't write him off too hastily, if I were you. You know what they say about absence making the heart grow—"

"I don't care what absence makes his heart do," Rachel said hotly.

"But the two of you were getting on so well! What happened?"

"He got a little surprise during exam week. His family flew in to see him so they could all drive home together."

"His family?"

Rachel's throat tightened as she remembered the mortifying scene that had taken place at Douglas's apartment. "It seems he has a wife and a four-year-old daughter, minor details that he never got around to mentioning to anybody—least of all to me—while he was at Giblin."

"But that's despicable. The man should be ashamed of himself!"

"The state of Douglas's conscience is his problem," Rachel said firmly. "But you can rest assured that the relationship is definitely over. I'm not planning to change my last name or anything else about my life at any time in the foreseeable future, so unless the library staff gets caught in more budget cuts, there's no reason why I can't send you a bigger check each month. I just didn't realize you needed more money."

"Well, I don't," Aunt Carrie protested. "Not at the moment, anyway. But I'm getting older, and I don't ever want to be a burden to you, so when this opportunity came up—"

"Taking in boarders, you mean?"

"Yes. When Pastor Milligan came to me, I didn't see any reason to say no."

"Wait a minute. Let me get this straight. Pastor Milligan asked you to rent a room to Sandor Pulneshti?"

"Well, not exactly. He'd received a letter from one of our sister churches in New Jersey, telling him about a parishioner who was leaving the Newark school system and wanted to retire to the country. She needed a place to stay, at least temporarily, and Pastor Milligan asked if I'd be interested in renting a room to Miss Jones. And I said yes."

A retired schoolteacher from New Jersey? That sounded safe and dull, not at all the sort of thing to inspire an anonymous letter. "All right," Rachel said thoughtfully. "You said yes to Pastor Milligan, and Miss Jones moved in. When was this?"

"In January, when you went back to the university after your Christmas break. And then, in February, Mr. Pulneshti and Max came."

"And Max is the one you drove to Milford with, tonight?"

"That's right. But Mr. Pulneshti came first, at the beginning of the month. He was working on Mrs. Gilcrest's house and—"

"Oh! Is he the one who's fixing it up? I noticed that the For Sale sign was finally gone. When is he planning to move in?" she asked, relieved. At least that would get rid of *one* problem.

"No, you misunderstand me, dear. Mr. Pulneshti isn't going to be living there. He's one of the carpenters repairing the house."

Ah, Rachel thought, *a carpenter. That explains the muscles.*

"Lately," Aunt Carrie continued, "he's been working on a new house out by the township limit, too, but he'd just begun the Gilcrest repairs when he came looking for a room. He offered to help with the outside chores in addition to his rent, shoveling snow and so on, and that seemed like a good idea, so I told him he could stay. Then Max—"

"Just like that?" Rachel interrupted in disbelief.

"Just like what, dear?"

"This man walked up to your door and asked if he could move in, and you said yes, just like that? Did you talk to his employer?"

"No, of course not. What business was it of mine—"

"Sweetheart, did you know anything at all about this man except that he was working on the old Gilcrest place?"

"Well, no. That is to say, I didn't actually know he was working there until he told me."

Rachel fought to keep her voice level. "And was that before you rented him the room, or after?"

"After, I think. Yes, I'm sure it was after. When we sat down to dinner, Miss Jones asked him what he did for a living, and he said—"

"You didn't even know if he had a *job*?" Rachel demanded, her determination to stay calm going up in smoke. "Did you at least ask him for a month's rent in advance?"

"Of course not," Aunt Carrie said, sounding scandalized. "That wouldn't have been very friendly of me, especially when he'd been so nice, offering to help out around the house since neither Miss Jones nor I are as young as we used to be."

In retrospect, the scenario chilled Rachel's blood: a strange man coming to the door, learning that the house was inhabited only by two elderly spinsters, convincing them to let him stay there with them.... If he had turned out to be some drifter intent on brutalizing them or stealing their money, what could they have done to stop him? It was almost enough to make her grateful to Sandor Pulneshti for being who he said he was and not taking advantage of two such helpless innocents.

"And then, within a week, we met Max, and she agreed to—"

"She?"

"She," Aunt Carrie confirmed with a smile, and continued, "Max volunteered to take over most of the actual housework in exchange for her room and board. I declare, Rachel, between Max and Mr. Pulneshti, I don't know when I've felt so rested. And Miss Jones is a highly educated woman, wonderful company. So you see, it isn't just the money, it's the companionship and the help they provide, as well. Looking back, I hardly know how I got along on my own, these past few years. When you meet them all tomorrow morning, you'll see that there's really nothing for you to worry about. It's all worked out wonderfully."

But Rachel was only listening with half an ear to her aunt's effusive words. "There's another one," she said. "You said all the other bedrooms were being used—that must mean you have four boarders, not three. Who haven't you told me about?"

"I was getting to him," Aunt Carrie insisted. "You didn't give me a chance to finish." But Rachel thought she detected a new note in her aunt's voice; the older woman sounded flustered. "My fourth boarder is Mr. Hudson, Mr. George Hudson. He's an older gentleman, semiretired."

"Semiretired from what?"

"Mr. Hudson deals in antiques and curios. He and his nephew have a shop in Cincinnati. He's a charming man, wonderfully friendly."

"I'm sure," Rachel said bleakly, wishing her aunt would send all four boarders packing, but Aunt Carrie clearly had no intention of doing so. Still, precautions needed to be taken, however belatedly. The situation just called for diplomacy and compromise.

"You know, Aunt Carrie," Rachel said. "I'm sure Mr. Hudson and the other boarders will understand if we ask them for a list of references."

"References? What do you mean?"

"Just the names and addresses of a couple of people who can vouch for them. I'd like to see something on paper that tells us that these people are all who they say they are."

"But—"

"There's nothing unusual about it."

"But I don't think—"

"We could ask them in the morning. I have to catch the afternoon bus back to Cleveland tomorrow and I'd really like to have the list by then so that I can begin to—"

"Rachel, wait. I just don't think I could do that. Perhaps from now on I could ask each new tenant to provide me with a list of names, but these people have been living here with me for months. How will it look if I suddenly start demanding character references from them? Their feelings would be hurt, I'm certain of it. It's insulting. I'm sorry, dear, but I just couldn't."

It wasn't an argument Rachel could afford to lose, but she knew equally well that it wasn't one she could win by force. Her aunt wasn't a child; she couldn't be ordered, only persuaded. Taking a deep breath, Rachel tried again.

"Aunt Carrie, it isn't just a matter of character references. What if Miss Jones got sick, or Mr. Pulneshti was injured in a construction accident? Would you know who to notify if they were unconscious and couldn't tell you? Even worse, what if one of them died? Would you know how to contact their families?"

"Dear me, I never thought about that," Aunt Carrie admitted, sounding distressed by the thought of one of her boarders falling ill.

"With luck, it won't ever be an issue," Rachel said soothingly, "but it could be. The background information is for their benefit as well as yours. You have a responsibility to them."

"Well..."

"In the morning, I'll explain to them what we need and why we need it, okay? They don't know me, so they won't have any reason to take it personally. Just leave it to me." *And if any of them refuse,* she thought, *or their references don't check out, then you and I will have to talk again. But this is a start, at least.*

It was also enough unpleasantness for one night. The mystery of the anonymous letter could wait until morning. Rachel's eyelids felt as if they'd been lined with sandpaper, and she could hear Aunt Carrie yawning beside her.

"Get some sleep." Rachel fought back a yawn of her own. "And don't worry. Everything's going to be fine."

"Everything is already fine," her aunt corrected her gently. "You'll see. But it is wonderful to have you home again."

"It's good to be here," Rachel said.

The room was hot and stuffy despite the rising breeze. The mattress was too soft to suit her, and the pillow too hard. Acutely aware of her aunt resting beside her, Rachel willed herself not to toss and turn, but the night's traumas and unresolved problems continued to crowd her thoughts, competing for attention.

Soon, Aunt Carrie's breathing fell into the slow, deep rhythm of sleep, leaving Rachel feeling wider awake and more isolated than ever. *I'm just too used to sleeping alone,* she concluded, and found the realization a sad one. Was she destined to follow in Aunt Carrie's footsteps, never finding a man she could love with her whole heart, never having children of her own, eventually depending on a group of total strangers for companionship?

No, she reflected, *your life will be even harder. At least Aunt Carrie has you to love her. Who will you have when she's gone?*

A flicker of distant heat lightning brightened the room for an instant, then faded. Resenting it, she closed her eyes. The farmland around Dalewood needed rain, not flashy pyrotechnics. Heat lightning was nothing but an empty promise, as misleading as Douglas Chadwick's romantic words had proven to be.

Some things were too important to live without. And some were too important for lies.

IN HER DREAM, rain was falling in sheets across the land. The heavy, drenching torrents soaked deep into the parched soil and splashed around her bare ankles as she ran across the freshly plowed furrows. She was fleeing from a gang of swarthy giants who pursued her, calling her name, their voices reverberating in her ears like summer thunder.

Waking with a start, Rachel opened her eyes to the glow of morning sunlight. She felt a brief stab of disappointment when she realized that the rain existed only in her dream, but it was hard to stay unhappy for long; a sweet chorus of bird song rose from the redbud trees outside her aunt's open window, and a cool breeze ruffled the curtains. Beside her, Aunt Carrie slept on, serenely undisturbed.

According to the alarm clock, it was half-past six. Although she had had only a few hours of sleep, Rachel was too tense to lie back in the hope of dozing off again. Moving as quietly as she could, she pushed back the sheet and slipped out of bed, doing her best to ignore an assortment of pangs and twinges from her abused muscles, souvenirs from her wrestling match with Sandor Pulneshti.

When Rachel looked in the mirror over Aunt Carrie's bureau, it reflected a pale, puffy-eyed face, half-hidden behind a tangled mass of curls—hardly an inspiring sight. With a grimace of distaste, Rachel ran her aunt's brush through her hair, subduing it, then opened the closet and reached for the skirt and blouse she'd arrived in. The comfort of shorts and a halter top would have to wait a few more hours. This morning, facing her aunt's boarders over the breakfast table, she wanted to look like an authority figure, fair but firm, not just the landlady's niece.

Shoes were another matter. Sighing, she wondered when she'd have a chance to reclaim her sandals from the other room. The selection of left-behinds on the floor of Aunt Carrie's closet was distinctly limited: paint-stained sneakers, battered huaraches and a pair of black suede pumps that looked lovely but would invariably blister her heels within minutes.

Nobody's going to be looking at your feet anyway, she rationalized, and stepped into the huaraches.

Armed with clothes and shoes, Rachel opened Aunt Carrie's door and peered out. As she'd hoped, no one was in sight, and the bathroom door stood open. Mustering her courage, she dashed down the hallway to claim the shower first.

Once inside, with the door locked securely behind her, Rachel found indications that someone else in the house was an early riser: traces of misty condensation lingered on the mirror, and the inside of the plastic shower curtain was beaded with moisture.

Remembering her rain dream, Rachel wondered if her sleeping brain had translated the sound of water thundering through the pipes into a storm for her inner landscape.

As to the source of the deep-voiced giants who had pursued her, it seemed distinctly unfair of Sandor Pulneshti to have multiplied himself. One of them was more than enough.

Ten minutes later, basking in the steamy spray, Rachel felt almost human again. Not even the sight of the purplish bruises on her left forearm could seriously interfere with her mood as she savored the water's soothing caress. Last night, she had assured Aunt Carrie that everything would be fine; this morning, she even believed it.

She was rinsing the soap from her body, letting the hot water and lather cascade down her back, when she first heard the pounding. It stopped after a moment, then started again, sounding almost as if the person doing it were in the room with her. There was another pause before a third session of pounding began, even louder than the first two. Rachel turned off the water.

"Hey," a female voice called out, its aggrieved tone apparent even through the wall. "Leave a little hot water for somebody else!"

Not sure whether to apologize or defend herself, Rachel did neither. It was true, she hadn't given any thought to how much hot water she might be using, but that was only because there had never been any shortage of hot water in Aunt Carrie's house. With six adults making use of it, Rachel could see why conservation might have become a necessary evil. She simply hadn't had a chance to think through all the ramifications of her aunt's overextended hospitality.

Blast. Now she felt as if she'd lost the moral high ground before she'd even met her aunt's other tenants. Drying herself briskly, she hurried into her clothes, glad that she'd decided against the lengthy process of washing and drying her hair, as well.

When Rachel unlocked the bathroom door and opened it, she half expected to find a disgruntled boarder waiting there, shower cap in hand, but the hallway was empty. Each bedroom door along it was closed, leaving her no way to guess how many of the rooms were still occupied, but the aroma of percolating coffee rising from the stairwell warned that at least one of the boarders was already downstairs.

Rachel hesitated, speculating. If it was Sandor Pulneshti down in the kitchen fixing coffee, this would be a golden opportunity to slip in unobserved and reclaim her shoes, purse and overnight case.

On the other hand, he might still be in bed. She had no wish to be caught a second time tiptoeing into the room where he slept. Surprising him was too dangerous an occupation. At least until her bruises faded, she didn't intend to confront Sandor Pulneshti unless he was wide awake, fully clothed, and in the presence of witnesses.

All told, the risks outweighed the benefits. With a wistful sigh, Rachel turned her back on temptation and headed downstairs, wondering how many of the tenants she would find there. Now that she was up and dressed, she was anxious to speak her piece and have it over with. If there was going to be any unpleasantness over her request, she didn't want Aunt Carrie involved.

The front door stood open, allowing the cool morning breeze to pour in through the patched screen. Inhaling a deep breath of the sweet air, Rachel marched down the hallway to the kitchen.

She found all of the boarders there, seated around the kitchen table, deep in conversation: three unfamiliar faces and her nocturnal adversary. Unnoticed by the group, Rachel stood still for a moment, observing them as they talked, mentally matching their faces to Aunt Carrie's descriptions of them.

An elderly woman with skin as dark and lustrous as polished walnut and a tight-cropped head of grizzled gray hair sat at the far end of the table, listening attentively to the others; Miss Jones, at a guess, the retired schoolteacher from New Jersey.

To her left was Sandor Pulneshti, silent as well, sipping coffee from a mug that seemed dwarfed by his huge hands. Even seated, he looked larger than life, although daylight made him seem marginally less threatening. He was no giant, but he was a big-boned man, and Rachel knew, with a clarity of memory that set her pulse pounding, that the padding on those bones was all muscle and sinew.

This morning, he wore a faded blue work shirt and, knotted at his open throat, a red bandanna that lent him a rakish air. Beneath the charcoal slashes of his eyebrows, Rachel was wryly pleased to see dark circles beneath his eyes; at least she wasn't alone in feeling the effects of their late-night clash.

At the head of the table, addressing the others, stood a little man Rachel could only describe as dapper. His white hair and moustache were meticulously groomed, and his cheeks were as pink as a department store Santa's. This, then, was George Hudson, the antique dealer who had so impressed Aunt Carrie. "...looking forward to meeting this young woman," he was saying. "If she's half as delightful as her lovely aunt, I'm sure we'll all—"

"She's a shower hog, that's all *I* know!" the fourth member of the party interrupted him hotly. The speaker, a young woman whose long auburn braid marked her as the donor of the strand of hair from the bathroom sink, sat with her back to Rachel. She was "Redhead"...and, by the process of elimination, "Max."

As soon as Rachel had identified the roomful of strangers to her satisfaction, she found her attention drawn back, inexorably, to Sandor Pulneshti, who was still brooding silently over his coffee. He looked as out of place among the other boarders as a panther in a room full of housecats. The top four buttons of his work shirt were unfastened, and his bandanna hung limp and loose. His clothes looked as though they'd been thrown on as an afterthought, only to satisfy convention. The deep V of the open shirt revealed a tanned expanse of chest, and his smooth umber skin was visible beneath the whorls of dark hair that grew there in profusion. Of its own volition, her brain supplied a graphic memory of the way that hair traced downward to his navel and then plunged lower still to gather densely again....

As if her gaze had been a touch, he looked up. When he saw her standing in the doorway, his face became suddenly animated, as if the caffeine from the coffee he was drinking had just hit his bloodstream.

"Speak of the devil," he said in the sardonic tone she remembered from the night before.

At Sandor's words, Mr. Hudson's gaze focused on Rachel as well. "Ah, here she is," he said to the others. "Good morning, Miss Locke! Allow me to introduce our little band of—"

"Thank you, Mr. Hudson, but that won't be necessary," she said firmly. "I think I've figured out who all of you are." Dragging her gaze from Sandor's face, Rachel focused on the quiet woman at the end of the table. "You, for instance, must be Miss Jones."

"Integrity Jones," the older woman replied, her voice a startling, resonant alto. "I'm glad to make your acquaintance. Your aunt speaks very highly of you. I trust no harm was done last night?"

"Just a broken leg," Sandor said before she could reply.

Rachel's heart lurched. "What?"

"The left front leg on my drafting table," he clarified.

The girl seated with her back to Rachel laughed.

"And you must be Max," Rachel said.

"If you say so," the girl retorted, without turning around.

Not wanting to stir up trouble unnecessarily, Rachel let it go at that, taking a moment to look the group over. Black and white, young and old, male and female; it was hard to imagine how Aunt Carrie could have taken in a more diverse cross section of people. "My aunt told me a little bit about each of you, last night," Rachel said. "Now that we've met, I'm looking forward to learning a lot more."

Sandor Pulneshti smiled, as if he detected the double meaning of her words.

Rachel stiffened defensively. *Let him mock me if he wants to. I've got a responsibility to Aunt Carrie.* And yet she had a nagging feeling that the expression beneath his smile was something softer than ridicule. For a crazy moment, she thought it might have been approval, but that made no sense at all.

Doing her best to ignore him, she continued, "This is the first time my aunt has taken in boarders, so I hope you'll all bear with us for doing things a little out of sequence."

"What's that supposed to mean?" Max demanded, twisting in her chair for the first time to look over her shoulder at Rachel.

My God, she's just a kid, Rachel realized as she looked at the girl's elfin features. Abruptly she remembered the anonymous letter's reference to "juvenile delinquents and vagrants." Max didn't look old enough to be living on her own. Had Aunt Carrie saddled herself with a runaway?

"That means," Rachel elaborated warily, "that Aunt Carrie and I would appreciate it if you could each write out a short list of references for us this morning—bank managers, former landladies, past employers, people like that. Or in your case, Max, how to contact your parents and one or two of your teachers."

"And what if we don't?" Max asked pugnaciously.

I should have known this wouldn't be easy, Rachel lamented, wondering how to short-circuit the girl's interference before it could spread into a general mutiny. "How old are you, Max?"

"Eighteen."

Rachel had seen hundreds of eighteen-year-old freshmen. None of them had looked as young as Max. "Would you mind showing me your driver's license?"

"Why should I?" Max challenged her. "I already told you, I'm eighteen. Don't you believe me?"

The girl was leaving her no out. "No, I don't," Rachel admitted. "But feel free to prove me wrong."

Max glowered at her. "You didn't answer my question. What happens if I don't give you this magic list you want?"

"Aunt Carrie and I might have to ask you to leave," Rachel replied, determined not to lie just to avoid an awkward situation.

"Jeez! Who died and made you queen of the universe?" the girl asked rudely, looking Rachel up and down. "We've been doing just fine here. We don't need you showing up and sticking your nose in."

"Maybe you don't, but Aunt Carrie does."

"Bull. You just want to throw your weight around. I don't have to listen to you," she declared, and lumbered awkwardly to her feet.

Rachel stared at the girl's distended abdomen, her jaw sagging in astonishment. "You're pregnant!"

"Gee, really? I hadn't noticed," Max said acidly, and pushed past her into the hallway.

Rachel watched her go, amazed that her aunt hadn't said a word about the girl's pregnancy. Of course, thinking back, her aunt hadn't said much at all about Max. *Trust Aunt Carrie to attract a stray,* Rachel thought ruefully, listening as Max stomped up the stairs, *but this is a lot more serious than taking in a homeless puppy or kitten.*

To her right, George Hudson cleared his throat. "I, for one, would be happy to supply you with a list of names," he said, and smiled at Rachel, revealing a mouthful of teeth too gleaming and symmetrical to be natural. "Or, if you prefer, I can contact my references by phone and ask them to forward their letters directly to you."

"Whichever you prefer, Mr. Hudson," Rachel said, grateful that someone was taking her request seriously. "Mr. Pulneshti?"

Across the table, Sandor leaned back in his chair, watching her with an air of casual interest. "Sure. You want references, I can get some together for you."

"I have my employment file upstairs in my room," Integrity Jones volunteered. "Some of the names may be outdated but I'll amend it for you. Shall I get it now?" she asked, starting to rise from her chair.

Smiling, Rachel shook her head. "Thank you, but there's no need for that much of a rush. Finish your coffee. I'll be taking the bus back to Cleveland this evening. If you could have your list to me by then, that would be fine."

"Leaving so soon?" Sandor asked.

"I have a job to get back to, Mr. Pulneshti." She spoke the words sternly, but she could imagine all too well what she must look like to him: an absentee niece who breezed in just long enough to disrupt the status quo and then breezed out again.

In this case, though, appearances would be deceiving. She intended to use her time in Cleveland to follow up on the boarders' references, and to be back in Dalewood within a week—on her next day off, or sooner if she could convince someone to trade their work schedule for hers. Besides, what ax did the man think he was grinding? News of her imminent departure should have made his morning.

"All I want—" she started to explain, then broke off at the sound of footsteps on the stairs. Rachel sighed. With her luck, Max was returning for Round Two.

"Rachel?" Aunt Carrie called.

"In the kitchen," Rachel answered, glad she'd settled the matter of references before her aunt came down for breakfast. Max was going to be a problem, that much was clear, but the other boarders seemed perfectly willing to—

"Oh, good," her aunt said, bustling into the room. "You're all here. Good morning, Miss Jones, Mr. Pulneshti, Mr. Hudson, Rachel, dear. I wish you hadn't started without me," she added, sweetly reproachful. "I could have spared everyone this little misunderstanding."

Oh, no, Rachel thought with a sinking sense of foreboding. *Oh, Aunt Carrie, you wouldn't*— But, as her next words proved, she would.

"What I'd like from each of you is just the name and phone number of a person I could call for you in case of emergency, not—"

"Aunt Carrie—"

"—not an actual list of references, you see."

"Aunt Carrie—"

"Because that would be silly, after all the wonderful months we've had together," her aunt said stubbornly. "So let's consider the matter of references closed, shall we?"

"It really wouldn't be any imposition," George Hudson said slowly. "But if you're sure it won't be necessary..."

"Positive," Aunt Carrie said. "I'm glad all of you are here, and I hope you'll think of this as your home for a long time to come. Now I'm sure you're all anxious to have breakfast and get on with your day. Who'd like pancakes?"

CHAPTER FOUR

HALF AN HOUR LATER, with a generous helping of Aunt Carrie's pancakes sitting undigestibly in her stomach, Rachel excused herself from the forced civility of the kitchen and slipped outside.

She was surprised to find that it was already intensely hot. *If this is May,* Rachel thought despondently, *Heaven help us come July.*

For that matter, she could have used a little celestial intervention at the breakfast table. As it was, Max's shrewd tactic of throwing herself on Aunt Carrie's mercy had cast an emotional cloud over the issue of references. In a day or two, when the situation had had a chance to cool down, Rachel knew she would have to try again to reason with her aunt. For now, however, the subject was emphatically closed.

Rachel walked briskly along Spruce Street, hoping to burn off the bulk of unwanted pancakes knotting her stomach and the burden of frustration knotting her muscles. Tomorrow, she would contact a realtor in Cleveland, someone who knew what sorts of apartments and condominiums might be available around the campus—

"Rachel?"

Startled, she looked around to see who had called her name.

Across the street, a car was pulling over to the curb in a hasty maneuver that would have caused a five-car pileup in Cleveland's congested morning commute. In Dalewood, by contrast, it merely startled a squirrel. As Rachel watched, the driver shut off the engine and climbed out into the sunlight to greet her.

Tom Gaines. Rachel's shoulders sagged as recognition came to her. Then, stubbornly, she lifted her chin and waved a welcome as he bounded across the street to join her.

From a distance, he looked disconcertingly boyish, as if only one summer, not fifteen, had passed since they'd acted out the foolish passions of first love together. In reality, she had last crossed paths with him two years earlier, but when Tom reached the sidewalk beside her, Rachel realized that he had changed quite a bit even in that relatively short interval. His straight blond hair was thinner than she remembered it, and subtle lines—of what? Tension? Frustration?—had begun to etch themselves into his pale skin.

"Hello, Tom." She put out her hand.

"Rachel. Damn, it's good to see you," he said, and pulled her against him in a hug.

Despite her first impulse to pull away, she made a conscious effort to relax and let the embrace run its course. It was years since she and Tom had gone their separate ways. By now, he had to be as relieved about it as she was. Any pleasure, any pain that had existed between them was ancient history. This was nothing but an old acquaintance eager to say hello.

But the hug was a little too tight, and it lasted a little too long. When he released her, Rachel took an involuntary step back, struggling to regain her composure.

"So how's the career girl?" Tom asked expansively, as if it were a fine joke. "I see you finally got tired of the big city and came back home. Did your aunt tell you about the job opening?"

"I'm just in for the day," Rachel said, retaining her smile with an effort. "I have to head back on the six o'clock bus."

"No," Tom scolded her, "you're supposed to ask '*What* job opening?'"

"All right," she said cautiously. "What job opening?"

"Mrs. Sawyer is scheduled for a hysterectomy next week," he said, his gaze intent. "That means we're going to have to shut the library down for the summer...unless we can find someone to fill in. So, of course, I thought of you."

"Of course," she echoed bitterly, disappointed in him. "What could be more natural? Why, I'll phone my resignation in to the university right away. I'm sure they'll understand, once I tell them that I have a chance at a part-time, temporary position here. What an opportunity! How can I ever thank you?"

"Whoa there," Tom said, looking startled by her outburst. "Quit putting words in my mouth, would you? I thought of you because I hoped you might know some student who needed a summer job. Give me a little credit! I know how hard you worked to get that university position. There was no offense intended. Just forget I mentioned it," he said, turning away.

"Wait." Mortified, Rachel reached out to touch his sleeve. "I'm sorry, Tom. Really. It's just been one of those crazy mornings where you start to believe the whole world has it in for you. I didn't mean to shriek at you like a banshee."

He grinned. "I've had a morning or two like that, myself, from time to time. Apology accepted."

Rachel breathed a sigh of relief, knowing she could take him at his word. Tom had always been even-tempered to a fault, never holding a grudge, always willing to grant people the benefit of the doubt. In the past, his affability had sometimes driven her crazy, but she was grateful for it this morning. "Well then, since you're still speaking to me, how have you been?"

"Okay, I guess."

"You're looking good," she said automatically.

"So are you," he said with disconcerting sincerity. "But then, you always did."

"Tom—"

"Well, it's the truth. You can't hang a man for speaking the truth, can you?" He shook his head. "In a way, I wish you didn't look so wonderful. Then I'd have an excuse to drive up to Cleveland some night and steal you away."

His tone was jocular but she had the uneasy feeling that he meant every word. Searching for a change of topic, Rachel said, "I wouldn't think it would be so tough to find somebody to fill in at the library."

"I know. After all, it's just for the summer. But it looks like I was being naive again. Remember the story of the little Red Hen?"

"Everybody wants to eat the bread but nobody wants to bake it?"

"Exactly. The teachers are too busy with summer school, and everybody else has an excuse—crops, kids, businesses, vacations, you name it. But they all holler at the idea of the library being closed...and frankly, so do I. There's a superstitious part of me that's afraid to lock that library door for fear we'll never find a way to open it again." He frowned. "Too many things in this town have already shut down and disappeared for good. People keep moving away—and it always seems to be the young, bright, ambitious ones who leave. You should know—you were one of them. And that's no way to keep a town alive."

"People have to do what's right for them," Rachel said.

"And what about what's right for the town? Doesn't that matter? Isn't anyone accountable? Isn't anyone responsible for—" He held up his hand, as if to stop the flow of his own words. "Sorry. I didn't mean to climb up on my soapbox, but I get so damned frustrated sometimes, and right now this library thing has really got me worried. Will you see what you can do? Try to find us somebody who can step in, just until we get Mrs. Sawyer back on her feet, okay?"

"I'll do my best," she promised.

"Fair enough. In that case, I'll drop it from my worry list for a few days and keep my fingers crossed."

Wondering what else was on his worry list, she asked, "How's your father doing?"

"Better," Tom assured her. "Strokes are scary things, but Dr. Ames says that Dad's coming along better than any of us have a right to expect."

"I'm glad," Rachel said, feeling the inadequacy of the words. "I'm sure this hasn't been an easy time for either of you."

He shrugged away her sympathy. "Don't worry, Gaines men are stubborn. If sheer pigheadedness counts for anything, Dad's going to make it all the way back. His speech is a little fuzzy, and his right hand's still weak, but he doesn't let that stop him from putting in a full day at the store, six days a week."

"That's great, Tom. It must have been a relief to him, knowing you were handling things at the drugstore while he was in the hospital."

Tom shrugged again. "You know how it is. When times get rough, family makes all the difference."

Rachel made a noncommittal sound, wishing his observation hadn't hit so close to home.

"Dad and I were on our way to open the store when I spotted you," Tom said, brightening. "Why don't you let me give you a lift uptown?"

"You mean your father's been sitting in the car all this time?"

"It's okay, he doesn't mind. Come with us, Rachel. I've been wanting to show you some of the improvements we've made at the store."

His eagerness worried her. "No, I'm sorry, Tom. I can't," she said, and watched his smile fade. "Not today. Maybe next time," she added, afraid he would try to insist.

But he took the refusal with good grace, saying only, "Come and say good morning to Dad, at least. He said he wanted to talk to you."

"All right," she agreed reluctantly, and headed toward the car.

As they walked, she wondered what Archibald Gaines could possibly have to say to her. He had operated the Dalewood Drugstore for as long as Rachel could remember, presiding over the prescription counter in his white pharmacist's jacket, as much an authority figure as the township policeman. During her senior year of high school, when she and Tom were dating seriously, he had spoken out against Rachel's plans to go away to college, stating that his wife had never worked and neither should any wife of his son's. Now, as Rachel peered in to where he sat ensconced in the front passenger seat of his son's Oldsmobile, she saw the same austere profile she remembered, unsoftened by time or circumstance.

"Good morning, Mr. Gaines," she said through the open car window.

"G'morning, Rachel." His diction was slurred, but his bird-bright gaze passed over her with disconcerting thoroughness, renewing her awareness of her wrinkled blouse. "You look weh. Your aun' tehs me the university fines you idispesiba."

"Indispensable," Tom murmured beside her.

Rachel smiled wryly. However distorted Archibald Gaines's speech might be, his intellect—and his determination to goad her about her career—seemed unimpaired. "Well, you know how Aunt Carrie likes to exaggerate," she equivocated. Then, because she no longer felt compelled to submit to his jibes, she added pointedly, "Tom said there was something you wanted to talk to me about?"

The craggy face contorted briefly in a grimace . . . or perhaps it was meant as a smile. "Escuse me if I speak blunly," he said, "buh does she nee money?"

Rachel frowned, not sure she understood. "You mean Aunt Carrie?"

He nodded. "Tom tehs me she has ren'ed out her house."

Damn those boarders, Rachel thought angrily. The whole town must be speculating about her aunt's finances. Trying to sound calm, she replied, "Not the whole house, Mr. Gaines. Just the extra bedrooms."

"An' you approve?" he asked, his tone making it clear that he certainly didn't.

To almost anyone else in town, Rachel might have been tempted to talk about her run-in with her aunt's boarders and her determination to send them on their way as soon as possible, but Archibald Gaines wasn't a man who invited confidences. Instead she fixed him with a determined smile. "Aunt Carrie says it isn't a question of money. She says her boarders have been a big help around the house. Besides, she enjoys their company."

"Wouldn' need 'em if you stayed home," he said reprovingly. Lifting his chin stiffly, he looked into Rachel's eyes. "Going away again, I s'ppose?"

Just as stiffly, she returned his look. "This afternoon."

His nostrils flared in disdain. "So—t'hell with her, jus' like you said t'hell with my boy, eh?"

"Dad!" Tom protested.

Feeling sick, Rachel straightened and took an unsteady step away.

Tom caught her arm, his fingers pressing urgently into the bruises Sandor Pulneshti had left there. "Rachel, I'm sorry. I didn't know he was going to—"

"Thomas?" the old man snapped.

Shaking off Tom's hand, Rachel kept walking.

"He lashes out," Tom said wretchedly, pursuing her. "There's so much frustration bottled up inside him these days...."

Taking pity on Tom, Rachel said, "It's all right. I understand. You'd better go. You'll be late opening the store."

He hesitated, clearly torn. "All right, but I'll call you before you head back and we can—"

"No, I think it would be better if you didn't." She took a steadying breath. "If I find a student who's interested in the library job, I'll pass your name along. Aside from that, let's just let matters rest for now, okay? No hard feelings?"

"No hard feelings," he echoed, sounding wistful.

"Thomas!"

"Coming, Dad," Tom said, but his eyes held hers a moment longer, full of emotions she didn't want to acknowledge. Then, with a sad smile, he climbed into his car and drove away.

IN THE RELATIVE PEACE and privacy of midmorning, when the boarders had scattered to their day's activities, Rachel took her aunt into the living room. "Sit down. I have to show you something."

Aunt Carrie obediently sank onto the sofa.

"Here," Rachel said, holding out the envelope she'd received at her Cleveland apartment. "I got this in the mail yesterday. It's why I tried to call you last night."

Aunt Carrie removed the sheet of beige stationery from its envelope and unfolded it, silently reading the words typewritten there.

"Oh, dear," she said when she was through.

"Oh, dear," Rachel concurred. "Somebody around here doesn't seem to think your boarders are such a red-hot idea."

Her aunt pursed her lips, reading the letter again. "This is really very strange," she said at last. "Why would someone write to you instead of just talking to me directly? And why leave it unsigned, if they feel this strongly? In a way, I suppose it's really rather sweet."

"Sweet?" Rachel repeated incredulously.

"Sweet of them to worry about me," Aunt Carrie continued. "But whoever wrote this is being dreadfully unfair to Max and the others. 'Undesirables' indeed! They're a lovely group of people. Why would anyone be upset about them?''

Rachel gave a derisive hoot of laughter. "Where shall I start?" she asked. "Come on, Aunt Carrie, don't be an ostrich about this. Your tenants certainly aren't the kind of people who are likely to blend into the background in Dalewood.''

"Why not?" Aunt Carrie demanded stubbornly. "They're perfectly nice, all of them.''

"Maybe so, but they stick out like sore thumbs. Didn't it occur to you that eyebrows might be raised if you rented out rooms in your house to a couple of unmarried men? And not just any men! Sandor Pulneshti must have every female from fifteen to fifty fantasizing over him, and George Hudson is any widow's dream come true, with his ivory teeth and sweet-talking ways.''

"He can't help wearing false teeth," Aunt Carrie reasoned. "And it isn't right to criticize him for being pleasant and polite. What am I supposed to do, ask the man to move out because he's too well mannered? What sort of sense would that make?''

"As for the other two," Rachel went on, refusing to be sidetracked, "you were right about Integrity Jones, she does seem well educated and interesting, but she's probably the only black woman in a fifty-mile radius of Dalewood.''

"Are you saying that I shouldn't rent a room to her because her skin is a different color than mine?" Aunt Carrie asked, her face a picture of astonishment.

"No, of course not. That's not what I'm saying at all. But you wanted to know why your boarders weren't likely to blend in here in Dalewood, and I'm saying that Integrity Jones is bound to stand out, at least superficially. And as for Max—''

"What *about* Max?" Aunt Carrie challenged, the light of righteous battle in her eyes.

Searching for the right words, Rachel said earnestly, "Max is a very young girl in very big trouble, Aunt Carrie. She belongs at home with her parents. Letting her hide here isn't going to solve anything in the long run. Besides, keeping her here could land *you* in a lot of trouble. Did she go to school this spring?"

"Max has already graduated," Aunt Carrie said. "She's eighteen."

"If Max is eighteen, I'm Queen Victoria. Has she told you where she's from?"

"I haven't asked her."

"Well, don't you think you'd better? Her parents must be frantic. She does *have* parents, doesn't she?"

"Yes, but she can't go back to them."

"Why not?"

Aunt Carrie's gaze lowered. "She hasn't said."

"What about this little jaunt the two of you took to Milford, last night? Were you driving or was she?"

"Max drove. She's a very good driver."

"Did you stop to think about the fact that you'd be liable if she got in an accident? Does she have a license? Or even a learner's permit?"

"I'm sure she must, but—"

"But you don't really know. What were the two of you doing in Milford anyway?"

"If you must know, we were attending Max's first Lamaze class."

It was a more distressing answer than any that Rachel had been able to imagine. "Oh, Aunt Carrie, don't do this to yourself," she protested, but she could see that she was already too late; despite Max's rough manner, Aunt Carrie had taken the girl under her wing.

"Why shouldn't I? Max has her heart set on a natural delivery, and the class requires that she have a partner to coach her through the breathing and relaxation techniques."

"I know what Lamaze is, Aunt Carrie. I also know that the coach is usually the prospective mother's husband, not her landlady."

"In this case, the baby's father isn't available. If you want the truth, I was flattered to be asked," she said, her face aglow. "It should be a fascinating experience."

Rachel shook her head. "I wish I could believe that. I can see that Max needs somebody. I just don't agree that you're the somebody she needs. Don't you understand? I don't want you hurt."

"Caring is always risky," Aunt Carrie conceded calmly, "and it's true I do care about Max and her baby, but I hardly think I'm in any great danger of being hurt. What is it you're so afraid will happen?"

Hardening her heart, Rachel said, "I'm afraid Max will sponge off of you until she's had the baby, and then pack up and disappear. She might even leave you holding the bag— or, in this case, the baby."

"I don't think that's very apt to happen," Aunt Carrie said in much the same tone she had once used to assure Rachel that there were no monsters hiding in her closet. "And if it did—" she lifted her plump shoulders in a gentle shrug "—it isn't as if I've never raised a child, now is it? And I quite enjoyed myself the last time."

"That's a low blow," Rachel protested, but she couldn't help smiling. "Point granted, you brought me up and you did a wonderful job of it, but you were in your thirties then, not your sixties. Besides, I was your brother's little girl, a blood relation. Max is a total stranger. It's obvious she won't be able to raise the baby herself, but that doesn't make it *your* responsibility."

"Suppose you let me worry about that?" Aunt Carrie suggested with kindly determination.

"But—"

"Whatever else may happen with my boarders," she said with uncharacteristic force, "I intend for Max to stay here as long as she needs to. I don't want you upsetting her or asking her questions. If I'm making a mistake, it's mine to make. It's my house and my heart. I can see that this silly letter has upset you, but Max's situation is more important than neighborhood gossip. She made a mistake, yes, but I see no reason why that mistake should be allowed to ruin her life."

"Aunt Carrie, listen to me, please—"

"No, I think you should listen to me. You've known Max for four hours. I've lived with her for four months. She's a guest in my house. I'll thank you to remember that." She handed the anonymous letter back to Rachel. "And now, unless there's something else you think we need to discuss, I'd better get out to the kitchen and start on the potato salad, or lunch will be late today. Would you like to give me a hand?"

Never before in Rachel's experience had Aunt Carrie taken so adamant a stand. The boundary lines were clearly drawn. If she went on fighting her aunt's involvement with Max, she'd find herself on the outside, branded as a hard-hearted villain who had to be outwitted and kept uninformed. On the other hand, if Rachel could manage to bite her tongue for the time being, Aunt Carrie would at least feel she could still turn to her for help and comfort if the situation with Max turned out as badly as Rachel feared it would.

The choice was really no choice at all. "Luckily for you, I can still peel a mean potato," Rachel said, and shoved the anonymous letter into her pocket, out of sight but not out of mind.

THIS WEEK, they were creating the roof.

Sandor stood on the temporary scaffolding at the top of the wall, sweating steadily as he and his partner waited, shirtless, in the afternoon sun. Below, the other two-man crew began their climb up the paired ladders, holding an eighteen-foot rafter of Douglas fir.

The four of them had already hauled more than half of the sixty rafters skyward, taking turns as ladder men and catchers so that nobody could complain of getting stuck with the "dirty" end of the job. Half a dozen small interruptions had plagued their morning, but they'd been working in a steady rhythm since the lunch break, saying little, each man intent on his own solitary thoughts.

Sandor's, for once, had little to do with the details of the house beneath his feet. Instead he found himself reliving the raw blend of fury and fear he'd experienced when he woke in the night to the sound of someone in his room, and the shock that had fizzed through him when he'd grappled with the intruder and felt the unexpected stroke of silk and satin-smooth skin against his bare body.

For a strange, suspended moment, the remembered scent of Rachel's perfume seemed more real to him than the pungent fragrance of the pine resin that stuck to his palms.

"Yo! Sandor!"

"Sorry," he said gruffly, embarrassed to have been caught daydreaming. There were safer places for it than twenty-five feet up in the air. Bending down, he fielded his end of the rising rafter, determined not to let his mind wander again.

The pattern of the day's work was hurry-up-and-wait, and the intense heat had an almost narcotic potency. By late afternoon, he was doing a stint as ladder man, manhandling two-by-eights. Thinking about the shower he planned to take before dinner, he grinned at the memory of Max's outraged accusation that Miss Caroline's niece was a "shower hog." If Rachel Locke was in the bathroom when he got back, she'd better be prepared to move over; as hot as he was, he'd push her to one side and share the cooling water, rather than wait his turn.

What had begun as a humorous thought swiftly took more substantial form in his mind. He could almost feel the stinging spray of cool water against his overheated skin and hear its blurring hiss, and he could imagine, with a clarity that stole his breath away, just how Rachel would look with her slender body free of all restraints, glistening and wet as she turned to him. . . .

"Hey, Sandor, we gonna work all night?"

The words rudely jolted him out of his fantasy. "Had all you can take?" he asked defensively. Squinting, he looked measuringly at the sun's position above the horizon and saw, to his surprise, that it was quitting time and past. "All right," he said, secretly relieved. "Let's call it a day. The rest of this lumber can wait till morning."

Most days, he was the last to leave the site, lingering to assess the day's progress long after the others had driven away. Tonight, he packed his tools with quick efficiency and walked without a backward glance to where his pickup truck was parked.

He'd left his shirt draped over the steering column, but the wheel was still almost too hot to touch. Sandor turned the ignition key and touched his foot to the accelerator, coaxing the tired old engine to life. When he had it grumbling along fairly smoothly, he slipped the truck into gear and pulled out, leaving the rest of the crew to curse at the cloud of dust his tires kicked up.

"Hot date?" one of them called after him.

Sandor ignored him. *I just want to get home and cool off,* he told himself. *It's been a long, hot day and I didn't get much sleep last night. I've earned an evening off, haven't I?*

Reaching down to where his shirt lay crumpled on the seat beside him, he patted the pocket, making sure that the piece of paper he'd written on at lunchtime was still tucked safely inside. Then, satisfied, he turned his attention back to his driving, guiding the big truck down the hill into town.

In less than five minutes, he was on Spruce Street, parking his truck behind Miss Caroline's dusty sedan. Climbing down, he pocketed his keys and let himself through the back door into the kitchen.

Max was there, moving slowly as she set the table for the evening meal. She looked up at his entrance and made a sound that Sandor chose to interpret as a greeting.

"I'm parched," he said, reaching into the cupboard for a glass. By confining their talk to externals, he and Max had long since evolved a pact of mutual noninterference. "When's dinner?"

"Fifteen minutes. There's lemonade in the refrigerator."

Pulling out the pitcher, Sandor observed, "Only five plates? What about our guest?"

"Gone home," Max said, with a palpable air of satisfaction.

The news stopped him with the glass halfway to his lips. "Already? I thought she wasn't going back until—"

"Caroline said she was taking the six o'clock bus."

Sandor glanced up at the clock on the wall: five forty-seven. "Damn." He set the glass on the counter and fished in his pocket for his keys. "I'll be back in time for dinner," he said over his shoulder as he pushed the screen door open. "If I'm not, go ahead without me."

His one regret, as he backed the truck out of the drive-way, was that his shower would have to wait.

RACHEL STOOD BEHIND the wooden bench, toying unhappily with the handle of her overnight case. The last thing she wanted to do was go back to Cleveland, leaving Aunt Carrie behind with a houseful of boarders and a handful of unresolved problems.

Not that her aunt seemed to mind, particularly. She had driven Rachel to the bus stop, but when Rachel suggested that she needn't wait with her for the bus to come, Aunt Carrie had been quick to say, "If you wouldn't mind, dear, perhaps I will head back. Tonight's the monthly meeting of the County Historical Society in Milford, and Mr. Hudson has agreed to take me, but the guest speaker starts promptly at seven. We'll never make it in time if I'm late getting supper on the table.''

"Let them get their own supper," Rachel had suggested testily.

"Oh, I couldn't. It wouldn't be fair. 'Bed and board,' that's what they're paying me for and that's what I mean to provide. No, no, we'll make it, one way or another...but I could use the extra time, if you really wouldn't mind."

And so Rachel was waiting on the corner alone, wondering how she could possibly turn her schedule inside out and be back in Dalewood again by the end of the week.

Across the street, the picture window of the Dalewood Drugstore stared at her like a reproachful eye. The bus was due any minute; with luck, it would arrive before Tom or his father noticed her standing there. She wasn't in the mood to talk to either of them after the emotional excesses of that morning's encounter.

Four years ago, she had left Dalewood behind with a sigh of relief, and now, despite her better judgment, she was being forced to plot her own homecoming. The ghosts of her past must be laughing, she thought.

Hearing the loud growl of an approaching engine, Rachel turned, expecting to see the six o'clock bus bearing down on her. Instead a battered pickup truck jolted to a stop in front of her bench, and Sandor Pulneshti climbed out.

He looked like what he was: a man who had put in a long day of manual labor under punishing conditions. His pale blue work shirt was dark with sweat, his jawline shadowy with the stubble that had sprouted since that morning. And yet, despite his obvious weariness, energy seemed to rise from him in tangible, intimidating waves, like the rippling heat mirages that distorted Main Street's sun-baked pavement.

"Here," he said without preamble, holding out a piece of paper.

Down the street, the bus drove into view.

Rachel's gaze traveled from the half circle of garnet marks her teeth had left in his tanned forearm down to the paper he offered. "What is it?" she asked, made wary by the intensity she read in his eyes. Last night she had labeled him a dangerous man and let it go at that. What she had failed to take fully into account, however, was the fascination that that danger exerted over her. Sandor Pulneshti was a walking enigma, his aloof manner and air of self-sufficiency a provocative challenge. If she were wise, she'd refuse the paper he offered and dismiss him from her thoughts now, while she still could . . . but the odd blend of humor and severity she sensed in him enticed her to solve the mystery contained within the man.

"I said I'd get them to you." His hand was unwavering as he thrust the sheet toward her. "Take it."

Rachel reached out, then hesitated as the bus sounded its horn, the driver gesturing in obvious annoyance at the pickup truck parked squarely in its way.

As if his patience had run out, Sandor pressed the paper against her palm and folded her fingers around it.

It was a gentler touch than they had shared the night before, but its impact was as great. As if a channel had been opened, Rachel immediately sensed the tension and determination that had driven him to track her down; she could almost feel the ache of the muscles in his back and shoulders, taste the salty dryness of his lips as his tongue flicked out to moisten them, experience the burning hunger that fueled him and the icy inner core of loneliness that allowed him no peace.

Sandor stepped back abruptly, breaking the contact. "Take it," he repeated, and then said, "I'd better go," as the bus horn blared again. Without another word or glance, he climbed into his truck and drove away, leaving her feeling bereft.

Rachel watched his turn signal blink at the corner. In the sudden void created by his departure, she felt a pang at the thought that he was driving back to Aunt Carrie's to sit at her kitchen table, eat her cooking and share the news of his day, while she was going to be riding the bus back to Cleveland, eating cold chicken and potato salad for supper, going home to an empty apartment.

The bus stopped in front of her, emitting a hot cloud of diesel fumes, but Rachel's thoughts were still on Sandor Pulneshti's pickup truck.

It was ridiculous to feel shut out; Aunt Carrie would welcome her back in a minute if she decided to stay. It was equally ridiculous to feel homesick. Returning to Cleveland tonight was entirely her own choice. And it was worse than ridiculous to wish that Sandor hadn't taken his hand from hers—she should have been relieved to see him go. So why did she feel like plopping down on the bench instead and bawling like a baby. . . or, worse yet, going after him?

"Coming, miss?" the bus driver asked.

It's only for a few days, she counseled herself, *just until you can sort things out at work. Then you'll be back for another try at talking some sense into Aunt Carrie. Face it, the boarders have already been here for months. Another week won't be the end of the world. And some geographic distance is probably just what you need between you and that man.*

"Yes," she said firmly to the driver, and climbed the steps to hand him her return ticket.

The bus was half-empty. Settling gratefully into a window seat, Rachel tucked her overnight case beneath it and laid her copy of *Publishers Weekly* on the empty seat beside her. Only then, as the view through her window began to shift and move, did Rachel unfold the piece of paper Sandor Pulneshti had forced upon her.

Benjamin Pierce. The name was printed in neat, square letters, dark pencil on yellow paper. *Assistant Manager,*

Bennington National Bank, Fifth Avenue Branch, Cleveland. Elizabeth Katharine Ramsey, Chapter President, Builders Association of Northern Ohio. And, below that: *In case of injury or death, notify the above. No next of kin.*

His references. Despite Aunt Carrie's turnabout at the breakfast table, Sandor Pulneshti had written out his references.

I said I'd get them to you, he'd told Rachel at the bus stop, his tone sober, his gaze direct. And so he had.

Troubled, Rachel bit her lower lip. She'd known from the first that Sandor Pulneshti was different, and she'd used a fair number of terms to describe him to herself in the past eighteen hours, most of them as uncomplimentary as they were colorful.

But now, looking down at the paper in her hands, she had to consider the unsettling possibility that he might also be that rarest bird of all: a man of his word.

CHAPTER FIVE

"RACHEL? Line three's for you."

Each year, Rachel expected the summer session to be less hectic than the winter session, and each year she received the same rude awakening as May thundered into June. In the wake of her day off, she had returned to find her desk piled high with faculty requests and books on loan from other universities. Now, wishing she had four hands and at least two heads, she marked her place on the page in front of her with an ink-stained fingertip and lifted the receiver. "Research Desk."

"This is Dr. Winston," a woman's voice announced. "I'd like to speak with Rachel Locke."

There was a Dr. Winnington who taught Greek and Latin, but who was Dr. Winston? The name rang no bell. Disconcerted, Rachel tried to match it with a department. Political Science? History?

The lapse of memory was annoying but it didn't surprise her. In the forty-eight hours since her return, she had found it increasingly hard to keep her thoughts from straying back to Dalewood . . . and to Sandor Pulneshti. Checking out his references had yielded some startling results—results that were reassuring, in a way, but definitely not what Aunt Carrie's thumbnail sketch of the man had led her to expect.

"This is Rachel Locke, Dr. Winston," she said, reaching for a bookmark. "How may I help you?"

"Miss Locke, I'm on the staff here at Milford Memorial Hospital. I'm calling about your aunt, Caroline Locke."

It took a moment for the words to register. "About Aunt Carrie?" Rachel asked, and a panicky voice inside her head began to chant, *You shouldn't have left her. You never should have left her.*

"Yes. Your aunt fell earlier this evening and broke her hip. We've admitted her here at Milford Memorial and her condition is stable now, but she'll be needing surgery to repair the damage."

Around Rachel's desk, the bustle of the library continued, oblivious to her distress. She pressed the receiver to her ear more tightly. "Surgery? When?"

"Tomorrow morning at nine. I've examined your aunt and she's basically in good health, so there's no undue cause for concern, but it would still be best if you could be here to see her tomorrow before the procedure. The break was high on the head of the femur, so we'll be doing a complete hip replacement. I can meet with you in the morning and answer any questions you may have about that procedure... unless you plan to come by tonight."

Rachel looked up at the clock on the wall: nine-thirty, half an hour from the library's closing time. "I'll be there as soon as I can," she assured the doctor, "but I'll be coming down from Cleveland by bus, so I probably won't get in much before midnight. Will I be able to see Aunt Carrie that late or will they make me wait until morning? Will you still be there then?"

"You'll still be able to see your aunt, or at least look in on her if she isn't awake, but I'm leaving in a few minutes. The nurses can answer any general questions you may have tonight about your aunt's condition, and I'll be glad to fill you in on the details in the morning before we take her down to the O.R."

"Are there papers I need to sign?" Rachel asked, wishing she didn't feel so ignorant about how hospitals worked.

"No, that won't be necessary. Your aunt was conscious when she was admitted. I met with her and explained the situation once we had the X rays back, and she signed all the necessary consent forms. But I see that you're the only relative she listed, so I'm sure you'll want to stay on top of what's being done for her. I expect you'll be pretty extensively involved in her convalescence these next few months. Unless there's someone else...?''

In one sense, there were plenty of "someone elses," in the form of George Hudson, Integrity Jones, Sandor Pulneshti and the infamous Max. But they were outsiders. Tom Gaines had been right, after all: when times got rough, family did make all the difference. Whatever upheaval it might cause in Rachel's life in the months ahead, she didn't intend to leave her aunt's care to strangers.

"I'm the one who'll be there," she said firmly.

"Well, I'll see you in the morning. Good night, Miss Locke."

"Good night, Dr. Winston. Thank you for calling me."

Hanging up, Rachel tried to organize her whirling thoughts, but the overriding one was the thought of Aunt Carrie, injured and in pain. Until tomorrow morning's surgery had been safely accomplished, nothing else mattered at all. Someone else would have to deal with Rachel's bookladen desktop; if she was going to catch the bus, she would barely have the time to pen a hasty note of explanation to the head librarian.

When the note was written, Rachel slipped it into an envelope, painfully aware of the bridges she was burning behind herself. With luck, the university would grant the emergency leave she was requesting, but she knew that the restrictions of the new budget had already cut the library staff drastically. It was unfair to expect them to carry on shorthanded for months in her absence. Mr. Cunningham, the head librarian, might fill her position on a temporary basis...or he might decide that the only reasonable solution was to deny her request and, if she refused to come back to work, hire a permanent replacement for her.

It was pointless to worry about it. She couldn't influence the library's decision; she could only make her own. Right now, Aunt Carrie was her first priority. As soon as she had put her note on Mr. Cunningham's desk, she'd head for her apartment to pack...and this time it would have to be more than just an overnight case. For better or worse, it looked as if she'd be spending the summer in Dalewood.

THE HOSPITAL, when she finally reached it, was smaller than she'd expected and less modern than she'd hoped. The passage of countless feet had worn away parts of the pattern on the linoleum floor, and the high ceiling sent distorting echoes after her as she left the information desk and boarded the elevator. It was disconcerting to realize that her expectations of what the hospital would look like—high tech and gleaming—were based largely on the occasional medical shows she had watched on television.

For as long as Rachel could remember, she and Aunt Carrie had had no serious illnesses, no broken bones, no injuries that couldn't be tended by Dalewood's sole practicing physician. They'd both been lucky, and Rachel realized belatedly that she had taken their luck and their good health for granted. She was a grown woman with a job and an apartment of her own, but tonight she felt thirteen, not thirty, ill at ease and ill prepared for the ordeal ahead. She wanted someone to hold her close and promise her that everything would be all right...but that was her role, now. Aunt Carrie was counting on her, leaving Rachel no choice but to cope as best she could.

With a creak and a groan, the elevator reached Aunt Carrie's floor. Rachel stepped out into the hallway and looked toward the nurse's station, but there was no one in sight. She supposed she ought to wait for someone in authority to appear, but the woman at the desk downstairs had said that Aunt Carrie was in Room 343, and the doors to the rooms were clearly numbered.

Rachel walked down the hallway and around the corner. The door to Room 343 stood open, but a pale green curtain hung just inside the doorway. On tiptoe, Rachel approached the curtain and pulled it back.

The room beyond was dimly lit. Peering in, she could see the end of a narrow bed with someone's foot suspended above it, wrapped in elastic bandages. Hesitating, she heard the low drone of some sort of motor in the room, and beneath the sound of the motor, another kind of humming, a human voice tracing a delicate, barely audible tune.

Drawn by it, Rachel stepped beyond the curtain.

From her new vantage point, she could see that there were two beds, and that the one against the far wall was empty, but her view of the patient whose leg was in traction—the patient who must be Aunt Carrie—was blocked by a man sitting beside the bed, a man whose wavy dark hair and broad shoulders were as familiar as they were unexpected.

A warming wave of relief cut through the dark blanket of Rachel's anxiety. It made no sense for her to feel reassured by Sandor Pulneshti's presence in Aunt Carrie's hospital room, and yet the mere sight of him was easing the nauseous knot of concern in the pit of her stomach. Too grateful to question the reasons beneath her response, she walked slowly forward.

The quiet room had a dreamlike quality, intensified by the muted light and the mesmerizing repetition of the song Sandor hummed. He seemed completely oblivious to her presence; it was as if her steps made no sound and her body cast no shadow, allowing her to pass ghostlike through the room, undetected.

She stopped behind his chair, close enough to reach down and rest her fingers against the corded column of his throat, and still he seemed unaware of her. Looking over his shoulder, Rachel drank in the sight of her aunt's sleeping face, smiling when she saw that Aunt Carrie's limp hand was cradled within Sandor's callused one.

The melody faded to silence.

"Sandor?" Rachel said softly.

She had been afraid that her voice would startle him, but he turned his head and offered her an unguarded smile of welcome, as if he'd been expecting her. The intimidating air of tension and fatigue that had radiated from him at the bus stop was gone. Remembering the odd, electric moment of communication when he'd touched her hand, Rachel wondered again whether it had been reality or illusion. Tonight, Sandor looked different—younger, somehow, and surprisingly accessible. If she touched him now, would she be able to sense what he was feeling?

But she had waited too long. Lowering Aunt Carrie's hand carefully to the mattress, he rose from his chair and, with a tilt of his head, indicated the open doorway.

Rachel nodded and walked with him to the entrance. Left alone on the other side of the room, Aunt Carrie looked small and fragile against the crisp white sheets, her closed eyes deeply shadowed.

"I'm glad you're here," Sandor said so quietly that the sound of his voice was nearly lost in the buzz of the electric fan that stirred the room's warm air. "She's been asking for you. The doctor told her you were coming but not until late."

"I took the bus," she said, unwilling to launch into a full explanation. Her worst fears had been put to rest, but it seemed to her that Aunt Carrie was lying unnaturally still. "Is she unconscious?"

"No, just sleeping. They gave her something for the pain a while ago and she's been drifting in and out ever since."

"Dr. Winston didn't say how the accident happened. Do you know?"

He shrugged. "Just what George Hudson told me. Apparently it was one of those fluke things. They were coming out of choir practice together and she missed her footing on the church steps and fell. When he tried to catch her, he took a tumble, too, but he got off with nothing worse than a few bruises and a good scare.''

"What are *you* doing here?" she asked Sandor.

"Miss Caroline is a friend," he said. "I didn't want her to be alone. Don't worry. Now that you're here, I'll go home."

She had asked out of curiosity, not intending her words as a challenge to his presence in Aunt Carrie's room, but she doubted whether he'd believe her if she tried to explain. Choosing instead to steer the conversation into safer waters, she asked, "That song you were humming when I came in— what was it?"

Sandor looked startled. "Humming?"

"It went like this," she persisted, and shaped the deceptively simple melody softly on the air.

At the sound of it, Sandor's eyes widened in surprise. Gruffly he said, "It's an old Romany tune. A lullabye. I didn't realize—"

She wanted to press him for more of an explanation, but a flicker of movement drew her eyes to the bed instead. As she watched, Aunt Carrie stirred, then froze with a moan of pain.

Rachel hurried to her side. "Aunt Carrie?"

Aunt Carrie's eyelids fluttered, her hands moving restlessly over the sheet that covered her.

"Aunt Carrie, it's Rachel." Sitting down on the chair Sandor had vacated, she took her aunt's hands in her own.

Aunt Carrie's eyes opened, cloudy and unfocused.

Rachel leaned forward, into her aunt's line of sight. "Hi, there. You've had quite a night." She squeezed her aunt's hands gently. "How are you feeling?"

"Rachel! Oh, Rachel, I'm so glad you're here." A tremulous smile lit Aunt Carrie's face. "Such a silly thing, falling like that. So careless...." Her smile faltered. "I'm afraid I'm going to be a dreadful nuisance to everyone for a while."

"I suppose I should thank you," Rachel teased her gently. "I've been looking for a good excuse to come home."

"Home? Oh, no, dear. You mustn't. Your job—"

"I'm on leave," she said, hoping it was true. "Just relax. I'll take care of everything."

"Will you, dear? Will you really?" A tear slid from the corner of her eye. "They say I can't go home for a week or so, but I can't be away that long, there are things I have to do...."

"It's all right," Rachel soothed. "I don't want you to worry. Whatever needs doing, you can count on me."

With a deep sigh, Aunt Carrie closed her eyes again. Her breathing slowed and grew steadier, as if she were slipping back into sleep, but she roused after a minute and said, "You'll be there, then?"

"At the house, you mean?"

Aunt Carrie nodded.

"Yes," Rachel assured her, "I'll stay at the house."

"And you'll be there for them until I can come home again?"

"Them?"

"The boarders, dear. You'll look after them for me, won't you? I try to have breakfast on the table no later than seven—"

Forget about the damn boarders, Rachel wanted to shout. *It's you I'm worried about!* But she bit her tongue. For tonight, the important thing was to put Aunt Carrie's mind at peace.

"Don't worry about us, Miss Caroline," Sandor said from behind Rachel's chair. "We'll get along just fine."

Aunt Carrie's forehead furrowed anxiously. "But the four of you shouldn't have to—"

"I'll take care of everything," Rachel promised.

"And the groceries—"

"Hush. We can talk about all that tomorrow. You need to rest. It'll be morning before you know it. For now, sleep is just what the doctor ordered."

"Sleep, yes...for all of us." She raised her voice slightly. "You'll see Rachel safely home, won't you, Mr. Pulneshti?"

"No, I'm staying here," Rachel said.

Aunt Carrie shook her head, then frowned as if the movement had caused her pain. "Go on home, dear. I want you to. Sleep in my bed tonight, and be sure the others get their breakfast in the morning, and then come back to see me again before the operation. Will you do that for me? I'll be able to sleep tonight if I know you're there, looking after things. Truly. Mr. Pulneshti...?"

"My truck's downstairs," Sandor volunteered mildly. "You can ride back with me if you want to."

"Please, Rachel."

"All right," Rachel said with as much good grace as she could muster. "If that's really what you want—"

"It is. And you can bring a few of my nightgowns with you in the morning. And my hairbrush."

"I'll bring them." She bent forward to kiss her aunt's cheek. "I'll talk to the nurse on my way out, and I'll be back first thing tomorrow." Reluctantly she rose to leave. "If you need me before that, just call. Promise?"

"Promise," Aunt Carrie said, closing her eyes again. "Good night. Oh, and Rachel...?"

"Yes, Aunt Carrie?"

"Perhaps you could fix waffles in the morning. Max is really very fond of waffles."

"I'll remember that," Rachel said, making an effort to keep the sarcasm out of her tone. Then, picking up her suitcase, she followed Sandor Pulneshti out into the corridor.

CHAPTER SIX

FOR RACHEL, the next few days were a forceful reminder of what small-town life was all about. Neighbors were continually stopping by the house with gifts of food and anxious inquiries, and at the hospital, Aunt Carrie played hostess to a steady stream of visitors. Pastor Milligan, who seemed to feel responsible for Aunt Carrie's fall, arrived in Milford early on Saturday morning and stayed until the close of visiting hours. That evening, Rachel reached home to find that a long list of well-wishers had called in her absence.

When she arrived at the hospital Sunday morning, she saw that Archibald Gaines had sent a tall vase of rainbow-hued gladiolus to brighten Aunt Carrie's room. Even George Hudson's extravagant offering of yellow sweetheart roses looked faded and insignificant by comparison.

There were other surprises in store, as well. Tom Gaines had delivered his father's flowers personally, and it quickly became apparent that Tom and Aunt Carrie had been busy hatching plans in Rachel's absence.

"I've had the most wonderful idea!" Aunt Carrie announced. "It's amazing how things work out for the best, you know. I wouldn't have chosen to break my hip, of course, but now that I have, Libby Sawyer won't have to worry about the library while she's recuperating. *You'll* be there to look after it for her and—"

"Wait," Rachel said. "Hold it right there. Who said anything about me looking after the library?" She cast an accusing glance at Tom. "I only promised to look for a replacement."

"But you haven't found one yet, have you?" Aunt Carrie asked anxiously.

"Well, no. Frankly it got lost in the shuffle. Work was a zoo when I got back on Thursday, and then—" she gestured at the hospital bed "—then something else came up, as you may have noticed."

"And now you'll be in Dalewood for the summer, and that changes everything!"

"I'm staying in Dalewood this summer to take care of *you*, not the library."

"But you can do both! Lately Libby's only had the library open a few afternoons a week. Surely you'll have that much time free. After all, you can't expect to sit with me around the clock."

"She's right, you know," Tom said, joining in for the first time. "You shouldn't tackle looking after your aunt single-handedly."

Rachel scowled at the unwelcome intrusion. "I'll manage."

"I mean it, Rachel. It isn't smart to try to do it all yourself. I found that out the hard way after Dad had his stroke." Tom walked to the window and leaned one hip against the sill. "By the time he'd been home a week, we were ready to kill each other. I needed a break...and so did he. We ended up hiring a private nurse to come in during the day. That way I could get back to work at the drugstore, and Dad and I weren't getting on each other's nerves all the time."

"And we wouldn't even have to hire anyone," Aunt Carrie added. "I'm sure Miss Jones and Max would be willing to take turns helping me when you were at the library, Rachel. It would give you something to do, and the whole town would benefit."

"It sounds as if you two have this all worked out," Rachel said, but there was no heat behind her accusation. As ideas went, it wasn't the worst one Aunt Carrie had ever had. And finding a solution to the library's problems was important. Rachel remembered all too clearly how much she had looked forward to choosing her new books each week, especially in summer. In all good conscience, could she turn down an opportunity to return that favor in kind?

Still, it bothered her to think of leaving Aunt Carrie at home with no one but the boarders to look after her. They had no medical training. Then again, in all honesty, neither did she. If skilled care was necessary, Rachel would have to hire someone. But if it turned out that all Aunt Carrie required was companionship and a helping hand, would it really be to her benefit for Rachel to introduce another stranger into the household, even on a part-time basis?

"Speaking for the town council," Tom said, venturing a hopeful smile, "I can offer you the hourly rate we've been paying Mrs. Sawyer, but it's barely enough to buy you lunch uptown."

"Somehow that's about what I expected." Rachel looked from Tom to her aunt and back again. What chance did she have when those two visionaries started scheming together? "Don't worry, Tom. I wasn't expecting to earn anything this summer. But before I agree to anything, I need to know what the council expects. Are they just looking for someone to sit at the front desk and check books in and out?"

"Sure, I guess so. Why? Did you have something more in mind?"

"I'm not sure yet, not until I've seen the place for myself. But if I find things that need to be done, I'd like to know whether I have the authority to do them or not."

"Look," Tom said earnestly. "We never dreamed we'd be able to find somebody with your qualifications to take over for the summer. If you decide you want to tackle this, I'll guarantee to run interference for you with the rest of the council. Most of them won't care what you do, as long as it doesn't cost the township any extra money. With me in your corner, you should be able to count on doing anything you want to with the library, as long as you stay within the budget.''

''Anything I want?'' After the red tape and departmental politics Rachel had endured at the university library, the thought of being given a free hand was intoxicating. Surely she could find a way to manage a few hours a week without seriously neglecting Aunt Carrie. And she intended to hold Tom to his promise of noninterference and support. Besides, if the university released her, as she was afraid they might, a summer spent as a librarian in Dalewood would look better on her resumé than a summer of unemployment. ''All right, then, Tom. So be it.''

''Are you sure? Don't you want to think it over for a day or two? I wouldn't want to push you into anything—''

''Don't worry about me, Tom. As far as the library is concerned, I intend to be the pusher, not the pushee. Can we settle this between us or do you need to clear it with the other council members?''

He held out his hand to her. ''The decision's mine to make. And the job is yours if you want it.''

''In that case,'' Rachel said, accepting his handshake while Aunt Carrie looked on approvingly, ''it's a deal. You and the council have got yourselves an interim librarian.''

''Great.'' Reaching into his pocket, Tom pulled out a key. ''I picked this up from Mrs. Sawyer on Thursday night,'' he said, handing it to her. ''You may as well take it with you now.''

''The key to the city?'' Rachel teased, feeling light-hearted now that the decision was made. ''Thanks, Tom. Maybe I'll drive by the library on my way home tonight—if I can still find it! I'd be embarrassed to admit how many years it's been since I last walked through the door this key will open.''

"Well, that's one advantage Dalewood has over Cleveland," Tom said reassuringly. "You can't possibly lose your way."

MARRY IN HASTE, *repent at leisure.*

The old cliché came forcibly to Rachel's mind that evening when she unlocked the door and propped it open, letting herself in to what passed for the Dalewood Public Library.

Thankfully it wasn't a marriage she had undertaken, just a part-time summer job, but her first survey of the library convinced her that she'd have the grounds—if not the time—for plenty of repentance in the weeks ahead.

The air trapped inside the big room was hot and stale, smelling of floor wax and old paper, but the library itself was neat and tidy. There was no dust on the shelves, no dirt on the floors, no clutter on the tables and countertops.

There was also no computer to monitor book circulation, no microfiche system and no microfilm reader. For that matter, there was no card catalog, computerized or otherwise. The *Milford Messenger* was the only newspaper in the rack, and the library's reference section, which she would normally have regarded as her personal bailiwick, consisted mainly of a set of ten-year-old encyclopedias and an equally outdated world atlas. Only the almanac was current.

Walking slowly along the nonfiction shelves, Rachel saw that Dewey decimal numbers had been inked onto some of the spines, but many of the books were unmarked, and entire areas of study were completely unrepresented.

The fiction section wasn't much of an improvement. Most of the books were neither classics nor best-sellers; they fell into that gray zone of books that had been written, published and then forgotten. It was an undistinguished assortment, and the military precision with which the books were aligned led her to believe that few of them were ever checked

out, or even looked at. *I've agreed to preside over a corpse*
Rachel thought unhappily as she continued her tour.

It wasn't until she reached the end of the row that sh
discovered the first real signs of life. Jumbled together there
in no particular order were hundreds of paperback books—
an eclectic mix of celebrity biographies, romance novels
adventure stories and murder mysteries. Pulling out severa
at random, she saw that the circulation cards glued inside
their covers attested to a lively readership.

She smiled, as pleased by the sight of them as a gardener
who had spotted the first green shoots of spring. Finally here
was proof that the Dalewood Public Library was still a living part of the town it served. As long as people were willing to come through its doors in search of entertainment and
enlightenment, there was a chance for improvement and
community involvement.

The children's corner fed her optimism further. Settling
herself on the floor in front of the low shelves, she let her
gaze roam, picking out titles she remembered from her
youth: *Old Yeller* and *The Black Stallion*, to feed her love of
animals; *Little House on the Prairie* and *Girl of the Lim-
berlost* to satisfy her sense of wonder and adventure; *Kim*
and *National Velvet* to prepare her for the leap into adult
fiction, and dozens more, each one memorable in its own
way. And here, as on the paperback shelf, she found welcome indications that eager hands and eyes had recently
foraged through these books, searching for satisfaction.

Pulling out a battered copy of *The Secret Garden*, Rachel
smiled. If she could be here for the children, to listen to their
ideas and answer their questions, that would be justifica-
tion enough for a summer's work. Wooing the adults was
the key to the library's survival, that was plain, but win-
ning the children over would be the more important task, an
investment in Dalewood itself.

Tom hadn't yet revealed the details of the library's operating budget, but she knew it wouldn't be much. She'd have

to capitalize on her contacts at other libraries, begging for first look at any books they planned to discard, and she would certainly continue Libby Sawyer's approach of supplementing the library's holdings with paperbacks. They weren't a good long-range investment, but they were an affordable way to revivify the current collection. And she'd need to study the library's acquisitions list, to see what had been purchased over the past few years. With luck, a few gems had gone unnoticed in the—

"Hello there."

Rachel jumped. "Mr. Pulneshti!"

He stood just inside the doorway, balanced and watchful. Although he offered no apology for startling her, his body language made it clear that he was unsure of his welcome. He wore white canvas shorts that emphasized the sinewy length of his legs, and a pair of battered running shoes. A red T-shirt was draped around his neck, reminding her of the bandanna he had worn on the morning after their first encounter. Below it, Rachel could count the subtle corrugation of his ribs.

"I saw your aunt's car parked out front."

She knew she should dilute the tension of the moment with casual conversation, but an odd sense of expectation stole the words from her mind, leaving her silent.

"The library door was open," he added, as if she had questioned the propriety of his presence. "I can leave, if you want me to."

"No, stay," Rachel said.

Her words hung there on the air between them, irretrievable, saying too little . . . and too much.

She cleared her throat and added, "After all, this is a public library. You have as much right to be here as anyone else."

"Even after hours?" Sandor looked around the empty room and grinned. "Or is this the Dalewood equivalent of a convenience store, open twenty-four hours a day?"

Why did his sense of the absurd have to dovetail so neatly with her own? It was hard to remain distant with a man who could make her smile. "Hardly. From what I've been told, people have had to be pretty quick on their feet lately to find a time when this poor old library was open at all. But I'll be changing that, now that I've taken over."

It was a decision she hadn't realized she'd reached until she spoke the words aloud, but the rightness of it was undeniable. Libraries weren't meant to be like trains, run on tight schedules. They needed to be open often enough for people to stop by on the spur of the moment, when the urge to browse or the need to know struck them. A few afternoons a week just wasn't enough. Let Tom and the town council think what they liked; she'd donate her time, if it came to that.

Don't start making this harder for yourself than it has to be, the little voice in her head cautioned. *You can't afford to be away from Aunt Carrie for long stretches of time. If you start extending the library's hours, you'll have to find somebody else to man the desk when you're not—*

"Miss Jones!" she exclaimed as the idea crystallized.

"No, you had it right the first time," Sandor corrected with elaborate patience. "I'm Mr. Pulneshti. Miss Jones is a foot shorter and wears dresses. She's an alto and I'm a bass. But try not to let it worry you. You'll get us all straight, eventually."

Again Rachel found herself smiling. "Thanks," she assured him, "but I know who you are . . . or at least I'm beginning to. You know, when I first asked Aunt Carrie about you, she said you were a carpenter."

His big hands lifted in acceptance of her statement. "I am."

"But you're also an architect."

He nodded.

"And a general contractor."

"So?"

"So you're not exactly the itinerant workman I'd been led to assume you were."

"Sure I am. I travel from job to job, from site to site, wherever the projects take me. That makes me a walking dictionary definition of 'itinerant,' wouldn't you say, Madame Librarian?"

"You must have an office somewhere."

"Not really."

"Then how do your clients get in touch with you? By carrier pigeon?"

"Nothing so inventive. I use the architectural firm I used to work for in Cleveland as a contact point for mail and meetings, and their switchboard takes messages for me when I'm out in the field on a job."

"Like you are now."

"Like I am now," he agreed. "Like I nearly always am, for that matter."

Rachel tried another tack. "Cleveland...is that where you live?"

"Since February I've been living here in Dalewood."

"But your home base," she persisted, "your apartment, that's in Cleveland, isn't it?"

"I don't have a home base. Not in that sense."

No next of kin. The final words from his reference sheet came back forcibly to Rachel's mind. She supposed she ought to be tactful and let the matter drop, but there was something challenging in Sandor's reticence, as if he were daring her to push beyond the polite facade of social interaction. "No permanent address?" she asked skeptically. "No house? No apartment? What on earth do you do with all your things? Store them at a warehouse?"

"Things?"

"You know—belongings. Clothes, books, pots and pans, birthday presents, old income tax returns...?"

"I'm not big on possessions," he said. "Business records get stored at the office. Money goes into the bank. Beyond that, what I have travels with me."

"You're telling me that, except for money and documents, everything you own is in your room at Aunt Carrie's?"

"Well, I don't take my truck upstairs with me at night," he said teasingly, "but essentially, yes. Does that seem so unusual to you?"

"Maybe not if you're a Martian. But this is America, land of the free, home of the charge card and the three-car garage. It's your democratic responsibility to acquire as many toys as the guy next door."

"Sorry. It's a little late for this leopard to change its spots. Citizenship may not be enough. Maybe you have to be born on U.S. soil for the buying gene to be properly dominant."

"And you weren't?" she asked, intrigued.

Her question seemed to jolt him. "No," he said and then, without elaborating, changed the subject. "Look, I didn't mean to take up so much of your time. I was just out for a walk, trying to cool down. When I saw your aunt's car and the door standing open here, I figured I'd stick my head in and see what you were up to. Small-town curiosity seems to be contagious, even if conspicuous consumption isn't."

"Ah, but you didn't follow through," Rachel observed. "A true small-town gossip would have found an excuse to leave as soon as they found out I'd agreed to fill in as librarian this summer. The telephone lines would already be humming. Never mind, Mr. Pulneshti. I'm sure you'll do better next time."

Her foolishness won a smile from him, a smile that erased the stiffness that had settled over his features when the question of his origins had arisen. *He must really have meant it when he said there was no next of kin,* Rachel reflected. *He's alone in the world . . . and not from choice.*

She couldn't have said what made her so certain that his isolation was involuntary, unless perhaps it was the remembered sight of his hand cradling Aunt Carrie's as he sat beside her hospital bed. Intuition seemed to be shouldering logic aside where her opinion of Sandor Pulneshti was concerned.

You're getting as bad as Aunt Carrie, the inner voice warned. *A sucker for every stray dog and orphaned kitten.*

She wished it were true, but she knew that the attraction she felt was anything but maternal.

He wasn't like Tom. Tom was predictable, as comforting as fresh-baked bread. There was nothing predictable about Sandor...unless perhaps it was his stubborn determination to keep the promises he made. He wasn't like Douglas Chadwick, either—glib and two-faced—and she thanked heaven for that.

Sandor was himself, a blend of sharp brains and tanned brawn, and the combination was intoxicating. If she wanted to escape involvement, caution would definitely be her wisest course—caution and as much distance as she could manage, under the circumstances.

If.

Sandor thrust his hands into the pockets of his shorts. "Would you do me a favor?"

"I will if I can," Rachel said, wondering what he could possibly want from her.

"Do you suppose you could stop calling me Mr. Pulneshti?"

"You've decided you prefer Miss Jones after all?" Rachel asked, but the banter was mechanical, a smoke screen to hide behind while she tried to interpret his request.

"You know what I'd prefer," he said, with a quiet intensity that sent a shiver through her.

She could have taken his words as a joke, or acted affronted by them; she could even have pretended to ignore him. Instead, not sure where the path between them might lead but determined to find out, she said, "Then maybe you should start calling me Rachel." When he didn't respond, she tucked *The Secret Garden* back into its place on the shelf and, trying to sound casual, said, "I was getting ready to call it a night when you showed up. Would you like a ride home?"

He hesitated, and Rachel felt her confidence ebb. Had she misinterpreted his mood, read too much into his request?

"Thanks," he said after an uncomfortable silence, "but I think I'll finish my walk."

It was silly to feel hurt and disappointed; nothing had really happened. Nothing at all. And yet, leading the way to the door, she was unable to shut out her awareness of Sandor, who stood close behind her, watching her. Self-consciously she slid the doorstop out of the way and turned off the lights.

In the darkness, he said, "Rachel."

"Yes?" She stood still, waiting, the weight of the door a steady pressure against her hands.

"Nothing," he said softly. "I just wanted to see how it would sound." Then he stepped past her, through the open doorway, and disappeared into the night.

IT WAS PAST MIDNIGHT before Sandor finally returned to the big white house on Spruce Street.

When he'd left Rachel behind on the library steps, his plan had been to walk until he could forget what an ass he'd just made of himself, but it soon became obvious that he was apt to reach Miami Beach before that happened. Of all the lamebrained, weak-willed, libidinous mistakes he'd made in his life, launching a summertime flirtation with his landlady's niece ranked right up there near the top of the list. Before he was free to get romantically involved with anyone, he had to find another woman, one straight out of his past. Until he succeeded at that, his future wasn't really his own....

But that hadn't stopped him from fantasizing about Rachel, nor had it stopped him from investigating when he'd spotted a light on in the library and saw Miss Caroline's familiar car parked out front. And he'd found exactly what he'd gone looking for: trouble.

You're a fool, Pulneshti.

And so he walked. If anyone had asked, he'd have told them that he was wandering without purpose or destination, but eventually he found himself out beyond the edge of town, standing in front of the moonlit form of the house he was trying so hard to create. These days, he rarely had a chance to be alone at the site, and he had never seen it at night. Unprepared for quite how different everything looked, he stood gazing at the half-constructed building for several minutes, absorbing the sense of its monochromatic silhouette. Then, walking inside, he climbed to the second story, intrigued by the way the moonlight filtered through the riblike rafters.

As always, the work-in-progress drew him out of himself. By the time he climbed down to ground level again, the sullen fever in his blood had cooled, leaving a comfortable weariness in its wake. Sitting down on a pile of lumber, he considered the house, wondering yet again where he had failed in his design.

The door.

Sandor blinked and sat up straighter.

It was the door that was the problem...or rather the space where the door would soon hang. He'd specified a standard frame in his plans, and a nicer-than-average oak door was on order, but he could see now that the imbalance between the house's soaring elevation and his conventional solution to the entryway lay at the core of his subtle, persistent dissatisfaction with the facade. Windows alone couldn't compensate; he needed more height, more breadth. More door.

Sandor stood and began to walk again, increasingly restless as his mind hummed with possibilities. Double doors might be the best solution, or perhaps a single massive portal, its imposing dimensions lightened by leaded-glass panels. Or maybe...

He walked the miles back to Miss Caroline's house in a trance. As he climbed the stairs to his room, he told himself that in the morning he would put pencil to paper and see which solution was most pleasing. Now that he had pinpointed the problem, he could afford to sleep for what little remained of the night.

At peace, he opened the door to his room and stepped inside, then stopped.

Someone was stretched out on his bed, barely visible in the moonlight. *Rachel,* he thought, and his heart slammed against his ribs, stuttering in a quick new rhythm that obscured his solemn resolve to leave her alone. But in the next instant he realized that the silhouette was all wrong. This wasn't Rachel; it was— "Max?"

Sandor sat down on the edge of the bed and reached out to touch the teenager's arm, bewildered and concerned. By mutual agreement, the tenants in Miss Caroline's house never went into one another's rooms. Any interaction that occurred between them took place downstairs; there was no chummy sharing of confidences behind closed doors. It was beyond belief that Max had come into his room like this, at night and uninvited. Something had to be seriously wrong.

Sandor nodded in slow comprehension. Something was wrong, and Miss Caroline was gone, closed away in her hospital room in Milford, leaving Max without a protector. From the day when Max had first arrived, snow-damp and shivering, looking more like a sick kitten than a girl, it had been apparent that Caroline Locke was the only person in the house that she liked or trusted. What need did she suddenly have that couldn't wait for Miss Caroline's return?

Turning on the bedside lamp, he shook her shoulder. "Max?"

She woke with a jolt and sat up on one elbow, her eyes wild for a moment as she looked around. Then, with a little moan, she dropped back against the pillow. "I fell asleep," she said, her tone startled and belligerent.

"So I see. Is something wrong? Do you feel okay?"

Max's hands closed protectively over her abdomen. "I'm fine."

"Good, I'm glad. But what are you doing in here?"

"Waiting for you." Moving ponderously, she scooted higher on the bed, levering herself up to lean against the headboard. "Don't get mad. I didn't touch anything. I just needed to talk to you."

"I'm not mad," Sandor said cautiously, "just curious. What did you want to talk about?"

Her right hand dropped down to move restlessly over the chenille bedspread, stroking back and forth along the fuzzy ridges. Watching the nervous motion, Sandor saw that her fingernails were bitten to the quick. "I've got a problem," she said.

You've got several, he was tempted to say, but he bit his tongue and waited for her to go on.

"It's my class," she said as a blotchy flush made its way up her neck to her cheeks. "I don't have anybody to go with me now."

"Class?"

"About having the baby," Max said. "Everybody's supposed to have a partner, but now with Caroline breaking her hip and everything, I don't. So I thought..." She looked up at him, her eyes dark-shadowed. "I was wondering if... maybe... you..."

It was a crazy notion. He couldn't be Max's labor coach. He was a stranger, a man who didn't know the first thing about babies. He couldn't possibly go with her to her class. How would it look? People might even assume that he was responsible for her pregnancy. And if he was embarrassed at the thought of going with her to class, he didn't dare envision what going with her to the hospital for the actual birth might entail. No. It was too crazy. She'd have to find somebody else.

Like who, Pulneshti? Her options aren't exactly limitless.

He hesitated, and in that moment Max took his hand and pressed it to the wrinkled cotton of her blouse, just above the bottom hem. "There," she said. "Did you feel it?"

"Feel what?" Sandor asked, trying to draw his hand back.

Max's grip on his wrist tightened. "Wait a second. Just wait."

"What am I supposed to—" He froze in surprise as something nudged against the palm of his hand.

Max grinned, releasing him. "There."

"Was that...the baby?" he asked, and realized that until that moment, the child growing inside Max's body had had no reality for him. Yes, he'd known she was pregnant, but somehow he had only thought about it in terms of Max herself. He hadn't taken into account the presence of another individual, a tiny person, still not fully formed, who would have a life independent of him or Max or anyone else.

Beneath his hand, the baby moved again.

I'm thirty-five, Sandor acknowledged. If life had been kinder, he might already have had children of his own. Instead this would probably be his only chance to claim a front row seat at an undeniable, dyed-in-the-wool, Grade A miracle.

"So," Max ventured, "how about it? They'll teach you everything you need to know at the class. Will you do it? Will you come?"

"Are you kidding?" Reaching out, Sandor gave her braid a tug. "I wouldn't miss it for the world."

WHEN RACHEL CAME DOWNSTAIRS to fix breakfast the next morning, she resolved to keep her mind on her cooking and her eyes on her plate, in the hope of avoiding any more embarrassing private encounters with Sandor Pulneshti.

She needn't have worried. He didn't step into the kitchen until everyone else was already seated, and he paused just long enough on his way out to snatch two hot blueberry muffins from the basket on the table and say, "Did you sleep okay, Max?"

"Yeah. Thanks."

"See you tonight," George Hudson called out cheerfully as the screen door banged shut.

Rachel stared after Sandor indignantly. What was she, the hired help? He could at least have greeted her, even if he wasn't going to thank her for the muffins. And he ought to get a new muffler for that rattle-trap truck of his, before one of Aunt Carrie's neighbors registered a complaint.

Damn the man.

As she and Max finished cleaning up the breakfast dishes, Monday morning's mail arrived. Sorting through it, Rachel found the usual clutter of junk mail and magazines for Aunt Carrie, an important-looking package addressed to Mr. Hudson and two envelopes bearing her own name.

The first was from Mr. Cunningham, Giblin's head librarian, informing her that her request for a three-month leave had been denied. Her remaining vacation days would cover her absence through the first week of June. He would expect her to return to work at that time, as required by her contract. If, for any reason, she did not intend to return at that time—

Rachel folded the letter and stuffed it back into its envelope. She knew that it wasn't fair to be angry with Mr. Cunningham. Under the circumstances no other response had been likely, but she'd still dared to hope that they could reach a compromise.

It was obvious now that that wasn't going to happen. In five more days her job at Giblin University would be gone and, with it, her paycheck. It was time to cut back radically on her expenses . . . and that meant doing something about her Cleveland condominium. It might already be too late to find someone to rent it for the summer, but she'd have to try. And what about next fall? Would Aunt Carrie still need her then?

Preoccupied, she opened the second envelope and found a single sheet of beige stationery inside, with nine words typewritten on it.

A broken hip, it said. *What next? I hope you're satisfied.*

CHAPTER SEVEN

IT SEEMED TO RACHEL that her aunt's Spruce Street residence took on the feel of a genteel social club in the week following Aunt Carrie's homecoming from the hospital. Friends dropped by daily, and Dalewood's Monday evening card party announced that it would move its activities to Aunt Carrie's house for the duration of her convalescence.

Contract bridge was the town's current obsession. Rachel wasn't surprised to learn that George Hudson and Integrity Jones knew how to play, as well. Given Aunt Carrie's devotion to the game, it was probably the one question she had remembered to ask before agreeing to rent rooms to them.

Tonight, four card tables had been crowded into the living room. Rachel greeted the card players as they arrived, fielding their eager questions about the library while she searched their smiling faces, wondering which of these people she had known since childhood was capable of having written the anonymous letters.

Agnes Denihee and a tall, unfamiliar man were the last to arrive.

"I do hope we haven't kept everyone waiting," the scrawny little woman exclaimed. Dragging her escort inside, she said, "This is Rachel Locke, dear. Our hostess's niece. And this," she said proudly to Rachel, "is my Walter. Isn't he a handsome devil?"

Privately Rachel found the description inaccurate to the point of hilarity, but she swallowed her smile and held out her hand to Walter Denihee. "It's very nice to meet you."

"And *speaking* of handsome men," Agnes said loudly, "what about Madame Zora's prediction? Has Cupid's arrow struck yet?"

"Not yet," Rachel said, acutely aware of the amused interest of her aunt's friends. "Would you like me to take your sweater? I think we're ready to start."

To her relief, they settled into their seats and the evening of card playing began. The participants changed partners after every fourth hand according to some elaborate rotation system that remained a mystery to Rachel. She simply sat where she was sent and played with whoever appeared across the table from her.

In the third rotation Integrity Jones was her partner, with Pastor Milligan and Aunt Carrie as their opponents. When her partner took the bid, Rachel was able to spread her cards faceup and excuse herself from the table. "I'll bring out another pitcher of lemonade," she volunteered, and headed for the kitchen, leaving Integrity Jones to play the hand.

Circulating from table to table, refilling people's glasses, Rachel saw that the bright little woman had already won enough tricks to fulfill their current contract and, to judge by Pastor Milligan's unhappy expression, was managing an overtrick or two, as well.

Aunt Carrie was looking tired. Since stairs were more of a challenge than she would be able to handle for a while, Rachel had listened to the doctor's advice and transformed the sewing room next to the kitchen into a temporary bedroom. With the aid of a walker, the new arrangement gave Aunt Carrie the run of the downstairs, allowing her to be as involved in the house's daily activities as she wished to be. But Rachel suspected that her aunt found the hospital bed they had rented to be a poor substitute for the comfort of her own mattress.

Going to her, Rachel knelt beside her aunt's chair. "You look like you're ready to call it a night."

"Oh, no, dear, I couldn't," she said, although the remaining card in her hand was trembling visibly. "It would ruin everyone's evening."

"I'm not worried about 'everyone,' I'm worried about you. You promised Dr. Winston you wouldn't overdo things, remember?"

Pastor Milligan leaned across the table with a solicitous smile. "It's your play, Caroline. Is anything wrong?"

Taking the card out of her aunt's hand, Rachel laid it faceup on the table. "Aunt Carrie's worn out. She's going to bed now."

"Well, not quite yet," Aunt Carrie amended. "There's still one more hand to be played in this rotation. I'll just—"

"No," Rachel said obstinately, worried by the light, quick rhythm of her aunt's breathing. "It's just a game. Your health is the important thing."

Gathering the cards into a neat pile, Integrity Jones said, "I believe Mr. Pulneshti plays bridge. I'm sure he wouldn't mind sitting in. Shall I go upstairs and ask him?"

Rachel bit back a protest. Since her encounter with Sandor at the library, she had scarcely seen the man, and no words more personal than "Pass the salt, please," had passed between them. She hadn't anticipated having to play cards against him when she had agreed to fill in for the ailing Libby Sawyer at the bridge table, but she couldn't think of any other solution that would pry her aunt away without an argument. "Good idea," she said staunchly to Integrity Jones. "Come on, Aunt Carrie. I'll help you get settled for the night."

But her aunt waved her away. "No, you'll be needed to play out the next hand. Max can help me. You and I can't *both* desert our guests. Perhaps Miss Jones wouldn't mind knocking on Max's door when she goes up to get Mr. Pulneshti.''

Rachel settled for escorting Aunt Carrie to her room and waiting with her there until Max arrived, but it was hard to smile a convincing welcome to Sandor when she came back to claim her place at the table a few minutes later.

Her cool reception didn't seem to worry him. "All right, ladies and gentlemen," he said, dealing the cards with a casual skill that drew Rachel's eye, "the game's Five Card Stud. Eights and aces are wild, minimum bet's a ten spot."

Smiling grudgingly at his nonsense, Rachel sorted out her hand, hoping that she and Integrity Jones would be able to give him a run for his money. She was rewarded with the sight of the strongest hand she'd held all evening. All she had to do was weather the bidding until it came around the table to her, then she would communicate her good fortune to her partner and together they could reap the benefits.

As the dealer, the right to open the bidding went to Sandor. "Three no trump."

It was an outrageous opening bid, indicating that he had enough points in his hand to assure the game, regardless of what his partner held. *Beginner's luck,* Rachel thought bleakly.

"Pass," said Integrity Jones, and Rachel folded her cards together. Her hand was good, but not good enough to justify a high-level bidding war when her own partner had already passed.

"Pass," Pastor Milligan said contentedly.

"Pass," Rachel said, the word bitter on her tongue.

Her strong hand gave her the necessary weapons to make Sandor fight for what he needed, but the outcome was never really in doubt. Playing in a steady rhythm, he collected the nine tricks his contract called for, and the remaining four were little solace to Rachel.

To make matters worse, the group of card players were determined not to call it a night. "One more rotation,"

Pastor Milligan instructed. "North stays put. South and West exchange seats, then East and the new West move one table to your left."

"Miss Caroline was North," Integrity Jones explained to Sandor, and turned to Rachel. "That means that you and Pastor Milligan exchange seats, and then he and I move along to the next table. Good luck."

Like patterns in a kaleidoscope, people altered their positions. When the bustle of movement subsided, Rachel found herself partnered by Sandor Pulneshti, with George Hudson and Agnes Denihee as their opponents.

"Weak Twos, Stayman, Blackwood and Gerber?" Sandor asked, making the names of the bridge conventions sound like a law firm.

"I'd rather not tackle Gerber," Rachel answered. "I'm pretty rusty, but I think I can manage—"

"None of you are going to be*lieve* what happened to my friend Myrtle McCreedy over in Milford," Agnes Denihee interrupted, dealing the cards. "You remember Myrtle, don't you, Mr. Hudson? I introduced the two of you at the Historical Society meeting."

"Yes, of course. A lovely lady."

"Well, two men came to her door last week and offered to asphalt her driveway. They told her they'd just finished a job over on the next block and had just enough left to do her driveway and so they offered her a bargain price, seventy-five dollars, and they'd do it right then."

Stifling a yawn, Rachel looked across the table and saw, to her surprise, that Sandor was listening closely to Agnes Denihee's story.

"Naturally she said yes. When they were through, they told her to be sure to give it a day or two to get thoroughly dry, and so she did, of course, and—did I say that all of this happened last week? Anyway, when she went out to get her newspaper yesterday morning, she checked and it *still* wasn't dry, and so she called me up and asked if Walter could come by and take a look, and he did, and *he* said it wasn't asphalt at all! Can you guess what it was instead? Can you?''

"Used motor oil, probably," Sandor said. "Count your cards before you look at them, everybody. I'm one short."

Agnes Denihee glared at Sandor. "Yes, well, used motor oil. I ask you! Have the rest of you ever heard of such a thing? And as sticky as these cards are it's a wonder if you're only *one* card short."

"Here, I seem to have fourteen," George Hudson said. "Shall we deal over again or—"

"Oh, just give him the extra card," Agnes sputtered, and turned her attention back to Sandor again. "You know, I really don't think I'd be so quick to admit I knew how their little tricks worked, if I were in your position. People might begin to wonder about the quality of the work you're doing on that old house down the street."

Rachel had heard enough of Agnes Denihee's nasty brand of chatter. "You've got no right to accuse Mr. Pulneshti of doing something wrong," she asserted. "In a town this small that sort of unfounded rumor can ruin somebody's business. If I were you, I'd want to be pretty sure of my facts before I started making accusations."

Across the table, Sandor looked astonished by her defense.

Faced with such strong opposition, Agnes Denihee backed down. "Well, now, I'm not saying that he cuts corners or does anything he shouldn't," she equivocated, "but he even *looks* like he's one of them, and so—"

"Looks like he's one of whom?" George Hudson asked before Rachel could object again.

"Why, those gypsies, of course. Myrtle says they've been as bad as a plague of locusts this past month or so, showing up all over Milford, doing odd jobs and generally causing a stir. Frankly I think they're behind all those burglaries we've been reading about in the paper. Yesterday, when I was driving back from visiting Myrtle, *I* saw—"

"I think you owe Mr. Pulneshti an apology," Rachel interrupted.

"That isn't necessary," Sandor said coldly.

"No, of course not," George Hudson added soothingly. "I'm sure Mrs. Denihee meant no harm. As a matter of fact, Pulneshti, I should introduce you to Mrs. McCreedy. She lives in a lovely old Federal-style home in Milford, and she was saying at the meeting that she would like to have it inspected by a qualified architect so that it could be added to the county's historical list. That would be right up your alley, wouldn't it?"

Rachel expected Sandor to dismiss the suggestion, but he said, "Have her get in touch with me, then. It's your bid, Mrs. Denihee."

"Mine? Oh, yes, well..." She consulted her cards hastily. "Pass. And I certainly meant no—"

"One diamond," Sandor said firmly, closing the matter.

Rachel was braced to endure the next hour of play, but she soon began enjoying it, in spite of herself. Sandor was a quick and audacious player, one who bid his hand aggressively and then played it to its full potential.

It was exhilarating, like dancing with an agile partner. On the final hand, she and Sandor carried the bidding from level to level until, at last, Rachel was committed to play out a grand slam in diamonds, a contract that required her to take all thirteen tricks.

To her left, Agnes Denihee's lead was the ace of spades.

Sandor spread his cards out on the table for Rachel to see: first the diamonds, then the clubs, then the hearts.

George Hudson sighed. "A void in spades. I do believe you're going to pull this off, Miss Locke."

And she did. When all fifty-two cards were stacked neatly in front of Rachel and the game was theirs, Sandor reached across the table to shake her hand. "There were at least three ways to lose that contract. If this is how you play when you're rusty, you can be my partner anytime."

His fingers were warm and strong around her own, his palm rough, and she found herself accepting both the handclasp and the compliment with genuine pleasure. He was a good player, arguably the best she'd ever been paired with and, therefore, his compliment meant something to her. As for the handshake, that definitely meant something to her as well, judging from the way her nerves were jangling, but she wasn't ready yet to think about what that meaning might be.

The other tables had finished the final game of the evening as well, and people were rising stiffly from their chairs, congratulating each other or bemoaning their bad luck. Agnes Denihee pushed back her chair and got to her feet, looking disgruntled. "A tall, dark stranger in*deed*," she said to Rachel disapprovingly, under cover of the other voices. "I'd watch my step with that one if I were you, dearie." Turning away, she smiled brightly at George Hudson. "Well, we were certainly given a lesson in humility tonight, weren't we? I'd better go find my Walter and see if he fared any better."

Troubled, Rachel watched her go, wondering whether the woman's outspoken nature made her the likeliest or the *least* likely source of the anonymous letters. What would be the point of writing them since she felt so free to speak her mind? And yet, if she thought her opinions and advice were being ignored, then perhaps—

"Is something wrong?" Pastor Milligan asked solicitously, joining her. "Sometimes after a lively night of cards, I can't help mentally replaying the last hand, trying to squeeze out that one last trick."

"That won't be Rachel's problem tonight," Sandor said from behind her, his voice rumbling an octave deeper than the minister's. He touched her arm, and Rachel fought down an impulse to look around the room to see if Agnes Denihee was watching. "Grand slam, bid and made."

"Well, then, my congratulations. You make a formidable pair. I'll have to be on my mettle when I play against you next week."

"No," Sandor said. "I only filled in tonight as a favor."

"Well, then, Rachel—"

She shrugged. "Same here, I'm afraid. A temporary stand-in. I'll settle for going out in a blaze of glory."

"Are you sure? It would be a shame to lose two such worthy adversaries, especially when you've begun so well together. I really think the two of you should reconsider."

"You may be right," Sandor said.

Rachel looked up at him in surprise.

He didn't smile, but the laugh lines at the corners of his eyes deepened. "Good partnerships are rare. Maybe we should explore this one a little further before we write it off. What do you think?"

As suddenly as if it had never been severed, the thrill of connection was there between them again, strong and enticing. He stood very still, watching her, waiting for her to answer. To respond. *Oh, I'm responding, all right,* Rachel thought ruefully. If she was going to rebuff him, now was the time... but a rebuff was the last thing she wanted to offer. Beyond caution, she smiled into his eyes. "I guess I'm game if you are, partner."

GYPSIES IN MILFORD.

Long after the house had fallen into its night silence, Sandor sat by the open window in his room, thinking about Agnes Denihee and her tale. Was she right about the gypsies? Using motor oil on roofs and driveways was an old trick, known to swindlers of all sorts. There was nothing conclusive there. And by her own admission she was only passing on a second-hand account.

A month ago, he would probably have shrugged off her story. Over the years, he'd followed many stronger leads in his ongoing attempt to track down one particular family of gypsies. Usually it turned out to be a wild-goose chase. Occasionally he did succeed in locating a band of traveling Rom, but never the right group and never anyone who was willing to aid him in his quest. And twice his questions had resulted in a scuffle as he was forcibly turned out of whatever gypsy camp he'd found. *Never again,* he had vowed to himself, nursing a split lip after the last encounter.

But that was before he met Rachel Locke.

Sitting across from her tonight, he had found it impossible to maintain the illusion of cool distance that he'd worked so hard over the past two weeks to create. After the final game, standing with her, he'd experienced a wave of towering anger at the circumstances that held him separate from her. Until such time as he could find the Demetro family—a task that had confounded him for nineteen years—he had no future to offer any woman.

But Agnes Denihee said there were gypsies in Milford.

Tomorrow, he had a full day's work scheduled, and he was committed to going with Max that evening to her Lamaze class. But after work on Wednesday, he'd drive over to Milford and take a look for himself. And he would drop in on Myrtle McCreedy to examine her house and see if she could add any useful details to Agnes Denihee's story. The trip would probably be a waste of time... but he'd never know if he didn't go.

And suddenly not knowing was unbearable.

CHAPTER EIGHT

WHEN RACHEL WALKED into the Dalewood drugstore on Wednesday morning, the gossip mill was operating at full flood. Several of Monday night's card players were settled comfortably at the soda fountain with midmorning doughnuts, and the supposed asphalting of Agnes Denihee's friend's driveway was still a hot topic of conversation. Tom was cheerfully refilling cups and wiping up spills while his father sat enthroned beside the cash register at the back of the room, typing up a prescription, listening but remaining aloof.

"Rachel!" Tom called, spotting her. "How about a cup of coffee?"

"Have you bought a new coffeepot yet?"

"Of course not. Old Reliable's going to last through the end of the century."

"In that case, thanks but no thanks. I've lost my taste for battery acid."

"Yeah, well, Cleveland's made you soft. What if I said I've got an apple Danish over here with your name on it?"

"Apple? Oh, Tom, you don't fight fair."

"All's fair in love and war," he quoted, and smiled hopefully as he held up the pastry.

Rachel's spirits sank. How many times would she have to say no before Tom quit trying to rekindle the spark between them? In Dalewood it wasn't possible to avoid him entirely, and she couldn't very well drive to Milford every time she needed a tube of toothpaste. And if she did, it would only hurt his feelings. She didn't want to humiliate him or make things more uncomfortable between them than they already were, but he seemed hell-bent on misreading every little civility as a sign of reconciliation.

"No," she corrected, smiling for the benefit of the people sitting at the counter. "All's fair in the battle of the bulge. I've already had one breakfast today. That's my limit." She held up her shopping list. "I just came by to pick up a few things. Thanks anyway."

The little bell that hung above the door jingled, and all eyes turned to inspect the newcomer, a dark-haired woman with a bag of groceries clutched in her arms. Rachel took advantage of the moment to start down the aisle of non-prescription drugs and cosmetics, searching for the shampoo Aunt Carrie had requested. To her left, the topic of conversation at the counter had changed. "Yeah," one of the men was saying. "I hear where a whole pack of 'em have been doing field work for Charlie Grabemeyer. Good workers, he says, and there's no taxes to figure. You just pay 'em while you need 'em, and then they move on."

"That's fine, I guess," another voice said skeptically, "so long as they don't rob you blind while they're at it."

"Naw, it's no worse than those migrant workers that came through last year. They've got some old guy in charge who handles all the dickering with Charlie, and he pays 'em by the piece so they can't fleece him. Don't you worry, if anybody's gonna get the short end of the stick, it won't be Charlie."

Shampoo, aspirin, dental floss... Rachel consulted her list again. Vitamins. That's what she was forgetting.

When she had gathered everything she needed, she surveyed the shelf of office supplies. As she'd expected, packets of blank envelopes and beige paper were stacked along with the other stationery. Anyone from Tom Gaines to Pastor Milligan could easily have bought paper in the Dalewood Drugstore that matched the anonymous letters she had received.

Frustrated, Rachel walked to the back of the store, swallowing a sigh of exasperation as she joined the slow-moving line that had formed there. She wanted to open the library at ten, but she knew, in all honesty, that that was only the surface excuse for her impatience. In a deeper, truer sense, she was chafing at the hours that had to pass before she could see Sandor that evening at the dinner table.

After the tantalizing sense of promise that had blossomed between them after the Monday-night bridge game, it had been a disappointment to come down to breakfast the next day to find that he was already on his way to the building site. By the time he got home that evening, there had barely been time for him to shower and eat a hasty meal before he drove off with Max to her class. By the time he finally returned, hours later, Rachel was hopelessly entangled in a cutthroat game of Scrabble with Aunt Carrie and Integrity Jones.

But tonight would be different. One way or another, she was determined to win some privacy for the two of them, determined to get a chance to explore the insistent longing that filled her whenever she thought of him, determined to satisfy the urge she had to learn the texture of his jet-black hair beneath her fingertips.... She needed to understand the mysteries that haunted his gaze.

Flushed, Rachel shook free of the dark, sweet fantasies that stalked her and took her place in line.

The unfamiliar woman with the groceries was standing in line ahead of her. Looking at the back of her head, Rachel hoped it was no one she knew. At the library, she had already embarrassed herself by failing to recognize a few of the patrons. How could you tell someone that they were fifty pounds heavier than you remembered them, or that they didn't look quite the same now that they'd gone bald?

But this woman was quite young, certainly not much over thirty. Whoever she was, no one had greeted her when she walked in. She might be new in town, or visiting. *Just don't let her be somebody I sat beside in high school,* Rachel prayed, moving slightly to the side in an effort to see her more clearly.

The woman's sun-darkened skin was pulled tight against her bones, and her face was made to look even thinner by a brown birthmark that followed the curve of her left cheekbone. Her long hair was haphazardly parted, caught back in a rough braid. She was small, with the delicate bones of a child, but the way she carried herself gave an impression of wiry strength—a farmer's wife, maybe. Her mouth was slack, and she looked tired. Her gaze was fixed on the shoulder blades of the person in front of her.

When the stranger reached the head of the line, she set her purchase on the counter. Then, holding her bag of groceries with one arm, she reached into the pocket of her faded housedress with her free hand and held the money out to Archibald Gaines.

Standing so close, Rachel could see that his movements were slow and clumsy as he took the bill and punched the keys of the cash register. "Nine'y-three, nine'y-four, nine'y-five…" he said, counting coins into the woman's palm, then hissed in exasperation as the final nickel slipped from between his fingers and fell to the floor.

Stooping, Rachel picked it up and handed it back to him. She hadn't expected any effusive thanks, but she was unprepared for the look of black resentment he gave her, as if the aftereffects of his stroke were somehow her fault. He reached out to complete his counting…and again the nickel fell.

This time the woman bent to retrieve it herself, nearly spilling her groceries in the process. Then, sweeping her purchase off the counter into her bag, she murmured her thanks and started for the door.

"Wait!"

She turned back. "Yes?"

"You gave me a twen'y," Mr. Gaines said.

"I did?" She walked back to the counter, glancing shyly at Rachel as she stepped past her and took her place at the head of the line again. "Thank you for being so honest, mister," she said in accented English as he counted the remaining bills into her hand.

"No need t'thank me."

"But you could have kept my money and I wouldn't have noticed."

Rachel hid a smile. No one in Dalewood was more unwaveringly honest than Archibald Gaines. It would never occur to him to keep a customer's money. Indeed, if she knew him, he was probably feeling affronted by the mere suggestion.

The woman reached into her pocket and drew out a folded single on top of the straightened bills he had handed her. "There, you see? It was folded just like the twenty. How stupid of me. Oh, well. No harm was done, thanks to you. Could I please give you these and have a ten-dollar bill for them?"

"Certainly."

"You are very kind," she said, and kept up a constant stream of talk as the money changed hands, not seeming to mind the hesitations and slurring of Mr. Gaines's speech. Pocketing her money at last, she turned to leave, smiling brightly, the earlier air of weariness gone from her expression. *She's pretty,* Rachel realized with a shock.

"Next?" Archibald Gaines said gruffly. When Rachel had set her purchases on the counter, he turned the vitamin bottle over to expose the price sticker, then rested his hand on the counter, making no move to enter the amount on the cash register.

"Mr. Gaines?" she said uncertainly when a long moment had passed. An unhealthy flood of color mounted in his cheeks as she watched. "Are you all right?" When he didn't respond, she turned anxiously, trying to catch Tom's eye. What did someone look like when they were having a stroke? "Tom? Could you come over here for a second?"

He started across the room, but her voice seemed to have jolted the older man out of his daze. "That woman," Archibald said hoarsely, looking past Rachel's shoulder. "Where is she?"

"She left."

"Where did she go?"

"I don't know," Rachel said, bewildered. "Why?"

Tom arrived at her side, concern etched clearly into his features. "Are you okay, Dad?"

"Find that woman. Stop her!"

"All right," Tom said, moving toward the door. "But why? What's wrong? What did she do?"

Archibald flicked a glance at Rachel and the other people standing in line behind her, and the hectic flush stained his face again. "Never mind what she did," he bellowed at his son. "Just find her!"

"By the time I got out to the street, she was long gone, of course," Tom told Rachel when he stopped by the library at closing time, "along with ten dollars' worth of the day's profits."

"You mean that woman shortchanged him?"

"Yeah. Dad's fit to be tied. Nobody's ever flimflammed him before. She must have been pretty smooth. Didn't you notice anything while it was going on?"

"No, not really," Rachel said, looking up from the inventory she'd begun. "Of course, there was a lot of confusion at first, because she thought she'd given him a single when it was actually a twenty...." Rachel smiled wryly. "I guess that was all part of it, huh?"

"It looks like it. Dad says she asked him to give her a ten in exchange for a stack of smaller bills, and she kept him talking the whole time, and she had this big bag of groceries she kept juggling, and he was trying to hurry, and somehow, he's not quite sure how or when, she got two tens out of him instead of just one.'' Pulling out a chair, Tom dropped into it. ''He can't pin down exactly how she managed it, but we checked the cash drawer and we are ten dollars short. Not that ten dollars is the end of the world—it's just the principle of the thing. Dad doesn't think much of himself these days, anyway, and now—well, he's really embarrassed. That's why I came by. I wanted you to know what happened, but I thought maybe you wouldn't mind keeping it to yourself. He'd hate it if your aunt found out.''

''Aunt Carrie wouldn't tease him.''

''I know, but . . . Well, he wouldn't want to look foolish in her eyes. Dad's proud. And he cares a lot about what she thinks.''

''What are you saying?'' Rachel asked, feeling that she'd been missing something. ''Do you mean that your dad and Aunt Carrie—''

Tom stood, looking flustered. ''He admires her, that's all. Just forget it, okay? I've got to be going.''

''Okay,'' she agreed. ''Consider it forgotten.'' But as she closed the library for the afternoon, she found herself thinking back, trying to recall just how many years had gone by since Tom's mother had passed away. Could it be that Archibald Gaines and Aunt Carrie . . . ?

Impossible, she told herself. *It would be like Ebenezer Scrooge courting Pollyanna.*

She felt better then . . . until a memory came to her of the vase of rainbow-hued gladiolus in Aunt Carrie's hospital room. And suddenly she wasn't quite so sure, after all.

LATE THAT AFTERNOON, at least an hour before he should have called it quits for the day, Sandor gave in to temptation and started out, taking the back roads to Milford.

The past day and a half had been formed of one frustrating delay after another, task following task as the hours crawled past. But he was free now, free to pursue the elusive answers he needed, the answers that would allow him to pursue his feelings for Rachel with a whole heart and a clean conscience.

And if he failed, if it was just another promising lead that came to nothing, he would somehow find the strength of purpose to break cleanly with her, once and for all.

He scanned the passing countryside as he drove, slowing frequently to peer into the stands of trees that separated one man's fields from the next, looking for an unexpected spot of color or the reflection of the setting sun glinting off a half-hidden windshield. Stopping at a produce stand along the way, he made inquiries, but the teenage boy at the cash box had no news to offer, just early strawberries. Philosophically Sandor bought a pint and ate them in place of the dinner he was missing as he continued his drive.

In Milford itself, the problem became one of too much information rather than too little. It seemed that every grizzled farmer and soft-palmed store clerk had a tale to tell. Like Agnes Denihee, however, none of them seemed to be speaking from personal experience. At best, they knew someone who knew someone, and the directions and suggestions they offered were vague and often contradictory.

Finally Sandor admitted to himself that he was wasting time. Climbing back into his truck, he headed east, toward the river.

The first sign that he might be getting closer to his quarry came as he drove past the brick wall of an abandoned factory in the poorer part of town. At eye level on the weather-smoothed brick, just dark enough to be visible, someone had chalked a seemingly random pattern of lines and dots.

Hitting the brakes, Sandor backed up and studied the marks.

It was a message, scrawled on the wall in the same way his ancestors would have arranged sticks and pebbles or gouged the soft ground at the side of some country road. Different places, different methods, but the purpose was the same—to offer warning or encouragement to others who traveled the same path and knew enough to interpret what they were seeing.

Food and shelter; the first part of the message was easy to read. But where were the food and shelter to be found? What did the final crosshatch of symbols represent? Sandor stared at the wall in frustration. Luck had brought him as far as it could. Now he was being thrown back on the very memories he had tried for so long to obscure.

Determined, he got out of the truck and walked over to the wall, reaching up to trace the faint chalk marks with his fingertips in the hope that doing so might trigger some half-forgotten association.

Water. With a surge of relief, he remembered that the pattern before him had something to do with water. And it made sense, with the river so close by. But what exactly...?

The bridge. Yes, he thought with satisfaction, that was it. *Food and shelter at the bridge*.

Smiling grimly, he climbed back into the cab of his truck and started the engine.

WHEN RACHEL RETURNED from the library, she found Aunt Carrie seated with Max and Integrity Jones on the back porch, listening to the eighth inning of a Cleveland Indians game on the radio while they sipped iced tea.

"Who's ahead?"

"The bad guys," Max said in tones of disgust.

"What's the score?"

Integrity Jones smiled. "It might be kinder not to ask. Would you care for a glass of iced tea?"

"Thanks. I'm parched. How long has the drinking fountain at the library been out of commission?"

"If I may quote my boarder," Aunt Carrie said with a twinkle in her eye, "it might be kinder not to ask."

Miss Jones took an empty glass and the pitcher of iced tea off a tray table in front of her, poured some for Rachel and passed the glass to her.

Rachel took a long swallow. "So where's Mr. Hudson? I thought he was the big baseball fan."

"Oh, he is, dear, but he's making a quick trip uptown to buy a gallon of ice cream for tonight's dessert. His nephew is going to be joining us for dinner, and he wanted to do a little something extra."

"When did all this get arranged?" Rachel asked, annoyed. "I only bought enough chicken for the six of us."

"That's all right. Mr. Pulneshti phoned an hour ago to say that he wouldn't be home for dinner, so it all works out perfectly."

Suddenly the tea tasted flat. "I'm going to go change out of these clothes," Rachel said, and went inside, leaving the three of them to their ball game.

Was it just bad luck and bad timing, or was Sandor avoiding her? If his absence was intentional, he was playing a complex little game of cat and mouse, arousing her interest and then pulling away. But if it was pure coincidence, a matter of circumstances working against them, then he must be feeling as frustrated as she was.

Resolving to give him the benefit of the doubt one more time, she poured her tea out into the kitchen sink, set her glass on the drain board and started down the hallway toward the stairs.

The sound of quiet footsteps overhead stopped her.

Rachel cocked her head, listening. Was Mr. Hudson back from his errand already? If so, why hadn't he come into the kitchen to take care of the ice cream?

The footsteps stopped.

Maybe it wasn't Mr. Hudson at all. His room was at the back of the house; these sounds were coming from the front, from her old room.

From Sandor's room.

In spite of herself, Rachel felt a thrill of anticipation. Had he found a way to make it back for dinner, after all? Eagerly she went to the foot of the stairs and started up. "Sandor?"

At the sound of her voice, the footsteps began again, coming toward her along the upstairs hallway. "Hello?" a male voice said inquiringly, and Rachel hesitated; it was the voice of a stranger.

A moment later, a tall blond man came into view, neatly dressed in a light gray summer suit. Seeing her, he smiled engagingly. "Could you help me? My uncle asked me to meet him here for dinner, but I can't seem to find him anywhere. I knocked, but nobody answered. The door was unlocked, so I let myself in and went up to look for him, but—" Coming down the stairs toward her, he looked at her more closely and said, "Uh-oh. You look annoyed. Shouldn't I have come in? I thought since this was a boardinghouse—"

"This is my aunt's house," Rachel said, trying not to be disarmed by his contrite expression. "If nobody answered, it would have been better if you'd rung the bell or gone around to the back porch."

He gazed down at her apologetically, his dark eyes and wavy blond hair making him look like a cocker spaniel puppy enduring a scolding.

"But I don't suppose any harm was done," she said, relenting, and held out her hand. "I'm Rachel Locke."

"And I'm Jeremy Hudson. Pleased to meet you." He shook his head ruefully. "Uncle George will probably rake me over the coals for barging in here like this. If you'll introduce me to your aunt, I'll apologize to her and—"

"Oh, forget it," Rachel said. "It's too hot for apologies. Come on out back and we'll find you some iced tea. Do you like baseball?"

THREE DIFFERENT BRIDGES forded the Cowles River in Milford, and it wasn't until Sandor reached the third of them that he saw what he was looking for: a huddle of trucks and vans sheltered by the thrust of the bridge abutment, and a flicker of firelight.

Parking under the sole functioning streetlight in the area, he climbed down from his pickup truck, closing the driver's door with a firm slam that carried through the warm evening air. He approached openly for the same reason that he wore his working clothes: he wanted the gypsies in the gully below to recognize him as a fellow Rom deserving of their help, not some *gajo* troublemaker intent on sticking his nose in where it didn't belong.

Sandor climbed down the embankment and started toward the group, disappointed to see that there were only half a dozen men sitting there, some young, some old. He raised his hand and one of the older men returned the gesture. The others sat stolidly, watching him.

"Sarishan," Sandor said in greeting as he neared the camp fire, hoping that his Romany sounded less rusty than he feared it did. "I was glad to see your message back there on the wall. Do you have room for another by your fire?"

"That depends on what you seek," one of the older men replied cautiously. "You don't look like a man who has missed many meals."

There was no point in denying the obvious. "True enough," Sandor said. "For now, I have work that provides me with money enough for food, and a truck to take me where I need to go. All I really ask tonight is news of other Roms you may have met on your travels."

The man considered this request. "Is there someone special that you're looking for?"

"I'm hoping for word of the *vitsa* of Lulash and Celie Demetro," Sandor said, deciding that the word for "extended family" best defined his complex relationship with them.

Several of the men exchanged glances. Sandor waited uneasily, unable to read their faces.

"Demetro? Perhaps I know of these people," the group's spokesman said. "Then again, there are many who go by that name. What else can you tell me of this *vitsa* you seek?"

Sandor hesitated. There were so many things he couldn't say.... "Well, I last had dealings with them many years ago in Chicago. Lulash Demetro and his wife have two sons and a daughter named Laza."

"Then their family cannot be the one, for the husband and wife I know of had three sons, not two."

His statement was enough to feed Sandor's hope that the old man knew Lulash and Celie, or at least knew of them. Schooling his impatience, he said, "They may yet be the same. It is true, as I said, that there were two sons, Lazlo and Gunari, born of their own blood, but there was also another taken into the family many years ago. Might that not be the third son you heard mentioned?"

The man's gaze was cool and distant. "Perhaps. I don't suppose it matters. The boy died." His shrewd eyes searched Sandor's face. "Or so I was told."

The boy died. The words were a shock, rocking Sandor's view of his own past. At the age of sixteen, he had stood alone and listened to the sentence passed against him by the judges of the *kris*: banishment from the world of the Rom. It was a decree that relegated him to the status of a nonperson, as if he had never been born.

What he felt now was surprise and a sort of bittersweet gratitude. That the Demetros had talked of his death to these men and not denied that he'd ever existed was a backhanded compliment, an acknowledgement that he was remembered with some fondness by the Demetro family in spite of the *kris*'s ruling.

If I can see them, even for a few minutes, he thought with renewed optimism, *I can make them understand why I need to talk to Laza. All I have to do is find them. And this man can tell me where to look.*

·'Well, then,'' he said as calmly as he could manage, ''it would seem that the crossing of our paths tonight was fortunate. You have my gratitude. When you have told me what you know of Lulash and Celie Demetro, I will seek them out and—''

''No. I cannot do what you ask.''

''But I only want to talk with them,'' Sandor said, hoping to temper the flat refusal.

''I will tell them of our talk. If you are known to them, then surely they will welcome news of you. What is your name?''

Sandor shook his head. ''It isn't that simple. There was a misunderstanding. Hard words were spoken. Harsh deeds were done. All I wish is to atone for the past and assure myself that they are well. I mean them no harm.''

''Then be at peace,'' the old man said. ''I have seen them and they are well. Be on your way with a clear conscience and a light heart.''

''It's a question of honor,'' Sandor insisted. ''I mean you no disrespect, but this is not a situation where I can take another man's word for something I have not seen. I must meet with Lulash and Celie Demetro myself and talk with them.''

''Then give me your name and tell me how they can find you, if they decide to do so.''

The impasse was maddening. ''Surely you can understand,'' Sandor pleaded. ''We parted with ill feelings between us. It will not gladden them to hear my name. I wish them no unhappiness, but they have no way of knowing that. The only way the old wound can be healed is for me to go to them humbly and offer my apologies. They'll be glad of it in the end, I promise you."

"Liar," one of the younger men said, and spat into the fire.

Startled, Sandor looked down at him, but all that he saw was a belligerent, muscular Rom of little more than twenty. The only thing familiar about his face was the expression of disgust and anger he wore, a look that roused a host of painful memories in Sandor's mind. Nineteen years ago, Lulash Demetro's upper lip had curled in that same way as he had cursed Sandor's name, and the assembled faces of the *kris* had worn a similar look of close-minded condemnation when they'd passed their sentence upon him. That look had dug a deep and bitter place for itself in Sandor's soul, and the unexpected sight of it on a stranger's face made his fists clench reflexively. "You're quick to condemn, for a green boy who knows nothing of my situation."

"A green boy?" The youth stood with slow menace. "Think again, worthless one. I was a boy then, yes, a little boy who could do nothing but listen helplessly in the night as Laza cried. But I am a man now, and I will protect my family against you. You will leave here, and you will not come back again."

But Sandor hardly heard his final words, so intent was he on searching the young man's features for a trace of the small child he must have been. "Lazlo?" he asked uncertainly.

"No. I am Gunari."

Gunari? It seemed impossible. The sight of him forced Sandor to a harsh new acknowledgement of the passage of time. Gunari had been the baby of the Demetro family, only five years old when the *kris* had delivered their ultimatum. Sandor could still remember the look of delight on Laza's face on the morning when she first held her baby brother in her arms. How could he reconcile that memory with the sight of this angry, broad-shouldered young man?

"Gunari, I am glad to see you again after so many years," Sandor said, "but there is more to this matter than you can possibly understand. Take me to your father, please, so that he and I can reason together. What harm can there be in that?"

"What harm? The same harm you have done to these honest Rom by joining them in this camp as if you had the right!" Looking around at his companions, he pointed an accusing finger at Sandor. "This man's name is Sandor Pulneshti. The elders of my *kumpania* declared him *mahrime*—unclean. He pollutes us all by his presence here."

A rumble of disapproval rose from the men circled around the fire.

"Go now," Gunari ordered with angry self-importance, "or I will make you go."

Sandor tried again. "Gunari, hear my words. I won't turn and walk away from here. I can't. If you won't say where I can find your parents, then I must ask you to take a message to Laza for me."

"Go," Gunari repeated forcefully, and two more of the men rose to their feet. "Leave us. I will not say it again."

Despairing, Sandor said, "If I agree to go, will you at least tell me what has become of her? Is she happy? Is she well?"

"You have lost the right to ask."

"Then tell your father what happened here tonight," Sandor entreated, watching warily as Gunari moved around the fire toward him, clearly poised for a fight. "Tell him what I have said. Tell him—"

"I will tell him nothing. Nothing! You are *mahrime*. Your words are poison in my ear."

"Tell him I need to speak with him, damn it. I'm working in Dalewood. He can find me north of the town at the crest of a wooded hill where a new house is being built. It's easy to find. I'm there every day. Tell him to come, for Laza's sake—"

"Mahrime," Gunari shouted in fury, and charged at him.

Sandor stood his ground, partly from stubbornness and partly from a hope that Gunari might be more willing to listen once he'd been given a chance to vent his anger.

For whatever reason, it was a mistake. The impact of Gunari's fist sent Sandor staggering backward over the uneven ground, his arms flailing, his balance lost. He fell and his head struck the rocks with a sickening jolt. Dimly he saw the others closing in above him, their faces frenzied, like a pack of dogs who had caught the scent of blood.

"Mahrime!" they chanted. *"Mahrime!"*

Sandor opened his mouth to try to reason with them, but the toe of a heavy work boot struck his ribs, driving the breath out of his body. Then another boot landed, but this time his head was the target, and it was thought that was driven out of him—thought, then sensation, and finally, blessedly, consciousness.

CRICKETS.

It took Sandor several long minutes to identify the sound. Laboriously, he began to puzzle out a line of logic.

He was outdoors, sprawled on bare ground. In all likelihood, he was still by the riverside encampment of Gunari and his friends. The only nearby sound was the chirping of crickets; the others must already have gone, leaving him behind. His head was pounding and his side ached fiercely, but he was alive. Considering Gunari's rage, it was a dispensation he hadn't been altogether sure of receiving.

Since he had no wish to spend the rest of the night huddled beneath a bridge, he supposed he would have to get up.

Reluctantly he opened his eyes.

He was indeed alone. The elderly trucks and vans of the gypsies were gone, and the cheerful camp fire had been extinguished, leaving only cold, damp ash. Gritting his teeth, he sat up and found that the pockets of his jeans had been emptied and pulled inside out. The watch had been stripped from his wrist, and someone had taken his belt and the laces from his boots. His wallet lay on the ground beside him, gutted. The cash he had carried was gone, along with his driver's license and social security card.

The social security card alone would have been enough to condemn him in their eyes. No self-respecting Rom would have applied for such a card, at least not in his own name. It was printed proof that Sandor had broken with their way of life and embraced the *gaje* world. Therefore, they owed him no loyalty or aid. Anything he owned was fair game, theirs for the taking.

Anything I own. . . .

The truck.

Standing was hard; walking was harder. Weaving unsteadily, Sandor floundered up the embankment, afraid of what might await him at the top. They'd already taken all his money and identification. Without his truck, how was he going to get back to Dalewood?

Worse yet, his tool chest had been stowed in the storage locker in the back of the pickup. It had taken him years to amass those tools, buying some new and some used, caring for them, repairing them, utilizing them through the long hours of a hundred projects until they were like extensions of himself. Without them—

Bracing himself as he reached the lip of the rise, he looked down the road toward the distant streetlight.

In the garish glow, his truck sat waiting for him. Amazed that it had escaped Gunari's retribution, Sandor stumbled gratefully toward it.

As he drew nearer and the damage became more visible to him, he began to understand. One headlight had been smashed, and the safety glass of the windshield on the passenger side was a crisscross of stars and cracks. Inside the cab, the upholstery had been slit with a knife.

The keys were in the ignition. *Go now,* Gunari had demanded, and had left Sandor the means to do just that, contenting himself with other expressions of anger.

They hadn't bothered to unlock the storage compartment; they seemed to have used a rock instead to break the hasp. The tool chest was upside down in the street beyond the truck, its contents strewn in all directions.

Stiff and dizzy, he carried the empty chest back to the truck, then began the slow job of gathering the tools, moving along the pavement on his knees like a man doing penance for his sins, returning each recovered hammer, saw and rasp carefully to its proper place.

The glass in his level was broken, and half of the drill bits seemed to have disappeared, but most of the tools were unharmed. Sandor concentrated on the task at hand, refusing to acknowledge the pain it cost him, just as he refused to acknowledge the turbulent emotions bottled within him. *Later. You can think about all of it later.*

When he was finally through, he hauled himself onto the driver's seat and turned the key, hoping that they hadn't decided to sabotage the engine. To his relief, it proved no harder to start than usual. By the light of the single headlight, he started home.

On the way, he allowed himself one detour. Reaching the deserted factory, he angled the truck so that the beam from his headlight struck the redbrick wall.

As he'd expected, the chalk marks were gone.

SPRAWLED ACROSS Aunt Carrie's big bed, still dressed in her shorts and blouse, Rachel was almost asleep when she finally heard the distinctive rumble of Sandor's truck pulling into the driveway a few minutes after midnight.

Drowsiness fled. Swinging to her feet, she made her way across the room, letting herself out into the darkened hallway. Her feet were quick and sure as she descended the stairs and doubled back along the long downstairs hallway, past Aunt Carrie's closed door, into the kitchen, eager to tell Sandor about the strange happenings of her day and curious to learn what had kept him away throughout the evening.

He was fumbling with the back door when she got there. Rachel turned the knob and opened the door for him. "Hi, stranger," she said teasingly, keeping her voice low in deference to Aunt Carrie, asleep in the next room. "Too drunk to fit your key in the lock? Come on in. I was beginning to think—"

Sandor took a staggering step into the room.

At the sight of his face, Rachel forgot the rest of what she'd been about to say. The little light above the stove cast only a soft glow, but it was enough to show her the dirty scrapes and swollen eye, the torn clothing, the general stiff posture of pain endured. Alarmed, she reached out to put a steadying arm around him.

He shied away from her touch, nearly overbalancing in the process. "Don't touch the ribs," he warned her harshly, then offered a strained semblance of a smile. "Sorry to bark," he said, his breath coming in shallow gasps, "but a bullet to the brain would be kinder than an arm around my waist right now."

"What happened?" Rachel asked in horror. "Who did this to you?"

"Nobody. Forget it. I'm—" He took a lurching step, then recovered his balance. "I'll be fine. Go back to bed."

She pulled out a kitchen chair, aching to touch him. "Here, please, sit down before you fall down."

"No," he said with weary patience, "if I sit down, you'll never get me up again. Climbing out of the truck was bad enough."

"But—"

"No detours," he interrupted her, looking haggard. "I'm going to my room while I still have the strength to get there."

"In that case," Rachel said firmly, "I'm coming with you."

CHAPTER NINE

SANDOR WOULD HAVE REFUSED her help if he'd thought he could manage without it; Rachel could read that much in his face. But after a silent moment he gave a small nod and said, "Just get me upstairs without either of us breaking our necks, okay?"

She relocked the back door, watching anxiously as he leaned against the refrigerator and bowed his head. "I'll do my best," she promised him. "But first I'd better call the doctor."

Sandor's head came up sharply. "No doctors. I just need—"

"I can see what you 'just need,'" Rachel said in concerned exasperation. "A hot bath, an ice pack, and a fistful of painkillers...and that's just for starters. Seriously, Sandor, I think you'd better let me drive you to the hospital in Milford."

Without warning, his answering chuckle turned into a muted groan. Putting a hand gingerly to his side, he took a shallow breath and said, "No. I've had as much of that town as I can take for one night. I'm going upstairs. You can either help me or get out of my way."

His tone was grimly determined, despite his glassy gaze. "All right, tough guy," Rachel said with misgiving. "Upstairs it is."

It seemed at first that there was no way to steady him on the stairs without adding to his pain. Finally, after a frustrating interval of trial and error, she climbed the steps ahead of him, letting him rest his hands on her shoulders for balance and support.

She was so intent on trying to sense how he was doing behind her that she forgot to be careful on the fifth step. It creaked loudly as it took her weight, and again when Sandor stepped on it. Rachel looked up toward the landing, braced for the sight of one or more of the boarders coming out of their rooms to investigate the piercing squeaks, but the upper hallway remained dark and silent.

At the head of the stairs, she guided Sandor's hands down from her shoulders and placed them on the level railing that bordered the stairwell. "Stay here and catch your breath for a second," she whispered. "I'll be right back."

Closing the bathroom door behind herself, she turned on the light and spread a bath towel on the counter, quickly rifling the medicine cabinet for antiseptic, cotton balls and a bottle of aspirin.

What else might she need? After a moment's thought, she turned on the hot-water tap and dampened one washcloth while the water was still running cold, then wet a second one when the flow began to steam.

Certain that she must be forgetting something but unsure what it might be, she gathered everything into the towel, turned out the light and let herself out to rejoin Sandor.

He was standing exactly where she'd left him, his breathing audible in the darkness. "Okay," Rachel murmured, wishing she could enfold him and take away his pain. Instead she touched his arm gently and promised, "One last effort and you're there."

The hallway had never seemed longer. When they finally reached the door to Sandor's room, Rachel stood aside to let him pass through first, then followed him in. Flipping the light switch, she set her bundle on the floor, walked to the windows and pulled down the shades.

Sandor moved toward the bed like a man in a fog.

Rachel hurried to intercept him. "Don't lie down yet. Let's get you out of those clothes first."

He gripped one of the uprights of the four-poster bed. "Somehow," he drawled, his voice raspy with pain and fatigue, "this isn't quite how I hoped to hear you saying those words."

"Beggars can't be choosers," she informed him tartly. Then, seeing that cooperation was beyond him, she began unbuttoning his shirt.

It was sweat-damp and dirty, and the material that stretched across his shoulder blades was torn in several places, as if it had been dragged over something rough. Through the rips and tears, she could see that the skin beneath was scraped raw, and once the shirt was completely unbuttoned, more scrapes and bruises over his ribs were revealed. "Can you let go for a minute?" she asked him, unsure of his equilibrium.

Slowly his fingers uncurled from the bedpost.

"This shirt is a total write-off," she said. When he didn't respond, she peeled it down his arms and tossed it into the wastebasket beside his drafting table.

Uncovered, his injuries looked unreal; it was as if he were in stage makeup for some violent B movie. Heavy bruising had already begun to discolor the skin over his rib cage, and the sight of the dozens of dirty little wounds that covered his back made Rachel's stomach lurch queasily. Unable to stop herself, she reached up to rest her hand against his cheek in silent sympathy.

His tight-lipped expression softened at her touch, and he swayed toward her as if seeking solace, but he straightened again almost before the motion had begun. "That's enough," he said, his voice a raspy whisper. "Go away now."

Troubled by the rebuff and his growing unsteadiness, she took Sandor's hand and wrapped his fingers around the bedpost again. "Hang on. We have to get your boots off, at least."

"Then do it," he said, the tremor in his voice robbing it of rudeness.

She'd promised herself not to badger him with questions, but what she found when she knelt at his feet jarred her out of her resolve. "Why would somebody take your boot laces?" she asked in bewilderment.

His eyes closed, his mouth set, Sandor said nothing.

"All right, sorry, forget I asked." She tapped his right foot. "Lift it up."

He did as he was told, as numbly patient as a horse being shod. *Thank heaven I heard his truck,* she thought, watching him. *He couldn't have done this for himself.*

Rachel tugged the first heavy work boot off and peeled away the white cotton sock beneath it, then repeated the procedure on the other side, unexpectedly struck by the sight of the high-arched delicacy of Sandor's narrow feet on the rug.

Delicate? her inner voice questioned skeptically. *Those boots must be size 12s at least. You're pretty far gone when you start admiring a man's feet.*

With his boots out of the way, the removal of Sandor's dusty blue jeans was Rachel's next task. She supposed the thought should have been daunting, or at least have prompted a maidenly blush. Instead, in all honesty, she had to admit to a thrill of anticipation. *What's the point in false modesty? You've already seen him in the altogether. Just remember, you're here to play Florence Nightingale, not Jezebel.*

She knew that perfectly well. She just hadn't counted on the aura of forbidden intimacy that being alone with him in this room was creating, nor had she foreseen how provocative she would find it to undress him, with his smoldering energies banked down for once to an unintimidating flicker.

Reaching up, she gripped the waistband of his jeans.

His eyelids flew open at her touch, exposing her abruptly to the startled and startling intensity of his gaze. *What was that about banked energy levels?* she wondered shakily, meeting his bleak stare. Obviously she'd been wrong about his state of mind, mistaking introspection for passivity.

Clearing her throat, she said, "Once we get your jeans off, you can lie down."

"That would be nice," he said dryly. He was looking down in her general direction, but the focus of his stare was slightly left of center now, and Rachel revised her opinion of his expression yet again, deciding that at least a portion of what she had interpreted as blind anger was blinding vertigo.

"Did you hit your head tonight?" she asked uneasily.

"Somebody hit it for me. Do you suppose we could hurry this up a little?"

Rachel unfastened the snap at the top of his fly and grasped the brass tab of the zipper. "Maybe I'd better call for an ambulance, after all," she said, drawing it smoothly down. "You probably need—"

"—to have my head examined? No thanks."

"Be reasonable, Sandor. You may have a concussion."

"No."

"No, you don't have a concussion?" she asked, tugging the stubborn denim down his long legs. "Or no, you don't want me to call?"

"Both." The corded muscles of his thighs tensed and bunched as he fought to keep his balance. "Forget it. *J'y suis, j'y reste.*"

"Yes, well, 'Here I am and here I stay' sounds good," Rachel said, surprised by the quotation, "but it may not be the safest decision you ever made—not to mention the fact that I may end up behind bars for criminal neglect if you're found dead in this bed tomorrow morning."

"Nobody'd press charges."

Not quite sure how to take his response, she ignored it, running her palms down the length of his calves, forcing the tight pant legs down around his ankles. His skin was warm and taut beneath her hands, the curve and slope of his muscles sharply defined. She tapped his right foot and he lifted it obediently, his thigh grazing her cheek as his point of balance shifted.

The contact only lasted for a moment, but Rachel felt her pulse redouble. "You aren't making it any easier for me to keep this strictly business," she scolded him as he swayed again. The sight of his white cotton briefs was having more of an impact on her than she'd bargained for. She had no intention of removing them, of course. There was no reason to, none at all. But like a fig leaf on a statue they drew her attention inexorably to the area they covered. The first time she and Sandor had been together in this room, he'd been furious and she'd been terrified. Tonight, he was battered and she was full of conflicting emotions, wavering from anxious concern to unruly desire.

Third time's the charm? her inner voice queried.

Maybe so, she admitted to herself with surprise. Maybe so. There was no way of knowing. What she *did* know, unfortunately, was that tonight was not the night. What Sandor Pulneshti needed right now was a friend, not a bedmate.

"Now the other foot," she said, and freed him from the grubby jeans. "There. Just one more minute. Let me turn down the covers." She folded back the familiar chenille bedspread and the top sheet, refusing to dwell on the thought that she was preparing to tuck Sandor Pulneshti into the bed of her childhood. The notion was too hot to handle, too fraught with hopes and memories intermingled, at once too real and too ephemeral. *I want you in my bed,* she thought, gazing up at him. *I want you in my life. And I don't have any idea whether that's going to be possible.*

"So," Sandor said unsteadily, "can I collapse now?"

"Soon. I brought some aspirin." She retrieved the bottle from her towel bundle, then realized what she had forgotten. "You'll need a glass of water. Hold on while I—"

"Forget it. Give me the aspirin. I'll take them dry."

Rachel's taste buds tingled unpleasantly. "Don't be silly. It'll only take a minute to run down the hall and fill a glass."

He held out his hand. "Just give them to me."

"But—"

"Do I have to spell it out for you?" Sandor asked, clearly annoyed. "If we keep running around here like a French bedroom farce, somebody's bound to wake up and notice, which won't do either of our reputations much good."

"But we haven't done anything wrong."

"How much difference do you think that would make to somebody like Agnes Denihee? When did the truth ever stop a good rumor? I wouldn't enjoy trying to prove our innocence to the world at large, would you? And I don't suppose your aunt would be very happy if somebody started telling tales about you. She's already taken more than enough flack about the rest of us."

"What do you mean?" Rachel asked, wondering if Aunt Carrie had confided in him about the anonymous letters.

"I'm not deaf or blind," he said. "I've heard the things people say to her. I've seen the looks they give her. I've even been the target of a few comments myself, although most folks would rather play it safe and snipe at Max or Miss Jones. Small-town America isn't used to being part of the melting pot." He looked sad and thoughtful and Rachel could see the exhaustion gathering in his face, draining it of color and sapping the vigor from his voice. "And you're twice as vulnerable to gossip as your aunt is. What if somebody outside saw you pulling down the shades in here? What if one of the other boarders decided to buy their own acceptance at the expense of your reputation?"

"You've got troubles of your own," Rachel reminded him. "Don't start worrying about me." For some reason, he seemed to find that funny. "I can take care of myself," she insisted, affronted.

His smile faded. "I told you to go back to bed when I first came in, and that's what you should have done, but you were determined to come along and be helpful. Fine. I'm grateful, but enough is enough. Now it's time to exercise a little self-preservation instead. So hand me the aspirin, okay?"

She didn't have the heart to go on arguing with him. Opening the bottle, Rachel said, "How many do you want?"

"Half a dozen should do."

She opened her mouth to protest, then closed it again. Half a dozen aspirin was a stiff dose, but it wouldn't kill him. She placed the tablets on his palm and watched, wincing, as he took them.

With a series of visible efforts, Sandor swallowed them down. "So *now* can I collapse?"

"Sure...but collapse face-first, could you? I need to disinfect those scrapes on your back."

"Don't you ever give up?" he asked, the challenging words belied by his look of startled gratitude.

"No. Why should I? To hear you tell it, I'm relatively safe in here—it's *leaving* that's going to get me in trouble. Besides, I can't have you bleeding all over Aunt Carrie's sheets, can I?"

He smiled wanly. "Heaven forbid. Face-first it is."

Carefully she helped him to ease himself facedown onto the mattress, then began the task of cleansing the cuts and abrasions that marred the skin over his spine and shoulder blades.

"I don't know about this," she said dubiously as she worked, trying to be both deft and thorough. "What you really need is a hot shower, or a long soak in the tub."

"Not tonight," he said, as she'd known he would. "Don't worry, I had a tetanus shot last month. Just clean off the worst of the dirt."

When she was finally satisfied, she ran her fingers gently through his hair, tracing over his skull until she found a large lump on the back of his head.

"Good grief, this is huge! Your head must be pounding. I'm going to get some ice for you to put on it."

"No. If I didn't want you going down the hall to get a glass of water, I certainly don't want you traipsing down to the kitchen for ice. Besides, don't waste your pity. That isn't where it hurts."

"What?"

"That's just where I hit my head against a rock. It's the place where they kicked me that really hurts, behind my left ear."

Hoping that it was another of his mordant jokes, Rachel slid her fingers to the side...and encountered another swollen knot.

"Sandor, this is serious. I can't believe you managed to drive yourself back here in this condition. Let me call a doctor."

"No."

"Or the police."

"No!" He reached up, groping until his fingers found her wrist and closed tightly around it. "Listen to me. You're not my mother. You're not even my landlady. This is my business and nobody else's. I want you to turn off the light and get out of here, now. Understand?"

"At least let me help you turn over again."

Sandor let go of her wrist. "Why bother?" he asked wearily, the anger fading from his voice. "All that's left are bruises. You can't do anything about them anyway. Just pull the sheet up over me and go on to bed while I pass out, okay?"

She didn't want to leave him. In spite of all the bluster and flippancy, she could sense his underlying distress. It turned her stomach to think that while she'd been spending a dull evening in Dalewood, serving chicken to Mr. Hudson's nephew, Sandor had been in Milford, where someone—or several someones—had beaten him up. Why had it happened? And why didn't he feel he could talk about it? If it had been a random mugging, he should have been howling for the police. Instead he didn't even want her to call a doctor.

There was so much she didn't know about him, so much she didn't understand...and now he expected her just to walk away. Well, she wouldn't. She was going to stay and do her best to find out what kind of trouble he was in and how she could help. But it didn't seem to be Sandor's style to cry on anybody's shoulder about his problems. Offering him a sympathetic ear wasn't apt to get her anyplace.

Instead, she did her best to adopt a stern tone and said, "At least tell me whether I need to spend the rest of the night on the porch with Aunt Carrie's shotgun across my lap, guarding the house."

His heavy-lidded eyes opened slowly. "What?"

"You heard me. What's the story, Sandor? Have you got union trouble with your carpenters? Did you take out one too many building loans and now the sharks are upping the interest rate? Somebody spent a lot of time and energy messing up your body tonight, and I'd like to be prepared for the guys in the black hats if they walk up and ring our front doorbell, wanting to finish the job."

"It wasn't like that," he said dully.

"Oh? What *was* it like?"

He sighed. "A personal matter. Don't worry, it's over."

"Given the way you look, can I afford to take your word for that?"

"I'm afraid you're going to have to. Look, I'm grateful. Really. But as far as anyone here is concerned, the matter is closed."

There was a limit to how far she was willing to badger him in his present sorry condition. Conceding defeat, she said, "You're a stubborn man, Sandor Pulneshti. Did you at least get the satisfaction of breaking somebody's jaw?"

"You want the truth? I didn't land a single punch." He closed his eyes. "Good night, Rachel."

She pulled the sheet up, settling it carefully over the raw places on his back. "Good night," she said reluctantly, and turned out the light. Then pausing with her hand on the doorknob, she added softly, "Sandor, if you need anything in the night—"

"I won't," he interrupted. "And if I do, I'll get it for myself. Go to bed, Rachel."

There was no way to stay, after that. Frustrated by her inability to break through his barriers, she stepped out into the hallway, leaving him alone with his pain and his problem, whatever it was.

On tiptoe, she retreated to her temporary quarters in Aunt Carrie's room and slipped between the sheets. "Honestly, Gertrude," she said to the solemn-faced doll sitting primly on the other pillow, "if this is the peaceful country life, I don't think my heart is strong enough to take it."

But she knew, even as she spoke the words, that the real danger to her heart was lying awake at the other end of the hall, with the bitter taste of aspirin and secrets on his tongue.

CHAPTER TEN

"MR. PULNESHTI?" Caroline Locke's voice broke the early morning stillness. "Mr. Pulneshti, is that you?"

So much for getting an early start. Already holding the kitchen door open, Sandor said, "Yes, Miss Caroline, it's me."

"Could you possibly come here for just a moment?"

There was no way he could refuse a request so politely made. "Of course," he said, and dropped the keys to the truck back into his pocket, letting the screen door slap shut again.

For Sandor, the week since his run-in with Gunari had been an endurance test. With grim determination, he had pushed himself to do what was necessary, arranging to have the truck's broken windshield and headlight replaced, buying a new level, working on the new house as efficiently as his battered body would permit.

But it had been hard, just as it had been hard to fend off the concerned questions from Miss Caroline's boarders. "An accident at the construction site," he'd told them, hating the lie. "I fell off a ladder." To his work crew, he'd said nothing, doing his best to ignore their increasingly ludicrous guesses about what he had been up to, just as he tried to ignore the vivid discoloration of the bruises that greeted him in the mirror each morning, and the searing doubts and worries that plagued his nights.

He couldn't escape the feeling that his encounter with the gypsies in Milford had been disastrous. Stumbling upon

Gunari Demetro had been a one-in-a-million fluke, and he worried that it might have done more harm to his cause than if he and Gunari had never met at all. The Demetro family rarely stayed in one place for long. If the other Rom who had been with Gunari that night had kept their silence, the boy might well have persuaded his family to move on without ever telling them the reason he wanted to do so. Still, Sandor held out a slim hope that the group remained nearby, and that Gunari had told Lulash Demetro what had transpired that fateful night. For a week now, he had made it his business to arrive at the building site soon after dawn and to stay long after the others had gone home, in the hope that Lulash would come in search of him. But so far, he had hoped in vain.

He had, of course, done more than stand by quietly and hope. He had pursued George Hudson's suggestion, making time to visit Myrtle McCreedy's house and question her about the men who had "asphalted" her driveway. And five times in the past seven nights, he had driven to Milford on his own and searched for other encampments, but he had returned each time unsatisfied. He could find no more subtle messages, no secluded camp sites, no gypsy faces, familiar or unfamiliar. Only the occasional rumor or complaint gleaned from the townspeople convinced him that the Rom were still somewhere in the area.

It left him precious little opportunity to see Rachel. Last night had been the first time in a week that he'd gotten back to Spruce Street in time for supper, and only then because he had promised to pick Max up for her Lamaze class. It hadn't been a comfortable meal. Across the table from him, Rachel had been silent, her eyes downcast as she ate. *Fine thanks you've given her for the way she took care of you,* Sandor berated himself.

Over the past seven days, there hadn't even been a private moment in which he could try to explain his extended absences. In spite of that, or perhaps because of it, his awareness of Rachel seemed to increase each time he saw her, and his desire for her became more insistent. A longing had welled up within him in spite of all logic and caution, and he knew he'd have to put even more distance between them. He wanted her, yet he had to draw away; he felt love growing, yet he wasn't free to speak of that love....

More than once, driving back from a night of fruitless searching, he had considered moving out of the boarding-house and taking a motel room in Milford...but that would mean abandoning his hopes for a relationship with Rachel, and his heart refused to accept that possibility. There had to be a way. And he intended to find it.

Very impressive, he thought dryly as he walked to the doorway of the sewing room to answer Miss Caroline's summons. *But when? And how?*

"You're up awfully early," he said, surprised to see that she was already out of bed, wrapped in her robe.

"I could say the same for you." She waved her hand toward the window seat. "Sit down, won't you? This will only take a few minutes."

"Yes, ma'am." He sank onto the flowered cushion she'd indicated, taking care not to jar his side. "What can I do for you this morning?"

"It's about your rent," she replied. "It comes due again next week, but I just don't feel that I can let things go on this way."

"What way?" he asked, but his heart sank. *What way do you think, Pulneshti? If you can see that Rachel is unhappy, Miss Caroline must see it, too. You had a chance to do the right thing and leave here voluntarily—but did you? No. You let things drag on, and now you've forced her to take the decision out of your hands.*

"After all," she said, her tone one of gentle regret, "it wouldn't be fair to act as if nothing had changed."

"No, of course not," Sandor agreed, feeling miserable.

"I want to be absolutely fair about this—"

"It's all right, Miss Caroline, I understand."

"Good. Then you understand why a reduction is necessary."

Sandor looked at her. "Reduction?"

"Yes, of course. The rent we originally agreed on was for room and board. If you aren't going to eat your meals with us anymore, it wouldn't be right for me to go on charging you the same amount."

It hurt to laugh, but he laughed anyway. "Miss Caroline, believe me, that won't be necessary."

"I think it's entirely necessary, Mr. Pulneshti. I have no intention of taking advantage of you." Dimples appeared in her plump cheeks as she smiled at him. "Well, actually, I *am* planning to take advantage of you in one small respect, but certainly not by charging you more than is fair for your room. If your schedule won't let you eat here regularly, then your payments deserve to be adjusted. I'll expect your July check to be written for half of the usual amount—unless this past week was just an aberration. Was it?"

Say no, you idiot. Tell her you're moving out. Instead he heard himself saying, "I—I'm not sure, yet."

"Well, then, we'll try the reduction for a month and see how it goes." She dusted her hands together briskly, dismissing the topic. "Now as to that favor, do you suppose you could spare a few hours on Saturday? There's an important errand that needs running, and it's going to take a pickup truck like yours to get it done, and so I thought I'd ask—but I want you to feel free to tell me no if you're already tied up."

Tied up on Saturday? He ought to be, he thought. He'd spent most of the previous weekend cruising the country roads around Milford, checking out the rural areas where it was too dark to search efficiently at night. But searching for Lulash Demetro and his family was a task that might stretch on indefinitely. If Miss Caroline needed part of one day, the least he could do was oblige her. "I don't have anything planned for Saturday," he replied. "The truck and I are at your disposal."

Miss Caroline beamed. "Wonderful. Rachel will be so relieved!"

"Rachel?" When would he learn to look before he leaped? "The favor is for Rachel?"

"Yes, her realtor called last night to say that someone wants to rent her condominium for the rest of the summer. She's delighted, of course, but the tenant wants to move in on Sunday and most of Rachel's things are still there. She claims she can cram everything into my car, but that's ridiculous. The place is being rented furnished, so the bed and couch and the kitchen things aren't a problem, but she has boxes and boxes of books, and all her winter clothes, and—"

"—and the truck would help," Sandor said. "I understand."

He understood, all right. He understood that he was being offered an unexpected opportunity to drive Rachel to Cleveland and back, to spend those hours alone with her . . . and he understood that the chance was too tempting to pass up. *You're a masochist,* he told himself savagely. *A masochist and a fool.*

But he didn't feel like a fool; he felt like a man clinging to the ragged edge of a dream, a man who couldn't bear to let go a moment before he absolutely had to. Lulash Demetro might still come before the end of the week. If he did, and if he was willing to listen to reason, then Sandor would have a chance to straighten out his tangled past.

Miss Caroline smiled up at him hopefully. "Well, then, can we count on your help?"

Tell her you can't do it. Tell her—

Ignoring his conscience, Sandor said, "Sure. My pleasure."

"Thank you. I hate to ask, but I feel terribly responsible for Rachel having to change all of her plans and move down here this summer to look after me. Not that I don't think she was glad to leave Cleveland, in a way," Miss Caroline qualified, her eyes bright and canny as she smiled at Sandor. "She'd been dating a visiting professor there, a charming man. She even brought him here for Thanksgiving dinner. I began to think it might be serious, and so did Rachel... until she found out that he wasn't nearly so available as he'd led her to believe." She sighed. "You can say what you like about the advantages of city life, but some things are simpler in a small town where everyone knows everyone else."

"I'm sure you're right," Sandor responded automatically, but he felt sick inside. *You can drive Rachel to Cleveland,* he told himself despairingly, *and you can pack up her things and bring her back home again. But how in hell are you going to make her understand when you tell her that you've been spending all these nights in Milford searching for your wife?*

THE FIRST INKLING Rachel had of Aunt Carrie's private arrangement with Sandor came after breakfast on Saturday morning when she looked down from her bedroom window and saw George Hudson below in the driveway, his sleeves rolled fastidiously above his elbows, preparing to wash her aunt's car.

By the time she got downstairs, water from the garden hose was thundering into a pail. "Excuse me," she said loudly. "Mr. Hudson?"

Soapy sponge in hand, he turned at the sound of her voice. "Yes? Just a moment." He twisted the nozzle of the hose, cutting off the noisy flow. "There. That's better. What can I do for you, my dear?"

She smiled apologetically. "Well, I guess it's a question of what you can *not* do for me. It's awfully nice of you to think of washing Aunt Carrie's car...but I've already made arrangements to borrow it this morning. In fact, I'm planning to leave in just a few minutes."

"Really? That's odd. After breakfast, your aunt suggested we take a quiet drive before the day grew too hot. We were going to leave as soon as I'd finished here." He sighed. "Perhaps your plans slipped her mind—"

"Nothing slipped my mind," Aunt Carrie said, appearing at the door, supported by her walker. "Isn't it a lovely morning for a drive?"

Rachel eyed her with misgiving, fighting the feeling that she was about to be outmaneuvered again. "What's the story, Aunt Carrie?"

"Story? I don't know what you mean. I already told you, dear, this poor old car of mine isn't big enough for everything you'll need to bring back with you today. It's going to take a truck."

"Aunt Carrie, we've been through all that. The car will have to do. I may need a truck, but I don't have one."

"Oh, but you do," her aunt said, and looked past Rachel's shoulder. "Doesn't she, Mr. Pulneshti?"

Turning, Rachel saw him standing at the corner of the garage, watching her, his arms folded. She gave him a look of her own, one that asked, *How long have you been standing there listening to all this?*

A glimmer of a smile passed over his face and vanished.

Rachel hesitated. The thought of spending the day with Sandor was tantalizing, especially after the invisibility he'd practiced for the past week. She had watched and worried for the first few days, concerned about his injuries and about his safety... but his actions had made it clear that he wanted no part of her concern.

Why, then, was he offering the use of his truck? Had Aunt Carrie pressured him into it? Not wanting to be a burden or an object of pity, Rachel held out her hand and said with false cheer, "I guess a truck would come in handy, after all. How nice of you to lend me yours. Luckily I know how to drive a stick shift. Toss me the keys and I'll be on my way."

"No need," Sandor said laconically. "The driver's included."

"A package deal? Thanks, but no thanks," she said firmly, determined to give him an out. "It's a generous offer, but I couldn't possibly take up your Saturday."

"Why not? It sounds like you could use a hand."

"And you think you're in any shape to give me one?"

Because she was beginning to learn how to read his face, she had the satisfaction of watching her question hit home, but it only took him a moment to recover his composure. "After a week of construction work," he said calmly, "I guess I can load a couple of moving boxes without fainting in your arms."

"Many hands make light work," Aunt Carrie added from her vantage point on the porch.

George Hudson smiled at her. "The more the merrier."

"They can keep this up all morning," Sandor warned her. "Wouldn't it be simpler just to hit the road and get it over with?"

He was right, of course. Aunt Carrie could be tenacious, and George Hudson, for whatever reason, seemed prepared to back her to the hilt. The morning was slipping away.

And, questions of injured pride aside, she wanted to go with him.

"Oh, all right," she said ungraciously. "There's a stack of broken-down boxes in the garage—"

"They're already in the truck, along with the tape."

"Well, then, hold on while I get my purse—"

"It's right here," Aunt Carrie said.

"I'm going, I'm going," Rachel muttered, climbing the porch steps to claim her purse.

Aunt Carrie kissed her cheek. "Don't work too hard, now. It's supposed to break a hundred by this afternoon.

We'll have supper waiting for the two of you when you get back."

"Don't worry if we're late," Rachel cautioned her, returning her kiss. "I don't know how long this is going to take."

"I know, dear. I'm just glad you'll have someone to help you."

"So I gathered," Rachel said. "The next time, wouldn't it be easier just to—"

Sliding in behind the wheel, Sandor started the engine.

"All right, all right, I can take a hint!" Rachel ran to the noisy truck. Taking the hand Sandor extended, she clambered up onto the high seat. "Let's roll," she said, and waved goodbye to Aunt Carrie and George Hudson as the truck backed down the driveway.

"Thanks for letting me come along," Sandor said as they drove along Spruce Street.

Rachel looked across at him suspiciously, expecting to see a mocking glint in his eye, but he seemed to mean what he was saying. "Well," she answered cautiously, "we'll see if you still feel like thanking me after you've spent the day packing and loading. Frankly I'd have thought you'd be grateful for a day off instead of volunteering for *more* hard work."

"I'm where I want to be," Sandor said with quiet conviction. "And I'm doing what I want to be doing. Nobody's twisting my arm. Besides, I've been wanting a chance to talk to you."

Rachel waited expectantly, but Sandor lapsed into silence. Content for the moment, she turned her head to gaze out of the window. The last time she'd ridden in Sandor's truck, it had been the night before Aunt Carrie's surgery, and she had traveled through the darkness to Dalewood with a heavy heart. By contrast, this morning felt like a celebration. The colors of the passing houses and lawns seemed unusually vivid, as if the June sunshine were a spotlight.

Later the day would be meltingly hot, but the morning air still held a hint of coolness as it washed over the bared skin of her arms and legs. She shifted, savoring the sensation...then looked down as something pricked the backs of her thighs.

Beneath her, the woven fabric of the seat was covered in several places by long strips of electrical tape.

"I'm sorry I haven't been around much all week," Sandor began, but his words barely registered as Rachel twisted to look at the seat back and found more tape pressed there, making an ugly black pattern against the material.

"To tell you the truth, part of the reason I volunteered my truck for today is that I've been wanting a chance to talk to you without anybody else around. To be open with you. To... explain what's been going on."

There had been no tape on the upholstery when Sandor had driven her home from Milford, she was sure of that. She could remember being surprised by the truck's tidy cab, in contrast to the noisy engine and dusty exterior. The seats had been unmarred, she was sure of it.

"I've been in Milford just about every night," he was saying, "looking for... for someone I need to find. Someone I know from a long, long time ago—"

Strangely disquieted, Rachel reached down and peeled back the edge of the nearest piece of tape.

"Don't!" Sandor protested, but it was too late; she could see a long rip in the fabric, arrow straight and deep enough for the padding to show through.

"How did this happen?" she asked, seeing that he, too, sat on a crosshatching of tape. He was looking straight ahead, but she could sense that his attention was fixed on her, not his driving. When he didn't answer her, she said, "There's too much damage here to be accidental. Who did this?"

"It happened in Milford."

"The night you got hurt," she said in a challenging tone.

FIRST-CLASS ROMANCE

Mail This Heart TODAY!

And We'll Deliver:

**4 FREE BOOKS
A FREE GOLD-PLATED CHAIN
PLUS
A SURPRISE MYSTERY BONUS
TO YOUR DOOR!**

HARLEQUIN DELIVERS
FIRST-CLASS ROMANCE—
DIRECT TO YOUR DOOR

Mail the Heart sticker on the postpaid order card today and you'll receive:

- **4 new Harlequin Superromance® novels — FREE**
- **a lovely 20k gold electroplated chain — FREE**
- **and a surprise mystery bonus — FREE**

But that's not all. You'll also get:

Money-Saving Home Delivery

When you subscribe to Harlequin Reader Service®, the excitement, romance and faraway adventures of these novels can be yours for previewing in the convenience of your own home at less than cover prices. Every month we'll deliver 4 new books right to your door. If you decide to keep them, they'll be yours for only $2.74* each. That's 21¢ less than the cover price. And there is *no* extra charge for shipping and handling! There is no obligation to buy — you can cancel Reader Service privileges at any time by writing "cancel" on your statement or returning a shipment of books to us at our expense.

Free Monthly Newsletter

It's the indispensable insider's look at our most popular writers and their upcoming novels. Now you can have a behind-the-scenes look at the fascinating world of Harlequin! It's an added bonus you'll look forward to every month!

Special Extras — FREE

Because our home subscribers are our most valued readers, we'll also be sending you additional free gifts from time to time in your monthly book shipments, as a token of our appreciation.

OPEN YOUR MAILBOX TO A WORLD OF LOVE AND ROMANCE EACH MONTH. JUST COMPLETE, DETACH AND MAIL YOUR FREE OFFER CARD TODAY!

You'll love your elegant 20k gold electroplated chain! The necklace is finely crafted with 160 double-soldered links and is electroplate finished in genuine 20k gold. And it's yours free as added thanks for giving our Reader Service a try!

 Harlequin Superromance®

FREE OFFER CARD

4 FREE BOOKS

FREE GOLD ELECTROPLATED CHAIN

FREE MYSTERY BONUS

PLACE HEART STICKER HERE

MONEY-SAVING HOME DELIVERY

FREE FACT-FILLED NEWSLETTER

MORE SURPRISES THROUGHOUT THE YEAR — FREE

☑ YES! Please send me four Harlequin Superromance® novels, *free,* along with my free gold electroplated chain and my free mystery gift, as explained on the opposite page.

134 CIH KA9U
(U-H-SR-03/90)

NAME _____

ADDRESS _____ APT. _____

CITY _____ STATE _____

ZIP CODE _____

Offer limited to one per household and not valid to current Harlequin Superromance subscribers. All orders subject to approval. Terms and prices subject to change without notice.

© 1989 HARLEQUIN ENTERPRISES LTD.

HARLEQUIN "NO RISK" GUARANTEE
- There is no obligation to buy—the free books and gifts remain yours to keep.
- You pay the special members-only discount price and receive books before they're available in stores.
- You may end your subscription anytime by just writing "cancel" on your statement or returning a shipment of books to us at our expense.

PRINTED IN U.S.A.

Remember! To receive your free books, gold electroplated chain and mystery gift, return the postpaid card below. But don't delay!

DETACH AND MAIL CARD TODAY.

If offer card has been removed, write to: Harlequin Reader Service, 901 Fuhrmann Blvd., P.O. Box 1867, Buffalo, NY 14269-1867

MAIL THE POSTPAID CARD TODAY!

BUSINESS REPLY CARD

First Class   Permit No. 717   Buffalo, NY

Postage will be paid by addressee

Harlequin Reader Service®
901 Fuhrmann Blvd.
P.O. Box 1867
Buffalo, NY 14240-9952

NO POSTAGE
NECESSARY
IF MAILED
IN THE
UNITED STATES

He nodded grudgingly.

"And the people who did this are the ones you've been looking for all week?"

He hesitated, then nodded. "In a way."

"Then why won't you go to the police? Sandor, this was done with a knife," she said, her mind filling with violent images. "A knife that could have been used on you!"

"Could have been, but wasn't," he said dismissively. "I'm sorry, but it's a private matter, and it'll have to stay that way."

Resenting the rebuke, Rachel bit her tongue to keep from replying. Hadn't she patched him back together a week ago? Hadn't she held her silence since then? She had respected his right to decide what to do—or not to do—about the attack. However reluctantly, she had kept her distance and allowed him his precious privacy. *He* was the one who had volunteered to drive her to Cleveland. *He* was the one who claimed he'd been looking for a chance to explain things to her. And now he had the nerve to shut her out when she voiced a fraction of her very real concern. So much for his fine talk about being "open." He didn't want to take her into his confidence. He only wanted the opportunity to deliver a prepared speech about his activities.

They drove in silence until they had left Dalewood behind. As the truck picked up speed on the open road beyond the township limits, the breeze coming through the open windows built into a warm wind. Wishing she'd brought a scarf, Rachel gathered her billowing hair at her nape and began plaiting it into a braid.

"Sorry," Sandor said over the rumble of the engine and the rush of the wind. "No air conditioning."

"That's okay," she said, relieved that the silence had been broken, however prosaically. As hard as she tried to be angry with Sandor, she found worry overwhelming her temper. He was in some sort of trouble; that much was clear. And she knew how alone he was in the world. Surely it was understandable that he was out of the habit of being able to share his problems with anyone. She would have to let him take his time and find his own way.

"What I said before…" he began hesitantly, and cleared his throat uncomfortably. "About it being a private matter?"

"Mmm?"

"What I meant was 'private from the police.' Not private from you."

Rachel's heart warmed. He did trust her… or at least he was trying to. "It's a long way to Cleveland," she said. "And there's nothing I'd rather do than sit here and listen if there are things you want to tell me. I'm sorry if I came on strong about going to the police, but I don't want to get up one morning and find out that something horrible has happened to you."

He shook his head. "Don't worry, it's been a very uneventful week. A lot of effort expended for no visible return. How about you? What sort of week have you had?"

He was sidestepping again, but Rachel didn't blame him. There was, as she'd said, plenty of time before they got to Cleveland. If he wanted her to break the conversational ice, she was willing. The act of braiding her hair had stirred a memory, and she decided to begin by sharing it with him. "Actually it's been a pretty odd one. I saw the strangest thing the other day when I was at the drugstore…."

She'd been afraid that the anecdote would bore him, but by the time she was halfway through her tale of Archibald Gaines and the shortchange artist, Sandor had moved his foot from the accelerator to the brake, and was steering his truck onto the dusty shoulder of the road.

"What is it?" Rachel asked. "What's wrong?"

"Nothing." He turned off the engine. "Tell me what happened."

"This is really important to you," she said in soft surprise.

"It could be," he admitted.

"All right, then." Hesitantly she picked up the thread of her story again. When she'd reached the end, she said, "So Tom went outside and looked, but there was no sign of her...and that's all. Why? Did she cheat you, too? You look like you've seen a ghost."

He ignored her questions. "You were there while all this was going on?" he asked intently.

"Yes, I already told you I was."

Sandor rubbed the back of his neck. "I'm sorry. I didn't mean to be insulting, but the woman you saw might be somebody I know."

"One of the people you've been trying to find?"

"I...ran into her brother around here recently, so it isn't as farfetched as it sounds. It could have been her. It really could. You say she was tiny with long, dark hair. Did you notice anything else about her? Her clothes? Her jewelry? Anything?"

Rachel thought back. "I don't think she was wearing any jewelry, and her clothes were ordinary, just a housedress and a pair of sandals."

"You don't remember anything else about her?"

"Like what? Is there something special I should have seen?"

Sandor shook his head stubbornly, the motion short and jerky. "You tell me. I don't want to put any ideas in your head."

The confusion and frustration that his withdrawal had put her through in the past week seemed unimportant in the face of his present intensity. Closing her eyes cooperatively, Rachel tried to recreate the woman's appearance in her mind: her hair, her clothes, her skin....

The focus of the memory sharpened. "She had a birthmark," Rachel said, opening her eyes as she remembered.

"What kind of birthmark?" Sandor asked, and Rachel knew by the timbre of his voice that it was the answer he'd hoped for.

"On her face, under her cheekbone, almost like somebody had taken a brown marking pen and drawn a smudgy line there."

"Which side?" he asked, moving closer still, but he was smiling now, his face alight with an excitement that Rachel found contagious.

"The left," she said.

Sandor's hands came up to frame her face. "The left," he confirmed exultantly, and kissed her.

It was a kiss of gratitude...or at least that was how it seemed to Rachel when it began. But his lips courted hers as the moments slipped past, betraying his hunger so disarmingly that she was powerless to resist him. As she responded, his fingers sank into her hair, loosening the braid she had just created; he seemed to revel in the abundant curls freed by his touch.

Rachel felt the last of her caution fall away. How could she cling to doubts when all she really wanted was to cling to Sandor?

A dizzying minute later, he brought the kiss to a gentle close. "Thank you," he said, his voice barely audible over the roar of the traffic flashing past his open window. "Thank you."

"For what?"

"For noticing. For telling me. For being you, and being here."

"If that's a sample of how you thank people," she said shakily, "it's a wonder they aren't lining up for the privilege of helping you."

"Really?" Pulling back slightly, Sandor grinned. "Maybe I should have tried kissing Gunari."

"Who?" Rachel asked, feeling an unexpected spurt of jealousy at the thought of Sandor kissing anyone but her.

"Gunari Demetro. The young man whose handiwork you helped me recover from last week."

"The one who beat you?"

"One of half a dozen, as ego compels me to point out. But the main one, yes."

"And he was the one who sliced up the seats? Why would he do all this to you? Who are these people?"

The amused undertone was gone from Sandor's voice when he answered. "I guess you'd have to say they're family, in a sense."

"Family?" It wasn't a word she'd expected to hear from him, least of all in regard to the injuries he'd suffered. She shook her head, perplexed. "Well, they say any family is better than none at all...."

"I don't know," he said. "I'm not exactly an authority on the matter. When I said they were only family 'in a sense,' I meant it. And when I wrote 'no next of kin' on my references, I meant that, too. As to why Gunari did what he did—" a shadow crossed his face "—let's just say it's a very long, very old, very sad story. If you don't mind, I'd rather not tell it to you quite yet. But if I can find the girl you saw in the drugstore—"

"The woman," Rachel corrected.

"What?"

"She was a woman in her late twenties or early thirties, not a 'girl.'" Seeing his look, she explained, "I just want you to be sure this is the right person before you get your hopes too high."

"Oh, it's the right person, all right. But it's been almost twenty years since I've seen her, and I guess I've been remembering her the way she looked back then, not the way she would be now. A woman. So," he said with a determined smile, "if I can find the *woman* you saw in the drugstore, I think I can give that old story a whole new ending— one that I hope you'll like as much as I will." Moving back behind the wheel, he reached for the ignition key. "Right now, though, I'd better get us back on the road, or tomorrow will catch up with us and we'll have to fend off your new tenant while we finish packing."

As they merged onto the highway again, Rachel kept her gaze averted, certain that her jumbled emotions were written plainly on her face for Sandor to see. Away from him, it always seemed so simple: he was her aunt's boarder, an outsider whose past life and present intentions were a mystery to her. *Stay away,* she had told herself time and again. *For once in your life, use your head and keep your distance.* And she meant to, each time.

But then he would come near her, and all her neat reasoning would begin to unravel under the inexorable pressure of his presence. He had a way of finding the chinks in her armor, a knack that seemed to grow more sure each time they were together. He could undo her with a look, a word, a touch—and now a kiss. What next? She was afraid to find out . . . and more afraid that she wouldn't.

What was he thinking right now as he steered his rattletrap truck along the highway? Rachel stole a glance at him, wishing she knew. Why had he kissed her? Why had he stopped kissing her? Was the memory of that embrace dominating his thoughts the way it was dominating hers?

"Do you know any of the farmers around here?" Sandor asked.

Well, Rachel thought glumly, *I guess that answers that question.* "Most of them," she said, resolutely turning her attention to the fields beyond her open window. The families who owned land along the highway were considered a part of Dalewood; the children attended the Dalewood schools, and their parents came into town to shop, to attend church, and to use the library. "That's Ben Stewart's place," she said, pointing as a massive barn came into view. "And the one across the road used to belong to the Jessups, but they sold it a couple of years ago, and moved to Cleveland. Why?"

"I have no idea," Sandor said, "although I've heard that farming's a pretty hard life. Maybe Mr. Jessup just got tired."

Rachel punched him lightly on the shoulder, picking a spot that she knew was unbruised. "No, I mean why the sudden interest in the denizens of Dalewood?"

Reaching up, Sandor adjusted his visor, and Rachel knew he was taking a moment to choose his words, deciding how best to answer her. Finally he said, "I've been assuming that the group of gypsies I'm looking for is based near Milford. After all, that's what Agnes Denihee said, and that's where I found Gunari Demetro. But you saw his sister Laza—the woman I'm looking for—in Dalewood. If the main camp is somewhere down here, it would explain why I've been coming up so empty in Milford. I only saw a few other men there with Gunari that night. And no Rom worth his salt minds a little traveling. They wouldn't think anything of driving up to Milford every day, or anywhere else in the area, for that matter. The more I think about it, basing themselves in Dalewood would have its advantages if they're doing much scam work like that driveway. It's never wise to foul your own nest. Do you suppose any of the farmers you know would be willing to talk to me? They might know if one of their neighbors has given permission for anybody to camp out on their land."

"I may be able to do you one better," she said. "The day I saw that woman shortchange Mr. Gaines, I heard one of the men at the coffee counter talking about a man who's hired a group of gypsies to work in his fields. Would that help?"

Sandor shot her a wild glance. "Help? Are you serious? Of *course* it would help. Who was it? Where does he live? Good grief, woman, you're a walking miracle. What *else* do you know? Talk about irony! I've been running around for a week now like a chicken with its head cut off, doing my level best to avoid you, knocking myself out, getting absolutely nowhere, and all that time—''

"Why?" Rachel interrupted, gathering her courage. "Why were you avoiding me?"

He looked away, the animation draining from his face.

"Why?" she asked again, watching his profile.

"Because."

"That's not an answer."

Making a face, he took one hand off the steering wheel and gestured at the seat between them. "Because of knives, then," he said reluctantly, frustration roughening his voice. "And oiled driveways. And 'Change for a twenty, please, mister.' Because my life's a mess, damn it, and you deserve better."

She captured his gesturing hand with her own. "Don't," she said, disturbed by the dark and dangerous world that his words described. "Don't talk about yourself like that."

"Rachel, I—"

"Hush." Twining her fingers in his, she let her free hand stroke the tense muscles of his forearm. "Just for today, give yourself a break, all right?" She moved her hand higher, rubbing her thumb across the smooth rise of his biceps. "Listen. The man I heard them talking about is Charlie Grabemeyer. His farm is halfway between here and Milford. We can stop there on our way and ask him about—"

"No," Sandor said, his muscles tightening beneath her touch. "Not with you along. Not after what happened with Gunari. Just show me the place. I'll come back tomorrow and talk to him on my own."

"But I've known Mr. Grabemeyer since I was a kid," Rachel argued. "He'll be more apt to talk with you if I'm—"

"No. I'm not taking you there."

"All right," she conceded, warmed by his concern but chilled by the frightening implications his decision conveyed. "I'll back off. But only on one condition. I want you to tell me when you're going to Mr. Grabemeyer's farm."

"Why?"

"So somebody will know where you are in case you run into Gunari Demetro again. Or his knife."

RACHEL AND SANDOR worked like demons throughout the day, only stopping for a hasty bite of lunch. By six o'clock all of her belongings except the contents of her bathroom and the linens from her bed were packed into labeled boxes and taped shut, ready for transport.

Through the long hours of packing, Sandor allowed himself the pleasure of watching Rachel as she moved with smooth grace, wrapping glassware in protective layers of newspaper or folding clothes into cartons. He felt over-sized and clumsy beside her, working up a sweat in spite of the efforts of the air conditioner. It pleased him to do the heavy work, using his brawn to spare her the worst of the effort. On her own, she would have faced a back-breaking day; together, they made steady progress, moving from bookshelf to closet to bureau, and back to bookshelf again.

She had a million books, or so it appeared, and she was taking them all back to Dalewood. Some, she explained, were personal favorites she was reluctant to leave behind. The rest could be used to supplement the depleted shelves at the library, at least temporarily.

Sandor tried to concentrate solely on the job at hand, suspending his speculations about Laza for the space of an afternoon. Now that he knew she was so near, he was filled with renewed confidence. He would find her, she would free him, and that would put an end to the matter, once and for all. There would be no reason to burden Rachel with the details of his troubled past. Soon those dark years would be nothing more than a dream, and would cast no shadow on the future he hoped to share with Rachel.

But that new optimism made him increasingly vulnerable to the siren call of Rachel's presence as they worked side by side. Time and again their eyes met and mirrored the attraction between them. More than once, Sandor found himself on the verge of covering her hand with his or brushing against her for the pure pleasure of feeling her skin against his, and he knew she felt the same way. Yet he held back, balked by the invisible line that circumstance and society had drawn between them.

He wanted Rachel, wanted her in every way, but he would be taking unfair advantage of her if he turned his desires into action now, before he severed his connection with Laza. There was no need for a formal divorce, since they had never been legally married in *gaje* terms; only in the eyes of the Rom had they been truly married. Nevertheless, honor compelled him to make sure that Laza had gone on with her life after his banishment. He hadn't even been given the chance to speak with her after the *kris*'s pronouncement. Only when he was sure she was well and happy would he be able to freely commit to another. If only context and consequence could be ignored! he thought. Then he would take Rachel in his arms and savor her strength and fragility; he would kiss her properly, using his mouth to create more than the empty words they had exchanged over the past few hours. And if she was willing, if she longed for it as he did, it would be his almost unbearable pleasure to take her into the empty bedroom and remove her clothes, and his, and learn her body as he wanted her to learn his, and then—

"What now?" Rachel asked. "Shall I pack the bathroom while you start loading the truck?"

His hands were shaking. Sandor thrust them deep into his pockets. "No. I think we should take a break first and find some supper." He had to put some distance between them before he did something reckless. He groped for an explanation she would accept. "Once we've loaded the truck, we won't want to leave it parked someplace while we eat."

"Well, if we both work on the bathroom, it won't take long to get it packed, and then we can go and eat before we start loading."

"I'd rather go now," he said flatly.

"All right," Rachel said, giving in with good grace. "I know a great place just a short walk from here if you like Chinese food."

"Fine." Anything was fine if it got him out in the open air where there were other people to diffuse the atmosphere of intimacy.

"Just hold on while I grab a shower, okay?"

A fresh surge of desire pulsed through him as he envisioned Rachel standing naked beneath a spray of water. To wait outside the bathroom door, knowing that she was in there just a few feet away, was a refined form of torture he didn't think he could endure. "Rachel, I don't—"

"You don't have to run away from me," she told him, suddenly very serious, and he saw that she had read his reaction with alarming acuity. "If there's something you want—or don't want—all you have to do is say so."

She was too trusting. Too honest. He sealed the box in front of him and tossed the roll of tape aside. "Label this," he ordered roughly, hardening his heart against the wounded look in her eyes. "Then mark the boxes you want kept on top when I load. We'll both shower before we go eat, and I'm taking first shot at it."

In the bathroom, he stripped out of his clothes with angry efficiency. Then, sliding back the clear glass door of the shower stall, he stepped in and turned the cold water on, full force.

The sudden shocking chill made it hard to breathe, and his outraged nerve endings shrieked in protest, sending insistent messages that his brain interpreted as pain. *You'll survive,* he told himself unsympathetically. *It's your own damned fault.*

He plunged his face into the spray, letting the water beat on his closed eyelids, wishing he could use the force of it to wash the aching desire for Rachel out of his mind. One way or another, he could beat his body into submission, but what weapon could he use against his own emotions? It wasn't just a question of wanting a woman in his bed; he wanted Rachel, wanted her beside him as a talisman against the terrible loneliness, wanted to make her a part of his life in a way no woman had ever been. But "wanting" didn't mean he could make it so. Between the present moment and any possible future with Rachel hung the forbidding shadow of his past. The shadow of Laza.

Depression settled over him, and was more effective than cold water. Shivering, he backed out of the worst of the flow and opened his eyes, reaching for the soap. *As long as you're in here, you may as well—*

He froze. Beyond the water-spattered barrier of glass, Rachel stood barefoot on the bathroom rug, her eyes trained on him solemnly as she unfastened the final button on her blouse.

Say something, the strident voice in his head insisted. *Stop her.*

The blouse fluttered to the floor.

Turn off the water and tell her to get out of here—or get out of here yourself if she won't listen to reason.

Shorts followed blouse. Mesmerized by the sight of her, Sandor remembered how she had looked when they first met. That night, she had been dressed only in a provocative silk teddy. She had been beautiful then. She was beautiful now.

Have you gone crazy? His inner voice was growing shrill. *Quit staring at her.*

A rosy blush had risen to color Rachel's face, but she didn't hesitate as she unfastened the clasp of her lacy bra and slid the straps down her arms. Revealed, her breasts were small and full, the nipples gathered tightly, deep pink against her pale skin.

You can't do this, Pulneshti. Damn it, you can't!

But his body had opinions of its own, despite the icy water.

Slipping her thumbs into the waistband of her panties, Rachel pushed the wisp of material down and stepped free.

Sandor's heart beat painfully at the sight of her naked perfection, offered up for his eyes alone.

Rachel opened the glass doors and sampled the spray with her fingertips. "A cold shower? That seems counterproductive." She adjusted the taps and smiled impishly. "Let's warm things up in here instead," she suggested, and stepped inside to join him.

CHAPTER ELEVEN

SANDOR RETREATED until his back was pressed against the cool tile wall. "We shouldn't be doing this."

"I got tired of waiting," Rachel said, and reached for the soap.

"I'm not talking about the shower, damn it."

"Neither am I."

Her response jarred him, but Sandor tried again. "I think you'd better leave."

"Do you?" She placed her lathered palms against his chest. "Then say it like you mean it." Her hands drifted lower, moving gently over the yellowing bruises on his ribs. "You're sending out mixed signals. Again. It's a bad habit you have."

"Rachel . . ." he said raggedly.

"Mmm?" Her hands were at his waist now. He couldn't talk coherently, couldn't think things through, couldn't find the strength of purpose to argue against the blinding delight her touch was bringing him. How could he expect her to listen to his hypocritical objections when his body was giving the lie to everything he said?

He groaned.

"Where does it hurt?" Rachel asked solicitously, reaching lower still. "Here?"

After the long months of abstinence, he found the caress of her soap-slick fingers almost more than he could bear. Spasms of sensation shot through him, pleasure verging on pain. He captured her hands with his own, suspending the delicious torment before he lost control entirely. "Why?" he demanded, searching her face. "Why are you doing this? Why now? Why here? Why me?"

"Because I want you," she said breathlessly, "and I don't know if we'll ever have a chance like this again."

I want you. Not I love you.

Her words tore at him . . . and yet they brought relief, as well. *I love you* would have forced him to a confession of why he wasn't free to make her his own. But if it was only a question of her wanting him—and she must to have come to him here—then perhaps he could allow himself this moment after all, adoring her with his body without doing her any lasting harm. He could give Rachel everything she wanted . . . as long as he held himself back from trying to give her more than she was asking for. When she was ready to leave, he would have to open his arms and release her without hesitation until he could come to her freely. Besides, she was more right than she knew: if Laza continued to evade him, or refused to release him, then this might be the only chance he and Rachel would ever have to be together.

He remembered how the High Priestess had smiled up at him enigmatically from the Tarot deck. *The one woman in all the world . . .*

"Rachel," he whispered, and bent to cover her mouth with his own.

The steamy water beat a counterpoint to the silken invitation of her hands as she embraced him. Dizzy with need, Sandor knelt and pressed his face against her skin, greedy for the taste and the touch of her. He kissed the shimmering beads of water on her breasts, closing his lips around each stiff nipple in turn, using his tongue to tease and please her. Each moan that escaped her sent a thrill of excitement through him; each gasping breath heightened his own arousal. He ran his fingertips down the slender column of her spine, following the curves of her flesh, sliding his palms to either side to encompass the gentle flare of her hips.

"Come up here and kiss me," Rachel entreated him, stroking his damp hair back from his forehead.

"In a minute," he promised unsteadily, kissing his way slowly down her rib cage. "I'm busy."

She was utterly desirable, endlessly appealing. With his cheek pressed to the flat plane of her abdomen, he could feel the rapid rise and fall of her breathing. Reaching her navel, he explored it with the tip of his tongue. Then, pressing Rachel gently into the corner where the tiled walls of the shower joined, he nuzzled the triangle that flourished between her parted thighs, and felt her pulse skitter and leap as he deepened his tender assault.

Once he had made his way through the protective barrier of chestnut curls, he found her taut and liquid, already eagerly aflame. Tracing his way with unerring care to the heart of her living maze, he was rewarded by a whimpering cry and the sudden restless thrust of her hips toward him.

He slid his hands up to encompass her breasts, rubbing the swollen nipples roughly with his thumbs as he continued to stroke her with his tongue. Rachel writhed, her fingers cramping rhythmically in his hair as he relentlessly stoked the fire he had created within her.

"No, please," she panted, "Sandor, I—"

He barely heard her, lost in the wonder of her responsiveness as he sent her flying toward the glory, so close, so close....

Instead Rachel crumpled beside him, clinging to his shoulders as the water cascaded over them, half sobbing as she insisted, "Not here, not like this, I want you with me, in me, please, please...."

Astonished, he covered her face with kisses, tasting her frustration and desire. "I wish we could. It would be wonderful, but I don't have any way to keep you safe. Let me—"

"No, it's all right, I have something you could use...if you don't mind."

"Mind? Do I look that crazy?" he asked, and helped her to stand, his legs almost as unsteady as hers. She wrenched the taps closed and he slid the shower door aside, waiting while she opened the medicine cabinet and took out a small package, then following willingly as she opened the door to the hallway and led him to the bedroom at a stumbling run.

Still dripping, she collapsed onto the mattress and pulled him after her, wrapping her arms around him with fierce possessiveness, rolling over and over until she was on top of him, kissing him. She raised herself on hands and knees so that she was straddling him, her nipples just grazing the curling hair on his chest, her lower body brushing over his with maddening persistence.

He reached for her breasts, wanting to feel their dainty weight against his palms again, but she sat up and opened the little box, saying, "In another minute, you'll have me too crazy to stop." She slipped the protective sheath into place, the touch of her hands intoxicating as they moved over him.

He groaned in pleasure.

"Sandor, please," she said, pressing against him with subtle pressure, "I want you now. Not an hour from now, or ten minutes from now, but now. Right this instant." She was beautiful, her cheeks flushed with arousal, her breasts lifting in quick rhythm with each erratic breath. Rising on her knees, she positioned herself over him, poised for the joining.

His entire body seemed to be throbbing. "Consider me—" his breath caught in his throat as she shifted slightly "—your willing slave," he finished, watching her hungrily as she swayed above him, thinking that she was the most exquisite sight he had ever seen.

It was his last coherent thought. His world broke down into a series of crystalline beads, each bead encapsulating a precious instant. There was the moment when Rachel first lowered herself onto him fully, welcoming him into the tight enchantment of her body; the moment when he finally saw her face transformed in joyous release; and the moment when his own deliverance welled up within him, too overpowering to be contained any longer, searing along his frenzied nerves like a fire storm.

Then the moments stopped, and there was only a sweet gray oblivion that cradled him, holding him at peace with himself and the world.

When time began again, the arms that held him were Rachel's. She was asleep, her face inches from his own. Unable to help himself, he edged closer and kissed her.

It woke her, and she blinked owlishly in the darkening room. "Hi," she said shyly, hiding her face against his neck.

Sandor slipped a hand beneath her damp hair and massaged her nape. "Hi, yourself."

She shivered at his touch.

"Are you cold?" he asked, aware of the air conditioner's hum and the quilted bedspread trapped beneath their naked bodies.

She shook her head in denial, her curls tickling against his jaw. "Could you . . . could you just hold me for a minute?"

He smiled in wry amusement. "I could try."

Rachel raised her head in surprise. "Try to hold me?"

"Try *just* to hold you," he clarified, and saw her answering smile grow as she took in his meaning.

His body's impetuous response to hers seemed to reassure Rachel. Kissing his chin, she said, "So you aren't going to throw me out of bed for being bossy?"

"Hardly. In the first place, I wouldn't have the strength. In the second place, I seem to remember being pretty pleased with where your 'bossy' behavior got us. And besides, in case you've forgotten, this is your bed. If anybody gets thrown out of it, it should be me."

"Says who?" Rachel snuggled closer invitingly. "I'm just sorry to hear you're feeling so weak. Still, they say that bed rest can do wonders for a man in your condition."

"Do they?" Sandor asked, sorely tempted. Sitting up, hating his self-appointed role as the voice of reason, he asked, "And what do they say about packing a pickup truck in the dark? Or finding something to eat? Or keeping your aunt from worrying?"

Closing the gap he had created between them, she stroked him seductively. "They say streetlights, drive-throughs and a quick phone call. Any more questions, Mr. Pulneshti?"

I tried, he thought despairingly as his pulse rate soared. *I did try.* "Dozens," he said, reaching down to knead one of her breasts. "Hundreds, in fact." He tweaked the soft satin of her nipple as it rose to greet his touch. "I'm sure I'll remember them in just a minute or two. You don't mind waiting, do you?" he asked, and bent his head to take the tip of her breast into his mouth.

"Not at all," he heard her say as he used gentle suction to draw her in more deeply. "I'm sure we can find some way to occupy ourselves in the meantime, if we just—" as he caught her nipple between his teeth with gentle force, her breath snagged sharply, then escaped in a blissful sigh "—just put our minds to it. Take your time, Mr. Pulneshti. Take all the time you need."

ON MONDAY, Sandor drove into town on his lunch break, anxious to see the Dalewood Drugstore for himself.

It looked disconcertingly ordinary, not at all the sort of setting where a miracle might occur... and yet it seemed to him that Laza's appearance there bordered on the miraculous. How else could he explain the coincidence of time and place that had brought Rachel and Laza within touching distance of one another? It was unbelievable good fortune—and fortune twice over that Rachel had been present to hear Mr. Grabemeyer's name, as well. It was as if the Fates had finally tired of their relentless persecution of Sandor Pulneshti and decided to allow him one slim chance to reclaim his future.

Sandor smiled. All in all, his view of the Fates had mellowed considerably since he had wakened in Cleveland to find Rachel asleep in his arms. Now *there* was a miracle: a miracle of beauty and pleasure, the golden treasure at the end of the quest. All he had to do now was earn the right to stake his claim to the paradise they had found together, by finding Laza. Once that was accomplished—

"Can I help you?"

The question made him jump. "No," he said to the clerk behind the counter, "I just came in for a few things. I can find them myself."

Why had he said that? There was nothing he needed. He had only wanted to see the place where Laza had been...but some guilty holdover from his childhood made him feel that he had to legitimize his presence in this store with a purchase. After all the years, memory still had the power to compel him. He was the juggler, poised uneasily between two worlds, no longer viewing all *gaje* as sheep deserving to be shorn, but vulnerable still to the shadowed memories of his past attitudes and actions. Maybe a part of him was still atoning for old transgressions, or maybe it was a simple case of overcompensation. Whatever the motivation, he was on the hook. Resigned, he scanned the shelves and in the end settled for a pair of nail clippers and a new comb to replace the ones Gunari had taken from him.

At the back counter beside the cash register stood a discreet display. Remembering how unprepared he had been in Cleveland, Sandor made his selection and added it to his other purchases.

"Will tha' be all?" the clerk behind the counter asked. Sandor decided his earlier reaction might have been justified; there was a chill in the white-haired man's tone, as if he disapproved of Sandor and would breathe easier once he was gone.

"That'll do it," Sandor said, laying down his money.

The man picked up the ten-dollar bill, then paused, looking past him to say, "G'morning, Mrs. Denihee. How are you?"

Sandor stiffened.

"Not very well, I'm afraid," the familiar voice said nasally. "Not very well at all. If there's anything I hate, it's a summer cold. Walter had one last week, and so I suppose I shouldn't have been surprised to wake up with one myself, but—"

She rambled on. Sandor felt as if he had somehow become transparent, a ghost hovering invisibly in the air between Agnes Denihee and the elderly man behind the counter. If the bridge party had been a reliable indication, the woman was capable of holding them captive for hours with the story of her head cold. "Excuse me," he said firmly to the clerk, unwilling to wait her out. "If you'll finish ringing these things up, I'll be on my way."

The man offered no apology for the delay, but after a further moment of hesitation he did begin to sort through the items, entering the prices on the cash register keys with painstaking care.

"Why, Mr. Pulneshti! I didn't realize that was *you* standing there," Mrs. Denihee said, her tone of surprise unconvincing. "We certainly missed your talents at the bridge table this week." She stepped closer, peering around him. "What brings you here? I hope you aren't feeling poorly, too...."

Damn, Sandor thought with a feeling close to panic. *Once that old busybody sees what I'm buying, she'll probably faint. Or scream. Or, worse yet, make a beeline out of here, eager to spread the word.*

The clerk swept Sandor's purchases clumsily into a bag, inadvertently knocking the pocket comb to the floor. He stooped laboriously to recover it, then thrust the bag into Sandor's hands.

Trying to sound calm and unconcerned, Sandor said, "I believe I have some change coming."

Glaring as if he'd been insulted, the man opened the register again and counted out the necessary coins and bills.

"Thank you," Sandor said, the words grating in his throat. Turning, he added, "I hope you feel better soon, Mrs. Denihee," then walked to the front of the store and out into the midday sunshine.

The image of the old man's scowl and Agnes Denihee's fish-eyed stare followed him. Sandor's shirt was damp with a cold sweat that owed nothing to the day's dry heat, and his fists were as tightly clenched as when he had faced Gunari across the camp fire. *Fight or flight,* his body had decreed . . . and he had chosen flight.

What other choice did you have? A brawl with a pair of senior citizens? Don't be so thin-skinned, Pulneshti. Nobody said anything.

But the uneasy feeling refused to go away.

IN DALEWOOD, Independence Day was a major holiday, second only to Christmas in its popularity. As a child, Rachel had thought it wonderful that the town threw a parade for her birthday. Each year, she had wound colored crepe paper through the wheels of her bike and proudly taken her place in the procession with the other children, reveling in the cheers and applause of the bystanders as she pedaled past.

She could still remember her disillusionment when she was finally old enough to realize that it was the country's birthday, not her own, that was being celebrated with such fanfare. The trauma of learning Santa Claus's true identity had been pure anticlimax by comparison.

"Of course, as an adult I'm prepared to take a more enlightened view," she explained to Integrity Jones as they stood on the corner of Main Street, waiting for the high-school band to march into view. "Dalewood just hasn't realized that its parade has served a dual purpose all these years.''

The older woman's laugh was musical. ''That's very big of you, Rachel. I like your attitude.''

The liking was mutual. In the course of their shared duties at the library, Rachel had developed a genuine fondness and admiration for the retired schoolteacher. It was hard to remember, sometimes, just what her objections to the boarders had been back in May. Integrity Jones and George Hudson now seemed like fixtures around the big house on Spruce Street, ever cheerful, ever eager to please.

Rachel wished she could say the same about Max. The girl's pregnancy was advancing into its eighth month, and her bad temper seemed to be growing as quickly as her waistline.

''Leave the poor child alone,'' Aunt Carrie had said with ready sympathy when Rachel commented on Max's increasing surliness. ''She can't help but worry. The other night, I found her holding Gertrude, rocking that old doll and crying. When I asked her what was wrong, she said, 'What if my baby gets sick? What if *I* get sick, and there's nobody to take care of it?' I swear, Rachel, it was enough to break a heart of stone to hear her go on.''

''I'm sure it was,'' Rachel had agreed mordantly, and asked, against her better judgment, ''How is she planning to pay her hospital bill?''

Aunt Carrie's silence had been all the answer she needed.

Still, as worrying as Max's situation was, it was balanced by the joy Rachel felt whenever her thoughts touched on Sandor. The memory of the hours she had spent in his arms in Cleveland still had the power to bring a flush of pleasure to her cheeks. She felt no guilt over what they had given each other; it was only her concern for Aunt Carrie's feelings and an uncomfortable awareness of small-town mores that had made her listen when Sandor urged her to maintain a discreet distance upon their return to Dalewood.

As a result, there had been no midnight trysts while the rest of the house slept, no knowing glances exchanged across the supper table, no kisses stolen in the hallway when no one was there to see. *Be patient,* he had counseled her, and Rachel was doing her best, but she was powerless to prevent the leap of her pulse when he entered the room, or the warmth that flooded through her at the sound of his voice.

She wasn't sure her resolve would have held through the week if he hadn't given her his promise to take her to the building site that evening to view the fireworks and discuss the talk he'd had with Charlie Grabemeyer. *It went fine,* was all he had said upon his return the previous Sunday night, and there had been no opportunity since then to press him privately for the details.

Integrity Jones applauded enthusiastically as the band played "The Stars and Stripes Forever." "It's like a time warp," she said to Rachel when the tubas had passed by and she could make herself heard again. "I've read about Fourth of July celebrations like this in history books, but I never expected to be a part of one."

"Oh, come on. We're not *that* quaint."

"No? Your Aunt Caroline tells me that there's a pie raffle in the town square when the parade is over, with the proceeds going to the library. Your idea, I suppose?"

"No, the pie raffle happens every year. All I did was convince Pastor Milligan that the library deserved the profits this year, instead of the Ladies' Aid Society."

"And then, as I understand it, there will be recitations by the students from this past year's Honor Roll, with the Declaration of Independence being read by the valedictorian." She smiled. "In fact, your aunt tells me that you were the valedictorian of your graduating class. Did you read the Declaration of Independence aloud?"

"Well, yes," Rachel admitted, embarrassed, "but—"

"And finally, to wrap up the afternoon, everyone competes in a spelling bee. I wouldn't mind taking part in that,"

Integrity Jones said, "if you think the townspeople would stand still for it."

"Of course they will. We'll both take part. As town librarians, it's practically our civic duty, don't you think?"

"Our civic duty," Integrity Jones concurred, with a twinkle in her eye. "By the way, did you bake a pie for the raffle?"

"Three," she admitted, and shrugged. "Maybe we are 'quaint.' Who knows? In Cleveland, all of this seemed pretty silly to me. But when I'm back here...well, I turn into a hopeless traditionalist, I guess."

"There's nothing wrong with tradition."

"But it sounds hokey!"

"Oh, only from the outside, don't you think?"

In the wake of the band, a group of boys and girls were riding by on decorated bicycles, waving energetically. At the sight of them, Rachel felt a hard knot of resistance deep within herself relax and begin to give way. "Only from the outside," she agreed, and raised her hand to wave back.

"YOU SHOULD HAVE SEEN the spelling bee," she greeted Sandor that evening as she took her place on the high seat of his pickup truck. "I held on until the tenth round," she told him, "but then I got tripped up on 'moxibustion.' Pastor Milligan missed 'decemvirate,' and that brought it down to just Archibald Gaines and Integrity Jones."

Twilight was setting in, and the worst of the heat had begun to dissipate. Riding along, Rachel felt relaxed and content as she thought back over the day. Only Sandor's absence had marred it. Now that he was with her, she felt complete.

"The two of them plowed through words I'd never even heard of! Finally Mr. Gaines had to spell 'psittacine.' He got the *ps* part right, but he only put in one *t*. If Integrity had spelled it wrong, too, they would have gone on to another word to break the tie, but she got it right. You should have heard Aunt Carrie cheering."

"Your aunt was there?" Sandor asked as he turned the corner at the end of Spruce Street.

"Yes, I drove her down. She and Mr. Hudson watched from the car, and everybody came by to say hello. I think she had a good time."

"Did Max go, too?"

"No," Rachel said, a little irked by the mention of the teenager's name. "She stayed at the house."

"Mmm. Too bad."

"I looked for you today," she said, trying not to sound reproachful. Now that they were alone together, she wasn't quite sure how to break the ice and regain the sense of intimacy they had shared in Cleveland. "I think you would have enjoyed yourself. It's too bad you couldn't make it."

"I was working."

"But it's a holiday."

"When you're your own boss, holidays don't mean much. With the rest of the crew off, it was a good chance for me to get busy on the finish work at the Gilcrest house. We should have been done a month ago. Originally I told the boys we'd work there on rainy days, but we haven't *had* any rainy days, and I got too involved in the new project to break away. So today seemed like a good chance to get caught up."

"And did you?"

"I made a start, anyway."

"You don't sound very happy about it."

Sandor shrugged. "It was a beautiful day outside, a day I wanted to spend with you, and instead I spent most of it on my hands and knees, inhaling varnish. Still, I need to finish the renovations and get that house on the market. Next week, the crew and I will get the exterior scraped and painted."

"It already looks a hundred times better than it did," Rachel told him. "I just hope you'll be able to find a buyer for it. Real estate isn't exactly a booming commodity in Dalewood."

"Shouldn't be a problem," Sandor said laconically as they turned, headed for the edge of town.

"No? Well, I hope you're right, but that house sat empty for a long time before you came along."

"That was before. Not many people want to tackle a true fixer upper. But the house will be better than new by the time I get done with it." He looked across at her and smiled reassuringly. "Don't worry—I'm not just indulging in wishful thinking. I supervised a string of renovations like this in Clarkston over the past few years, and they sold as fast as we could finish them."

"But this is Dalewood," Rachel reminded him. "Most people who live here have been in the same house for decades. The work you're doing can't be cheap. Who's going to be able to afford—"

"New blood," Sandor said as they reached the county road. "People from the city who are willing to commute."

"You mean people from Cleveland?"

"Akron and Canton, too. Professional couples who've done well for themselves and have finally gotten around to starting a family. Cities are hard places to raise children. For what those people would have to spend to buy a condo or a little starter home in Cleveland, or even in the immediate suburbs, here they can have two thousand square feet of house, a big yard and a crime rate that's a tenth of what you'd be faced with in any good-sized city. The trade-off is the commute, but there are a lot of people who'll think that's a pretty attractive deal if they can just find the right kind of house."

It was one of the longest speeches she'd ever heard him make. Rachel smiled. "Ah. I'm beginning to see the light.

They're looking for the right kind of houses . . . and you'll make sure they find them."

"Supply and demand," Sandor affirmed. "And it tends to snowball once it gets going. In Clarkston, we did twenty renovations before the demand leveled off. In a town that size, it's a significant number."

Rachel tried to imagine the impact it would have if twenty new families moved into Dalewood. "There must have been some culture shock to deal with," she said thoughtfully. "From what you've told me, none of those new people were intending to find work in Clarkston—they were just treating it as a bedroom community."

"That's what made it work. The new households added to the tax base, but the people living in them didn't flood the local job market. Oh, a few people may have looked for work locally, but most of them were only able to finance the move because of their city jobs. The kids are enrolled in the local schools, the parents shop at the local stores and the whole thing bolsters the town's economy."

"But have the people in Clarkston really accepted the newcomers?"

Sandor grinned, his teeth gleaming white in the encroaching dusk. "I could be hard-hearted and say 'That's not my problem,' but I'll settle for reminding you that things take time. At first, I'm sure the new families will stick together, just like the old guard will, but eventually I think it will work out."

"And that's what you're planning to do here in Dalewood? Buy up old houses that have been neglected, fix them up and sell them to families like those?"

Sandor steered them off onto a gravel road. "Not necessarily. I'm not a social worker. I'll gladly sell the Gilcrest house to anybody who wants to buy it and can meet the price. After all, this isn't charity work I'm doing. It's business. My business."

"When work is a pleasure," Rachel quoted, *"life is a joy. When work is duty, life is slavery."* Seeing Sandor's quizzical look, she said, "Maxim Gorki. Sorry. Librarians like to quote. It's an occupational hazard. All I meant is that you sound sort of burned out when you talk about the renovation work."

"Burned out?" He looked surprised, then pensive. "Maybe I am a little." They were close to the crest of the rise. Pulling over to the edge of the road, Sandor turned off the engine and set the emergency brake. "But what I'm doing up here at the site more than makes up for it. If I can start to interest more people in building from scratch, it'll be the best of both worlds. Come on. I'll show you."

They climbed the final slope on foot. Slowly a half-finished structure came into view, more fully revealed with each step they took.

"Renovations may be business," Sandor said as they reached the top, "but this is pleasure, and the renovation work helped me finance it. Take a look and tell me what you think."

The house was nothing like what she had expected. It inhabited the hilltop, demanding and defining its space as inexorably as the trees around it. The lines were simple and deceptively clean, but the dimensions were massive, giving an impression of strength and solidity.

"It's wonderful," she said, impressed.

"You sound surprised."

"Well, I guess I was assuming it would be some sort of Victorian, like Aunt Carrie's."

Sandor turned to her, wearing an expression of indignant surprise. "What are you talking about? Your aunt's house isn't a Victorian."

"It isn't? Then what is it?"

"Greek Revival. It was built around 1830, and that predates anything Victorian. Actually it's a pretty specialized design, even for Greek Revival—a style called a gable-front-

and-wing house. As a rule, you only find them in western New York State and here in the northeastern part of Ohio. There are almost a dozen good examples of gable-front-and-wing houses here in Dalewood. The first time I walked down Spruce Street, it was like stumbling across a living museum. That's why it's such a crime for a place like the Gilcrest house to be allowed to fall into disrepair. We ought to—'' He broke off, looking chagrined. "I'm lecturing. Sorry. Talk about occupational hazards! If I do it again, stuff a sock in my mouth or something, all right?"

"It's okay," Rachel said. It was more than "okay," actually—she found it endearing to see how passionately his interests were engaged. "I guess I assumed that this house you were building up here would just be a variation on the other houses in Dalewood—Greek Revival, or whatever. I didn't realize it would be so...so individual. Organic, like something that grew up out of the ground. It should have a name of its own," she said impulsively. "Not the style, the house itself."

Said aloud, it sounded silly. Rachel braced herself, waiting for Sandor's laughter.

Instead he nodded, as if he understood what she meant and agreed with her. "Maybe when it's bought the owners will give it one. In the meantime, for a little while longer, it's all ours. Come inside and let me show you around."

"In a minute," she said. "First, tell me what happened when you drove out to Charlie Grabemeyer's farm."

"Now?"

"I've been waiting for almost a week," she said. "I want to see the house, really I do, but I won't be able to give it my full attention until I know what you found out." When he hesitated, she said, "Humor me, Sandor. How long can it take?"

"Not long," he agreed with a humorless smile. "Mr. Grabemeyer was very cooperative, under the circumstances. I told him who I was and what I wanted to know, and he explained to me that he didn't know where the gypsies who have been working for him were living. In fact, he says he's never even laid eyes on most of them, except at a distance. They have a *phuro*—a man named Kalia Kaslov—who acts as their representative. He's the one who deals with the business end of things and comes by at the end of the week to collect everybody's pay.''

"Do you know this Mr. Kaslov?"

Sandor shrugged. "Who can say? The name isn't familiar to me, but that doesn't mean much. Most Rom use an assortment of names, depending on the situation. Anyway, Mr. Grabemeyer agreed to pass along a message to Kalia Kaslov for me, saying that I'm looking for Lulash Demetro and telling him where he can find me." He rubbed the back of his neck. "The message may never get to him. Or, if it does, he may decide to ignore it. But worrying won't change that. And I'll go on looking in the meantime." Reaching out, he took her hand in his and gave it a gentle squeeze. "And that's all there is to tell for now. Come inside and let me show you around before we lose the light."

It was nearly dark inside, but Sandor led her through the labyrinth of empty rooms without hesitation, explaining the floor plan and pointing out special touches that he had designed. "It's a big house—four bedrooms—and so I tried to anticipate some of the extra demands that a family that size puts on a house. The work island in the kitchen means fewer traffic jams when a meal's being fixed and everybody's underfoot. And there's a laundry room upstairs where most of the dirty clothes and linens are generated. That lets me take the part of the basement where you'd expect to find hookups for the washer and dryer and put in a shelved storage room and pantry instead, with the rest finished off as a recreation room, a place where kids can play without having to be too careful or too quiet."

On the second floor, Rachel exclaimed aloud with pleasure when she stepped into the high-ceilinged master bedroom and saw the balcony that stretched along the back wall of the house. "I shouldn't admit this," she laughed, "but when I was little, I used to crawl out and sleep on the porch roof when the weather got too hot. Here, you could do that without even having to risk life and limb. And look at the view! You can see halfway to Crawford County."

"I figured we could watch the fireworks from here," Sandor said. "I threw a couple of your aunt's lawn chairs in the back of the truck before we left. Why don't you finish looking around while I go down and get them?" he suggested, starting for the door.

"Sounds like a deal to me," she said happily. "I could stay up here all night."

Sandor stopped in midstride.

Mentally replaying her words, Rachel realized how they must have sounded to him. Not entirely displeased, she smiled and said, "Feel free to read that any way you like. Just because the township's throwing a celebration doesn't mean we can't set off a few sparklers of our own . . . or even a Roman candle or two. Are you feeling combustible?"

"Definitely. I hope you brought your matches."

Rachel patted her pockets in a mock search. "I know they're here somewhere . . . but you may have to help me find them."

"Hold that thought," he said, his deep voice warm with promise. "I'll be right back."

Left alone, she listened to the hollow echo of his footsteps on the stairs, surrendering to the pleasant shivers rippling through her. Judging from the hungry light in Sandor's eyes, the worries that had assailed her during the past week had been pointless. Any distance she had sensed between them must have been due to her aunt's crowded house, not any second thoughts he was having.

Overhead, she could make out the graceful curves of a coffered ceiling. For that matter, graceful examples of fine workmanship caught her eye at every turn. It was obvious that Sandor had lavished more than his skill on this house; he had given it his love…and she had good reason to know just how artful his touch could be. How hard it had to be to invest so much effort and imagination, to watch a project grow beneath your hand, day by day, and then to have to part with the fruits of your labor. Money seemed an inadequate compensation under the circumstances. Did Sandor ever dream about claiming the house for himself? When he described the recreation room, did he envision his own children playing there? When he had lavished such care on the airy beauty of the master suite, had he imagined himself lying here at night with his wife asleep beside him?

She could wonder all she liked, but she had no way of knowing. So far, his dreams weren't something that Sandor seemed willing to share.

Rachel stepped onto the balcony. The western sky still glowed, but it was nearly dark overhead, and a single brave star was visible.

Unable to resist, she whispered the incantation Aunt Carrie had taught her when she was little: "Star light, star bright, first star I see tonight, wish I may, wish I might, have the wish I wish tonight."

The star glittered, waiting for her to voice her heart's desire.

I wish…

From below her came the sound of a snapping branch and a curse.

Rachel looked over the railing. If her presence on the balcony was inspiring Sandor to imitate Romeo Montague in the darkening yard, she hoped he wasn't going to break an ankle in the process. But no further sound rose to greet her.

Overhead, her star was still waiting.

I love him, she confided to it. *I love him. Please, let him love me back.*

CHAPTER TWELVE

WHEN SANDOR RETURNED, he had a folded lawn chair tucked under each arm and a blanket slung around his neck. "Well, did you find those matches?" he asked as he stepped into the bedroom.

"No, I'm afraid not," Rachel said softly, coming in from the balcony. "Maybe you'll have better luck."

He set the chairs aside and dropped the blanket to the floor. "Maybe I will. Come over here and I'll give it my best shot."

Step by measured step, she crossed the floor to him. "Where will you start?" she asked, trembling before he even touched her.

"With the obvious."

"The obvious?"

"Your pockets." He promptly slipped two fingers into the pocket of her plaid camp shirt. It was empty, but he made a thorough job of the search, his fingertips stroking the soft mound of her breast. "Well, there's definitely something in there," he said, tantalizing her aching nipple through the intervening layers of cloth, "but I don't think it's a book of matches." He withdrew his hand.

"That's a shame," Rachel said, her throat dry. "What next?"

"Your shorts, I think."

She was wearing an ancient pair of denim cutoffs, as soft as chamois from years of wear and countless washings. Sandor turned her away from him, then put his arms around her from behind and slid his hands into the deep front pockets. With his fingers splayed against her upper thighs, he drew her back, fitting his body firmly to hers. "Just hold still now. This won't hurt a bit."

Steadying her, he explored the depths of the pockets. Rachel leaned against him, surrendering to her role as the passive object of his attentions as his fingertips traced along the seams.

"A paper clip and two rubber bands," he said when the heels of his hands had come to rest against her hip bones, "but no matches. Not in front, at least." He kissed her throat, then nipped at her earlobe. "How about in back?" he asked, his breath warm against her skin.

Rachel lifted her chin and laid her head on his chest as she replied, "I guess there's only one way to find out."

"Right." Freeing his hands, he gripped her shoulders and turned her back around so that the tip of her nose was nestled against his shirt. "Once more into the fray," he murmured, and plunged his hands into the back pockets of her shorts.

Rachel chuckled, then sighed happily as he pulled her close.

"You find this search amusing?" Sandor demanded archly, taking the opportunity to knead the soft contours of her buttocks through the restrictive material of her shorts.

"Just the pun," she assured him as she adjusted to the rhythm of his hand and the heated pressure of his body.

"Pun?"

Each flexing of his hands deepened the intimacy of their embrace and the urgent fire of her response, and yet they were fully clothed, standing so that nowhere did his bare skin touch hers. Striving for control, she explained, "Fray. You said 'into the fray'..."

"You'll have to speak up," he said, rocking her against him. "I can barely hear you."

She felt as if a thousand fireflies were flickering around her, here and then gone, here and then gone. "...and my jeans...are frayed...." How long would he make her wait? How many delicious games would he insist on playing before he surrendered, merging his body with hers, blending her need with his, creating from their hunger a satisfaction almost too rich to be borne?

"Fray and frayed," Sandor acknowledged, and took his hands out of her pockets, breaking the magical cadence. "I see. But I'm not finding any matches. Wherever they are, they aren't in your pockets. You're sure you brought them?"

She was tempted to abandon the silly game of words and wits once and for all, but Sandor was watching her expectantly, his face alive with an expression of pleasure and whimsy. Relenting, she said, "Positive. So what do we do now?"

His answering smile was wicked. "Do? Why, we intensify the search, of course. No one likes a quitter." His gaze danced over her. "It was windy in the truck. Maybe they got tangled in your hair." Reaching out, he sank his fingers into her curls until his hands were linked behind her head, drawing her close. "Or maybe you got hungry and decided to snack on them. Do you suppose that could be it?"

"If I were you," Rachel said, "I'd leave no stone unturned."

With an appreciative smile, he tilted her head and lowered his mouth to hers, capturing it in a bold, probing kiss.

A throaty boom shook the air around her, and it took Rachel's beleaguered mind a moment to realize that the explosion was a part of the outer world. "It's just the fireworks," she whispered when Sandor lifted his head.

"I knew that," he claimed with transparent bravado, and kissed her forehead. "Have I mentioned how incredible you are? Or what it's doing to me being here alone with you?" A wobbly laugh escaped him. "And have I mentioned that you definitely didn't swallow the matches? The evidence was conclusive: no sulphur on your breath.''

Another rumble reached their ears, and they turned in time to see an explosion of green fire painting the sky.

"Keep an eye on the pyrotechnics," he instructed, "while I get started on stage three of the investigation."

"Stage three?"

"The strip search." He unfastened the top button of her blouse. "Strictly routine." He worked his way down. "Don't worry, I'm a fully-trained professional. The fact that I'm conducting a thorough examination of your unclothed body will mean nothing to me."

"Nothing?"

He slipped the blouse from her shoulders and traced the curve of her collarbone lingeringly with his fingertip. "Absolutely nothing."

"I find that very reassuring," Rachel said, feeling feverish.

"Yes, ma'am, I was sure you would. And now, if you'll excuse me, I have to get back to work." Reaching behind her, he unfastened the clasp of her bra. "Just enjoy the fireworks display."

Again there was a boom, followed by a brilliant spray of orange phosphorescence. Rachel felt an answering cascade of sensation deep within her as Sandor coaxed the thin straps down her arms.

The lacy cups of the brassiere fell away, exposing her breasts to the phantom touch of the warm night air, and then to the very real touch of Sandor's hands. "Too dark to rely on a visual assessment," he said in a businesslike grumble. "Can't be too careful, you know."

"Of course," she said, trying to sound equally detached as he massaged her distended nipples. "I understand entirely."

"Your cooperation is appreciated." He gave her breasts a last gentle squeeze, then dropped his grip to the snap of her shorts. "Gravity being what it is, though, I suspect this is a more likely site for the search."

"Well, then, you'd better get on with it," she said with a show of impatience. "I don't have all night."

That's right—you don't, she realized sadly. Soon the fireworks display would end and the crowd that had gathered to watch in the town square would break up, heading for home. If Sandor was still intent on being discreet, he would probably insist on leaving then, too, and returning her to Aunt Carrie's house.

But it was hard to worry about what might happen in an hour when, in the present moment, he was opening the zipper of her shorts and peeling the soft denim down her legs. Lifting each of her feet in turn, he removed her sandals and freed her from the shorts, leaving her dressed in nothing but a pair of pale blue bikini briefs.

"Small things, matchbooks," he observed.

"Very," she agreed, and felt the hot tingling between her legs grow more insistent as Sandor walked slowly around her, almost invisible in the darkness.

"If a job is worth doing, it's worth doing well," he said prosaically, toying with the waistband of her panties.

Rachel waited for him to draw them down, holding her breath, quivering as she thought about the moment when his touch would bring her to life, ending the tantalizing anticipation. She had had enough of teasing and games; her body was crying out for release.

But the memory of their time in Cleveland came back to her, a sharply evocative reminder of how she had dictated the pace of that first encounter and how erotic she had found it to be the one making the decisions and calling the shots. If Sandor was enjoying that same thrill tonight, and bringing her nothing but pleasure in the process, who was she to fight him?

His hands roamed over the silky material, gliding along her hips, across her tensed abdomen, and then delicately between her legs, the friction of his short nails against the smooth fabric sending ripples of excitement through her. He slipped one finger beneath the elastic, stroking with maddening leisure through the damp curls until he touched the center of her desire.

"Oh, Sandor..."

A second subtle touch followed the first, fizzing through her like champagne. Then his hand retreated. "Rachel?"

"Hmm?"

"They don't seem to be here."

They? Oh, yes. The stupid imaginary matches. Rachel's heart sank. "Oh, dear," she said, using Aunt Carrie's genteel exclamation of dismay to disguise her very real frustration. "Now what?"

Sandor smiled roguishly. "Maybe you gave them to me."

Her spirits rose again: it was too captivating a notion to pass up. "That must be it," Rachel said, reaching for the buttons of his shirt. "Unfortunately for you, I'm *not* a trained professional, so you may find my search methods a little haphazard." The uneven rhythm of his breathing assured her that it was the least of his concerns. "And I'm afraid I can't promise to equal your degree of objectivity. I have a tendency to get very involved in my work." Reaching the bottom of the line of buttons, she concentrated on his belt buckle. "Still, if it's results you're after, I may be just the woman for you." Unsnapping his jeans, she gripped the tab of his zipper and gave it a little tug. "What do you say? Are you willing to risk it?"

His hand closed over hers.

"Now, now, sir, you really mustn't interfere with—"

"Shh." His fingers tightened uncomfortably on hers.

Startled, Rachel looked up at him.

His face was turned toward the balcony. A volley of fireworks showed her his expression, distant and intent in the tinted glow.

"Sandor?" she whispered uncertainly.

"Somebody's down there."

"What?"

He gathered her discarded clothing and thrust the bundle against her bare midriff. "Take these. Get dressed. I'll be right back."

"I'm coming with you," she whispered, shrugging into her blouse.

He gripped her arm almost as tightly as he had on that first night, pulling her across the floor. "Wait in here," he whispered, pushing her through a narrow doorway. "Stay where it's dark. Don't make any noise. Promise me?"

"No!" she said, more loudly than she'd intended.

He pulled her against him, covering her mouth with his hand. "Listen to me," he said in her ear, his voice the barest rumble of sound. "Maybe this is nothing, but I'm not taking any chances, not where you're concerned. If I don't come back, wait here until morning when the work crew comes. They'll get you home safely."

Wait until morning? Wait, knowing that he lay somewhere below, unconscious or injured...or dead? She whimpered in protest.

His hand tightened over her face. "Damn it, Rachel, this isn't a game. Stay here. Stay quiet. *Do* it."

She nodded.

He released her and pressed a quick kiss to her lips. "Get dressed," he repeated. "I'll be back for you as soon as I can."

"Sandor," she whispered, stung by a sudden frightening memory, "when you went down for the chairs, I heard somebody down there. I thought it was you, but..." Reaching up gingerly in the darkness, she touched his cheek. "Please, be careful."

"Count on it," he said grimly.

And then she was alone.

SANDOR CREPT down the stairs, every sense alert. He had planned this house and spent months building it from the ground up, board by nail by beam; he knew every room, every turn of it, knew the places where it swallowed sound and those where sound should bounce back against a listener's ears. But he had never expected to need that knowledge so urgently.

Let it be a tramp, he thought as he reached the lower floor. *Or some kid and his girlfriend looking for their own private Lovers' Leap.*

But he knew it wasn't likely. If there was a trespasser—and it seemed certain, now, that there was—he could only hope it was Lulash Demetro. That would be awkward but not dangerous. On the other hand, if the man Rachel had heard was Gunari, come to warn him away once and for all, that could prove to be awkward *and* dangerous.

Of course, there was a third possibility. His nocturnal visitor might be the mysterious Kalia Kaslov, the man that Charlie Grabemeyer said was in charge of the gypsies working in his fields. If Kaslov had received Sandor's message, he might have felt compelled to come and find out for himself why a dishonored Rom such as Sandor was snooping around, asking questions about a member of his *kumpania*.

Sandor stood still for a long minute, listening, waiting, but the house seemed empty except for himself and Rachel. Moving to the front door, he stared out across the yard. Nothing was certain except the passage of time and the growing anxiety it was bound to cause for Rachel, waiting upstairs in darkness. *Please stay hidden,* he thought anxiously. Then, closing his mind to further speculation, he stepped over the threshold and walked into the clearing, scanning the area.

The leaves to his left rustled.

Taking a gamble, he turned his head toward the sound and said, "*Sarishan*, Mr. Kaslov. Have I kept you waiting long?"

"Yes," came the reply, "but I forgive you for it."

Twenty years was a long time, too long for him to be sure of identifying anyone on the basis of a few words. But it was apparent, at least, that the speaker wasn't Gunari. The voice was too old, the words too measured, with a dry underlying humor alien to Gunari's fiery pride. "Come out," Sandor invited. "Come out and we'll talk."

The leaves rustled again, and a figure emerged.

Overhead, a huge barrage of fireworks erupted, color upon color, illuminating the clearing and the stooped form of Lulash Demetro.

The years had aged him unmercifully. The unruly thatch of raven hair that Sandor remembered was white now, the dark skin deeply lined, stretched tightly over the bones. His arms were still well muscled, but his hands were gnarled, looking unnaturally large below his thin wrists.

"I wasn't sure you'd get my message," Sandor said. "Or that you'd come here if you did."

"Nevertheless, here I am. You have seen to that. Now tell me, what is so important that you must offend good Rom with your presence at their camp fire and beg favors from a *gajo* farmer?"

Any humor Sandor thought he had detected was gone, leaving Lulash's tone as harshly uncompromising as his words. Sandor wrestled with his pride, resisting the temptation to respond in kind. *Remember, you're the supplicant here, Pulneshti. Be grateful that he came at all.* It was too much to hope for the passing years to have softened the bitter disappointment and disapproval that existed between them. But it made it hard to know what words to use to explain his present need.

"If you sought me out because you wish to be taken back into the *familia*," Lulash continued, "you are worse than a fool."

To be taken back? The idea was ludicrous. Sandor almost laughed, then swallowed the sound, knowing that it would offend the older man. "No," he said carefully. "I realize that that would be impossible."

"Then what will it take to convince you to leave us in peace?"

"Nothing you can't afford," Sandor said. "A few minutes of your time. A few words to put my worries to rest."

"What words do you need from me?"

"Tell me what happened after I was expelled by the *kris*. Tell me how the family has fared these years gone by. Are they well? Happy?"

"Your concern is pointless."

"But harmless," Sandor persisted. "Do me this final favor."

Lulash shrugged. "Life has gone on. What did you think, that it would stop? That we would all wither and die in your absence? The little ones have grown. Lazlo is tall and strong, working the fields beside me every day. And you have met with Gunari yourself...or so he tells me. I see he did you no lasting harm."

It was Sandor's turn to shrug.

"My wife—your sometimes mother—is an important woman now."

Sandor smiled. Among the Rom "important" was a polite substitute for "heavy." Remembering Celie's penchant for food, he wasn't surprised that age had brought with it an excess of weight as well as wisdom.

"She is well, and respected within the *kumpania*," Lulash added, and then fell silent.

Making me squirm? Sandor wondered. *I suppose you want me to beg for it. Well, maybe I owe you that satisfac-*

tion. "And Laza?" he asked, knowing that Lulash would count his question as a sort of victory.

"Laza," the older man repeated.

Sandor held his breath. So much hinged on this one reply—a future. A life.

"She is happy. Married to a good man, with three children."

It was the answer he had prayed for. Cast out from his *vitsa* nineteen years ago, he had been given no opportunity to speak with Laza first, no chance to ask her if she wished to join him in exile, no chance to explain or apologize or explore whether any future was left for the two of them. For years after his banishment, Sandor had suffered from dreams of what Laza might be going through if she insisted on honoring her marriage to Sandor in spite of the *kris*'s verdict. Without a husband to protect and support her, she would forever be under her father's thumb, without social status, without children of her own, without the love that she deserved. By *gaje* law, they had both been underage at the time of their marriage, but Rom tradition judged things differently. Young or not, they had taken their vows seriously.

But Laza, it seemed, had done the prudent thing. Faced with the *kris*'s unbending decree, she had made a new life for herself...and by doing so had set him free to do the same.

Elated, Sandor opened his mouth to offer his thanks and give his solemn promise not to interfere further in the lives of the Demetro family—but Lulash wasn't through.

"She has settled in New Orleans with her husband's *kumpania*," he elaborated. "We hope to see her and the little ones again next winter when we move south with the harvest."

New Orleans? But that was a lie. Rachel had seen Laza in Dalewood. And if Lulash had lied about that, he might well be lying about all the rest: Laza's marriage, her children...her happiness. How could Sandor trust any of it?

"And so you see that we have no need of you, Sandor Pulneshti, and no wish to awaken old memories. Done is done. Past is past. You made your choice, and the *kris* made theirs, and that is the end of the matter. I have done as you asked, although I was under no obligation to do so. Now I must insist that you not trouble us again."

Anger burned in Sandor's chest like a physical pain—anger and frustration and a resentment that reached back nearly twenty years. As Lulash turned away, he said, "The Rom in Milford talked of your adopted son who died."

Lulash spat. "Celie's foolishness," he said without turning. "It means nothing. You are *mahrime*, now and for all time."

"Does she know where you are tonight?"

"No."

"Does Laza?"

"I told you, Laza is in—"

"Save your lies for the *gaje*," Sandor said in cold fury. "Laza was seen here on the day that Gunari and I fought. I ask again, does she know where you are tonight?"

After a heavy moment of hesitation, Lulash said, "No."

"Has she even been told that I'm here?"

"No."

"She is a grown woman. She has rights. If you won't tell me where she is, I'll find her on my own."

Lulash drew himself to his full height. "You will do nothing."

"You think not?"

"I am sure of it. You have worked hard to carve out this life for yourself, clinging to the edges of the *gaje* world. How long do you think they will continue to employ you to drive their nails and carry their lumber if accidents begin to happen? It is bad luck to hire a wandering Rom like Sandor

Pulneshti for such work—or so they will come to believe
before we are through."

Sandor realized that Lulash thought he was just a carpenter hired to work on the house. He didn't realize that
Sandor was an architect and builder...nor would it have
impressed him if his mistaken impressions were corrected.
If anything, he would disapprove more of Sandor devoting
his life to the creation of buildings than if he were working
as a laborer for hire. The same difference of values and desires that had driven Sandor to defy gypsy law and custom
would prevent Lulash from appreciating what he had accomplished for himself. The rift between them was too wide
to bridge.

"Do your worst," Sandor said stubbornly. "I'll take my
chances."

"Then you may as well begin," Lulash retorted.

He spoke the words loudly—far more loudly than necessary, Sandor realized uneasily.

"I told you, Father," a voice insisted, aggrieved, and
Gunari appeared at the edge of the clearing. "It is useless to
reason with him. Force is all he understands. He does not
think a Rom's thoughts anymore; he is as foolish as a *gajo*.
I spared him, the last time we met, and how did he thank
me? By making trouble for us with the farmer. I warn you,
Father, he will hound us as long as he is able. He will follow us tonight if we let him. Let me stop him now instead."

"Kill me, you mean," Sandor said, the back of his neck
prickling. "But then you will have the police to contend
with, and they will hound you far worse than I ever could."

"Stop it, both of you," Lulash snapped. "There is no
need to speak of killing or police. It will not be necessary.
We are leaving now." When Gunari started to protest, Lulash raised his hand peremptorily. "Sandor will not try to
follow us tonight. He will be too busy with matters of his
own."

"What matters?" Gunari demanded, putting Sandor's worried thoughts into words.

"All right, we can go," a new voice said before Lulash could answer, and then the muted whoosh of a small explosion swept through the still night. Whirling, Sandor saw a tall stranger emerging from the garage attached to the house, outlined by a vivid orange glow.

Fire.

Rachel.

"Well done, Lazlo," Gunari laughed. "Come. Father was right. It is time for us to be going."

"Damn you," Sandor shouted after them in frustrated fury as they left the yard. "Damn you all!" And then he ran toward the house to face the mounting flames.

CHAPTER THIRTEEN

"RACHEL? RACHEL!"

The sound of Sandor's voice calling her name was the deliverance she had been waiting for. Rachel burst from her hiding place, her knees rubbery with relief. "Coming!" she carolled.

Her relief was short-lived. "Hurry!" Sandor shouted. "The house is on fire!"

The first thing to strike Rachel as she ran down the stairs was the stink of gasoline. The second was the sound of the fire—like kindling being broken. But it wasn't until she reached the foot of the stairs and followed that sound along a corridor and through an open doorway that she felt the shimmering wall of heat and saw the towering blaze.

Sandor was there, skirting the edge of the bonfire in an uneasy dance, his face a mask of concentration as he darted forward again and again to pull away boards that hadn't yet begun to burn. "Go," Sandor said when he caught sight of her. "Take the truck. Get the fire department up here." He threw his keys her way; they clattered to the floor by Rachel's feet.

As her first wild flare of panic passed, Rachel realized that it was less a case of the house being on fire than there being a fire in the house. Boards and boxes had been piled together in the middle of the garage floor and ignited, but they were burning on concrete a safe distance from the walls. The only real danger seemed to be the height of the flames, the tops of which came perilously close to the low ceiling.

Sandor had already managed to reduce the size of the pyre by almost a third, but time was working against him; most of the remaining boards were already ablaze. If the fire was going to be successfully contained, the next few minutes would be critical.

"Is the water hooked up?" she demanded, raising her voice to be heard over the hollow roaring the conflagration made.

"The main is in." The beam in his hands was smoldering. Jerking it free, he dropped it and stamped out the fledgling flames. "I'll find something to use as a bucket in a minute. Get going, would you? It isn't safe in here!"

And that, she realized, was the real crux of the matter. Sandor wanted her to drive to town because it would keep her out of danger, not because he expected the fire department to arrive in time to assist him. With luck and hard work, the fire would be out before she could get to a telephone. But the job needed at least two pairs of hands, not one.

Making up her mind, Rachel turned and ran back down the hallway toward the stairs.

"Rachel!" Sandor's anguished shout floated after her.

"It's okay," she called over her shoulder. "I'll be right back!"

The flickering flames had dazzled her eyes. When she reached the master bedroom, she had to grope along the floor until her fingers closed around the reassuring bulk of the blanket Sandor had brought. Throwing it over her shoulders, she hurried downstairs again. "Where does the water main come in?"

He spared her a harried glance and Rachel braced herself for an argument, but all he said was, "At the left corner. Be sure that blanket's saturated or it'll go up, too."

It all took time, so much time. Rachel crouching impatiently in the darkness while water splashed out of the spigot, worrying about Sandor's progress inside. By the time she was satisfied that the blanket was wet enough, it was a soggy weight, unwieldy in her arms.

She stumbled back inside with it and found Sandor playing a dangerous game of Kick the Can with the solid heart of the blaze, using his booted feet to scatter the boards slightly, disrupting the core of the fire, trying to prevent it from feeding on itself.

"Good," he said when he saw her, and took the blanket from her. "Now look for some sort of bucket, okay? Anything that holds water, the bigger the better. Between us, we'll have this fire out in no time."

What he said sounded calmly confident, but his soot-streaked face was grim, and Rachel could see an angry burn on his left arm. "I'll see what I can find," she promised, and plunged out into the night again.

In another twenty minutes, the crisis was over. Rachel emptied a final stream of water over the last of the charred beams and walked back to join Sandor. With the fire extinguished, the scene of the fire was hidden by darkness, but the smell of smoke was still thick on the air.

"Come on," she said, leaning her head against his shoulder. "There's nothing else we can do until morning. We may as well go home...unless you think they'll be back...?"

"No." Sandor put his arm around her. "No, I don't expect any more trouble tonight. You're right—it's time I got you home."

They walked in silence down the road to the truck, caught in the lethargic aftermath of their efforts. Climbing wearily up onto the seat, Rachel asked, "Who *were* those people, anyway? Why did they try to burn the house down?"

Sandor shook his head. "They just meant to cause trouble, not destroy the building." He fumbled with the ignition key, sliding it home with difficulty. "Trust me, if they'd wanted that house to go up in flames, it'd be long gone by now."

The engine growled, sputtered, caught briefly and then died. Sandor waited a minute and then tried again with the same result.

"As to who they were," he said, leaning his head back against the seat, the cords of his neck stretching taut, "haven't you guessed? That was my loving family...such as it is. Such as it ever was."

Straightening, he tried again to start the engine. This time, it didn't even sputter. With an exasperated growl, Sandor turned the lights on and peered at the gauges on the dashboard. Then, painfully, he began to laugh.

"It figures," he said, shutting off the lights.

"What do you mean? What 'figures'?"

"I should have guessed." He got out and walked around to open Rachel's door. "That nice little camp fire we just put out? They used the gas from my truck to start it. The tank's empty." He held out his hand. "I'm sorry, but it looks like we'll be walking home."

WHEN RACHEL REACHED the library steps the next morning, three people were already there, waiting to go in.

She supposed it was a small thing in comparison with the malicious destruction she had witnessed the night before, but it made her feel like cheering. *I'm starting to make an impact,* she told herself, smiling at them as she unlocked the door. *The town's starting to notice that I'm here.* With an effort, she put all thoughts of the fire—and Sandor—out of her mind.

To her surprise, one of the people waiting for her was Max. The girl followed Rachel inside, moving slowly, saying nothing, peering at the roomful of books from beneath her long bangs.

"Is there something I can help you find?" Rachel asked.

Max shot her a hunted look. "No."

"Well, feel free to browse. I'll be right here if you need me."

Max nodded and looked away, rubbing her distended abdomen.

The month-end paperwork was waiting for Rachel on her desk. She tackled it eagerly and found that, as she'd hoped, the June circulation figures showed a slow, steady improvement. Thinking back, she realized that the increase matched the way her spirits had risen as the month wore on. At some indefinable point, she had begun to look forward to her arrival at work each day, instead of feeling like Sisyphus, doomed to roll his boulder to the top of the mountain each morning, only to have it roll down again at sunset.

Setting the papers aside, she had the feeling she was being watched. Looking around, she found Max standing just behind her, wearing her usual scowl.

Resisting the temptation to scowl back, Rachel said, "Did you want something?"

"I…" Max looked at the floor. "I… Yeah. That book."

"We have lots of books," Rachel said, striving for a straight face and a matter-of-fact tone. "What's this particular one about?"

"Babies," Max clarified. "It's by that guy. You know—"

Inspiration struck. "Dr. Spock?" Rachel ventured.

"Yeah."

"Come on. We'll find it over here. It may not be a very recent copy, but babies haven't changed much over the years."

As soon as she had Max settled with a ragged paperback copy of Benjamin Spock's *Baby And Child Care*, Rachel tackled the morning's next task: shelving. Pushing the wheeled cart of returned books along, slotting each one into its proper place, Rachel was pleased to see that a fair number of her own books had been checked out, along with those from the library's collection. And people were sometimes coming to her now for suggestions on what they should read next. She was finding ways to improve the library in spite of its money woes, and patrons of the library were beginning to believe her when she assured them that books Dalewood didn't own could be obtained at no charge by interlibrary loan.

Integrity Jones had proven to be inventive as well, augmenting Rachel's efforts by initiating a story hour for preschoolers three afternoons a week. A group of young mothers had begun to come in regularly, using the story hour as a chance to browse in peace for books of their own. They were in their early twenties, women that Rachel still tended to think of as schoolgirls, a decade younger than she was. It seemed impossible that the fresh-faced children that clustered at Integrity's feet while she read aloud could be theirs—almost as impossible to Rachel as the realization that her own chances of having a family were dwindling.

"Later." She could still remember saying it on the day she and Tom Gaines had finally put their differences into hard words. *"Of course I want kids. Of course I want a husband who loves me. But that isn't all I want. Do you find that so impossible to understand? If I don't get my degree now, the odds are that I never will."*

It had been the right decision; she didn't doubt it. And she had seen enough professional women in her years at Giblin to know that a blending of career and family was possible. But she had never found a way to achieve that magic balance for herself. When Tom proposed, all she had been able to see was a trap closing slowly around her, cutting her off forever from the world of fine literature and higher education. However sweet a man he was, she hadn't been able to face the thought of living contentedly as Mrs. Dalewood Drugstore.

And so the solitary years had begun; she'd lived on her own and learned all the things she had wanted to know for so long. When she could spare the time, she dated, enjoying herself but finding no one who stood out particularly from the crowd. She studied, and she graduated, and eventually she landed her job as research librarian at the university, the culmination of a thousand dreams. But there were nights when the victory seemed hollow.

Then Douglas Chadwick had come along, tempting her with a new dream of a marriage built on courtly romance and intellectual compatibility. Too late, she had learned that that reality already belonged to someone else.

The discovery had outraged her and injured her pride, but her heart had been suspiciously unaffected. Hindsight was finally allowing her to see that she had used Douglas as a focus for her fantasies; she'd cared more for the life she thought he could make possible than for the man himself.

But now there was Sandor, who didn't fit into any neat, predetermined fantasy but caused her head to spin with new ones. She sighed. Pushing him out of her mind was proving impossible. He offered nothing and made no promises, and yet her heart persisted in its stubborn longing for him, just as her body ached for his touch. What they shared was a summertime affair, destined to vanish with the birds when the cold weather came...and yet it felt like so much more that she hardly dared to put a name to it.

Don't kid yourself, she thought sadly. *Consider what happened last night. It's not even safe for him to stay in one place. And as for his work, there are run-down houses all over Dalewood, but there's a limit. It's inevitable that he'll move on...and what will you do then?*

"That's a pretty long face," Tom Gaines observed. "Problems?"

Disconcerted at being caught off her guard, especially by Tom, Rachel said, "Nothing fatal. Just a passing case of the blues. What brings you here in the middle of a workday?"

"Well, I had a call from Libby, and I wanted to talk to you about it, if you've got a minute to spare. She and I are both so grateful for what you've done here...."

Rachel fought to keep a smile on her face. *The Dalewood Library is Libby Sawyer's domain,* she lectured herself. *You knew that when you agreed to fill in for her.* But she wasn't ready for her time at the library to end. The summer was only half over; the changes she'd tried to institute at the library were just beginning to pay off. She didn't want to walk away from it.

"I'm just glad I've been able to help," she said, trying to sound unruffled. "How's Libby doing?"

"Fine. Real well, in fact, but . . ." Tom looked over his shoulder at the patrons, then said quietly, "Rachel, she isn't coming back."

"What?" It took instinct and training combined to keep her voice a low murmur in spite of her astonishment. "Not at all?"

"It doesn't look that way. Her sister from Phoenix came out to take care of her after the operation, and I guess she's talked Libby into going back there with her. I told Libby she should take her time and think it all through, but you know how she is. She's got her mind made up. Talk about burning your bridges! She says she's putting her house up for sale next week."

Sandor will want to hear about this.

The thought flashed into Rachel's mind irresistibly, but in its wake came dark doubts. Libby Sawyer's house fit the profile of the sort of house Sandor was interested in buying and renovating, but was her own eagerness to tell him of its availability just a way of grasping at straws? Was she searching for any bait she could dangle to keep him in Dalewood a little longer? It was a humiliating possibility.

"So what do you think?" Tom asked.

Rachel looked at him uncertainly. "About . . . ?"

"About the library," he said, looking hurt. "About staying on here in Dalewood. You'll consider it, at least, won't you?"

She smiled encouragingly at him. "Of course I will . . . but it's a big decision. I figured I could tighten my belt a notch and live off my savings this summer but I can't do that indefinitely—and as you said yourself, being a librarian here doesn't pay a living wage. I'd have to find other work to supplement my income, work that would still leave me time to run the library properly. That's a pretty tall order. Not impossible, maybe, but a tall order."

"Rachel, it doesn't have to be that hard," Tom insisted with longing in his voice. "Maybe—"

She held up her hand, afraid of what he might say. "Let me think about it, Tom. We'll talk again before I make my final decision, okay?"

"Okay," he agreed with obvious reluctance. "As long as you promise to keep an open mind until you've heard me out."

"Cross my heart and hope to die," she said, trying to diffuse Tom's intensity with her flippant words. "Now get on back to the drugstore before your father sends out a search party."

He left, but Rachel found herself thinking about his news instead of concentrating on her work. When Integrity Jones arrived at one o'clock, Rachel was happy to turn the desk over to her and walk the sun-baked streets back to Aunt Carrie's house.

Her aunt had a cold lunch waiting when she arrived. Moving with more ease than she had a week ago, Aunt Carrie sat down across the table from Rachel. "So, dear, did you have a nice morning?"

Well, Tom Gaines came in and offered me a permanent job here in Dalewood. Somehow Rachel couldn't bring herself to put it into words. Not yet. She needed time to think. "Nice? I guess so. Max came down. How about you? How was your morning?" Rachel asked rhetorically.

To her surprise, Aunt Carrie blushed. "Fine . . . but it's a good thing you weren't at last night's celebration to see me making a public spectacle of myself. George and I got quite carried away by the excitement of the occasion."

"George?" Rachel repeated blankly, her mind still focused on Libby Sawyer's decision to move to Phoenix. Then understanding came and with it incredulous disbelief. "You mean George *Hudson*?"

Aunt Carrie nodded. "We began innocently enough, just holding hands, but I'm afraid I allowed him a few liberties. I may have led the poor man on. I hope he doesn't do something impetuous that will embarrass both of us."

"What could he possibly—" Rachel's jaw dropped as she realized what her aunt was implying. "You think he's going to propose to you? You think he wants to get *married*?"

Aunt Carrie dimpled. "My heaven, Rachel, don't look so horrified. Is it really so unthinkable that someone would want to marry me? As the saying goes, 'There's life in the old girl yet.'"

Rachel tried to rally her scattered wits. "Of course there is, Aunt Carrie. I didn't mean that I thought you were too old to get married. It's just...well...you haven't known him very long."

"That's what I told him—although, come to think of it, I've known him much longer than you've known Mr. Pulneshti."

Rachel froze, caught off balance by her aunt's unexpected perception.

The older woman smiled tenderly. "Now, now, dear, I don't mean to embarrass you."

"But I—We—" Rachel felt as if she were strangling. "Is it so obvious?"

"Well, it is to me, but I've known you all your life. If you're asking whether the neighbors are gossiping, then no, it isn't obvious at all. But I've seen the change in the two of you this past week." She sipped at her lemonade. "Why look so stricken? He's a fine young man."

"I know," Rachel said, blinking back an unexpected swarm of tears. "I know he is. It...just isn't quite that simple."

"It will be. You'll see."

It was the sort of blindly optimistic remark that had always exasperated Rachel. Now, however, she found herself clinging to the assurance like a talisman. "Do you really think so?"

Aunt Carrie's answering look was full of love. "It's bound to be. How could he possibly resist such a wonderful young woman?" She rose laboriously from her chair. "Now finish your lunch and read your mail while I take a little rest. George will be back from Milford soon."

"What's he doing in Milford?"

"I have no idea...but I have my fears. After all, there are no jewelry stores in Dalewood. But perhaps I'm doing him an injustice. It isn't as though he's a hasty man by nature. Perhaps he'll be wise enough not to let last night go to his head." Coming around the table, she touched Rachel's cheek. "And as to Mr. Pulneshti, remember that hope is a wonderful thing, my dear, and it doesn't cost a cent. There's such a thing as being *too* cautious."

Rachel watched her go, torn between concern and envy. Maybe Aunt Carrie was right. Maybe it was wiser to live on hope while you could, and let tomorrow's misfortunes take care of themselves. Maybe.

But George *Hudson*?

Sighing at the world's madness, Rachel reached for the mail.

A typed envelope sat on the top of the stack, addressed to her. With a sense of dread, Rachel opened it and drew out the single sheet of beige stationery, reading it slowly.

Rachel Locke, you should be ashamed. Instead of protecting your aunt, you have given yourself over to her enemies in exchange for an hour of wicked pleasure with that gypsy vagrant. I hope you will have the decency, at least, to get out of Dalewood before you do any more harm. Leave now, and don't come back. Ever.

Did the entire *world* know about her involvement with Sandor? Rachel dropped the letter, startled and embarrassed, but most of all she was angry—angry at the continued harassment by someone without the courage to sign a letter, and angry at being unfairly judged. Who was this person to order her out of her own hometown? Thrusting the letter into the pocket of her skirt, she stalked to the telephone and dialed.

"Dalewood Drugstore. May I help you?"

"Tom, this is Rachel. I've thought it over, and I want the library job. We can thrash out the details later, but I wanted you to know I'd made my decision."

"Fantastic! Let's drive to Milford tonight and—"

"I can't. Thanks anyway. Look, Tom, I have to run now. I just wanted to let you know. Talk with you later." Hanging up the phone, she slung her purse strap over her shoulder and walked to the door of her aunt's room. "Aunt Carrie, I'm taking the car, okay?"

"Fine, dear. Where are you headed?"

"Out to the building site," Rachel said firmly. "I need to talk to Sandor."

CHAPTER FOURTEEN

"HEY, SANDOR, there's a lady out front asking for you."

Sandor climbed down from his ladder, glad to be interrupted.

He had risen at dawn and walked uptown, waiting there until the town's one service station opened at six. Then, carrying a five-gallon can of gasoline, he had headed for the building site, anxious to assess the harm the fire had done before his men arrived for the day's work.

In the sunlight, the scene of the blaze was a depressing sight. He found no structural damage, but the ceiling that separated the garage from the storage space above was thoroughly blackened, and it reeked of the strange, acrid odor that fire always seemed to leave behind. At the very least, the plasterboard would have to be pulled down and replaced.

The work crew had accepted his sanitized version of the previous night's events: that a vandal had set the fire but been caught in the act when Sandor and a friend arrived to watch the fireworks. "Lucky timing," had been their comment as they cleaned up the charred wood. They'd promised to watch for anyone unfamiliar lurking around the site—probably a useless precaution, Sandor thought gloomily, but one he felt compelled to institute, despite the protection of insurance.

At the sight of Rachel waiting for him in the sunlight, he felt his black mood lighten. "As you can see, the house is still standing," he said, gesturing at it as he joined her in the front yard, "so I guess things could have been worse."

"I'm glad," she said, but there was little enthusiasm in her voice, and she looked weary and depressed.

Aware of the interested eyes of his men, Sandor said quietly, "Something's wrong. Can I help? Or am I the problem?"

That won a slight smile from her. "There's something I need to show you, but..." She looked beyond him at the crew.

Understanding her reluctance, Sandor said, "Let's go someplace where we can talk."

"Can you?" she asked, sounding relieved. "Just like that?"

"The boss gets to set his own hours," he assured her. "It's one of the perks of the job." He faced the house and called, "I'm heading into town, guys. Anybody need anything?"

No one answered.

"Good," Sandor said dryly. "I'm glad to see you're all so wrapped up in your work. I'll be back in a while. Hold down the fort."

"Thank you," Rachel said as she led the way to her aunt's car. "I'm sorry to break in on your day like this, but—"

"No apologies needed," he assured her, taking her hand. "You want to drive or should I?"

"I will. I know a place...."

They drove along the back roads until they reached an overgrown gravel driveway. Rachel parked at the end of it, in front of an abandoned barn, and turned off the engine.

"Okay," Sandor said gently, "tell me what happened."

She reached into the pocket of her skirt and produced a crumpled sheet of paper. "This came in this morning's mail," she said, holding it out to him. "I think you'd better read it."

Sandor read the typed words, then read them again with growing disbelief. "Do you know who sent this trash?" he demanded, incensed.

Huddled behind the wheel, Rachel looked woebegone. "No."

"A guess, then," Sandor said, frustrated that there was no proper focus for his anger. "You know these people. You grew up here. Who would write something like this?"

"I don't know...but this isn't the first time."

"What do you mean?"

"This is the third letter I've gotten. The first one was sent to my condo in Cleveland back in May."

It all made an unpleasant sort of sense. "Is that why you tried to call your aunt?" Sandor asked, remembering the first time he'd ever heard Rachel's voice. "Is that why you came roaring down here in the middle of the night?"

She nodded. "The first letter said that Aunt Carrie was in some sort of trouble, and then I called and you answered, and—"

"Why didn't you call the police?"

She shrugged. "Maybe I should have...but it was hard to believe that anything very nefarious could be going on in Dalewood. I didn't want to upset Aunt Carrie if it all turned out to be nothing, so I settled for coming down here to see for myself what was happening."

"And found a houseful of strangers."

"Well," Rachel temporized, covering his hand with her own, "some of you were stranger than others."

Her fingers were soft against his skin. Sandor clamped down tightly on his body's response. "When did the second letter come?"

"A few days after Aunt Carrie broke her hip."

He looked at the letter. "Does your aunt know about all this?"

"Sort of. I showed her the first letter, but that's all. When the second one came, she was still in the hospital and I didn't want to upset her. And today, when I got this...well, she was in such a good mood that I hated to ruin it."

"So she doesn't know about...us?" Sandor asked anxiously.

"Actually she seems to have figured it out for herself, but not because of the letter." To his surprise, Rachel's lips curved in a smile. "She assures me that you're a fine young man."

"Well, you know your aunt," Sandor said, disconcerted. "She likes everybody."

"Don't do that," Rachel said, sobering.

"Don't do what?"

"Run yourself down like that. You *are* a fine young man."

"Not as young as I used to be," Sandor said in his best Groucho Marx imitation. "And as for fine—"

"Stop it! You're a good person."

He shook his head. "Tell that to whoever wrote this letter. To them—to a lot of people—all I'll ever be is a 'gypsy vagrant.'"

"That's their mistake, and their loss."

"Maybe, but it's my problem—and now yours, I guess. Sorry."

She looked across at him as if he'd lost his mind. "Don't be ridiculous. You've got absolutely nothing to apologize for. I'm just trying to figure out who might have known about us, besides Aunt Carrie. I'm sure she hasn't talked about us to anybody else...unless maybe she said something to George Hudson. But even if she did, that wouldn't explain anything. The first letter was mostly a complaint about Aunt Carrie taking in boarders. George Hudson certainly wouldn't have written that!"

"No, it wouldn't make sense," Sandor agreed.

"*None* of this makes any sense. It isn't as if you and I have been carrying on all over town. I can't think of anybody who could have written it, let alone who *would* have."

From nowhere, the memory of Agnes Denihee's strident voice came to him. *Why, Mr. Pulneshti! I didn't realize that was you standing there.* "It's my fault," Sandor said, wishing the earth would open up and swallow him.

"What makes you think so?"

"Because I did a really stupid thing." His skin burned with embarrassment. "The day before yesterday, after you said you'd come up to the house with me to watch the fireworks, I got to thinking—hoping—that it might be a chance for us to... well, to have a little privacy again so that we could..."

"Make love," Rachel said. "I know. I was hoping so, too."

Her candor made it easier to go on. "I didn't want us to end up in a bind about protection again, so I went to the Dalewood Drugstore."

He had been braced for her fury; he wasn't at all ready for her astonished laughter. "You bought condoms at the Dalewood Drugstore? Oh, Sandor, you are a babe in the woods—or, more precisely, a babe in the backwoods. Even *married* men don't get their condoms at the Dalewood Drugstore. If there's a single item that everybody drives to Milford to buy, that's it. Buying something like that from Mr. Gaines is like buying it from God! I'm surprised you didn't rate a banner headline in the *Milford Messenger*."

"He did look pretty disapproving, but I assumed it was directed at me, not what I was buying." Sandor took a deep breath. "Anyway, that's not the point of all this abject confession."

"Sorry. Go on."

"Agnes Denihee was behind me in the line at the cash register, and I think she saw what I was buying, too. And frankly, if I had to put together a list of likely letter-writing suspects, she'd rank right up there at the top."

"I have to admit the possibility had occurred to me. She's certainly two-faced enough. And there was no love lost between the two of you at the bridge game. But she's fairly new in town. Why would she have gotten involved in the first place?"

Sandor spread his hands. "Beats me. Maybe I'm way off base and she hasn't got anything to do with it."

"Or you could be right and we just haven't figured out what makes her tick. I guess we may as well keep her a working hypothesis until we come up with something better."

Sandor looked at the sunlit field outside his window. "Being wrong wouldn't be as bad as convincing ourselves that we're right but never finding a way to prove it. We can't just walk up to her and accuse her. She'd deny it, and where would that get us?"

"Nowhere, I guess. Maybe I should fight fire with fire and start sending anonymous letters to *her*."

"Great, if she's the one. But she might not be."

"True. Well, then, maybe . . ."

"Maybe what?"

"No, it's crazy."

"Rachel, this whole situation is crazy. What were you thinking?"

"Nothing useful. I was just wondering who writes those horoscopes they print in the newspapers. Mrs. Denihee's pretty superstitious. If her horoscope warned her that it was bad luck to write anonymous letters, I bet she'd back off in a hurry. But those things are probably a syndicated column. There's no way the paper would let us tamper with it."

"No," Sandor agreed, his thoughts suddenly humming. He knew that the idea that had just hatched in his mind stood a good chance of working; he also knew that it filled him with a deep distaste.

So, scoffed the critical voice in his head, *you'll spare your own tender sensibilities and leave Rachel and her aunt to cope with this mess as best they can, eh? What sort of "fine young man" is that?*

He looked over at Rachel, pale and tense beside him. How could he let her suffer for his indiscretion? Swallowing his reluctance, he said, "It wouldn't have to be a horoscope. Not if she's superstitious."

"Well, no, I suppose not, but—"

Quickly, before he could change his mind, he said, "I could offer to do a reading for her with my Tarot deck. After all, I *am* a gypsy, however lapsed. The cards are genuine—they were my grandmother's. And I doubt that Agnes Denihee knows enough about the meanings of the Tarot to realize if I'm twisting the reading to suit our purposes."

Rachel looked thoughtful. "You know, it just might work."

"I'll make it work." *For you,* he wanted to add. *To protect you. Because I love you even more than my grandmother's memory, more than anything.* Instead he said, "I owe Miss Caroline that much, don't you think? Let's head back to the house. I'll show you the cards, and we can work out the details."

They drove back to town in silence.

When they reached the house, it seemed empty. "Maybe we could set something up for Monday night after the bridge party breaks up," Rachel suggested, following him upstairs to his room.

"Good idea," he said firmly, resisting the sense that what he planned to do would be a mockery. It was too late to back out; he might just as well carry the plan through with good grace. Besides, if there was one thing his grandmother had understood even better than her cards, it was love.

Offering Rachel a reassuring smile, he slid open the drawer of the bedside table and reached for the familiar chamois pouch.

His fingers met bare wood.

Startled, he looked down, opening the drawer farther. Then, shaken to the depths of his soul, he sat down on the edge of the bed. "They're gone. My cards are gone."

"OKAY NOW, FOLKS," said Paul Jefferson, the sole member of the Dalewood Police Force. He opened his notebook. "Just relax. Suppose you start by telling me what's been taken. I can get the details once we've got a list. Miss Caroline, you go first."

Aunt Carrie took Rachel's hand and recited unhappily, "A gold pin, my cameo brooch, a pair of earrings and Gertrude."

"Gertrude is an antique doll," Rachel explained, and gave Aunt Carrie's hand a reassuring squeeze.

"Anything else, ma'am?"

"I don't know," Aunt Carrie said, her voice quivering with distress. "It's hard to know where to start looking."

"I understand." The policeman looked at Rachel. "If you notice anything else, call and let me know, okay?"

"We will," Rachel assured him.

"And now you, Mr. Pul . . ."

"Pulneshti," Sandor said bleakly, standing alone by the living room window.

"Pulneshti. Right. What are you missing, sir?"

"A deck of cards."

Paul Jefferson looked up from his notebook as if he suspected Sandor of making a joke at his expense. "A deck of playing cards?"

"No. A Tarot deck."

"Tarrow? What might that be, exactly?"

Rachel watched as Sandor's air of defensiveness intensified, making him look cold and distant. Before he could reply, she said, "They're cards used traditionally for telling fortunes. This particular deck was very old, and I suspect it was worth quite a lot."

"Was it insured, Mr. Pulneshti?"

"No," Sandor said.

The officer grimaced unhappily. "Cards, dolls.... It sounds to me like you folks had an awful lot of antique stuff sitting around loose. When did the robbery occur?"

"We aren't sure," Rachel admitted. "Within the past day or two, but we haven't been able to pin it down any more closely than that. None of the things that were taken were things we used on a regular basis. Gertrude—my aunt's doll—was kept in the room where I've been sleeping, but I came home late last night, and I'm not sure whether she was there or not. And Aunt Carrie almost never wears her jewelry, so..."

"And what about those cards, Mr. Pulneshti? When's the last time you're sure you had them?"

"A few weeks ago," Sandor said. "Maybe even a month."

"Hmm. That's not much help. Was your room locked?"

"No."

"What about the house doors? Are they kept locked?"

Rachel sighed. "Not always, no. Lately we've been locking them at night when we go to bed, but they're open most of the day. And there may have been a night or two that we forgot about them."

As if to illustrate her point, the front door swung open, and Max and Integrity Jones came inside.

"Are these the other people you've been renting to?" Paul Jefferson asked Aunt Carrie, his gaze raking over them. Integrity Jones returned his scrutiny with a look of calm curiosity, but Max went pale, and fixed her eyes on Aunt Carrie's beseechingly.

"Come sit down, Max," Aunt Carrie said, patting the couch. "Officer Jefferson is here because we seem to have been robbed. Have you noticed anything missing from your rooms, either of you? No? Well, perhaps you wouldn't mind taking a quick look around, just to be sure."

"I didn't bring anything anybody could steal," Max said. "Can I go lay down? I don't feel good."

"I'll go up with her," Rachel volunteered, not liking Max's pallor. Suffering through the eighth month of pregnancy in the summer heat had to be almost unbearable. Max looked as if a strong breeze would topple her. Besides, Aunt Carrie would be upset if anything happened to her.

Oh, quit rationalizing, Rachel thought as they started their slow climb to the second floor. *You're worried about Max, too.*

"I'm okay," the girl said curtly when they reached her room.

"Can I get you something to eat?" Rachel asked. "Or a cold drink?"

"I just want to lay down," Max replied, and shut the door in Rachel's face.

You self-centered little twit, Rachel thought, her nerves strung taut by the strange happenings of the past twenty-four hours. *I was trying to be nice to you. Can't you at least be civil?* But when had Max ever been civil?

A new voice was rising loudly up the stairwell. Hurrying downstairs again, Rachel found that George Hudson had returned and was making his presence felt with a vengeance.

"Shameful!" he was insisting from his place on the couch beside Aunt Carrie. His arm was draped protectively around her shoulders, and his face was red with emotion. "There isn't a finer woman in this town. A person would have to be utterly without conscience to do such a thing! You might expect such behavior in Cleveland, and it's certainly true that Milford has had more than its share of robberies lately, but *here*?"

"Maybe the robbers from Milford are branching out," the policeman ventured, looking intimidated by George Hudson's righteous indignation.

"Then it's up to you to do something about it. I understand that the robberies in Milford have been committed by gypsies, isn't that right, officer?" When Aunt Carrie squeaked in protest, glancing with an expression of worried apology at Sandor, Mr. Hudson said, "In a situation like this, a man has to speak plainly."

"Let's speak plainly then," Rachel said in annoyance from the doorway. "Have there been any arrests for the Milford robberies, Officer Jefferson?"

"No, not yet, just a couple of folks who say they saw a dark-haired man hanging around."

"Then nobody really knows whether those robberies were committed by gypsies or—"

"Now, Rachel," Mr. Hudson interrupted patronizingly, "I'm sure we all find your loyalty admirable, but it's time to face facts, however unpalatable those facts might be. Don't allow personal considerations to cloud your judgment." He stood. "As a gesture of good faith, I would like this officer to search my room while he's here. I assume that none of the rest of you would object to making the same offer?"

"Are you saying one of us is the thief?" Integrity Jones asked.

"We certainly had the best opportunity. As to motive, who can say? But I, for one, will sleep better if I know that my reputation has been vindicated, and I would think the rest of you—including Mr. Pulneshti—would feel the same way."

"Do you think Sandor stole his own cards?" Rachel asked acidly.

Mr. Hudson's smile was condescending. "Thieves have done stranger things to deflect suspicion. Have you ever seen these cards of his?"

"No, but—"

"Have you, Miss Caroline? No? I daresay *none* of us has seen them. A skeptical person might question whether they exist at all. At the very least, their monetary value would seem to be debatable."

"Stop it!" Rachel ordered angrily, hating the skinned look of misery on Sandor's face. "Aunt Carrie, make him—"

"Search," Sandor said to Officer Jefferson, cutting her off. "You've got my permission. My room, my truck—whatever you want." He walked to the couch where Aunt Carrie sat huddled. "Miss Caroline, I don't steal, and I would never do anything to hurt you. If you need me, I'll be at the Firesign Motel in Milford."

Sandor, no! Rachel wanted to shout. *Don't let him hound you out of here. It isn't fair. I don't want you to go. And if there was ever a time when Aunt Carrie needed her friends around her, it's now. If you won't stay for my sake, stay for hers.*

As if her troubled thoughts had reached him, Sandor looked across the room at her and shook his head in curt refusal.

"And what about you, Miss Jones?" George Hudson was asking with an air of self-importance. "Would you have any objection to Officer Jefferson examining your room?"

"I don't approve of witch hunts," she said.

"Then you're refusing?"

She looked from Sandor to Aunt Carrie, then at Rachel and Office Jefferson, before finally facing George Hudson again. "No. I'm not refusing. We need to get to the bottom of this if we can—but that doesn't mean I like your methods."

"But what will any of this prove?" Rachel demanded, determined to defend Sandor against George Hudson's slurs. "If you find Sandor's cards under my mattress, does that mean I stole them and was stupid enough to put them there, or does it throw suspicion on everybody *but* me? Or does it mean I might *still* be the thief, but I'm clever enough to know that hiding them in my room will implicate somebody else?"

"It means I get my cards back," Sandor said grimly. "That's all I care about right now."

Rachel gave up. "All right, then. Let's look."

In the end, everyone but Aunt Carrie and Max followed along while the search was made, offering unasked-for suggestions and watching tensely as drawers and closets were explored. At George Hudson's insistence, the search extended to every room, then moved outside to include Sandor's truck and Aunt Carrie's and Mr. Hudson's cars.

Nothing was found.

"Which pretty well means there was nothing here to *be* found," Rachel said wearily to Sandor as the group trailed back inside. "Aunt Carrie's jewelry could be stashed almost anywhere, and so could your cards, but Gertrude's almost three feet tall. Unless somebody's got a wilder imagination than I do, I just don't think she's here."

"I never did. Those things have probably been sold off by now."

"Maybe not," Rachel said, hating the desolate look on his face.

Sandor shook his head. "Gone is gone."

Rachel touched his arm. "That doesn't mean *you* have to leave."

His gaze was unfocused. "I'd have been moving out soon anyway," he said dully. "Your aunt should be well enough to move upstairs again before long. You'll be wanting your old room back."

I don't want my room without you in it, Rachel thought sadly.

But he knew that. He knew it all.

And he was leaving anyway.

TWO OF THE MEN on Sandor's work crew had been staying at the Firesign Motel since the renovation work began in February.

After an hour, he wondered how they'd been able to stand it.

He'd eaten at a roadside restaurant on his way into Milford, more to make the time pass than out of hunger. When he reached the motel, it took him ten minutes to unload his pickup truck, and five to place his belongings in the flimsy bureau in his room. And then there was nothing left to do, no action to distract him from his despair.

He considered driving down the road to the nearest bar, but alcohol had never held much appeal, and going out again demanded more energy than he was willing to muster. It was as if some inner pendulum were swinging ponderously, slowing down, settling toward stillness. Stripping off his boots, he lay back across the bed and watched as the glow of evening turned to dusk, and then to darkness.

It wasn't just the cards. Their loss tore at him, a pain too raw to be ignored, but he felt an even deeper ache for the dreams that were slipping through his fingers. Stability...community...love. In his foolishness, he'd hungered for all three, seeing the embodiment of that hope in Rachel. At work, over the past week, he had even allowed himself the gentle fantasy that the house he was building could be theirs, a place where they could start a new life together. A place where they could start a family. A place where they could grow old in each other's arms.

For a gypsy, those were laughable ambitions...but then, he supposed he was a laughable excuse for a Rom, banned from one way of life, and shunned by the other. Prejudice was the natural enemy of dreams. His personal accomplishments could never defeat the subconscious web of folklore and suspicion that lurked in most people's minds when they heard the word 'gypsy.' Listening to George Hudson's accusation had forced him to admit that he'd been fooling himself all summer. He couldn't break free of his heritage any more than he could break free of the bonds that still held him chained to Laza. He could have his career, but that was all that he could have. Rachel was as lost to him as his grandmother's Tarot cards....

The weary cycle of his thoughts was interrupted by the sound of someone rapping on his door.

Sandor sighed. One of the crew had probably spotted his familiar truck and was coming by to see what was up.

The last thing he wanted was to explain his presence in Milford, but he knew that ignoring the knock would only postpone the inevitable. Sooner or later, the crew would hear about the thefts, or read about them in the local paper. They might as well hear it straight from the source.

Pushing to his feet, Sandor blundered through the darkness of the unfamiliar room and opened the door.

It was Rachel.

She stood on the threshold for a moment, backlit by the lights of the parking lot, then slipped past him without a word and pushed the door closed, enveloping them both in darkness.

Sandor groped for the light. "What are you doing here? You shouldn't—"

"Yes, I should."

"But—"

"Hush. It's going to be all right." She pressed her mouth to his in a deep, sweet kiss while her arms stole around him.

He would have pulled away from pity, but her embrace spoke of tenderness and passion. He touched his lips to her hair, her face, the slender column of her throat, and the pain within him began to recede.

As the pain ebbed, desire for Rachel rose to fill the void within him. He hadn't realized quite how alone and abandoned he had been feeling, quite how bereft at the thought of her absence, quite how hopeless when he wondered if he would ever have the chance to hold her again. Only now, when her presence put those fears to rest, did he recognize the extent of his need . . . and the force of his love.

The buttons down the front of her summer dress yielded easily to his shaking fingers. Beneath it, she was naked. The shock stoked his hunger, pushing him to a place where thought no longer played a part. He was body only, and his desire for her was overpowering. Struggling out of his clothes, he pulled her against him and then down onto the bed, pinning her beneath him, kissing her again and again, pressing his body against hers, desperate to feel every inch of her.

She rocked her hips against him and sent her fingers dancing over his back and buttocks, inviting him to close the final distance between them. Shifting, he braced himself and slid slowly in, unable to prevent the deep groan of pleasure that rose in his throat as her fevered body closed around him. Then he was moving, caught up in the rhythmic demands of their arousal, his breath coming short and sharp as he plunged and dived, driving himself harder and faster.

Within minutes, Rachel cried out, clutching at him wildly, but still the moment of his own release evaded him. He strained against her, desperate for completion, afraid suddenly that nothing would ever be enough to satisfy the raging need within him, that he was doomed to struggle forever on the edge, half a person, belonging nowhere, maddened by the loneliness and the hunger, always alone, never—never—

His climax hit him like a mortal blow, stunning him with its force. He collapsed onto Rachel, his limbs trembling, the air exploding from his lungs as aftershocks ran through him in ripples of sensation. It was too much, a deliverance he didn't deserve, a final burst of light before the long darkness. The shaky breath he drew escaped as a sob, followed quickly by others. A storm of grief swept over him inexorably, a bitter mourning for all of the treasures that had been torn from him, and all of the losses soon to come.

He expected Rachel to recoil; instead her fingers stroked gently through his hair while she hummed his grandmother's lullabye, the one he had used to comfort Miss Caroline at the hospital when the pain of her broken hip troubled her sleep.

At first, the fragile melody pushed him even farther beyond the edges of his control, but gradually a sort of numbed acceptance grew within him, easing the knot in his chest. Eventually he found the strength to pull back and sprawl beside Rachel with a murmured apology.

Her fingertips traced his lips. "No one can steal your memories," she promised softly in the darkness, and together they escaped into the sheltering oblivion of sleep.

CHAPTER FIFTEEN

"AND I'D LIKE the pancakes, with sausages and hash browns, whole-wheat toast and a large orange juice. And keep the coffee coming."

Rachel smiled across the table at Sandor as the waitress left. "How can you crawl around on scaffolds after a breakfast like that?"

"That's how we know if what we're building is up to code—climb up there and see if our feet go through the roof. Believe me, it's a stiffer test than some building inspectors require."

This morning, Rachel noted with satisfaction, he could make jokes, however halfheartedly. Last night, he had been too battered for levity. It had taken a night's sleep to help him find his balance again—a night's sleep in the arms of someone who loved him.

And there was no longer any question in Rachel's mind that love was what she felt for Sandor Pulneshti.

After he had driven off to Milford, she had been torn between her sense of duty to her aunt and her concern for Sandor. Aunt Carrie herself had resolved the dilemma after supper by dropping her car keys into Rachel's lap and saying, "I'm going to go read in bed and I intend to be oblivious to anyone else's presence, niece or burglar, until at least eight o'clock tomorrow morning. If you have half the sense I think you do, you won't be back before daybreak."

On her way to the Firesign Motel, different scenarios had run through Rachel's mind: Sandor might refuse to open his door; he might let her in but maintain the distance he had exhibited at Aunt Carrie's house; he might not be there at all; he might be there . . . but not alone.

She found that she put no credence at all in the last possibility. Whatever else she might find, it wouldn't be another woman in Sandor's bed. That place was hers, and hers alone. His actions and attitudes had given her the confidence to believe that. Although there had been no words of commitment, she sensed that she was as important to him as he had become to her.

But she remembered all too well the protective reserve that had settled over him after the theft of his Tarot cards and George Hudson's accusations, and she knew instinctively that he would be trying with all his might to feel nothing and to need no one. There would be no warm welcome waiting for her. Sandor didn't play games; if he had felt that he could allow himself the comfort of her presence, he would never have packed up his few belongings and driven to Milford.

And so she had planned her strategy during the final miles until, at last, she saw the garish neon sign that glowed above the Firesign Motel. When she pulled in, she spotted Sandor's truck parked alone at the far end of the parking lot, squarely in front of one of the units. Summoning her nerve, she shifted awkwardly on the car seat, shimmying out of her panty hose and briefs. She couldn't cause Sandor's lost cards to materialize, and she couldn't make him forget George Hudson's unfair words. But there was one kind of comfort she *could* offer, as long as she could maneuver around his stiff-necked pride. If she got beyond the door of his room, she thought resolutely, she fully intended to ambush him for his own good.

Now, with the light of a new day shining and the promise of breakfast on the horizon, Rachel was ready to pronounce last night's plan a success.

Across the table from her, Sandor was scanning the morning paper, somber but not withdrawn. As she watched him, his eyebrows suddenly rose as if something had surprised him.

"Don't tell me the *Milford Messenger* actually printed something newsworthy!" Rachel said. "If it's interesting, it must be a misprint."

"Maybe." Sandor folded the paper and held it out to her. "Take a look. Top right-hand corner."

With a flutter of misgiving, Rachel took the paper from him.

Dalewood Announces New Permanent Librarian, the headline read, and, in smaller print, *Libby Sawyer Retiring; Rachel Locke Accepts Post.*

"Well? Is it a misprint?"

"No," Rachel said, with the sinking knowledge that an identical copy of the *Messenger* was already sitting on Aunt Carrie's doorstep. She had missed her chance to break the news to people herself; the proverbial cat was out of the bag. "They offered the job to me yesterday morning," she said. "I told them I needed time to think about it…but then that anonymous letter came, and it made me so mad that I called back and took the job, just to spite whoever's been writing the miserable things." She sipped nervously at her water. "Not exactly a coolly reasoned career decision, I guess, but—"

"I'm not criticizing," Sandor said dispassionately.

I wish you would, Rachel thought. *How are we ever going to have any sort of future if we keep making unilateral decisions about our lives?* "I haven't signed anything yet," she said uncertainly. "I could ask for a one-year contract."

"You should do whatever you want to. I'm sure your aunt will be delighted to have you back in Dalewood on a permanent basis."

And what about you, Sandor? Are you delighted? Appalled? Indifferent? "Libby Sawyer is moving to Arizona," she explained. "I hear she's putting her house up for sale soon. You might want to go have a look at it. It's a beautiful place, but it's showing its age."

Sandor shrugged. "My hands are pretty full right now, and the cash flow will be tight until I get either the Gilcrest house or the new place sold. This isn't a good time to take on another renovation."

"Oh," Rachel said, disconcerted, and handed the newspaper back to him. Two days ago, he had been brimming with plans. Now he talked as if he were anxious to see the last of Dalewood. But why? Sandor cared about her. She refused to believe that he felt threatened by her new position in Dalewood. But something was definitely wrong.

"Here comes our breakfast," Sandor said, sounding relieved. "Then I've got to get going. The weather's looking strange, and we've got a full day planned out at the site."

"I understand," Rachel said as the waitress set their plates in front of them.

But she didn't. Not at all.

"I'M WORRIED ABOUT MAX."

It wasn't the comment that Rachel had expected to greet her when she arrived back in Dalewood.

Aunt Carrie was still seated at the breakfast table with the morning paper open in front of her. She must have seen the article about the library. Even if she hadn't, Rachel was sure that at least a dozen well-meaning friends must have phoned already to discuss the news.

"What's Max's problem?" Rachel asked, more testily than she'd intended. She couldn't help feeling that trying to cope with the repercussions of a robbery, a job offer, an anonymous letter and Sandor's unpredictable behavior was enough for any one person to try to tackle.

Aunt Carrie looked mildly reproachful, but all she said was, "She didn't come down for breakfast. I had Integrity look in on her before she left for the library, and Max claimed it was just this sudden mugginess that was bothering her, but with the baby only a month away, I can't help being concerned."

"I'll go up and check on her," Rachel promised. *Assuming she doesn't slam the door in my face again.*

Aunt Carrie ventured a smile. "And how is Mr. Pulneshti doing?"

It was the wrong question to ask. "Beats me," Rachel said in exasperation. "Why don't you ask him? Maybe he'll talk to you."

"I'm sorry. When you didn't come home last night, I assumed..."

"Oh, you assumed right," Rachel said, regretting her churlish outburst. "Everything worked out fine last night. I was glad I went. He needed somebody there. But this morning was another matter entirely." She sighed. Maybe talking out her confusion would help. It certainly couldn't hurt. "Look, let me go up and make sure that Max is okay. Then you and I can take our coffee out onto the porch and you can solve all my problems for me, just like you used to. Okay?"

"That sounds wonderful." Aunt Carrie smiled and added, "Not that I expect much advice to be necessary. As I recall, all you usually needed was a sounding board. Still, it's too nice an offer to pass up. We haven't had a heart-to-heart talk in a long time. I guess we've both gotten too used to living on our own."

"Maybe so. Anyway, hang tight and I'll be right back."

Rachel climbed the stairs and found herself unexpectedly short of breath. The morning *was* muggy, as if the rain that Dalewood needed so badly might finally be on its way. Was the sky already beginning to darken, or was it just wishful thinking on her part?

At Max's door, she raised her hand to knock, then hesitated when she heard the sounds coming from within.

Max was crying.

Lowering her hand to the knob, Rachel opened the door. After weeks spent together under the same roof, Rachel felt that she had come to understand some of the girl's ways. The last thing Max would want was a witness to her tears. But what she wanted and what she needed were two different things.

Max was huddled in the window seat, her long auburn hair unbound and disheveled, her skin blotchy from weeping. "So," Rachel said, sitting down on the edge of the bed, "what's the matter?"

It took several attempts for Max to find her voice. When she did, she wailed, "I didn't do anything wrong. I didn't steal those things!"

"Who said that you did?"

Max began to cry again.

"Are you upset because Officer Jefferson searched your room? He searched the whole house. Nobody was trying to single you out."

Max shook her head. "You don't know," she said in tones of despair. "I was the only one here, the only one—"

"When? When were you the only one here, Max? What happened?"

"I tried to tell you about it yesterday at the library," Max said with a flash of her old pugnaciousness, "but you were too busy."

A prickle of uneasiness ran up Rachel's arms. "I'm not too busy now. Tell me, Max. What happened?"

Tears brimmed in the girl's eyes. "Everybody was gone to watch the fireworks, and I guess he thought the house was empty because he took those things, and then he came in here and saw me, and he said that if I told anybody about it, he'd—he'd—" She pressed her hands to her abdomen and wept.

"Who, Max? Who did you see?" Rachel went to her, kneeling to stroke the hair back from her tear-streaked face. *Sandor's cards.* If they could identify the thief, there might still be a hope of getting them back. And it would clear Sandor of George Hudson's accusations. "Aunt Carrie wouldn't let anybody hurt you, Max. You know that."

"But he said—"

"Please, Max. Tell me. Who did you see?"

She blew her nose noisily and said, "It was that Jeremy guy."

"Jeremy Hudson?" Rachel asked, stunned. "Mr. Hudson's nephew?"

Max nodded. "When he came in here, he turned on the light, and he had the doll stuck under his arm. I told him it was Caroline's and he shouldn't take it, but he just laughed and said it was worth a lot of money and if I told his uncle or anybody else, he'd call the police and they'd find my folks and tell them where I was. Then he told me some other stuff he wanted, and he said if I brought some of those things to him today he'd pay me for them." She took a shuddering breath. "And I was going to. I need money so I can take care of the baby. But then I started thinking about how great Caroline's been to me, and I just couldn't. Besides, what would happen if I got caught? The police might put me in jail and take my baby away. But if I don't, he'll get mad and tell the police anyway, and then my folks will find me, and then . . . Rachel, what am I going to do?"

Rachel's throat tightened in sympathy, but she hardened her heart and said, "We'll do everything we can to help you, but you're going to have to tell the police what you saw."

"No! Don't call the police! If you do, I won't talk to them. I'll say you made it all up!"

"Max, Mr. Hudson is accusing Sandor of the robbery. Jeremy Hudson stole things from Aunt Carrie and Sandor that can never be replaced. He's a thief. We can't let him get away with this."

"But what about my baby?" She gripped Rachel's hand. "Please, can't we just go and try to get everybody's stuff back? Maybe if *you* told him he had to give it all back . . ."

Rachel could see a dozen flaws in the illogical plan, but she could also see that Max was too distraught to listen to reason. "Where is he?" she asked the girl, trying to pin down a fact or two.

Max shook her head obstinately. "If I tell you, you'll just call the police. But I can take you there." When Rachel didn't answer, she said, "Don't you want to get your aunt's doll back?"

It wasn't the prospect of finding Gertrude that tempted Rachel to cooperate. The doll was a sentimental keepsake; Aunt Carrie would feel nothing sharper than regret for her loss. But if there was any chance of recovering Sandor's Tarot deck . . .

"All right," Rachel said, not caring that it was madness. "We'll go. Get dressed. I'll be back for you in twenty minutes or so."

"Where are you going?" Max asked anxiously.

"Not to the police," Rachel said. "If I do, I'll tell you first, I promise. But I'm low on gas. How far are we going? Unless Jeremy Hudson is somewhere right here in town, I'd better get the tank filled."

Max eyed her suspiciously for a minute, then said, "Well, you'd better fill it up, then. We're going all the way to Cleveland."

"YOU AREN'T GOING TO DISAPPEAR on us again, are you?"

Sandor put down his hammer, wishing he could stop the pounding in his head as easily. "No. I already told you, yesterday was unavoidable. But I'm here now, so let's make up for lost time, okay?"

"Sure," his crewman said, smiling down mischievously from the top of his ladder. "But you may have to explain that to the lady who just pulled up out front."

Going to the window, Sandor saw Rachel walking across the yard toward the house.

Waking beside her at daybreak, he had watched with growing pleasure as dawn revealed the color and detail of her sleeping face. But his enjoyment of the passing moments had been marred by the weight of his guilt. Here was a woman who trusted him, who believed in him, a woman he claimed to love...and he rewarded her faith in him by hiding the truth from her out of the cowardly fear that knowing the facts would drive her away forever.

What he had learned at breakfast made it even worse. Rachel had already defended him publicly when it would have been easy to keep silent. She had come to him last night, sacrificing her pride to his need. She had listened to all his ambitious talk about the renovations he had completed in Clarkston, and his plans to do the same in Dalewood. She knew, at least in theory, that he was committed to working in and around Dalewood for a year or more. And now she had accepted the job of township librarian. He didn't doubt that Miss Caroline's age and health had been factors in Rachel's decision...but he had to believe that he was partially responsible, as well. He knew that his reticence at the breakfast table had hurt her, but...

But nothing. It was too late for self-serving excuses. On the lonely drive from Milford, he had vowed to bare his soul to Rachel the very next time he saw her.

He just hadn't expected it to happen so soon.

Still, expected or not, she was here. Before his courage could fail him, Sandor walked out to meet her.

Against a backdrop of black clouds, Rachel looked vibrant, her face aglow with whatever she had come to tell him. The dress she was wearing was still the one she had worn when she'd appeared at his motel door like an angel of mercy. He eyed its line of white buttons with longing, remembering the feel of them beneath his shaking fingertips, wondering if he would ever again have the chance to embrace the slender body hidden by the flowing material. *I can't do this,* he thought rebelliously, but he knew the choice was no longer his. However belatedly, he had to tell Rachel the truth.

"I'm glad you're here," he said firmly as soon as he was close enough to be heard. "There's something I have to tell you."

"I have something to tell you, too," Rachel said, her cheeks flushed with excitement. "I just talked to Max, and—"

Sandor held up his hand. "Wait. Please. Let me do this." He took a deep breath. "It's about that woman, the one you saw in the drugstore—"

"Laza Demetro."

"No," he contradicted her, "not Demetro. Pulneshti." He forced himself to meet Rachel's troubled gaze and speak the words he had hoped, above all others, to avoid. "Laza is my wife."

CHAPTER SIXTEEN

IT WAS PAINFUL to watch comprehension replace the confusion and disbelief on Rachel's face, but Sandor resisted the urge to turn away. "She's my wife," he repeated softly, "and I know how you must feel about that. I should have told you, should have explained it to you before this, but it's all so complicated—"

"Complicated?" She retreated a step. "No, it's really very simple. You're...married." Her voice wavered on the word, and the pounding in his head intensified.

"Yes, but Laza and I were just kids then. We haven't seen each other in years. Finding her is a question of obligation now, nothing more. It's you that I love, Rachel. You and only you."

He watched as she crossed her arms defensively over her breasts, the breasts he had kissed with such delight just hours before. "Don't," she said, backing away. "Don't make it worse."

"Loving you can only make things better."

"Not for me," she said raggedly.

"Rachel, please, I love you. I want to spend my life with you."

"Then come to me when you're free." Her tone was severe, but he could see the trembling that shook her. "Until then, I want you to leave me alone. I don't carry on relationships with married men—not knowingly, at least."

"I know that. Why do you think I've been searching for the gypsies in Milford? I'm *trying* to get free, but to do that

I have to find Laza. That's why I was so excited when you said you'd seen her in Dalewood. She's been that close! I swear to you, it's only a question of time before I track her down.''

''And then what?''

''Then I'll tell her that I want my freedom. But I have to see her and be sure that she's all right. I have to find out what her life has been like. I owe her that much.''

''Yes. But how much more do you owe her? Sandor, I know you. I know that sense of honor, and that pride. What if she doesn't want to give you up again? Could you walk away from her then? Even if you did, could you live with yourself?'' She shook her head sadly. ''Don't make promises to me that you can't keep, Sandor. Look for Laza. Find her. Talk to her. But until you've done that, I don't want to see you. And if you can't find her, then don't come back again, please, because I just can't...'' Trying to form the rest of the sentence, her soft lips twisted instead in a wordless cry that wrung his heart.

''Oh, Rachel,'' he lamented, reaching out to comfort her, ''sweet love....'' Unable to stop himself, Sandor caught her hand and pulled her to him, hugging her close, trying to shield them both from the black torment of the moment.

For one trembling breath, it seemed to him that she accepted his embrace, pressing her cheek to his chest; but then she struggled free and ran toward the car, her dark hair streaming behind her in the rising wind. As she drove away, the first fat raindrops fell around him, soaking into the dusty ground.

However bad you feel, you deserve it, he told himself, and ignored the desperate voice within that dared to argue otherwise.

RACHEL WAS HALFWAY TO TOWN before she realized that her blurred view of the road was due to something more than her own tears.

Rain. After all the parched months, finally there was rain. "You're too late," she told the storm as she groped for the knob that controlled the windshield wipers. "The crops are already damaged. Why couldn't you have come a month ago when it would have done some good?" And why, oh, why couldn't Sandor have admitted the truth before she had lost her heart to him? "You lied to me!" she shouted, finding some small crumb of release in speaking the words, even if he wasn't there to hear them. "'No next of kin'? You made a fool of me. You let me fall in love with you!"

Rachel, I love you.

She could still hear his voice, tenderly speaking the words that would have meant so much to her if he had said them five minutes sooner. She remembered his anguished expression, and the faint tremor in his voice, a tremor that conveyed vulnerability and sincerity.

"But you've got no right to," she cried, trying to cling to her anger. "You're breaking my heart. I can't help it if you're breaking yours, too."

She wanted to strike her fists against his broad chest and force him to witness her pain. She wanted to hear him try to excuse his irresponsible behavior. She wanted— A sob caught in her throat. What she wanted more than anything was to turn the clock back twelve hours, so that she could be in Milford, enfolded in his arms.

"Damn you, Sandor Pulneshti," she whispered, and surrendered to her tears as the rain redoubled.

As soon as it became apparent that the storm was more than a passing front, Sandor used it as an excuse to send his men into town to work on the Gilcrest house. He stayed behind, pacing from room to room in a search for leaks, listening to the melancholy drumming of water on the roof of the empty house, asking himself what new step he could possibly take to speed his search for Laza.

At first, he could think of nothing, but that was unacceptable. There had to be a way. If there wasn't, Rachel would be lost to him, and he had passed the point where he could imagine any sort of future for himself that didn't assume her presence. She had been entitled to her fury, and to her angry refusal to listen to his explanations. The only way to mend matters between them now was for him to succeed in severing the ties that bound his life to Laza's. Only then could he go to Rachel and beg her forgiveness. Only then would he have earned the right to explain the twisted shadows of his past.

And if he failed, then—for both their sakes—he would have to leave Dalewood as soon as possible. The Gilcrest renovations could be completed in less than a month if he kept the entire crew on it, and the new house would be finished by early autumn....

But failure was unthinkable. Finding Laza might be difficult, even dangerous, but it would be nothing compared to the effort of will it would take to force Rachel Locke out of his heart.

Sandor's tour ended in the master bedroom. *Well, did you find those matches?* he'd said teasingly two nights earlier, and Rachel had turned to him, eager and loving— How could he stay here, working in rooms that brought back so many memories of her? Worse yet, how could he bear to sell the house to some stranger knowing that it was his last tangible link with her? Damn it, he wouldn't lose Rachel. He *wouldn't*. He would find Laza and secure his freedom from her, even if it meant camping out on Charlie Grabemeyer's doorstep or combing his farm, field by field.

The low growl of a car's engine came to him on the damp air, overriding the quiet patter of the rain.

Stepping out onto the balcony, he looked toward the side of the yard, hoping to see who was driving up. Instead he caught a glimpse of someone on foot, moving out of sight through the trees at the edge of the clearing.

Let it be Rachel, he prayed as he ran downstairs. *Even if she's only here to tell me what a bastard I've been, let it be Rachel—*

When he reached the doorway, he saw that a police car had pulled into the yard. The driver sat motionless, but a uniformed officer had climbed out on the passenger side and was starting toward the house.

It wasn't the same man who had come yesterday to investigate the theft of his Tarot cards, Sandor observed. The face was different, and so was the uniform. He looked again at the patrol car. The painted insignia on the driver's door read Milford Police Department. Despite the suspicions that George Hudson had voiced, they were probably looking for some connection between the Milford robberies and the break-in at Miss Caroline's house.

"Sandor Pulneshti?" the policeman asked as he reached the house.

"Yes," Sandor said, and looked past the man into the trees, but there was no one there. Sandor sighed. Maybe he had been seeing what he wanted to see. For the moment, he owed the officer his attention. He was perfectly willing to spend the morning answering questions again if it meant there was some hope, however slight, that his cards might be recovered. "Come on in out of the rain."

Instead the man stopped at the foot of the porch steps.

"Sandor Pulneshti," he said, "you're under arrest for burglary."

He felt his jaw slacken in surprise. "Burglary?" he echoed in disbelief. "That's ridiculous."

"You have the right to remain silent."

"Who am I supposed to have robbed?" he demanded. He couldn't imagine Miss Caroline swearing out a complaint against him. And even if she had, he would be dealing with the Dalewood police, not a patrol car from Milford. It made no sense.

"If you give up that right, anything you say can and will be used against you in a court of law...."

Sandor's mind filled with an image of The Tower, reversed—the card the deck had thrown, all those weeks ago, to indicate his future. False accusations, it had warned. False imprisonment.

Troubled times.

He was innocent. In time, the confusion would be cleared away. But for now, he had little choice but to cooperate.

SHE'D HAVE TO GO HOME eventually, Rachel reasoned, but the prospect was unappealing. Aunt Carrie would be waiting for the heart-to-heart talk about Sandor that Rachel had promised her, a talk that would now be as pointless as it was painful. Max would be ready for their fools' errand, expecting her to drive to Cleveland in search of the larcenous Jeremy Hudson. And, for all Rachel knew, George Hudson might be underfoot. She could think of no more thankless task than enlightening him about his nephew's criminal activities. Let someone else break the news.

Still, avoidance had its limits. After half an hour of aimless driving along bumpy back roads, she circled back through town and drove into her aunt's driveway on Spruce Street.

As soon as she climbed out of the car, however, she regretted the decision. Tom Gaines stood on the back porch, clearly waiting for her. "Rachel, you and I have to talk."

"No." She stopped where she was, not caring that the rain was soaking her dress and dampening her hair. "I've had as many serious talks as I can handle for one morning. Whatever it is, let's tackle it tomorrow."

"This can't wait."

"Well, I'm afraid it's going to have to, Tom."

He shook his head stubbornly. "In another minute your aunt's bound to come out here inviting me to lunch. I'll say yes if it's the only way I can get a chance to talk to you.

Wouldn't it be easier to give me five minutes instead? Just five minutes.''

It wasn't like Tom to be so insistent. "Get in the car, then," Rachel said in weary surrender, and slid behind the wheel again. When Tom had belted himself into the passenger seat, she started the car, backed down the driveway and drove to the end of the block. "There," she said ungraciously, pulling over to the curb and shutting down the engine. "Now say what you've got to say."

It was only then that she took a moment to look closely at him, and what she saw stole her anger away. He looked ill, with dark circles beneath his eyes and an ashen pallor.

"I'm sorry to bother you, Rachel," he said quietly, "really I am—"

"What's wrong, Tom?" she asked more mildly. "Is it your dad?"

"No. Not the way you mean, anyway." He looked down at his hands. "I don't know how to tell you this. Isn't that crazy? All I've done for hours is rehearse this in my head, and I still don't know how to tell you." He smoothed his rain-spattered slacks. "I tried to call you late last night, but they said you weren't home."

No, I wasn't home. I was at the Firesign Motel, throwing myself at Sandor Pulneshti. "I was in Milford," she replied as steadily as she could.

"With that gypsy?" Tom asked, his hands suddenly still.

Rachel's temper rose. "Since when is it your job to run curfew checks on me? I told you I was in Milford. With whom, and doing what, is nobody's business but my own."

"I know that," Tom said in a choked voice. "You're absolutely right. But Dad—" Unfastening his seat belt, he reached into the pocket of his slacks and pulled out a crumpled piece of stationery. "I was straightening up the store last night, and I found this on the floor under the pharmacy counter, by Dad's typewriter."

Rachel took the paper from him and smoothed it.

The words typed there were all too familiar:

Rachel Locke, you should be ashamed. Instead of protecting your aunt, you have given yourself over to her enemies in exchange for an hour of wicked pleasure with that gypsy vagrant. I hope you wikk

It ended in midline, at the typographical error.

"I guess it was easier for him to type it over than to correct it," Tom said. "When I woke him up last night and showed him what I'd found, I expected him to deny writing it, or at least to be embarrassed. But he bragged to me about it. He told me he'd sent you other letters, too."

"A few."

Tom took the sheet of stationery back from her. "When I tried to talk sense to him, he said some pretty terrible things. And this morning when he saw the story in the *Messenger* about you staying on at the library—" Tom's shoulders sagged. "Maybe the stroke had more of an effect on his mind than any of us realized. Or maybe it's part of the same depression he went through when Mom died."

"Or maybe he just enjoys playing God," Rachel said, in no mood to be charitable.

"Maybe so. Anyway, I was calling last night to tell you about this, not to check up on you. Like you said, what you were doing in Milford is nobody's business but your own. I just wanted to apologize for the way Dad has invaded your privacy. I know that sounds feeble, but what else can I do? All I can say in his defense is that I know he's been worried about your aunt for a long time now . . . just like I've been worried about you. Maybe neither of us has been very good at finding ways to deal with that worry, but that doesn't make it any less real."

"I appreciate the gesture, Tom, but it doesn't excuse what's happened. Aunt Carrie and I have the right to make our own decisions without having to apply to anyone for approval.''

"I'm not arguing with that," Tom insisted. "But now that you're going to be living here again, I'd like to think that there's some chance that you and I..." Reaching out, he touched her hair. "Rachel, you know that I love you. When you went away it almost killed me, but I let you go because it was what you wanted for yourself. I've waited all this time. Hoping."

"I never asked you to wait," Rachel said with trepidation. "I never wanted you to."

"It doesn't matter. I'm not asking you for any promises—I know it's too soon for that. And Dad certainly hasn't helped matters any. But I want you to know that I still love you as much as I ever did. We had something wonderful together before you went away. I'd like to think we can find it again, if we try. I'd like to think we could be happy together."

Mrs. Dalewood Drugstore. If she wanted children, a chance at hearth and home and respectability, all she had to do was say yes to the question in Tom's eyes. It might outrage Archibald Gaines, but it would probably please and relieve Aunt Carrie. Tom would undoubtedly be a kind husband, affectionate and undemanding, happy for her to pursue her work at the library. In many ways, it sounded like a perfect solution.

Then why was she still crying for the moon, longing for a man who had lied to her, a man she could never have? Was she playing some perverse psychological trick on herself, only wanting someone because he was safely unattainable? Had she wanted Sandor Pulneshti so badly because she sensed, somehow, that he *was* unavailable? Would she have turned away from him, as she was turning away from Tom, if he had come to her with an offer of marriage?

No. She refused to believe that of herself. What she felt for Sandor was deep and true. His duplicity didn't change the nature of the love she felt for him. The sudden dashing of her hopes was no excuse for settling for second best. When she married—if she married—it would be because she was in love, not just for the other benefits that marriage might offer.

"Thanks for being honest, Tom . . . but I have to be honest, too." Hardening her resolve, she said firmly, "I'm fond of you, and I certainly don't hold any of this nonsense about your father and the anonymous letters against you, but I don't love you. Maybe I did once. At the very least, I thought I did. But I've done a lot of living since then, and I've had the chance to do a lot of thinking about what I want out of life."

"And I'm not it," Tom said bleakly.

"No. I'm sorry, but you're not."

They sat in awkward silence until Tom, rallying, said, "I've told Dad that the letters have to stop. He knows I'm here, telling you about it. I don't think you'll be bothered again, but I can't guarantee that he won't come up with some other way—"

"That's between your father and me, Tom. You can't hold yourself responsible for what he does. He's an adult."

And if it was true of Archibald Gaines, she acknowledged, it was doubly true of Aunt Carrie. Regardless of the final outcome of her aunt's decision to take in boarders, there came a point beyond which Rachel's own loving concern became interference. Now that she was going to be living in Dalewood again, it was a lesson she would have to take to heart.

If Aunt Carrie hadn't taken in the boarders, you never would have met Sandor Pulneshti.

It should have been a bitter thought. Instead Rachel felt something strangely close to gratitude as she remembered the beauty of the scattered days and nights the two of them had shared.

Stay angry, she warned herself. *Stay strong.* But she couldn't. Not if it meant despising Sandor. As ridiculous as it seemed, she still thought of him as an honorable man. *She's my wife,* he had said of Laza, and yet he claimed not to have seen her in nearly twenty years. If it was a lie, then it was an elaborate one, for he had spoken of her as a girl, as if the passing years had been powerless to age his memory of her. There was a story there, a story Rachel suddenly knew she had to hear, whatever the emotional cost to Sandor or herself.

But first, there was something she had to do.

Touching Tom's hand, she said, "Thank you for telling me about your dad. I know it wasn't easy. I'll come around in a day or two and talk to him. After all, you and I aren't kids anymore. If he's got something else to say, I'd rather he said it to my face. As to the rest, I'm sorry we don't want the same things. If I've done anything to lead you on, I'm sorry. I honestly thought you knew how I felt."

"I guess I knew," Tom said, his eyes downcast. "I just didn't want it to be true. I'm sorry if I've been a nuisance. Or an embarrassment."

Tears prickled in Rachel's eyes. "Through all of this, what you've been is a friend. You proved that today, and I'm grateful." She took her hand away. "But now I have to go. Can I take you back to the store?"

"No, my car's parked in front of your aunt's place."

"Well, then," she said, turning the key, "I'll drop you there."

"Aren't you going to go in and have lunch?"

"No, I'll just grab something to eat while I'm driving. I promised Max I'd take her to Cleveland this afternoon."

"Cleveland? On a day like this?"

"It's important," Rachel said. "We have to do a favor for a friend."

CHAPTER SEVENTEEN

"TURN LEFT," Max instructed Rachel. "We're almost there."

Rachel was glad to hear it. They'd been driving for over an hour on rain-slick roads, and her neck was tight with tension. Making a left turn from one busy street to another, she spotted the lit marquee of a shopping mall ahead of them.

ANTIQUE & JEWELRY SHOW
100 DEALERS
FRI THRU SUN—JULY 6,7,8

"So *this* is where he is," Rachel said.

"Yeah. He said he'd be here all day. But I was only supposed to come if I had the other stuff he wanted."

"We've been through all that," Rachel said firmly, turning in at the mall entrance. "If you'd taken something from the house, then the police would *really* have a reason to come after you. You don't need to add stealing to your troubles."

"But what am I supposed to tell him?"

Rachel guided the car into a parking space and turned off the engine. "Here." She unfastened the chain she was wearing around her neck and handed it to Max. "I'm giving you a present. Do you understand? This locket belongs to you now. If you decide to give it to Jeremy Hudson, that's your right. Tell him it was all you could sneak out with. And don't let him pay you for it—not that he's apt to offer! Tell him you brought it so that he wouldn't call the police and tell them about you. And while you're talking to him, take a good look around for Sandor's cards or any of Aunt Carrie's jewelry. You remember what I told you was missing from her jewelry box?''

Max nodded. ''A gold pin shaped like a basket of flowers, a cameo brooch, and a pair of earrings with diamonds and opals.''

''Good. If you see any of those things, come straight back and tell me about it. Be careful what you say, and don't let him give you anything. And if he gets mean about it, just walk away. Meeting him at a place like this, you should be safe. There'll be plenty of other people around. He wouldn't dare try anything here.''

''What are you going to do if he has the stuff?''

''I'm not sure. He may not even be here.''

''But if he is, what then? I don't want you to call the police.''

''No promises, Max. Let's just take it one step at a time. If he's here and we spot something we recognize, you and I can sit down together and decide what to do. Deal?''

Max nodded reluctantly. ''Deal.''

Rachel handed her the umbrella that Aunt Carrie kept stowed beneath the front seat. ''Then let's go in and start looking.''

The mall was enormous, and the display tables clogged the walkways, leaving only a narrow corridor on either side for the mass of rainy-day shoppers.

Max furled the dripping umbrella. ''Jeez, this is gonna take forever.''

''Maybe we'll get lucky,'' Rachel said, trying not to feel discouraged. The tables were arranged in a series of squares, with the vendors seated on the inside, giving the crowd access to the displays along each square's perimeter.

''We could split up and look for him,'' Max suggested.

Rachel was sorely tempted. Every minute of delay made it more likely that Jeremy Hudson would succeed in selling Sandor's cards, reducing her chances of recovering them from slim to nonexistent. But Max looked shaky and pale, and was breathing in sighing gasps as if the humid air were too thick for her lungs. Afraid to leave her, Rachel said, "No, we'd never find each other again in this mob. We'll just take our time. There's no rush. Stay back and try to blend with the crowd. I'm hoping we can spot him before he sees us."

As they moved slowly, scanning the dealers seated behind each table, they found that the meandering shoppers made an effective screen. Still, it was hard to be thorough; people were constantly shifting in and out of their line of sight, and the men and women seated behind the displays moved as well, rising to remove items from the glass cases or turning to make change from their cash boxes. Rachel was glad that Max was there to help her look.

They had covered more than half of the mall before Max grabbed Rachel's arm. "There—that might be him."

Rachel scanned the area anxiously.

"Over there," Max prompted, "looking the other way."

"Where?" Rachel asked in frustration. Then suddenly she saw where Max was pointing: on the far side of the next square of tables, there was a man with an eye-catching head of wavy blond hair. "You may be right. We'll have to go around to that side to be sure."

"No, I'll go. You wait here. I know what to do."

"You're sure?" Rachel asked, feeling less confident of their plan now that the moment was at hand.

Max nodded. "I'll go over and see if it's him. If it is, I'll give him the necklace." She looked down at it. "Is it something he's gonna want?"

"It should be," Rachel assured her. "I bought it a couple of years ago at an antique sale pretty much like this one.

It isn't worth a fortune, but it's old and it's pretty. He shouldn't have any trouble selling it.''

"Okay, then. I'll give it to him and see what I can see. Then I'll come back over here and fill you in. No big deal.''

"All right, then, go ahead . . . but be careful.''

"Of what?'' Max asked brashly. "The guy's stuck behind a table. What can he do, bite me? I'll be right back,'' she promised, and walked away, forcing a path through the milling crowd.

For Rachel, left behind, it was like watching a Hitchcock film and having the sound track fail as the final scene began. She could see Max making her way slowly around the square, coming closer and closer to the man until finally she was standing in front of him, her lips moving as she spoke. After a minute, she stopped talking and listened, looking wide-eyed and apprehensive. Rachel hoped it was just an act. There was more talking, and then Max held the necklace out to him.

When he took it from her, Rachel smiled grimly. So far, so good. All she had to do now was to be patient for another minute or two until Max could come back and tell her whether any of the missing items were on the display table.

Finally Max and Jeremy Hudson completed their conversation, but when Max walked away from his table she headed away from Rachel as well, vanishing quickly in the throng.

Rachel stared after her, unsure whether the move was just a preliminary precaution on Max's part to keep Jeremy Hudson from watching where she went, or whether she intended to lose Rachel, as well. If she wanted to disappear, the mall was a perfect place to do so. Rachel would stand no chance of finding her. Maybe Max wasn't as innocent as she'd claimed; she could even have been Jeremy Hudson's active accomplice in the theft. Or maybe, spooked by Rachel's talk of summoning the authorities, she was simply grabbing her chance to drop out of sight, once and for all.

And what am I supposed to tell Aunt Carrie? That I lost Max in Cleveland? No. Don't panic. She isn't gone. She'll show up in a minute.

But several minutes passed, and there was still no sign of her.

Rachel's stomach ached with tension. If Max had chosen this moment to vanish, the grounds for accusing Jeremy Hudson of the theft had vanished with her. The last link with Sandor's cards would grow weaker, turning half a hope into a mere glimmer. And what about Max herself? The baby was due in less than a month. Where would she go? How would she eat? Rachel fought against the thought of Max standing alone in the rain, soaked to the skin, thumbing for a ride while cars whizzed past her—

"You okay?"

"Max!" Rachel threw her arms around the startled girl, hugging her. "Are *you* okay? Where did you go?!"

"To the bathroom," Max said, looking embarrassed as she shrugged out of Rachel's grasp. "I have to go all the time these days." Her eyes narrowed. "What did you think I was doing? Running off?"

Rachel found that relief made it easy to smile. "Actually I figured you were laying a false trail to fool Jeremy Hudson."

Max grinned. "Sure, that's what I was doing. The bathroom was just an excuse, right?"

"Right. You're actually James Bond in disguise."

"Some disguise," Max said, looking more lighthearted than Rachel had ever seen her. "Anyway, he's got 'em."

"Them?"

"The cards, and some of the jewelry."

"Max, that's fantastic! Are you sure?"

Max shrugged. "Well, there's some sort of weird old deck, anyway, and he's got a cameo pin in one of the cases. So I figure it's probably the stuff he took. But I never saw any of it before, so I can't be really sure, you know what I mean?''

"I know," Rachel acknowledged, elation and apprehension warring within her. She, too, was a stranger to Sandor's cards . . . but the jewelry was another matter. Cameos were as distinctive as portraits—no two were alike—and Rachel had seen Aunt Carrie's hundreds of times. One good look would be enough to tell her if it was the pin in Jeremy Hudson's display case. But how was she going to get that one good look? After his talk with Max, he would never believe that Rachel's presence at the mall was coincidental. She was tempted to go with the odds and call the police on the basis of her suspicions, but she would be on much firmer ground if she—

"He's leaving!" Max whispered frantically.

"What?" Rachel's heart began to pound. Standing on tiptoe, she peered anxiously through the crowd.

Jeremy Hudson had risen from his chair and was speaking to the woman seated behind the adjacent table. Rachel crossed her fingers. Maybe he, like Max, simply had to go to the bathroom. On the other hand, if he started to pack up his display, she would have to do something to stop him, even if it meant facing him down in the middle of the aisle and accusing him of the theft. Surely the mall had some sort of security force; if she could only locate one of them in the crowd . . . but it would take time to explain the situation to a total stranger and convince him that he should help her. In the meantime, Jeremy Hudson might slip through their fingers.

Luck was with them. As Rachel watched, he stepped through the narrow gap at one corner of the square and strode away, leaving his displays undisturbed.

Rachel took a quick step, then stopped as Max took hold of her arm. "Where are you going?" the girl demanded.

"Over there to get a look for myself while he's gone. Don't worry, I'll be right back."

It wasn't easy to weave a hurried path through the browsing crowd. Stepping on a few toes in the process, Rachel did her best, murmuring apologies but losing no time. Arriving at Jeremy Hudson's table, she bent to scrutinize the bewildering array of jewelry displayed in a glass case on a bed of black velvet, searching until she spotted the familiar profile of Aunt Carrie's cameo brooch.

Jackpot, Rachel thought with giddy satisfaction, and straightened hastily to examine the larger display cases on either side of the jewelry. There on the left, prominently featured on the top shelf, was a large deck of cards, fanned out faceup. The top card depicted a woman seated between two massive pillars, one white, the other black. She wore ceremonial robes and an elaborate headdress, and she held a scroll in her hands. There were words at the base of the card, but they weren't in English or any other language Rachel recognized.

Sandor's cards. She was as sure of it as she could possibly be without having him there to identify them.

Rachel hesitated. She had accomplished all that she had hoped to. It was time to retreat prudently and plan her next move, safely out of Jeremy Hudson's line of sight. But she found that she couldn't bear to walk away and leave Sandor's cards behind, knowing what they meant to him. She was here, the cards were here, and Jeremy Hudson—however momentarily—was gone. If she was going to take action, she wouldn't find a better opportunity.

"Excuse me," she said to the woman sitting behind the next table. "I'd like to make a purchase."

"Well, the man who's running this booth will be back in just a minute, if you can wait. He just went to make a phone call."

"Gee, I'm already late," Rachel said ingenuously. "Couldn't you help me for just a second?"

The woman smiled. "All right. What were you interested in?"

"These cards." Rachel pointed. "I want to buy them."

"Cards?" The woman walked over. "Oh, I see. Sure. Just a minute while I figure out which key fits this case...." She tried several, her movements slow and methodical.

Rachel bit her lip, growing more and more uneasy, expecting at any moment to hear Jeremy Hudson's voice behind her.

The proper key slid into the lock and turned; the case opened and the woman reached for the cards, saying, "Okay, let's just see what the price on these little beauties is." She consulted a piece of paper taped to the back of the case and said, "Oh, my."

"What? Is something wrong?"

The woman's smile slipped back into place. "No, not at all." She cleared her throat. "The price is nine hundred dollars. A real find. I don't believe I've ever seen a deck quite like this. Will you be paying cash or would you rather charge it?"

Rachel was stunned. Nine hundred dollars? She only had seventy-five dollars in her purse, and the limit on her credit card was a thousand dollars—and she'd charged about two hundred in the past few weeks. She supposed she could write a check and then transfer money from her savings account to cover it, but the woman was unlikely to let her write a check without waiting for Jeremy Hudson's okay. It was maddening to have the cards close, so close....

"I'd like to examine them, please," Rachel said firmly, setting her purse on the table in a gesture of good faith. "The price is higher than I expected. I don't mind paying it, but I'll need a better look at the condition of the deck first."

"Of course." The woman handed them to her. "Ah, here comes Mr. Hudson. I'm sure he'll be able to answer any questions you may have."

The cards were a dense weight on Rachel's palm. She closed her fingers protectively around them. "I'm sure he will. Thank you. You've been very helpful."

"My pleasure." The woman's gaze shifted. "Mr. Hudson, this young woman is interested in your Tarot deck."

"Wonderful. Thanks for covering for me." He slipped between the tables and offered Rachel a polished smile. "Now then, let me tell you a little about . . ." The smile faltered as he recognized her, and his voice trailed away to silence.

"Actually," Rachel said coolly, "I know everything about this deck that I need to. But I would like to talk with you about the cameo in your display case. And about dolls, for that matter. Are you selling any dolls today, Jeremy?"

She used his first name intentionally, pressing her advantage. He was having to think fast, to decide what to do about her implied accusation. And his options, she realized, were limited. He could demand the return of the Tarot cards, but she had no intention of cooperating, and he had far more to fear from the police or security guards than she did. He could run, but that would mean abandoning all of his wares. He could confess, but she had done nothing to make him expect leniency from her.

Or he could try to bargain with her.

"You want the cards?" he asked, watching her guardedly. "Then take them and get out of here. I've got work to—"

"And what about my aunt's jewelry?"

He made a disdainful face. "Costume stuff. It's junk, really, but if you—"

"Junk? Then why did you steal it?"

He shook his head. "Hold on, now. I bought that jewelry, fair and square. You can't—"

"From my aunt? No way. From Max? She says not."

"And you believe her?"

"Yes. But who I believe really isn't the issue. A report has been filed on that stolen jewelry. It's up to the police to sort out who's telling the truth, and to do their best to trace my aunt's doll, as well."

Jeremy Hudson's face was ruddy with suppressed emotion. Producing a large sample case from beneath the table, he unlocked the jewelry display and began to fold up the lengths of velvet, bundling the pins and necklaces into convenient rolls.

"Oh, no," Rachel said. "If you think I'm going to let you walk out of here with my aunt's jewelry, you're crazy." Raising her voice, she said to the people around her, "We need a security guard over here, please. It's an emergency."

"Shut up," Jeremy snapped.

"Why should I shut up?" Rachel retorted, her voice still projecting strongly. "You're trying to leave here with stolen property."

Turning on his heel, he headed for the gap at the corner of the square. "This woman's crazy," he said to the woman at the next table as he passed her. "Watch my things. I'm going to call the police and have them—"

But before he could leave, a uniformed guard appeared with Max at his elbow. "All right now, everybody just stay put," the man said, blocking the gap. "The police are on their way. What exactly seems to be the trouble, sir?"

Rachel saw the belligerent squaring of Jeremy Hudson's shoulders begin to wilt. Catching Max's eye, she raised her thumb in a gesture of triumph.

Max's answering nod was subdued.

Joining her at the security guard's side, Rachel said quietly, "Thank you, Max. You're a lifesaver. He would have gotten away."

"I know."

With bravado, Jeremy Hudson was "explaining" the situation to the security guard.

Rachel touched Max's arm gingerly. "Don't look so worried, okay? Everything's going to work out."

Max shook her head in mute rebuttal, tears shining in her eyes.

"What is it? Are you afraid of what he'll say to the police?"

Again she shook her head, and the tears began to fall.

"Then what? What's wrong?"

"My pants are wet," she whispered, white-faced.

"Well, it isn't the end of the world," Rachel said soothingly, still listening with half an ear to Jeremy Hudson's elaborate lies. "Things like that happen. We'll buy you some dry ones before we—"

"I didn't say I wet my pants," she protested indignantly through her tears. "I said my pants are wet. Rachel, I . . . I think it's the baby."

CHAPTER EIGHTEEN

STANDING IN THE HOSPITAL CORRIDOR, Rachel dropped coins into the pay phone and punched out her home number. A series of electronic blips and clicks came over the line, followed by a burring buzz as the connection was completed and Aunt Carrie's phone began to ring.

It was answered immediately. "Locke residence," a melodious voice said, sounding uncharacteristically harried.

"Integrity? It's Rachel—"

"Thank God, child! Where are you?"

"In Cleveland. Why? What's wrong? Is Aunt Carrie all right?"

"She's fine, but we're both mightily perplexed. Here it is, past time for supper, and there's no sign of anyone to eat it with us. It's been a most peculiar day. Is Max still with you?"

"Yes... but her name isn't Max. It's Alison Maxwell. At least, that's the name she gave when we checked her in."

"Checked her in... where?"

"At the hospital. That's why I'm calling. She's in labor."

"Now? Already? I thought she wasn't due—"

"—for another month. I know. Tell me about it! I didn't dare drive her all the way back to Milford, so we're still here in Cleveland. When I called her doctor and told him that her water had broken, he said I should take her to the nearest hospital. It'll probably be hours before the baby's actually born, but Max needs Sandor now. She's really counting on him." *So am I,* Rachel thought fervently, *and not just for Max's sake.* "Could you ask Mr. Hudson to drive up to the building site and—"

"He isn't here. No one is, except your aunt and myself. I'd offer to go and find Mr. Pulneshti, but I don't have any way to get there. You have your aunt's car there in Cleveland."

"Damn. Well, when Mr. Hudson comes in—"

"Rachel, he isn't going to be coming in. He's gone. Moved out."

"What?"

"Some sort of family emergency, I gather. I was still at the library while it was happening, but Caroline says he had a call from his nephew this afternoon, and then he packed his things and left."

And to think I felt sorry for him! He must have known what Jeremy was up to all the time. She didn't know whether to be angry or relieved that he was gone. "His nephew is the one who robbed us," she informed Integrity Jones. "Max caught him in the act. That's why she and I were up here today, tracking him down."

"Well! You *have* been having adventures. But why on earth didn't Max simply—" Integrity Jones sighed. "On second thought, I begin to understand. She wouldn't be eager to bring herself to the attention of the authorities."

"And Jeremy Hudson capitalized on that, threatening her with all sorts of dire consequences if she told. She seems convinced that the whole world is plotting to take this baby away from her."

"I don't suppose it's too far from the truth, considering the circumstances. An unwed mother's lot is rarely an easy one, and I doubt that Max is quite as old as she claims. If she had been one of my students and she was determined to give birth to the child, I would certainly have been advocating adoption."

A metallic voice interrupted. "Please deposit twenty-five cents for an additional—"

Muttering to herself, Rachel shoved more coins into the phone. "Look, Integrity, I've got to get back to Max. I told her I'd only be gone a minute. But . . ." She hesitated. The last thing she wanted to do was impose on Tom, after their uncomfortable talk, but she didn't know who else she could count on. "Would you do me a favor? Could you call the Dalewood Drugstore and ask Tom Gaines to drive up to the building site and take a message to Sandor? Have him say that we're at Giblin Hospital, just off campus. It's on the map. And tell Aunt Carrie—" She hesitated again, wondering if she should pass along the news that Archibald Gaines was the source of the anonymous letters. Aunt Carrie would want to know . . . but right now it seemed like the least of their troubles. Perhaps it would be better to wait and tell her face-to-face. "Just say that I'll call again as soon as we know more, okay?"

"Certainly. And I'll phone Mr. Gaines right now and explain matters to him. I'm sure Mr. Pulneshti will get there just as quickly as he can. Give Max our best wishes."

"I will," she promised, and hung up.

When Rachel returned to the ward, she found that a new nurse had come on shift and was examining Max, moving her hands assessingly over the high dome of the girl's abdomen. "I don't know," the nurse said, her eyes focused on some distant point as she concentrated. "It just doesn't feel . . ." She pursed her lips. "I'm going to call down for an ultrasound."

Rachel came closer. "Why? What's that?"

"No big deal," Max said with studied nonchalance. "They just rub this microphone thing over my stomach so they can see the baby. It doesn't hurt. It's sort of neat."

"But why is it necessary?" Rachel asked the nurse, uneasy in her sudden role as Max's advocate.

The white-uniformed woman rested her hand several inches above Max's navel. "Because I think what I'm feeling here is a head, not a bottom. If I'm right... Well, there's no point in guessing. In a little while, with the help of the ultrasound, we'll know for sure." She tugged Max's hospital gown back into place. "I'll be right back, okay?"

"Okay," Max said meekly. As soon as the nurse was gone, she looked up at Rachel and asked, "Is he coming?"

"Someone's going to drive up to the building site and get him," Rachel assured her. "Don't worry. If I know Sandor, he'll drop everything as soon as he hears you're in labor. Did you have any more contractions while I was gone?"

"Just one, not very strong. They're getting farther apart, not closer together. I asked the nurse if they were going to give me something to make the contractions stronger, but she said the doctor would have to decide that. Maybe I should get up and walk again."

"We'd better wait," Rachel said anxiously. "If they bring the ultrasound equipment up here, they aren't going to want to have to hunt the halls for you."

In minutes, the nurse returned, accompanied by a technician and an unassuming-looking machine on a wheeled cart. As Rachel watched in fascination, a clear gel was spread over Max's skin. Then the technician ran a small hand piece back and forth across her abdomen, and an image began to take shape on the little screen.

At first, it was like watching a television without an antenna, but then, guided by the nurse's comments, Rachel adjusted to the quality of the picture. Magically the snowy form on the screen resolved into the vague but recognizable shape of a baby.

Rachel gripped Max's hand. "It moved its arm! See?"

"I see. I do. Oh, Rachel..."

"Definitely breech," the technician said.

The nurse nodded. "Thanks. I'll let the doctor know."

The image vanished.

"Breech," Max repeated. "That means head up, right?"

"That's right," the nurse said, moving aside as the technician wheeled his machine back out into the hallway.

"So what happens now?"

She smiled reassuringly. "We'll see what Dr. Anderson says, but I suspect he'll opt for a cesarean delivery."

Max looked horrified. "Can't you just turn it around? In my childbirth class, they said you could do that."

"It's true that sometimes we can turn the baby manually to improve its position, but in your case it just isn't feasible. You've been leaking amniotic fluid for several hours, and your baby is exactly opposite of where it should be for a normal vaginal delivery."

"But—"

"Let's see what Dr. Anderson has to say," she suggested kindly. "I'll go call him. Use your buzzer if you need me."

Left alone together, Max and Rachel continued to hold each other's hands. "I was going to do this right," Max said, her eyes glittering with tears. "I wasn't going to let them give me any drugs or anything, so the baby could be wide awake when it was born. I was going to—"

"You were going to do the right thing for the baby," Rachel said firmly. "And that's still what you're going to do. We'll talk to the doctor. It'll be okay, Max."

"But I'm scared." She squeezed her eyes shut.

Rachel wiped a tear from Max's cheek. "I'll stay right with you, and I'm sure Sandor will get here just as soon as he can."

"I want my mom," Max whispered shakily.

Rachel felt helpless. "Don't cry, Max. It'll be all right. This is a good hospital. I'm sure they know what they're doing. Don't cry."

"I can't help it! I want my mom." She choked back a sob. "Please," she entreated, clinging to Rachel's hand, "call her for me and tell her where I am. I need her, I do...."

"Of course," Rachel promised, astonished. "Just tell me the number. I'll call her right now." She copied down the number that Max recited and asked, "What area code should I dial?"

Max looked up at her, startled out of her tears. "You don't need one. This is where I'm from. They live here."

"Here? You mean right here in Cleveland?"

"Well, out in the suburbs, but my dad works downtown."

"Max, that's wonderful! If your mom is home, she can be here in no time. I'll go call her right now!"

Max's fingers tightened around Rachel's hand. "Wait. Maybe you better not call. Maybe—"

"Are you serious? Why not?"

Max turned her head restlessly on the pillow. "She doesn't know. About the baby, I mean."

"Oh, Max. You ran away and your folks don't even know why?"

"I couldn't tell them. I couldn't! My dad was going to be so mad, and my mom . . ." The words rushed out of her in a torrent. "The guy who got me pregnant is a total jerk, but I used to think he was fantastic. They told me not to go out with him, but I did anyway, and then I found out he was sleeping with another girl, too, so we broke up. When I found out I was pregnant, he just laughed and said I'd better get rid of it, and that I better not try to say it was his because everybody knew he was going with Sandy and he'd say he'd never gone to bed with me at all. So I left my folks a note that said I was running away to live with my aunt in New York, and I took all the money I had and borrowed some more from a friend of mine, and I got on a bus headed south instead." She swiped awkwardly at the tears on her face. "By the time the bus got to Dalewood, I'd figured out that they'd look for me mostly far away, so I decided to get off there and wait a few weeks while the excitement died down, and then go on. Besides," she said, venturing a watery smile, "it looked nice. And then I met your aunt. And I just...sort of...stayed."

"You know what I think?" Rachel asked softly.

"What?"

"I think you should let me call your mom."

Max nodded. "I feel bad about making them worry, but I was afraid to get in touch. What if they're so mad they won't come? What if they try to make me give my baby away?"

"What if they don't? Don't borrow trouble. You've been running from shadows long enough. Let me call."

Max's thin mouth tightened. "Another contraction," she said.

Rachel made a note of the time.

In less than a minute, Max said, "It's going away now. Damn. That nurse is right—the baby isn't going to get born at this rate. They've gotta do something...and I guess cutting me open is what it's going to be." She sighed shakily and groped for a tissue. "If my folks come, will you stay, too?"

"If you want me to. Shall I call them now?"

"Yes." Max closed her eyes. "Please."

AT THE END OF AN OBSTACLE COURSE of paperwork, procedure and frustration, Sandor found himself alone in a jail cell.

It was neat; there wasn't enough in it for it to be otherwise. And it was clean, smelling mostly of antiseptic. There was nothing barbaric about the cell at all...except its purpose. It was a box, a trap designed to hold humans against their will, and it made him feel ill to know that he had been forced to check his freedom at the desk along with his wallet.

Someone should have come for him by now. As soon as he'd arrived at the Milford Police Station, he had made his phone call to the boardinghouse in Dalewood and explained the humiliating situation, then settled back uneasily to wait. But burglary was a felony, and there was a limit to the police department's patience. When his call failed to produce any aid within an hour, they strip searched him and assigned him to a cell.

Sandor stretched out on the bunk, trying to think. Gunari. Lazlo. Lulash. Were they behind his arrest? Had they robbed someone's house and managed somehow to implicate him? They were angry enough to take a risk if they thought it might mean serious trouble for him. He supposed it was better than no theory at all. But it didn't feel right. Subtlety wasn't a Demetro trademark. The fire had been much more their style.

Still, where did that leave him? What could possibly have made the police think that he was involved in robbing someone's house? He was an architect, a builder, not a criminal... and yet here he was.

They'd wanted to know where he had been last night. In Milford, at the Firesign Motel, he'd told them truthfully. But then they'd asked if he'd been there alone... and Sandor had said yes. The half-truth bothered him, but he was determined not to drag Rachel's name and reputation through the mud simply to protect his own, especially now, knowing how she must feel about him. He didn't need the alibi she could provide. He was innocent of the charges against him. That would be proven, sooner or later.

That was what he had told himself, at least. But then the police had asked whether he'd been in contact with any of the other gypsies in the Milford area. Yes, he'd said, but only for personal, family reasons. They'd just nodded, looking grimly pleased.

Maybe he should have called an attorney, after all, but he didn't want to simply pick a name from the phone book, and he was reluctant to involve the Cleveland lawyer he used for professional matters. The less anyone in the business community knew about his present embarrassment, the happier he'd be. Besides, when he'd phoned the house on Spruce Street, George Hudson had been unexpectedly helpful, apologizing for his earlier accusations and telling Sandor not to worry, that he should just wait patiently while bail was being arranged.

Hours had passed since then. Something had apparently gone awry. But what?

As if summoned by his worried thoughts, a guard walked down the corridor and stopped in front of Sandor's cell. "You've got a visitor," he said, unlocking the door. "This way."

They walked through a maze of corridors, pausing at door after door while they were identified and buzzed through, until they came at last to a long, brightly lit room divided down the middle by a clear wall. On their side, prisoners in identical clothing sat at the long central table, communicating with the visitors on the other side of the barrier by speaking into telephone receivers.

"Down at the end," the guard said.

Sandor walked along the row of chairs, trying to see over the partitions that separated each phone from the next. Most probably, it would be George Hudson who had come to drive him back to Dalewood, but he couldn't help hoping that perhaps, just perhaps, Rachel had relented enough from her distress and anger to come after him. As much as he would hate for her to see him like this, his need to be with her was greater than his pride.

As he neared the end of the row, he caught a glimpse of dark hair above the final partition, and his heart filled with gladness. Against all reason, Rachel had come. Everything would be all right between them. He'd find a way to *make* everything be all right. It was just a question of— His knees felt suddenly weak. Dropping into the chair provided for him, Sandor reached out a shaky hand and lifted the receiver from its hook, staring through the glass at the woman who sat beyond it.

"*Sarishan*, Sandor," said Laza Demetro Pulneshti. "What sort of *gajo* trouble have you gotten yourself into now?"

CHAPTER NINETEEN

IT WAS ONLY NINE O'CLOCK when Rachel pulled into her aunt's driveway, but she felt as drained as if she had been up for days. The news she bore about Max and the baby was good, but her elation slid toward panic whenever her thoughts touched on Sandor.

She had known for hours, from her follow-up calls, that Tom's search at the building site had been fruitless. At her request, he had questioned the work crew at the Gilcrest house as well, catching them just as they were packing up for the day, but they had no idea where Sandor might be. When she'd phoned the Firesign Motel, the phone in Sandor's room went unanswered. She had even placed a call to Charlie Grabemeyer's farm, but that had proven equally unproductive. It was as if Sandor had dropped off the face of the earth.

Just like George Hudson.

No, she thought indignantly, *not like George Hudson.* Sandor was painstakingly honest. She refused to believe he had any guilty secrets beyond the one he had finally confessed to her: that he was married.

Married. That revelation still had the power to hurt her. Sandor wasn't the kind of emotional opportunist Douglas Chadwick had been, but the result was the same: she loved him ... and he was committed to someone else. There was no proper place in his life for her, however sincere his feelings might be.

When she had first learned the truth, it seemed that there could be no crueler fate. But the grinding concern of the past hours had taught her a further lesson: if she had to, she could find a way to adjust to losing Sandor, as long as she knew that he was alive and well. What she *couldn't* live with was the growing fear that his absence was involuntary, and that he might be lying alone in some dark field, dead or dying, a victim of Gunari Demetro's malevolence.

She had stopped at the Firesign Motel on her way home from Cleveland, and then at the building site just outside of Dalewood, searching desperately for some sign of Sandor . . . and she had found it. But now she had to figure out what it meant, and what to do about it.

The kitchen was brightly lit, and the welcoming scent of cinnamon greeted her as she mounted the steps. Integrity Jones opened the screen door. "Come inside and tell us all about the baby," she urged Rachel. "We thought you'd never get here!"

"Hot apple pie and ice cream," Aunt Carrie announced from her place at the table. "We're celebrating!"

Rachel's hopes rose. "Did Sandor—?"

"She meant that we were celebrating the baby's safe arrival," Integrity Jones said, her voice softly apologetic. "I'm afraid there's been no word from Mr. Pulneshti."

"Then I'm calling the police," Rachel said, heading for the phone.

"Whatever for?" Aunt Carrie asked in astonishment. "It's too bad he couldn't be there for Max, but you don't think something has actually happened to him, do you?"

"That's exactly what I think. I just drove up to the new house, and there's no sign of Sandor, but his truck is still there."

The sight of Sandor's pickup parked at the edge of the clearing had destroyed the last of the excuses—errands, emergencies, a drive to clear his mind—that she had been able to dream up in the course of the long afternoon to explain away his absence. Something was seriously wrong. She only hoped she could find out what that "something" was before it was too late.

As she began to dial the phone, the doorbell rang. "I'll get it," Integrity Jones said, moving toward the hallway. "Make your call."

Rachel's hand trembled as she finished dialing and waited for someone to answer on the other end. This late on a Friday night, Paul Jefferson would be off duty; her call would automatically be routed through to the county sheriff's department. In addition to describing Sandor, she would have to try to explain what she knew of Gunari Demetro's earlier attack and the fire that he and his family had set. It was all going to take time, time she wasn't sure Sandor had.

The phone rang once...twice...

"Rachel?" Integrity Jones called from the front of the house. "I think you had better come out here."

Rachel's nerves prickled at the guarded calm of the words. Haunted by the memory of Sandor's battered face on the night that he'd been beaten by Gunari, she hung up the phone and ran the length of the hallway, half expecting to find him crumpled in a blood-stained heap at Integrity's feet.

But it was Laza Pulneshti who stood there waiting for her.

Looking mildly disdainful, she met Rachel's anxious gaze. The entryway light burned brightly above her, making her dark hair gleam and throwing such deep shadows beneath her high cheekbones that the birthmark was obscured. "So then, you are Rachel Locke?" she asked in the accented voice that Rachel remembered from the drugstore. "Sandor has asked me to come and speak with you."

"You've seen him? Is he all right? Where is he?"

"Such concern!" Laza said, and the mocking tone of her words made Rachel hesitate. She was struck suddenly by the unwelcome realization that the woman she was questioning so ardently was Sandor's wife. The memory of Emily

Chadwick rose like a ghost in Rachel's mind. Was she about to be lectured again for attempting to steal another woman's husband?

Integrity Jones cleared her throat. "I'll be in the kitchen if you need me," she said, and vanished discreetly, leaving Rachel to face Laza alone.

At the Dalewood Drugstore, Laza had been plainly dressed and she'd projected an aura of weary endurance...until the moment when she knew her scam had succeeded. At that point, her eyes had begun to sparkle, and Rachel had been struck by her beauty.

Tonight, the sparkle and the beauty were very much in evidence. Her sleeveless blouse was a rich turquoise, and her full, calf-length summer skirt swirled gaily as she turned to watch Integrity's departure. There was nothing ostentatious about her clothing or jewelry, and yet the overall impression she conveyed was one of exotic mystery. By comparison, Rachel felt hopelessly ordinary. Small wonder that Sandor had married her. Small wonder that he remembered her so clearly and felt so concerned about her welfare, despite their separation.

Perhaps she had come to scold or accuse. Perhaps she had come out of curiosity. Whatever Laza's motivation, she claimed to have brought a message from Sandor. However unpleasant she feared their talk might prove, Rachel couldn't turn her away. "Would you like to come in and sit down?" she asked, gesturing toward the living room.

The suggestion seemed to surprise Laza. "Yes, please," she said, and added, "Somehow you are not what I expected."

Rachel said nothing, unsure how to respond, unwilling to risk offending her strange visitor when she was waiting to hear what Sandor's message to her might be and why he had chosen this woman, of all people, to deliver it.

Laza made her way gracefully to the couch, smiling mischievously as Rachel settled herself in the wing chair nearby.

"When I saw Sandor this evening, he spoke quite passionately about you. Are you in love with him?"

The question was short and unequivocal; it deserved a short, unequivocal answer. Gathering her courage, Rachel said quietly, "Yes. I'm sorry, but yes, I am."

Laza's raven eyebrows rose. "And why are you sorry about that?"

Rachel shrugged defensively. "It can't be pleasant for you to sit there and hear another woman say that she's in love with your husband. It certainly isn't pleasant for me to have to sit here and admit it. I..." *I didn't know he was married,* she wanted to explain, but if Laza wasn't interested in apologies she probably wouldn't be interested in explanations, either. Instead Rachel said simply, "I didn't mean for this to happen, but it did."

"And what do you intend to do about it?"

The woman was toying with her. Swallowing her anger, Rachel said, "There isn't much I *can* do now, except to stay away from him."

"But then both of you will be unhappy." Laza shook her head. "Poor little *gaja*. You are as bad as Sandor. You and he would find a way to choke yourselves to death on your precious honor if no one intervened. Is he not worth fighting for?"

Rachel's hands balled into fists of frustration; her fingernails pricked the soft flesh of her palms. "If he was in a position to choose, yes. But he isn't. Sandor made a vow to you. He won't break it, and I won't ask him to."

"You will simply do without him?"

"I'll do without him," Rachel said, the words bitter on her tongue. "But there won't be anything simple about it."

"Well, then," Laza said, smoothing her skirt, "it is fortunate for the two of you that there is no vow left to be upheld. The commitment Sandor and I made to one another ended nearly twenty years ago on the night when he was cast out by the *kris*. In my family's eyes, he is a dead man."

"And in your eyes?" Rachel asked cautiously, still not trusting where the conversation might lead.

"In my eyes, he is a fool—a sweet man, yes, but a fool. What do you expect me to say? Sandor was fifteen on the day we married—"

"Fifteen?" Rachel interrupted Laza, despite her best intentions.

"Among my people, we do not wait half our lives to marry," Laza said with a look that seemed to assess Rachel as an old maid in the final stages of decay. "I myself was thirteen. But within a year, he was gone. Should I have pined forever? I have married and buried a second husband since then, and I expect to be wed again soon."

"Then you and Sandor are divorced?"

"Are you asking whether I went to some *gajo* judge and obtained a piece of paper freeing me from Sandor? No. Why should I have? Your laws have no bearing on us. But we are no longer married to one another in the eyes of the *kris* and my *vitsa*. Be content with that."

"And if you change your mind?"

Laza shook her head impatiently. "My life is a good one. Sandor could never be accepted back into our world, and I have no wish to exchange what I have for the kind of life he lives. For that matter, I doubt that your laws and courts would have considered our marriage to be legal, since we were so young. And as for changing my mind, can't you see that after all these years he is a stranger to me? Be at peace, little *gaja*. As far as I am concerned, Sandor is a free man." Her mouth twisted wryly. "Well, not precisely free. He is in jail at the moment. But he is free of me, and I of him."

It was more than Rachel could absorb. "In jail?"

"Yes. He would like for you to provide bail, if you are willing."

"Of course I'm willing! But why on earth is he in jail?"

Laza rolled her eyes. "Some crazy *gaja* claims he robbed her house last night. It's a lie, of course, but what policeman ever believed a Rom? For weeks, they have been making these false claims about us, but this is the first actual arrest. My father says we are going to move on. There has been too much trouble, too many accusations. We work the fields and earn enough to stay alive," she insisted piously. "We mind our own business and hurt no one."

It didn't seem to be the wisest time to mention oiled driveways or the shortchange act Rachel had witnessed at the Dalewood Drugstore.

As if she had read Rachel's thoughts, Laza's shoulders moved in a sinuous shrug. "Of course, some people ask to be tricked, like sheep in need of shearing," she said with a sudden urchin grin. "But we have broken into no homes. Truly."

"And neither did Sandor," Rachel asserted. "He wouldn't do something like that. Besides, I was with him last night."

"Then I would suggest you tell that to the police in Milford." Laza stood. "And perhaps you can convince him to call a lawyer for himself. He would not be the first innocent Rom to be convicted of a crime. If he is going to live in the *gaje* world, he would be wise to play the game by their silly rules." She shook her head, walking toward the door. "He was always stubborn and full of pride. It is the cause of his troubles now, and it was the cause of his troubles then."

"What troubles? You say he was only fifteen when he married you, and sixteen when he left. Why did Sandor leave the gypsies?"

"He was forced to leave."

"Yes, but why? What did he do that was so terrible?"

"Hasn't he told you?" Standing on the threshold, Laza looked back over her shoulder at Rachel. "He read."

"What do you mean? I don't understand. What did he read?"

"Anything," Laza said disapprovingly. "Everything."

"But what's wrong with that?"

"He bought books. He studied. He wanted to stay in the city and go to school." She shook her head angrily. "We were happy together, Sandor and I, but it wasn't enough for him. There was a demon within him, determined to have its way. He was warned by my father, and then by the elders of our *vitsa*. He was told to stop, again and again, but he wouldn't listen. He even tried to teach some of the younger children. He left the *kris* no choice. How could they allow him to stay?"

"But everyone has a right to learn."

"We have our own language," Laza insisted stubbornly, "our own traditions. Already some of us must compromise and speak English, just to exist alongside the *gaje* world, to survive in spite of the *gaje* laws. The line must be drawn somewhere or there will be nothing left of us, no separate thing, no sense of who we are and what we have been."

"Would a little assimilation be such a horrible fate?"

"You are a *gaja*. You cannot be expected to understand." Laza took a step into the darkness. "Sandor told me of the life he has created for himself. He builds little boxes for people who have never traveled the land. And now he has lost his heart to you, a *gaja* who worships books. I suppose it should not surprise me." She moved to the edge of the porch. "In his heart, Sandor is no longer truly a Rom...but that does not mean I wish him unhappiness. There is much in him that is good. But then, you already know that. I can see it in your eyes. Shall I read your palm and tell you what lies ahead for the two of you?"

"Thank you for the offer," Rachel said carefully, "but no. Sandor and I will work out our own future."

At the bottom of the steps, Laza turned to look up at Rachel. "We leave tonight, my family and the others. I will not be seeing you and Sandor again. Treat him well, eh? He will make you a good husband." Again the corners of her mouth quirked upward. "Who should know that better than I?"

Rachel found herself smiling back. "Goodbye, Laza. And thank you. Have a good life."

"That is what being a Rom is all about," Laza assured her confidently, and slipped away into the night.

CHAPTER TWENTY

"ALL RIGHT, you're out of here."

With those sweet words still echoing in his ears, Sandor tucked his shirt into the waistband of his jeans, slipped his wallet into his back pocket and walked forward to reclaim his freedom.

Given the timing, he knew that Rachel must have been the one to post his bond and that she would probably be waiting for him at the end of the corridor. And that, in turn, meant that she had talked to Laza.

It still seemed like a miracle to him, although Laza had explained the bewildering sequence of events: Lulash Demetro had confided in his wife, and Celie, in her soft-hearted way, had in turn told Laza where to find Sandor in Dalewood. Following the sketchy directions, Laza had come, curious to see what sort of a man her boy-husband had grown into, arriving at the building site shortly before the patrol car had driven up to the door. It was Laza, not Rachel, that he had glimpsed standing among the trees at the edge of the yard, and Laza who had followed the police back to Milford and waited for the evening visiting hours to begin.

She swore that Gunari and the others had not framed him for the burglary of which he was accused, and he tended to believe her, even though it left him with no explanation for his arrest. *Tomorrow,* he promised himself. *You can get to the bottom of it tomorrow. Right now, just concentrate on Rachel, okay?*

It was what he wanted most to do, despite the uncertainties that still loomed between them. At least, finally, he could offer her his love. He and Laza had resolved their past; there were no ghosts to complicate his life and prevent him from acting on his wishes. If Rachel had any questions, now that she had spoken to Laza, he would answer them. And if she had any doubts about joining her life with his, he intended to dispel them without delay. For the first time in twenty years, he felt truly free...only to find that the best thing about his freedom was that he could lay it at Rachel's feet as a betrothal gift.

The final set of doors parted. Sandor hurried through them, eager to find Rachel, to embrace her, to open his heart to her and tell her exactly how he—

"You seem to have survived your afternoon of incarceration," Integrity Jones observed, her voice rich with friendly amusement.

Sandor struggled to control his disappointment and worry. He had been so sure that Rachel would come for him, so sure.... "I'm sorry to bring you out so late at night, Miss Jones," he said carefully, hoping she would take pity on him and explain what was happening.

She smiled warmly. "I know you must find me an odd emissary. Don't worry. Rachel is out in the car with Caroline." She cleared her throat delicately. "I think she was afraid you might not like for her to see you in here."

Reassured, Sandor appreciated her sensitivity. The past ten hours had been unsettling, and he wanted no taint on their reunion. But he hadn't planned on that reunion being quite so well populated. "It's awfully late for you and Miss Caroline to be out," Sandor said.

Integrity Jones laughed, walking with him toward the exit. "Well, I could tell you that it was entirely due to our concern for you...but that wouldn't be true. There's a bit more to it than that. I hope you won't mind too dreadfully, but we aren't going directly home. We have another stop or two to make."

"Oh?" Sandor opened the door for her, savoring the rain-washed scent of the cool night air. "Where are we going?"

"It's a surprise."

He didn't want a surprise; he wanted a chance to be alone with Rachel. Nevertheless, it looked as if privacy would have to wait its turn. Miss Caroline and Integrity Jones had already ridden all the way to Milford, set on whatever peculiar errand they had hatched. They weren't going to turn back now. *With a little luck, you'll be spending the rest of your life with Rachel,* Sandor reminded himself. *Sharing her for one more hour won't kill you.*

But the complacency of that thought rebounded within his mind, awakening a new uncertainty. It was possible that having a pair of well-intentioned observers present at their reunion was a good idea. Otherwise, in his present state of relief and excitement, he might be tempted to say too much, too soon. Rachel had every right to be angry with him for hiding the truth about Laza. He had some formidable fences to mend before he began counting too heavily on their future together.

At the edge of the parking lot, he looked out across the dark sea of cars and saw Rachel not far away, pacing back and forth with nervous energy. As she turned back in their direction, she stopped abruptly, and Sandor held his breath, waiting for her reaction, not sure whether she would come halfway or wait for him there.

His uncertainty died as Rachel started across the parking lot at a run. Dizzy with relief, he hurried to meet her and throw his arms around her. She captured his mouth in a welcoming kiss that exceeded his bravest expectations, chasing the shadowy fears from his mind.

It was a homecoming, something he had never expected to experience in his fragmented, rootless life. In spite of the pain he had put her through, in spite of Laza, in spite of everything, Rachel seemed willing to welcome him back and give him another chance.

"I'll be happy to drive," Integrity Jones said to them when he could finally bear to leave the sanctuary of Rachel's arms. "You've both had quite a day. Why don't you ride in back and have a catnap?"

"That's a wonderful idea," Rachel said promptly, and Sandor smiled his thanks, grateful for any chance to go on holding Rachel.

Climbing into the back seat, he welcomed her into the circle of his arm, resting his cheek against the fragrant softness of her hair, leaning back against the upholstery as the engine rumbled and the car moved slowly out of the parking lot.

There were a million things he wanted to say to her, but not with Integrity Jones sitting directly in front of him, and Miss Caroline turning her head to beam at them maternally from the front passenger seat. For now, it was enough just to hold Rachel close.

By the time the car passed the Milford city limits, the rigors of the day were beginning to catch up with him. Reassured by Rachel's nearness, Sandor slumped lower on the seat, closing his eyes against the glare of the oncoming headlights, letting his thoughts drift....

THE FIGURES *from his grandmother's Tarot cards had come to life, and the faces they wore were familiar. Integrity Jones wore the flowing robes of Temperance, the embodiment of maturity and moderation; beside her, Miss Caroline was Strength, representing the triumph of love over hate. Between them, the two woman grasped the wand of the Magician.*

"Sandor?"

Rachel appeared before him in the elaborate headdress of the High Priestess, but it began to shimmer and change as he ran to her. By the time he was close enough to reach out and touch her hand, the headdress had become a crown, transforming the High Priestess into the Empress, the perfect integration of physical and spiritual love. Smiling, she took the Magician's wand and held it out to him in invitation.

"Sandor."

He knew he didn't deserve it; a true Magician was able to translate ideas into flawless form and substance, creating order from chaos. But Rachel was unwavering. Honoring her confidence in him, he reached out to accept the wand—

"Sandor, wake up. We're here."

As the words penetrated his sleep-hazed mind, Rachel's dream image wavered and dissolved, replaced by the sight of her smiling face as he forced his heavy eyelids to open. "Where's 'here'?" he asked, and then covered his mouth as a yawn escaped him.

"In Cleveland," Rachel told him, climbing out of the car. "Aunt Carrie and Integrity are already inside."

"Cleveland? Why?" he asked, forcing himself to move. His brain barely seemed to be functioning, and his arms and legs felt incredibly heavy. "How long was I asleep?"

"About an hour," she said, steadying him as he swayed upright. "Come *on*. They're waiting."

He could ask questions or he could walk, but he couldn't seem to do both at once. Surrendering himself to the guidance of Rachel's hand on his arm, he followed her into the brightly lit building.

"This is a hospital," he said in surprise, looking around as they boarded an elevator.

"Brilliant observation." Standing on tiptoe, Rachel ran her fingers through his hair, finger combing it into some semblance of order. "Get the sleep rubbed out of your eyes, okay? You're going to want to see this."

The elevator came to a stop, and Rachel shepherded him out into another hallway. A small group of people stood a few yards away, talking excitedly to one another. As he came closer, Sandor recognized Miss Caroline and Integrity Jones, but the man and woman with them were unfamiliar.

Rachel slipped her hand into his as they approached the group. "Mr. and Mrs. Maxwell, I'd like you to meet Sandor Pulneshti. Sandor, these are Max's parents, Donald and Sylvia Maxwell."

The man shook his hand; the woman startled him by leaning forward and kissing his cheek. "Thank you for everything you've done," she said, her voice unsteady with emotion. "Alison has told us how kind you've been."

"Alison?"

"Max," Rachel supplied helpfully. "Her name is Alison Maxwell. You'll have to get used to it."

Sandor nodded, wishing his head felt clearer. Nothing was making much sense.

"And this," Rachel continued proudly, gesturing toward the picture window beyond them, "is Mr. and Mrs. Maxwell's new granddaughter, Caroline Alison."

He still didn't understand for a moment. Then he saw that a nurse on the other side of the glass was holding up a small blanketed bundle for their inspection. "Oh, my God... Max's baby?" He stumbled closer to the window, peering intently at the rosy face of the tiny infant. "She's beautiful... but what happened? It's too soon! And I wasn't here!"

"You have a lot of catching up to do," Rachel said. "But not right now. We'll come back and talk to Max and her folks tomorrow during visiting hours. Right now, though, Aunt Carrie and Integrity are going to wait here with the Maxwells while you and I run one final errand."

"But I don't want to leave yet," Sandor protested. "We just got here! I haven't even had a chance to—"

Rachel touched her finger to his lips. "Trust me on this one. You won't be sorry."

It was hard to imagine what errand could possibly be more important than staying to admire the new morsel of humanity on the other side of the window, but if it was what Rachel wanted him to do, Sandor wouldn't refuse. "All right," he said. "The sooner we go, the sooner we'll be back."

"We'll see you again in a little while," Rachel promised the others, and led the way back to the elevators.

This time, the drive was a short one. Rachel had barely finished explaining to him about Max's need for a cesarean delivery by the time they reached their destination.

"It's a police station," Sandor said levelly, resenting the uneasy flicker of alarm dancing through him. "If you're planning to revoke my bail, don't you have to return me to Milford?"

She squeezed his hand sympathetically, then unfastened her seat belt. "It's nothing like that, believe me. I just need your signature on something." Opening the door, she got out of the car. "It'll be okay. Really."

"Why the hell do you need my signature?" Sandor asked as he scrambled out of the car.

"Come on," Rachel said, and kept walking.

As far as Sandor was concerned, she was taking him on one wild-goose chase too many. "You know," he said to her moving back, "if it's a marriage license you're interested in, we should be at City Hall, not here."

At the very least, it got her attention. She stopped and turned, her stunned expression made visible by the glow of a nearby streetlight. "I didn't say anything about a marriage license," she said hoarsely.

"Well, I did."

As soon as the words were out of his mouth, Sandor's heart tightened with regret. Against his own best advice, he had blundered in before the two of them had had a chance to clear the air. Rachel stood frozen on the curb, looking small and fragile, obviously groping for a response.

Well, you idiot, he chided himself, *what did you expect? That was hardly the world's most romantic proposal.*

Finally Rachel's lips parted, but Sandor held up a peremptory hand. "Don't say anything yet," he entreated, afraid of the words that might come out of her mouth, words that could crush his dream out of existence. "Not tonight. Just think about it. You can give me your answer tomorrow when we're both feeling a little saner. Right now, I just want to sign whatever it is you think that I should sign so that we can get out of here and go home. All right?"

After a moment of hesitation, she nodded, looking as tired and confused as he felt. To his relief, she let him take her arm, and they crossed the street together.

Inside the front doors of the quiet precinct house, Rachel gestured toward a long wooden bench and said, "Why don't you wait for me there? This should only take a minute."

Sandor dropped down on the bench, watching with uneasy curiosity. Rachel spoke to the uniformed policeman behind the desk, who rustled through a stack of papers, then picked up the phone at his elbow and spoke into it briefly. He and Rachel exchanged a few more words before he separated a single sheet of paper from the sheaf and held it out to her.

Accepting it with a smile, Rachel beckoned.

Summoning one last burst of energy, Sandor pushed to his feet and went to join her.

"Sign this," she instructed him.

The document, whatever it was, was a blurred photocopy. The blanks on it had been filled in on a typewriter whose ribbon had long since earned retirement. After a glance, Sandor's sleep-sore eyes rebelled. "What is it?" he asked dully, taking the pen she offered.

"A promissory note."

He found that he still had the energy to register surprise. "What am I promising?"

"That you'll bring them back if they're needed as evidence at the trial," she said as another policeman approached them.

He wasn't sure whether he was being dense or she was being intentionally obscure. "What trial?" he asked.

"The one I'm going to tell you all about on the way home," she said, turning to the policeman.

"And what am I supposed to be bringing back?"

"These," she said softly, and turned back to him, offering his Tarot deck on her extended palm.

Sandor felt as if his heart had actually stopped for one dizzying moment. Then he was trying to do everything at once: kiss Rachel, reclaim his cards, sign the promissory note, thank the policemen, kiss Rachel again—

On the long trip back to Dalewood with Integrity Jones and Miss Caroline asleep in the back seat, Rachel explained Max's tearful confession and the ensuing quest to reclaim his Tarot cards from Jeremy Hudson. Listening, Sandor was free to run the cards through his hands again and again, reveling in the weight and texture of them, glimpsing their colors and images as passing headlights broke the darkness.

At the turnoff for Milford, he suggested that Rachel drop him at the Firesign Motel; instead she insisted that he pack his things and come back with them to Miss Caroline's house.

He didn't argue.

It was three in the morning by the time they reached Dalewood. "A day to remember," Integrity Jones stated as she clambered out of the car. "Good night, all." She made her way up the porch steps, leaving Sandor to lift a sleep-befuddled Miss Caroline in his arms and carry her into the house and down the hallway to her bedroom.

"I'm *so* glad everything has turned out all right," she said drowsily, patting Sandor's cheek as he lowered her gently onto her bed. "Good night, Mr. Pulneshti."

"Good night, Miss Caroline."

Rachel appeared at his elbow. "Here, Aunt Carrie, you won't be comfortable sleeping in your clothes. I'll help you get undressed."

Sandor left them alone together and went back outside to the car to retrieve his suitcase, filled with a sudden sense of trespass. As fond as he was of Miss Caroline, as relieved as he was to be back beneath her roof, he knew that she was premature in her assumption that everything had "turned out all right." His proposal to Rachel was still unanswered, and in that one decision rested the direction of his future.

When he came back in, he could still hear Rachel speaking quietly in Miss Caroline's room. *Just as well,* he thought. *Anything I say tonight would probably make things worse. Give her some time. Give her some time, and hope for the best.*

He climbed the stairs slowly and walked the length of the hallway to his room. Too tired to unpack, he set his suitcase beside the bureau and crossed the darkened room to open the windows, then shed his clothes and collapsed onto the bed. Tucking the Tarot cards beneath his pillow, he did his best to relax, welcoming the wave of sleep that reached to greet him almost as soon as his eyes were closed.

AFTER LOCKING THE FRONT DOOR, Rachel turned off the lights and took off her shoes, avoiding the squeaky fifth step as she climbed to the second floor. At the top of the stairway, she turned her back on Aunt Carrie's room and walked silently to the end of the hallway.

No light showed beneath Sandor's door. Opening it, Rachel stepped inside and closed it again behind herself. Then, smiling at the way circumstances had come full circle, she undressed in the darkness.

This time, no hand shot out to trap her wrist in a bruising grip. Unmolested, Rachel walked to the bed and stretched out on the cool sheets beside Sandor.

He was deeply asleep, his steady breathing just short of a snore. She longed to hold him close, to stroke his smooth, muscled body and feel the thrill of his touch, but she resisted the temptation. For tonight, it was enough to lie beside him where she belonged. She could afford to be patient.

Long after daybreak, she woke with a shiver of pleasure to the feel of Sandor tracing the curve of her breasts, first with his fingers, then with his lips. Smiling, she reached out to claim him.

They made love in silence, their bodies joining in a slow, healing rhythm. The room was filled with light; a breeze was warm against their skin. The sound of a lawnmower filtered in through the open windows, accompanied by the frothy scent of fresh-cut grass. It was Saturday, Rachel realized, and the citizens of Dalewood were busy putting the morning to use, oblivious to what was going on behind the white lace curtains of the front bedroom at Caroline Locke's house. Outside, everything was normal and industrious. Inside, there was only the sound of Sandor's voice whispering her name, and the intimate magic of her body molding itself to his.

Reveling in Sandor's gentleness and strength, Rachel abandoned herself to the combers of delight generated by the quickening pace of their lovemaking. But soon even that sweetness wasn't enough to satisfy the need building within her. She shifted slightly, angling her hips to allow him to sink even more deeply into her, gasping as the new position perfected the friction of his body against hers, igniting the gathered tension in her loins.

Like a chain reaction, the intensity of her climax rippled through her, building to a peak that blinded her for a moment to everything but the frenzy of her own release. By the time it began to ebb and she was able to snatch a breath, the moment was upon Sandor as well. He moved against her with renewed urgency, launching a last, glorious invasion that ended in his unconditional surrender.

Afterward, they moved apart, still breathing unsteadily, linked by the touch of his hand against her hip. Within minutes, Sandor had lapsed into sleep again.

Rachel turned her head on the pillow, savoring the sight of his relaxed features. Except for the dark stubble that lined his jaw, he looked absurdly young—not all that different, she suspected, than he had looked at the age of fifteen, when he had married Laza Demetro.

The thought no longer had the power to hurt her. Edging gently away from Sandor's lax fingers, Rachel slipped out of bed and consulted her watch, finding that it was nearly noon. She wanted a shower, fresh clothes and something to eat. Then while she waited for Sandor to wake, she could call the hospital in Cleveland and check on Max and the baby.

Downstairs, Aunt Carrie and Integrity Jones were nowhere in sight, but the morning paper and the day's mail were on the kitchen table. The envelope on the top of the stack bore the insignia of her Cleveland realtor's office. Reading the letter inside, Rachel felt a smile spread across her face. According to the agent, her summer renter was interested in buying her condominium, as was an associate professor in the history department. With any luck, a bidding war might ensue. At the very least, it appeared that a cure for her immediate money concerns was in sight.

Pleased, she sorted through the rest of the envelopes idly, trying to decide whether she would rather eat breakfast or lunch . . . but her appetite faded abruptly as she came to a plain, typewritten envelope addressed to her, with no return address.

Damn it, she thought despairingly, *Tom promised there wouldn't be any more anonymous letters. If this is anything but an abject apology, I'm going to march straight down to the drugstore and give Archibald Gaines a piece of my mind, and I don't care if the whole town hears me doing it!*

She ripped open the envelope and unfolded the sheets of paper she found inside, focusing angrily on the neatly typed text.

My dear Rachel
Please believe me when I say that I never intended for my list of "clients" to include your lovely aunt. I'm afraid most of her jewelry is gone, beyond recall—

With a chill, Rachel realized that Tom had kept his word: the author of the letter in her hand was not his father. Rather, this was a final communiqué from her aunt's innocent-seeming boarder, George Hudson. With renewed curiosity, she turned her attention back to the typewritten words before her.

—but I have made arrangements for Gertrude to be returned to her, under separate cover. I really am quite cross with Jeremy for ignoring my instructions and victimizing dear Caroline, but I trust his present difficulties will be a more effective chastisement than any I could have devised for him. I also trust that Mr. Pulneshti has managed to clear up his little misunderstanding with the authorities. I apologize for impugning his good name and encouraging Jeremy to adopt his appearance and identity for the burglary of Myrtle McCreedy's home, but Sandor and his fellow gypsies were too effective a red herring for us to resist. Like any good magic trick, our success depends largely on misdirection. I have greatly enjoyed my months in Dalewood...although, in retrospect, I must admit that you were quite right to be concerned about your dear aunt taking strangers into her home. At any rate, what with my nephew being temporarily out of the picture and all of the ensuing police interest, I have decided to move on to a new locale and sample true retirement . . . at least for a while. Best wishes to one and all. We shan't be meeting again.

GH

His closing line reminded her eerily of Laza's words: *I will not be seeing you and Sandor again.* They were two very different people, people who had never even met each other, and yet they had had a major impact on each other and on Rachel and the people she loved.

If nothing else, it all had served to remind her of just how unpredictable life could be. Chances at happiness whispered past like butterflies . . . and, like butterflies, they could drift away on the next contrary breeze. Sometimes you had to grasp the moment.

So decided, she moved quickly around the kitchen, assembling an impromptu picnic meal. When it was ready, she ran upstairs and down the hall to awaken Sandor.

"If you want a shower, now's the time," she announced as soon as she thought he was alert enough to understand her words. "In fifteen minutes, I'm going to come up here after you—wet or dry, dressed or not—and we're going to drive up to the building site and retrieve your truck. Do you read me?"

"Loud and clear," Sandor said, looking bewildered but amused. "I don't claim to *understand* you, but—"

"Yours is not to reason why," Rachel said, fighting to keep her face straight. "Oh, and one more thing—bring your cards. Now get moving. In fifteen minutes, we roll."

To his credit, he was ready in twelve. He had even shaved. Impressed, Rachel handed him the picnic basket. "Here. You're the muscular one. You can carry this."

"Breakfast?" Sandor asked hopefully. "Lunch?"

"A reasonable facsimile. Come on. Time to go."

"What's the rush?" he asked as he followed her outside, but he didn't seem to expect an answer.

As they pulled out, Rachel saw that her aunt and Integrity Jones were puttering among the rosebushes in the front yard. "We'll be back in just a little while," she called to them, then hesitated as she saw a delivery truck pulling up at the curb. The driver climbed down and advanced on Aunt Carrie, carrying a box roughly three feet long. Rachel smiled. If George Hudson's letter could be trusted at all, Gertrude was safely home.

Putting the car into gear again, Rachel drove slowly through town. When Sandor yawned beside her, she held the letter out to him. "Here—this should wake you up!"

He read it silently, shaking his head in astonishment.

"And on a happier note," Rachel said when he finally refolded the letter and slipped it back into its envelope, "Aunt Carrie has asked Integrity to stay on and I'm hoping she will. I don't know how we'd get along without her."

On the corner by the drugstore, Agnes Denihee stood at the curb, and Rachel slowed obligingly to give her time to cross to the other side of the street.

As the angular woman walked in front of Aunt Carrie's car, she started to nod her thanks. Then her gaze settled on Sandor, and her eyes widened in alarm as her mouth gaped open. Snapping it closed, she scuttled to the far curb and made a beeline for the little storefront police station where Paul Jefferson spent his mornings.

"I guess the news of my innocence isn't common knowledge yet," Sandor observed dryly.

Rachel giggled. "It may take a little while for Dalewood to recover from the excitement of the past few days. But don't worry. I'll bail you out again, if necessary."

"Well, I'm glad *you* think it's funny," Sandor said in a reproachful tone, then ruined the effect by grinning. "Do you think my picture is up in the post office yet?"

"In this town? Not a chance," she assured him. "The last time I checked, they were still displaying Dillinger's wanted poster. You'll have to wait your turn. Check back with them in a decade or two.''

Beyond the township limit, the trees along the roadside gleamed in shades of emerald and lime, their leaves washed clean by the rainstorm. Even the air smelled freshly scrubbed. Rachel drove up the hill to the building site and parked behind Sandor's truck.

In front of them, the new house rose proudly among the trees.

"Look at it," she said contentedly. "Isn't it beautiful?"

"If I agree, do I get to eat?"

"Philistine. If all you care about is your stomach, then by all means let's eat. I'd hate to have you fainting from hunger while I was trying to talk to you."

"Is that why you brought me up here?" Sandor asked as he opened the car door. "To talk to me?"

"Actually, yes," Rachel admitted, trying not to lose confidence. "Do you have a problem with that?"

"Not at all." He hauled the picnic basket out of the back seat. "I just think it's an interesting coincidence."

Rachel's pulse did a brief stutter step, then settled down again. "You had something you wanted to talk to me about?"

"It'll keep," Sandor said. "Ladies first."

"No, lunch first," Rachel replied, and retrieved Aunt Carrie's Hudson Bay blanket from the trunk. "Here. It's a little scratchier than a red-checked tablecloth, but it's better than eating off the ground."

Once the blanket was spread, Sandor began unpacking the basket, inspecting each item as he removed it. Uncapping the thermos, he sniffed its contents. "To begin, we have orange juice, to be followed by—" he unwrapped something in aluminum foil "—dill pickles. Guaranteed to wake the slumbering palate." The lid on the plastic bowl resisted his efforts for a moment, then slid off. "Ah. Cold chicken.

And then—'' another plastic container ''—cinnamon rolls. Do I detect a pattern of indecision?''

"Beggars can't be choosers.''

"That depends on what they're trying to choose,'' Sandor contradicted her, his voice deepening to a rumble as he set the basket of food aside.

"Oh?'' Again her pulse fluttered. "And what are you choosing?''

"You,'' he said soberly. "If you'll have me. I love you, Rachel. I want you to marry me.''

Her creature of the night was trapped in a pool of unwavering sunlight; he was her dream lover made flesh. Watching him closely, she said, "Yes, I'll marry you . . . on two conditions.''

She thought she saw him flinch at the words, but his voice was unshaken as he said, "Name them.''

"First, I want you to sell this house.''

"What?''

"You heard me. Have you had any offers on it yet?''

"No, but—''

"Then decide on your price . . . and then let me know, so I can meet it. I'm not about to let anyone live here at Tarot Hill but the two of us.''

"Tarot Hill?''

"I told you before, this house deserves a name of its own.''

She could see that she had caught him by surprise. His eyes seemed intent on peering into her soul as he said, "And your other condition?''

"I want you to use your grandmother's cards to do a Tarot reading for me.''

Again she had surprised him. "A reading?'' he echoed. "Rachel, you don't understand. I'm not an adept like my grandmother was. I've never done readings for anyone but myself.''

"Still, that's my second condition," she said firmly. "I went through a lot to get those cards back for you. They're important to you, and I want to understand more about them, and the best way to do that is to watch you use them. You brought them along, didn't you?"

"Yes, you told me to. But I've never—"

"I'm not going to report you to the Better Business Bureau if I don't like the results. I'd just like to see how it's done." She leaned forward to kiss his cheek. "It's nothing that has to be hidden, Sandor. If I marry you, I want to marry all of the things that make you what you are, not some homogenized, expurgated version of Sandor Puleshti. So show them to me. Please?"

Slowly he drew the deck from his shirt pocket. "Seriously, though, I'm not particularly good at this."

"Don't worry," she assured him. "That isn't the point."

"All right, then. Just relax and hold on to the cards for a minute. Then when you're comfortable with them, shuffle them until they feel right to you."

The cards were big in her hands, and she felt clumsy at first as she tried to mix their order, but soon she fell into a sort of rhythm, enjoying their cool smoothness. "Okay," she said when she had worked through the stack several times, "now what?"

"Set them down in front of you and use your left hand to cut the deck into three piles."

"How come I'm doing all the work?" she said teasingly, but she did as he instructed. When she had separated the cards, Sandor gathered them into a single stack again.

"The spread I use is one my grandmother taught me," he said. "It only uses four cards." Sandwiching the cards between his palms, he looked down at them and spoke in a low voice in words that Rachel didn't understand.

We have our own language, Laza had said, *our own traditions.*

"Is that Romany?" she asked when he fell silent.

He nodded.

"Can you translate it for me?"

Hesitantly he said, "One card for the days gone by, one for the present hour, and two to light the path into tomorrow." Then he removed the top card from the deck and turned it faceup in the sunlight. "The Six of Cups," he said. "Happy memories and new opportunities. A chance to renew old friendships."

He revealed the second card.

"In your present, the Queen of Pentacles." He looked up long enough to smile at her. "Maybe I don't know my own strength, after all. I couldn't have picked a better card to tell you how I see you. This is a woman of intelligence and talent, someone involved in her community on a variety of levels. Independence, generosity, strength...all of that and more is embodied in this lovely lady."

"I think you'd better go on to the next card," Rachel said. "I'm blushing."

But Sandor hesitated. "The past and present are one thing. Nothing we say can really change them. But the future..." He sighed. "Do you really want me to go on with this?"

"Absolutely. The third card, Sandor. Let's see it."

He turned it over, and Rachel exclaimed softly at the beautiful image revealed there.

"The Four of Wands. Harvest home. Peace and contentment. Romance finding its true culmination in marriage." He managed a small grin. "I'm not trying to exert any undue influence here. I'm just telling you what my grandmother would say."

"Of course. Go ahead. Three down, one to go."

"One to go," he affirmed, and turned the fourth card.

If the Four of Wands had been beautiful, the card that glowed before her now stole Rachel's breath away. On it, a rainbow arced across a sky of cloudless blue; beneath the multicolored ribbon of light, a man and woman embraced joyfully while two small children danced beside them.

"Good news," Rachel ventured.

Sandor nodded. "The best. Not as flashy as some other cards, but who needs flash when they have lasting happiness?" He touched the colorful card with his fingertip, then looked up at her with every appearance of shyness. "How do you suppose Miss Caroline would feel about becoming a great-aunt?"

"I think she'd bear up pretty well under the strain."

"And how would she feel about sharing you with a Romany wastrel?"

"If his name happened to be Pulneshti, I think she'd dance at his wedding, broken hip or no broken hip."

"Well, then . . . I'll ask you again." He clasped her hand gently. "I love you too much to go on without you, Rachel. Will you marry me?"

"Will I?" She smiled into his eyes. "Just try and stop me. I love you, Sandor Pulneshti, and I intend to marry you and be your wife for all time. And don't think you'll find a way to wriggle free just because you found a way to give Laza the slip. As far as I'm concerned, you're mine, and I'm yours, and that's the way it's going to stay."

"For all time," he promised, drawing her to him. "And we'll be as happy as two people can possibly be. I don't need cards to tell me that."

And then he kissed her, proving his point to Rachel's utter satisfaction.

Harlequin Superromance.

COMING NEXT MONTH

#398 BEHIND EVERY CLOUD • Peg Sutherland
Kellie Adams loved her position as head pilot of
Birmingham Memorial's air ambulance service. But
when VP Dan Brennan put the service and Kellie
under scrutiny, she knew she might lose her
job... and her heart.

#399 WHITE LIES AND ALIBIS • Tracy Hughes
Luke Wade had only touched her in a brotherly
fashion, but even as a young teen, Kristen's pulse
had raced whenever he was near. He'd been oblivious
to her undeclared emotions, too caught up in the
task of protecting her virtue to ever recognize her
desire. Now she was a grown woman and fate had
thrown them together again in a way that made any
secret between them impossible....

#400 A GENTLEMAN'S HONOR • Ruth Alana Smith
They were from different worlds. But the cotton
farmer-turned-model and the Madison Avenue
advertising executive seemed destined to be
together—until their worlds crashed. To Joe Dillon
Mahue, honor always came first—though Virginia
Vandiver-Rice was steadily gaining in importance....

#401 UNDER PRAIRIE SKIES • Margot Dalton
Kindergarten teacher Mara Steen sometimes
fantasized that she could marry Allan Williamson
and live with him and his young son on his Alberta
farm. But reality always intruded. She could never
abandon the grandmother who'd raised her, even
though her decision meant she'd never have a life of
her own....

Harlequin Superromance®

LET THE GOOD TIMES ROLL . . .

Add some Cajun spice to liven up your New Year's celebrations and join Superromance for a romantic tour of the rich Acadian marshlands and the legendary Louisiana bayous.

CAJUN MELODIES, starting in January 1990, is a three-book tribute to the fun-loving people who've enriched America by introducing us to crawfish étouffé and gumbo, zydeco music and the Saturday night party, the *fais-dodo*. And learn about loving, Cajun-style, as you meet the tall, dark, handsome men who win their ladies' hearts with a beautiful, haunting melody. . . .

Book One: *Julianne's Song*, January 1990
Book Two: *Catherine's Song*, February 1990
Book Three: *Jessica's Song*, March 1990

In April, Harlequin brings you the world's most popular romance author

JANET DAILEY

No Quarter Asked

Out of print since 1974!

After the tragic death of her father, Stacy's world is shattered. She needs to get away by herself to sort things out. She leaves behind her boyfriend, Carter Price, who wants to marry her. However, as soon as she arrives at her rented cabin in Texas, Cord Harris, owner of a large ranch, seems determined to get her to leave. When Stacy has a fall and is injured, Cord reluctantly takes her to his own ranch. Unknown to Stacy, Carter's father has written to Cord and asked him to keep an eye on Stacy and try to convince her to return home. After a few weeks there, in spite of Cord's hateful treatment that involves her working as a ranch hand and the return of Lydia, his ex-fiancée, by the time Carter comes to escort her back, Stacy knows that she is in love with Cord and doesn't want to go.

**Watch for *Fiesta San Antonio* in July and
For Bitter or Worse in September.**

JDA-1

Live the

Become a part of the magical events at The Stanley Hotel in the Colorado Rockies, and be sure to catch its final act in April 1990 with #337 RETURN TO SUMMER by Emma Merritt.

Three women friends touched by magic find love in a very special way, the way of enchantment. Hayley Austin was gifted with a magic apple that gave her three wishes in BEST WISHES (#329). Nicki Chandler was visited by psychic visions in SIGHT UNSEEN (#333). Now travel into the past with Kate Douglas as she meets her soul mate in RETURN TO SUMMER #337.

ROCKY MOUNTAIN MAGIC—All it takes is an open heart.